WHERE
MONSTERS
DWELL

WHERE MONSTERS DWELL

Jørgen Brekke

TRANSLATED BY STEVEN T. MURRAY

MINOTAUR BOOKS
NEW YORK

WHERE MONSTERS DWELL. Copyright © 2011 by Jørgen Brekke. Translation copyright © 2014 Steven T. Murray. All rights reserved. Printed in the United States of America. For information, address St. Martin's Press, 175 Fifth Avenue, New York, N.Y. 10010.

www.minotaurbooks.com

The Library of Congress has cataloged the hardcover edition as follows:

Brekke, Jørgen, 1968–
   [Nådens omkrets. English]
   Where monsters dwell / Jørgen Brekke ; translated by Steven T. Murray. — First U.S. edition.
     p. cm.
   ISBN 978-1-250-01680-5 (hardcover)
   ISBN 978-1-250-02604-0 (e-book)
   I. Title.
   PT8952.12.R455N3313 2014
   839.823'8—dc23

2013032457

ISBN 978-1-250-06080-8 (trade paperback)

Minotaur books may be purchased for educational, business, or promotional use. For information on bulk purchases, please contact the Macmillan Corporate and Premium Sales Department at 1-800-221-7945, extension 5442, or write to specialmarkets@macmillan.com.

First published in Norway by Gyldendal Norsk Forlag in 2011

This translation has been published with the financial support of NORLA

First Minotaur Books Paperback Edition: January 2015

10 9 8 7 6 5 4 3 2 1

To Eva, for her infinite faith

For thou shalt have full many a chance to roam
Seeking for something that all men love well,
Not for an unknown isle where monsters dwell.

—WILLIAM MORRIS

WHERE
MONSTERS
DWELL

PROLOGUE

There are no monsters under the bed.

The spaceship he spent almost a week building is wrecked, the pieces strewn all over the floor. Some of them are way down by the end of the bed where he's hiding. When he burst into the bedroom, he inadvertently swept the spaceship from the green plastic table that he and Pappa had bought at IKEA. Now he's afraid that the crazy person downstairs might have heard the crash when the LEGO pieces scattered in every direction. A Luke Skywalker figure, which he had wanted for so long and just got for his birthday from his parents, is standing right in front of his nose and staring at him with dark, empty eyes.

He's trying to breathe calmly and stay as quiet as he can. He mustn't make a sound. Then that raging person might not find him, might turn around and leave. But is that what he wants? If the person leaves now, Mamma will be taken away.

The only thing he saw was an arm and the crowbar that struck his mommy in the head, right above her ear. Her head was flung backward like a rag doll's, her neck so thin and white. Round drops of blood seemed to hover in the air. She fell to the floor without crying out, and he had to take a step back so she wouldn't fall on him. Then a shadow appeared, standing in the doorway. He didn't dare look at it. Not sure whether it was a man or a woman. He knew only that the person wanted to do them harm. For an instant, the time it took to draw a breath deep into his lungs, he thought he ought to protect his mommy. Then the figure took a step into the house, and the boy glanced at the crowbar. There was blood on it. Mamma's blood. He turned and ran.

I have to breathe softly, he thinks. Without a sound.

He hears footsteps on the stairs. Heavy steps, like Pappa's. Could it be him? Had his father come home just in time to save them? The footsteps stop at the top of the stairs. He tries not to breathe at all. Feels his chest tightening. Then he hears the footsteps again. They're coming straight toward him now.

Two feet coming across the floor. On the way to the bed they step on the pieces of the spaceship, smashing them flat.

There are no monsters under the bed. But there's one towering over it. Slowly the figure squats down. The boy hears the unfamiliar breathing come closer. Then he hears the voice:

"I am everywhere."

A hand grabs him by the hair and drags him out to the middle of the room. He doesn't want to scream and has only one thought: Now I can be with Mamma.

PART I

———◆———

The Edgar Allan Poe Museum

*God is an understandable sphere in which the center is
everywhere and the circumference nowhere.*

—ALAIN DE LILLE, CA. 1100

I

Bergen, Norway, September 1528

The mendicant monk had heard few good things about Bergen and even fewer about Norway, the land where he was born, about which he had forgotten so much. A lost and windswept land, it was said. The towns were far apart. But Bergen at least was a town of some size, and if the beard-cutter had settled here, it certainly meant that he had found what he sought among the young men of the town.

The coastal vessel on which he arrived from Rostock was the type that the Hanseatic seamen had used in the olden days, and some were still in use up here in northern waters. They were good at sea but could not compete with the Dutch and English trading ships. The ship was carrying flour, salt, and several casks of ale, of which the crew had partaken greedily during the crossing. On the last night of the voyage, during a boisterous drunken debauch on the foredeck, a seaman had fallen over the railing and drowned. The mood onboard was downhearted, because the drowned sailor had been only fourteen summers old and well liked. Not that the mendicant monk understood why. For his part, he couldn't help but be a bit amused by it all. The boy had wailed every single night of the voyage, so the monk hardly got a wink of sleep. But thanks to a sudden sea swell, the beggar monk now arrived rested in Bergen. All was as it should be. A sailor's life was short and dissolute. Few would truly miss the drunken little lapdog.

They glided into the harbor called Vågen, and the crew was busy taking down the sails and finding a spot to drop anchor. It was autumn, but winter had come down from the tops of the *fjells* above the town. He could count seven mountains, all capped by a thin white crest. Down in the harbor a light rain was falling; each drop described unbroken rings on the dark surface of the water.

The monk's gaze swept over the town. It contained no more than ten thousand souls. Apart from Bergenhus, the fortress overlooking the harbor entrance, a few churches, and scattered merchants' houses, Bergen was constructed exclusively of timber. He had never seen so many wooden buildings so close together. Even the town wall looked like it was made of bare logs. In the last stretch before the boat dropped anchor, he amused himself by imagining how well a town like this would burn.

Arriving at the wharf, he settled up with the first mate for the journey and hung his leather purse from the belt that held his cowl in place. He was a mendicant monk in possession of a heavy money purse. For an itinerant man like himself, it was occasionally necessary to stretch Brother Francis's commandments a bit. It saved him from unnecessary delays and detours.

The mate wished him well in his travels before heading for the nearest marketplace. The monk simply stood there, feeling the hunger that had afflicted him during the entire passage from Rostock. But fresh food would have to wait a while longer.

Sequence is everything, he thought. He had learned these words from Master Alessandro. Even though the master's words referred to the way one dissected a body and not to a hasty mission in an

unknown town, they were useful. Like nearly everything Alessandro said, they could be employed in many situations. And sequence
was truly more important than everything else if he were to come
away from this town with the booty he was after.

But first he had to find a swift way out of here.

Once he had possession of the knives he would continue north
in the direction of Trondheim. That's why he was looking for a
Norwegian vessel. There were not many of those along the German
Wharf this morning. A woman pushing a handcart past the docked
boats, trying to sell home-baked goods to the sailors, told him that
many of the Norwegian boats tied up along the strand side of the
harbor. As he stood there listening to a long and confusing description of the quickest way around the harbor of Vågen, he was surprised at how quickly the Norwegian language came back to him. It
was fourteen summers since he had been here last, and the language was the only thing he hadn't forgotten entirely from that time.
The language, and his mother's face.

He bought a small cake from the old woman and thanked her
for the help. Actually, he did not like the idea of going all the way
across town before everything was arranged. What if he ran into
the beard-cutter and was recognized? But it didn't look as though
he had any choice. He could clearly see all the cutters, fishing boats,
and dinghys that lay docked on the other side of the harbor. They
were precisely the sort of small vessels that carried passengers and
goods along the coast of this mountainous land. He pulled his hood
up and headed off.

It is said that the air of a town makes you feel free, but it certainly didn't smell good. After several days at sea he had almost
forgotten how a town could irritate the nostrils. Bergen was no
exception. On the contrary, the usual stench of drains, sewers, and
putrefaction was spiced by the odor of rotten fish and decaying
wood. The monk felt an urge to hold his nose as he walked down

the alleys at the end of the harbor, but he thought better of it. He did not want to do anything that might attract attention. He walked straight ahead without looking up and without making eye contact with anyone he encountered along the way.

When he reached the strand side there were even more people in the streets. Here they all spoke lilting Norwegian. The houses were smaller and there were more turfed roofs. He asked for directions and found a commercial house that did business in the north of the country.

"No, none of my boats are sailing this morning," said a diminutive merchant, giving him a skeptical look. The shopkeeper was a man of almost fifty summers. He stood inside the dim storeroom of his house, among barrels and stacks of dried fish. His skin had the same grayish-white color as the fish, and he spat on the floorboards to punctuate his words.

"Why is a grayfriar such as yourself in such a hurry?"

"I'm a grayfriar on a mission. I'm also a grayfriar who can pay his own way," said the monk, starting to loosen the money purse from his belt.

"Some people might claim that makes you something other than a grayfriar," replied the merchant dryly, but the monk could see that the weight of his purse and the jingle of the coins had made an impression on the man.

"There's a sailboat—a *fembøring*—sailing north to Austrått tomorrow morning. It's not my boat, but I'll talk to the first mate. But I have to warn you that the boat is owned by a high-born lady, and she's not particularly fond of grayfriars like you. You'd do well to disembark before the boat docks up north at Fosen," he advised.

"That might suit me well for several reasons. I have no desire to associate with noble folk who have renounced the holy Christian faith. Believe me, I've met enough of them in the German lands," he said with conviction. Then he promised to pay well for the journey, since the first mate would have to defy the ungodliness of his mistress and give passage to true Christian folk.

Then the monk went to buy what he needed for his continued journey: a good leather sack, some dried meat, and several bottles of wine. When he returned to the commercial house, he also bought some dried fish, which he added to the sack. At the same time he learned that an agreement with the mate had been reached, and he could now seek shelter for the night. The merchant told him the way to an inn.

"Are the proprietors well-known in town?" the monk asked before leaving.

"There is no Bergenser, living or dead, that the mistress innkeeper cannot gossip about," the merchant replied.

The merchant was right about that. The mistress of the inn loved to gossip.

The stories she told about the beard-cutter were not news to the monk, and he listened without interest. All he cared to learn was where the old master cutler did business. In between all the ridiculous rumors, half-truths, and exaggerations the innkeeper gave him enough information so he would be sure of finding his way the next morning. Now he knew where he would carry out his only real mission in town. He had to do it early in the morning. But not too early. It was important that there be little delay between completing his business and the time his boat sailed.

He lay on the bed in the room he had rented, letting a rosary glide through his fingers as he meditated over the seven joys of Mary and mumbled Our Father, and Hail Mary, Full of Grace. The inn was a drafty, timbered house. Autumn brought cold nights in Bergen, and the frosty air crept in through all the cracks. It turned out to be a sleepless night.

Before the cock crowed he was out on the streets of Bergen. Hoarfrost covered the turfed roofs, and the puddles left after yesterday's rain had a thin crust of ice. He cinched his cowl tightly about him and followed the innkeeper's directions from the night before.

When he arrived and opened the door to the dark room where the beard-cutter tended to his customers, the well-known artisan had just gotten up and was sharpening his knives. It was early. Nobody had yet arrived to have his hair cut, drink a glass of ale, or chat away the morning, as was the custom in places like this. The monk took a step into the room but did not lower his hood.

"I think you must be in the wrong place," said the beard-cutter. "Here we do no work without payment, and my cupboard is bare, I'm afraid."

The mendicant monk stood there looking at him from the shadow of his hood. The beard-cutter hadn't recognized him. Not so strange, perhaps. Many summers and winters had passed, and he was no longer a youth.

"I have come neither for food nor to purchase your services," said the monk.

The beard-cutter set down the knife he was sharpening on a little table next to a set of other knives meant for various purposes. He was a master with all these knives. For the moment he hardly did anything but trim beards and lance boils. But occasionally he might be called down to the wharves to amputate a gangrenous leg from a seaman. The time for great deeds was past.

Before he retired to this lonely town at the edge of the world, he had been assistant to Master Alessandro, down south in Padua. And his hands were behind many of the great master's discoveries about the human body. They had spent nights together in secret, bent over the stinking remains of criminals—the beard-cutter with his knives, the master with pen and parchment.

As a young boy, the monk had been forced to lie under the bier, listening and breathing in the smells until he fell asleep and the beard-cutter carried him to bed. The sight of the knives brought back childhood memories: the smell of wood and newly sharpened knives, and of almost suffocating on the stench of rotting human corpses.

"If it isn't food you want, there must be some other reason why you are here," said the beard-cutter.

"You're right," replied the monk. Then he sprang forward. His fist landed where he intended, and the beard-cutter slumped to the floor. The monk tore off his hood so that the light of dawn coming through a hatch in the wall lit up his face. The beard-cutter stared up at him in confusion.

"May God have mercy on my soul," he said. "It's you."

"I'm afraid it's too late for a heathen as rotten to the core as you to turn to the Lord," said the monk.

"You've returned from hell. What have you come here for?" It sounded more like a plea than a question.

"I've come for your knives," said the monk. "Better knives cannot be found in all of Christendom."

2

Richmond, Virginia, August 2010

Life can be a roller coaster. The first hill, when the cars are dragged up to the top, screeching, is the beginning. After that it's mostly downhill. At least, that's how life had been for Efrahim Bond. He'd been waiting a long time for the end, but the coaster had gotten a bit stuck on the last creaking curve heading toward the exit ramp.

How long had he been with the museum? It had to be more than twenty years, because he started here when he was still married and could remember what the kids looked like. Once he had been a promising student of literature, but he got bogged down writing a doctoral dissertation on Herman Melville that he never finished. Goddamn that white whale. So he'd ended up as a far less promising writer. In the decade after college he'd had two hopeless poetry collections published, which everyone including himself had long since forgotten. He also got married and had a couple of kids. Fine children. They had grown up to be fine human beings. Better than he was. He'd lost contact with them long ago.

After he stopped writing he got a job as a teacher at a Catholic school in Richmond, Virginia, but he couldn't stand the students. So he took on a whole series of other jobs before he finally wound up at the museum. And then his wife left him. So here he sat, in a dusty office that was only cleaned once a week, and then only the floors. He was surrounded by old books. Mostly he just looked out the window. Some days it rained, and other days the sun shone and it got unbearably hot in his office. He had no idea what had happened to the air-conditioning. It definitely wasn't working the way it should, but he didn't make much of an effort to find out what the problem was. For a long time he had imagined that this was how it would end. Up until now. Now he was finally onto something big. A free ticket for another ride on the roller coaster.

Until now Efrahim Bond had known only one thing about Norway. There was a little town there called Horten, and in that little town at the edge of the world, annual rock festivals had been held in the seventies. At that festival—could it have been in 1978?—a shivering Bob Marley had sung his tropical laments. It had been a wet and stormy summer day, the way summer days apparently often were in Norway.

He knew about the rain in Horten only because he had once listened to a lot of Bob Marley, enough to want to read a little about him, and in an interview in some magazine he remembered reading that the great reggae singer had complained about the weather and the cold in the middle of summer. He couldn't remember anything else ever being written about that concert in Horten; just that one complaint about the weather in some magazine.

He once fell into conversation with a visitor to the museum, something he used to do in the old days. The visitor was a Norwegian, and not particularly interested in the museum. He had been dragged there by his wife, who was more intellectual, better-looking, and more social than he was, a wife who would certainly not stay with him for the rest of her life. This Norwegian had been to the concert and was able to tell Efrahim that an organization called something like Red Youth had passed out flyers criticizing Marley, accusing him of being a traitor to his class. They thought that his most recent album, which must have been *Kaya*, was lacking a revolutionary sting, and that the foremost hero of the Third World had been corrupted. What these young upstarts didn't get was that *Kaya* contained several songs that Bob Marley had written and recorded nearly ten years earlier. Marley always alternated between rebellion and reconciliation in his songs.

This incident summed up all Efrahim knew about Norway and Norwegians, and it really didn't tell him very much. But several months ago his interest in this cold, long strip of a country had bloomed unexpectedly. In particular, he had started investigating various aspects of Norwegian criminality. The murder rate in the country was so low that he almost thought it could be politically controlled, that they were running some sort of social-democratic planned criminality. In contrast to all other Western countries he knew of, Norway had had only one serial killer, a melancholy nurse with syringes filled with curare and an overdose of mercy.

But that was no longer the case. After he'd compiled the results of his last month's work, it turned out that peaceful Norway possessed a serial killer of a far bloodier type. Actually, they'd had this killer for a long time without knowing it. He was sitting with the proof right in front of him on the desk. Not only the murderer's own confession to every single one of the killings, but also organic matter presumably from at least one of the victims. How this material came to be in his museum was a long story, but he was only a few lab tests away from confirmation of his theory.

He ran his fingertips over the rough paper on which the confessions were written. One bloody description after another, all jumbled together, but no longer indecipherable.

There was a knock on the door. Quickly, with an inexplicable feeling of guilt, he opened the top drawer of his desk and shoved the confessions inside, as if they were his own. He closed the drawer and said, "Come in!"

Efrahim had hoped it was the messenger from the university bringing the results of the tests, but it was not. At first he didn't recognize the person. When he finally did, it dawned on him that he had never seen this person in real life, but only in photographs. Pictures in which the visitor looked friendly. But this was no friendly visit, and it was the person he least wanted to see right now.

"So this is where you sit brooding over your big discovery," said the visitor with a surprisingly faint accent.

An unpleasant shock passed through Efrahim. How did the visitor know about the discovery? How was it possible? The plan had always been that they would keep this to themselves. How could they have been so careless? At the same time he understood that this was merely small talk. He understood that when he saw the crowbar the visitor held in one hand.

Efrahim Bond had never liked his office. It was much too small. There was such a short distance between the desk and the door that the legs of the desk were always pushing against the small Persian rug that was supposed to give the office some class. It would bunch up on the threshold so that he often tripped over it on his way in or out of the office. He sat so close to the door that anyone standing in the doorway was almost leaning over the desk. In other words, the visitor was one step away from landing a well-aimed swing with the crowbar. Provided the rug didn't get in the way.

"I took the liberty of closing up the museum for you. You had no appointments, and I thought it would be nice for you to work in peace and quiet." The tone was relaxed. The visitor was dressed informally in a light wool sweater with a V-neck, loose casual trousers, and deck shoes.

"Peace to work," Efrahim said hollowly. He glanced at the letter opener in the pen holder on the desk. He evaluated the distance between it and his right hand. How many tenths of a second would it take until the crowbar struck the first blow? Was it enough time to grab the letter opener, which was made of steel and was as sharp as a bayonet, and use it to parry the attack? Stab blindly and hope to get lucky? Maybe escape?

He had never been brave. Had never imagined attacking anyone, much less trying to disarm or even kill somebody who was attacking him. But this might be his only chance. It was no longer a question of courage. With Melville's white whale, with his writing career, with his wife and kids, there had always been an alternative to courage and strength. There were ways out even though he knew they weren't good choices. There were ways out for someone who gave up, someone who never bothered to try, someone who was afraid of adversity. But they were ways out that he could live with. Now, however, he was facing a simple choice: act or die.

For a fraction of a second he sat there hesitating. He was thinking about the thrill he'd felt this past month, impatient to reveal his discovery, the imagined press conferences, the book he was going to write that would be published in both Norwegian and English, the guest lectures, the seminars. Finally things would turn around. He had actually considered calling one of his kids to tell him about the whole thing before it came out. He had Bill's number. It was written in his address book lying next to the pen holder.

Again he glanced at the letter opener. He was sure he grabbed for it with lightning speed, but he wasn't fast enough. At the same instant the visitor swung the crowbar. It was done with such calm, such concentration, the way baseball players look when they're shown in slow motion on TV. The blow missed Efrahim, but that was intentional. The crowbar hit the pen holder precisely one inch in front of his fingertips. The pens and the letter opener struck the bookcase to his right, just below the spot where, with a little help, he had made his great discovery a few months ago. There was still a gap in the row of books where the volume with the peculiar leather spine had stood.

"No need to hurry," said the visitor, still holding the crowbar. "We have all the time in the world."

3

Trondheim, September 2010

The old wooden house on Kirkegata in Trondheim was a perfect place to go to the dogs, Vatten had decided, so he refused to move, even though people were constantly urging him to do so—to get some distance from the whole thing. He no longer used all the rooms in the house. From the hallway he could go straight into the kitchen. From there he could continue on to the bedroom and bath upstairs. The rest of the rooms on the ground floor he used only to store newspapers and books. He hadn't been to the third floor in several months, or was it years? He could hardly remember what it looked like up there. An architect he knew from his school days in Horten had helped him redesign the whole third floor when they moved in. He could remember almost word for word the discussions they'd had about space solutions, windows, and access to sunlight. Just as clearly he saw in his mind's eye the working drawings and little sketches of details like moldings and cabinet doors. He could even remember the colors of the paint spots he got on his old jogging pants, when he did the final finishing work himself. But that was all he remembered. The way the rooms had looked, the pictures on the walls, the broken LEGOs scattered all over the floor, the view of the cathedral that they had been so intent on showcasing, the telescope at the attic window, the Christmas trees that came and went every year, the dirty diapers, vomit, caresses, and reproaches—in short, the life they had lived up there. Now it lay in utter darkness.

He sat in the kitchen leaning both elbows on the table, warming the morning stiffness from his hands on a coffee cup as he looked at a fly dying on the windowsill. It gave up fluttering its wings sometime after his third cup of coffee. He poured a fourth and sat gazing at the dead insect. When he finished his coffee he carefully picked up the fly and dropped it in the trash. It was almost nine o'clock. Time to get moving and go out.

Out, as always, meant the Gunnerus Library. He never went anywhere but to work and back home, and he always took the same streets. If anyone, such as a colleague, had confronted him about never going anywhere, he might have protested and replied that he went for walks on Sundays. Sometimes he walked through Marine Park and along the riverbank of Nidelva, other times up to Småbergan to the fortress, and maybe even all the way up to Kuhaugen, the way they used to go three, four, or was it five years ago, when they were three. And he would have been right. He did go for walks on Sundays.

It was raining, which made the clapboard houses along Kirkegata shine. It was Saturday, and far too many people and umbrellas were on their way downtown. Vatten took it easy around the curve down Asylbakken, because the hill could be slippery on cold, rainy, fall days. His bicycle was what many would call cutting-edge, the kind that cost three or four months' wages brand-new. But now it didn't look so good. He had let it fall into pitiful disrepair. It was rusty, had loose brake cables, holes in the seat, and patched tires.

Once he safely reached Bakklandet, along the river, he sped up. Since nobody was around, he veered through the puddles on purpose, splashing water on both sides. His cuffs got wet underneath his rain pants, and the numbness that he usually had in his calves was replaced by a light prickling. But this modest childish behavior didn't make him feel wild or free. He felt only half alive, as if something inside him still retained some contact with the outside world.

The cathedral was grayer than its own shadow, like an enormous tombstone in the rain. It made him forget all thoughts that there might still be life in this body of his, only thirty-eight years old. He liked the cathedral, but it was so damned dismal that he seldom looked at it, just rode past through its shadow, focused and breathing hard. Maybe it was a bit far-fetched, but sometimes he thought that the shadow of the cathedral was what got him ready for work.

He liked Saturdays the best. No, actually he liked Sundays the best, though they weren't actual workdays, just days when he could have the whole library to himself after he finished his Sunday walk. Otherwise he liked Saturdays best, because they were only half days, a sort of transition period with fewer students, fewer questions, fewer coworkers. The office wing was usually deserted, and people never came up to the other wing, into the stacks themselves. There he could sit in peace and read all day if he wanted to. And on some Saturdays he did just that. Yes, that might be the best thing about Saturdays. He wasn't really working. He was simply inside and could do whatever he liked. Sometimes he stayed only an hour or two, but as a rule he was there for several hours. He had installed a very comfortable chair on the top floor of the library stacks, and once in a while he spent the night.

When he rode across the parking lot to the junior college and along the road between the Science Museum and the Suhm Building, with its exhibits from the Middle Ages, he got the best view of the Gunnerus Library. The building stood stoutly planted in the hillside. The wing where the books were shelved had rust-brown siding, possibly chosen to resemble the calf leather on the spines of books at a distance. The only problem was that no one could see the library from a distance, because it was squeezed in between other buildings. Up close the siding made you think of an abandoned, rusted, factory building. The slightly eerie air of decay and perdition it emanated still managed in an odd way to embody the dignity a library ought to have. It was almost as though you could sense the weight of all the books inside. The part of the building with the brown siding looked like it was sinking a few millimeters into the ground each day. In a hundred years it would presumably be underground, and nobody who worked inside would have noticed a thing. The rest of the building was a combination of siding and glass, and it was this that lent the Gunnerus Library its distinctive character, a peculiar combination of lightness and gravity, age and youth.

He parked his bike in the rack outside. Locked it with two locks, double-checked that they were both secure, and went inside. Veronika, a grad student working on her master's in archeology, was minding the counter. She smiled at him and he nodded back. As he opened the door to the administration wing, it dawned on him that he probably should have smiled. But he was familiar enough with his own reputation to know that it didn't matter much whether he did or not.

He took off his rain gear in the cramped cloakroom, which was actually only a coatrack in the corridor. It was important to hang up his jacket and pants slightly apart from each other and make sure that the sleeves and pant legs weren't twisted. Otherwise the rain gear wouldn't dry fast enough and would start to smell bad. He took some time doing this, even turning around at the door to his office and going back to check that he hadn't rolled up the sleeves of his raincoat.

The office wing consisted of a corridor with three small offices on each side. At the end of the corridor was a large room with beige *strié* painting on the walls and an atrocious green linoleum floor that was mopped every day but still looked dirty. A big, heavy table with metal legs stood in the middle of the room, seldom used for anything but holding piles of books or an assortment of coffee cups. From this room doors led into five additional offices. These were larger and brighter, with bigger windows. A sixth door was made of steel and had two combination locks. This was the door into the book vault. Inside were the library's most valuable manuscripts: vellum fragments from the Middle Ages, prayer books, first editions of Tycho Brahe, Descartes, Holberg, and Newton, things like that. Worth several million.

Vatten's office, with the control panel, monitors, and surveillance equipment, was at the end of the corridor, before the big room. He stopped and listened. At first he thought he was all alone in the office wing, but now he heard somebody inside the innermost room. He swore to himself. Then he took a step closer to where the sounds were coming from, stopped at the door, and scratched his nose. He took a deep breath, as if getting ready for a dive, took the last step, and went in.

Behind the table inside stood a woman in her midtwenties. She had curly blond hair, green eyes, and almost invisible freckles on her face. Her dress was dark green with a Mexican-inspired pattern over the shoulders. She was holding a steaming cup of coffee, or maybe tea, in one hand. With the other she was leafing through a book in front of her. When Vatten entered the room she looked up and smiled with dangerously intelligent eyes.

He tilted his head to one side, gave her an uncertain smile, and raised a hand, intending to wave in greeting, but the hand ended up in his hair instead. He stood there like that, smoothing his hair. I ought to say something, he thought, looking at the woman. She couldn't really be called beautiful. If a panel of a thousand Norwegian men were asked, most of them would have given an indifferent shrug. Still, there would have been a few willing to contradict the majority, and he was presumably one of them. He liked her at once. He had seldom seen greener or livelier eyes. Her face was round and a bit asymmetrical. And then there were those freckles that hadn't quite decided whether they were there or not. He had to say something before the situation grew more embarrassing.

"Who are you?" he asked.

Now she laughed. Apparently she had already gathered that he was unsure of himself and understood that he wasn't trying to be rude. She could sense such things, he thought, and he wasn't quite sure he liked that.

"Siri," she said with a friendly laugh, coming around the table and extending her hand. "Siri Holm."

Then it dawned on him.

"You're new here, aren't you?" he said with something resembling a smile. "Just wondering. We usually don't allow outsiders into this part of the library. But I'm sure someone must have told you that. So are you here on your own? You're not starting until Monday, right?"

She looked at him with a slightly amused seriousness.

"Dr. Vatten, I presume?" she said.

"Yes, of course," he said. "Jon Vatten, head of security." He was so used to his title that he didn't react to a stranger using it. Vatten had actually written a doctoral dissertation on Archimedes, yet he worked as a lowly security guard at the university library. He had always considered his title to be an expression of respect, sympathy, and a little Trondheim humor.

"I've heard about you," she said, with a smile that in no way revealed what she might have heard. "You're not a librarian."

He didn't reply, merely stammering, "You can just call me Jon."

"You look like a librarian," said Siri Holm. "Of all the people I've met here, you're the one who looks most like a librarian, which is kind of funny, since you're not."

Vatten felt dizzy. He looked around for a chair, but there weren't any around the table. There never were. He felt like turning around and going back to his office and sitting down, but he couldn't. It would be too brusque, even for him.

"And how does a librarian look?" he asked. He was almost sure he was still stammering.

"It's not your appearance, it's the way you move, the way you straightened your hair. Actually, I'm not quite sure what it is."

She laughed. Her reaction somehow convinced him that he needn't take what she said seriously, that it was just small talk. They were simply two strangers meeting for the first time. He admired her laughter. He stood there wishing that he could do things like that. Little social masterpieces. But he'd never been good at that sort of thing—not before and not now.

Some of his dizziness disappeared, and he was no longer so eager to get back to his office.

"You didn't answer my question," he pulled himself together to say.

"Which question was that?"

All at once the door to one of the offices opened and provided an answer. She wasn't here alone. Gunn Brita Dahle, the librarian Siri Holm was replacing, entered the room in all her abundance. Had she cut her red hair? Something was different about her today.

"Oh, hi, Jon," she said, hardly looking at him. She had her nose in some catalog. "I'm bringing Siri up to speed on some of her duties. I had to do it today because everything has already started at Rotvoll."

"Right, I was just on the way to my office," he replied, taking a step back. As he turned he felt Siri Holm tap him on the shoulder.

Again she gave a low laugh and said, "I suppose we'll be seeing a lot of each other."

He didn't answer, just left the room and closed the door behind him. In his office he quickly sat down on his desk chair. He didn't quite know what to think. Then he straightened the creases in his pants, which were still a bit damp from his bike ride.

Near Trondheim Fjord, 1528

He went ashore on the island of Hitra, several days' march from Trondheim. It suited him well, since he had been sitting in a boat long enough and yearned to use his legs again. The first part of the journey took him across the island toward a ferry landing, where he would be able to cross over to the mainland. From there he would follow the fjord toward the city. He was in no hurry to get there. In fact, he planned to make a lengthy stop on the way. He would spend the days out in the forest rather than looking for lodging. Not that he doubted that he could find an inn where a graybrother like himself would be treated well. The Lutheran heresy was mostly confined to the gentry in this country, the rich and powerful using it to justify their own avarice. But for the most part, people around here were true believers. Yet what he needed most of all was peace and quiet, free from the polite questions of a good host. When he wasn't proceeding toward the city farther up the fjord, he wanted to spend time on his work, and nothing else.

He wanted the vellum to be perfect. He still had not scraped it enough. First he needed to build a frame for it.

On the first day, he settled for the night on a ridge with a view toward the dark sea he'd come from. He lit a fire to keep warm. In the leather sack he'd bought in Bergen lay the beard-cutter's knives. In the firelight he picked up one of them and examined it closely. He imagined it in the hands of the beard-cutter. Those hands that had been so big and coarse yet could do such fine work. He did everything with his hands. Cut, made love, meted out punishment. The monk knew this man's handiwork well. He knew how the calluses on his fingertips felt. A fatherly pat on the shoulder, a casual touch at the workbench, and the Devil's claw around his neck. He fell asleep thinking of these things.

The next morning the monk grabbed one of the knives and went into the forest to find four good pieces of wood for the frame. He took his time and ended up with four slim branches from an ash tree, unusually supple for the season. He joined them together, fastening the corners with a solid hemp cord that he had bought in Bergen. Then he tested the frame by pulling and tugging it. When he was satisfied, he began to lash the skin to the frame.

4

Trondheim, September 2010

O*n the top floor* of the stacks stood Vatten's comfortable easy chair. Not an expensive item. Vatten had bought it at a flea market. It was upholstered in imitation leather, a bit too round and puffy to win any design prize, but it was extremely comfortable. In his opinion, anybody who ignored unimportant things like fashion and style trends would consider this chair a bargain.

In genuine La-Z-Boy style it could recline, and naturally it had a footrest that popped up when he leaned back. It was the kind of chair he would have scorned five years ago, for reasons he could no longer remember. But now he loved it. Most important, of course, was the placement of the chair. These were surroundings that most recliners were never destined to encounter; it stood between warehouse shelves full of books, artwork, notebooks, and old broadsides—all the words and opinions, truths and lies that gave life to the room. When Vatten spent the night up here, he always had such peculiar dreams. It was also important that the room had a high ceiling, because Vatten suffered from an unusual form of claustrophobia. He had fantasies about being buried alive. He imagined that he would mistakenly be declared dead, and then buried before anyone noticed that he was still breathing. This fantasy of his was based on a specific incident. Once he had taken an overdose of sleeping pills, and his heart had nearly stopped beating. He was almost dead, but only almost. His dread about being buried alive could take on a physical manifestation. Whenever it happened, he would literally feel an unbearable pressure on his lungs, smell fresh earth, and sense the narrow coffin, the blackness of the night, the silence like a lake that was overflowing. All this while he envisioned the air and the grass up above. These fantasies were usually triggered when he found himself in narrow, tight spaces. But never when he was in the book tower.

Now he was sitting quite calmly, bent forward with the chair in an upright position. He had brought along a book to make some notes about Edgar Allan Poe. So far he had just one page filled with a few recent scribblings. He often jotted down interesting passages he read, or ideas that popped up if he wanted to think about them further. The notes weren't meant to be used for anything other than to keep his mind agile. When he was done with them, he often put them in a folder, but sometimes he just threw them out. Not all ideas were worth saving.

With the passage of time and through painstaking research it has become rather clear that Poe's death was due to one of the following causes: meningitis, a brain tumor, syphilis, apoplexy, a deficiency of one or more enzymes, diabetes, some less common brain disease, alcoholism, an overdose of medication, opium abuse, cholera, mercury poisoning, lead poisoning, some other form of heavy metal poisoning, suicide resulting from depression, a heart disease, the fact that he was shanghaied, doped, and forced to vote for a particular party during the election of 1849, or rabies. But a definite cause of death has been impossible to determine.

P.S. Let us hope that he did not spend much time worrying about what he would eventually die of while he was alive. (Even though portions of his literary oeuvre lead one to suspect that such thoughts may have indeed plagued him.)

Vatten remained seated and read over his comments. He had actually intended to write more; in fact, he'd pondered writing a rather long text about the peculiar Edgar Allan Poe. With some indignation he thought about the fact that one of the greatest literary personages in the United States had died destitute, and then rested for years beneath a simple gravestone inscribed No. 80 before he finally received a suitable memorial. Today, a first edition of his first book, *Tamerlane and Other Poems,* was worth half a million dollars.

What Vatten wrote about Poe was merely supposed to be for his own use, to help his literary digestion, so to speak; nevertheless it had to be thorough. But when he looked over what he had scribbled down so far, he couldn't come up with a single meaningful remark. Yet he decided that this note was something he ought to keep, so he folded it up and put it in his pants pocket. Then he leaned back in his chair, extended his legs, and fell asleep, his body stretched out full length.

Much later than usual, he went downstairs to get his bag lunch. He'd expected to find the main building deserted. The library's closing time, 1:00 P.M. on Saturdays, had long since passed. So he was a bit surprised to find that the lights were still on in the office wing; both surprised and a little hopeful, perhaps. Was she still there?

First he went into his office and again read through his note about Poe. Then he checked the control panel on the wall next to the desk to make sure that the alarms had been activated the way they were supposed to be after the library closed. He ran his fingers through his hair to straighten it. Although he was pushing forty, his hair was thick and luxuriant. Curly. A bit disheveled.

The person he encountered was not the one he had anticipated or hoped to meet. Gunn Brita Dahle was still at work for some reason, standing in the middle of her office looking a bit bewildered. She was holding a bottle of wine, not the cheapest to be had at the state liquor store, but not the most expensive either. He recognized it as one of three farewell gifts she'd received at lunch the day before.

"Hi, Jon," she said as he entered the room. "I'm just packing up the last of my things." Then she looked around and sighed, with a melancholy smile that was half feigned, half genuine. "It's harder to leave than I thought. I've been sitting here for hours reading through old papers, emptying drawers, and looking at old photos. It's enough to make a person downright sentimental."

"We're going to miss you," Vatten said, and he meant it. He'd always felt comfortable with her somewhat strident feminism. At least she was honest. And they were the same age.

"So how'd you like to sample this before I go?" she said. "Jens is at the cabin with the kids, and I don't see any point in sitting at home on a Saturday night and drinking alone."

"I think it'll keep," Vatten said dryly.

"That's true. You don't drink, do you?"

"Very seldom."

"So you're not a complete teetotaler then?"

"I'm neither Christian nor of the dry persuasion, if that's what you mean."

Now she laughed. He realized that they had seldom stood around just talking as they were doing now, and that she really had a nice laugh. Maybe it was the laugh that made him open up a bit.

"But I actually have a problem with alcohol."

"You do?"

"I'm hypersensitive to it. One glass is enough to get me roaring drunk."

"Is that so?"

"I'm not making it up. As a matter of fact, I was just reading that Edgar Allan Poe might have had the same problem," he said, pleased that he was able to make use of what he'd read.

"So, the master of the macabre didn't drink as much as all the rumors say? He just got drunk fast?" she asked.

Vatten looked at her with interest.

"Do you know Poe well?" he asked.

"I've actually been to the Edgar Allan Poe Museum in Richmond," she replied. "I was there last spring."

Vatten was astonished. He vaguely recalled that Gunn Brita had taken a trip to the States, but he had no idea that she'd been to Virginia, or that she had visited the Edgar Allan Poe Museum. It struck him how little they had talked to each other about personal things. Damn, he'd been in the States last summer himself. The first vacation since *that* happened, and he hadn't even asked her for a single tip for his trip.

"Then you must know as much about Poe as I do. The main source for the claim that Poe was an alcoholic was one of his worst foes, a certain Rufus Griswold."

"Rufus Griswold?"

"Yeah, I know. It sounds like a made-up name. But Rufus Gris-wold was real enough, unfortunately for Poe's later reputation. He worked as an editor and literary agent in the mid-nineteenth century during the first flowering of American literature, when pamphlets, newspapers, and magazines came and went, and a poor writer often had to switch from one publisher to the next. This was the time of writing contests, feuilletons, and the penny press.

"Griswold succeeded Poe as the editor of *Graham's Magazine* in Philadelphia in 1843. No one knows why, but Griswold couldn't stand his predecessor; the main reason was presumably that Poe was a far more interesting editor than Griswold could ever be. One of the things he's notorious for is rejecting Poe's most famous poem, 'The Raven,' which was later published in the *Evening Mirror.*"

Now Vatten felt his cheeks flushing. He had read about Poe with great interest, but this was the first time he'd had an opportunity to talk about the author. He noticed how much the material fascinated him, as if it somehow had something to do with him personally.

"Griswold was even more notorious for acting as Poe's agent after the author died. He was the first to have a collected edition of Poe's works printed, but then he topped it all off by writing a damaging memorial as the foreword. That was where he presented the somewhat unstable author as a mad, alcoholic, and doped-up misanthrope. It was a real character assassination."

"Not a pleasant guy, this Mr. Griswold, I guess."

"Apparently not. But the sad thing about it all is that Poe's brief, brutal biography, which posterity has shown to have been partially based on forged letters, was long considered the official portrait of the author. Not until the 1900s did people begin to get a more nuanced picture of Poe. But many of Griswold's characterizations and assertions cling to Poe even today. One of them is the claim that he was an incurable alcoholic."

"And he wasn't, was he?" While Vatten talked, Gunn Brita had taken out a little corkscrew from her purse and opened the wine bottle. Now she slipped inside her office as he continued lecturing in a somewhat louder voice so that she would be able to hear him.

"I wouldn't want to say one way or the other. There's still a chance he was, but researchers are no longer certain. Poe's brother-in-law at the time, Thomas Maine Reid, does admit that a good deal of liquor was consumed, but he also says in one place that Poe was not addicted to alcohol and seldom drank very much. Today many people believe that Poe drank only during difficult periods, and there is evidence that he could stay sober for months on end. It was in conjunction with this discussion that I came across someone who claimed that Poe was hypersensitive to alcohol."

"So you have something in common." Now Gunn Brita came back from her office carrying two mugs. On one of them it said "World's Best Mom" and on the other "Fosen Water Ski Team." That mug had a picture of a tall, slim woman elegantly flying over the crests of the waves on a single ski. He couldn't understand why that mug had ended up in her possession.

"When did you discover that you were hypersensitive to alcohol?" asked Gunn Brita.

"It was actually something that came on gradually. It wasn't until I started at university that I developed the problem. I couldn't drink even half a liter of beer on Friday night without getting plastered."

"And when was the last time you took a drink?"

"Many years ago. It must have been . . ." Here Vatten stopped abruptly, but her eyes confirmed that she had understood what he had almost said.

"How do you know that you still can't tolerate alcohol?" she asked.

"Well, I actually don't know that," he replied, casting another skeptical glance at the two mugs. "Not without trying it."

"It's safe to test it here. If you get dead drunk from one mug of wine, I promise to take you home and put you to bed. It's your day off tomorrow, anyway."

"OK, why not?" said Vatten, taking the mug that said "World's Best Mom." He held it out, knowing that he might be making a stupid mistake.

5

Richmond, August 2010

The cleaning woman at the Edgar Allan Poe Museum had four different jobs. She tried to put together the wages from several lousy jobs to make one halfway decent income. She arrived at three in the morning and unlocked the door to the Stone House as usual but was startled to see that the lights in the display cases were still on. She had noticed that the curator had been oddly absentminded the past few weeks. He was often spaced-out when he arrived in the morning, as if he was brooding about some all-consuming secret. It hadn't mattered that much to her, because she seldom had time for small talk. Nevertheless, she was a bit worried about the circumspect old man. Not all secrets should be borne alone. Now he had begun to make mistakes, like forgetting to turn off the lights. Soon he might forget to lock up, so that some early morning she might discover the door open and a homeless person or two camped out on the floor.

As she worked her way through the Stone House and the Memorial House, she couldn't help thinking that Efrahim Bond had begun to lose his grip. After she was finished with the first two buildings, she always took a cigarette break in the Enchanted Garden, which was modeled after Poe's poem "To One in Paradise." When she sat down on a stone bench near the fountain, she noticed something odd in the dim light over by the Poe monument at the far end of the garden. She got up and went closer. Edgar Allan Poe's marble head was whiter than before, and no longer fastened to the five-foot-high pedestal of red brick. Edgar Allan Poe had acquired a body, a bloody body without skin; the sinews, muscles, and blood vessels all lay exposed. She noticed that below the flayed torso the corpse was wearing trousers, and that the boss's card key was attached to the belt.

She raced up to the offices in the exhibition building as if the Devil himself were at her heels. She grabbed the phone in the boss's office and dialed 911. Before she got an answer, she saw all the blood on the desk. Then she caught sight of the head in the wastebasket. There he lay staring up at her with bulging eyes—curator Efrahim Bond. He looked sadder than ever.

A voice said something at the other end of the line. All she could do was scream in reply.

Trondheim, September 2010

Vatten opened his eyes and stared up at the familiar light fixture. He had persuaded the janitor to change the fluorescent tube a few days ago, after it started blinking and disturbing him as he was reading. The fixture was mounted directly above his easy chair, between two rows of shelving. This was in a part of the stacks where there was no natural light. For the first time he found the artificial light irritating. He closed his eyes again and felt a thundering headache, as if his pulse had been amplified fifty times and was being pumped full blast through the tiniest capillaries of his brain. Vague memories flickered between beats. He remembered that he had said, Yes, thank you, to a sizable mug of Spanish red wine. He remembered drinking it as he and Gunn Brita kept chatting about Edgar Allan Poe. Then they had moved on to talking about the library's many rare books.

She had an astonishing amount to say about the book the so-called *Johannes Book*. It was an odd collection of texts from the 1500s, written on parchment by a priest at Fosen who had been a Franciscan monk before the Reformation. Second only to the diary of Absalon Pederssøn Beyer, it was an important historical source for the period following the Reformation. But it was strange and baffling. While Beyer's diary was systematic and scholarly and written with a larger public in mind, the *Johannes Book* was insular and cryptic, full of incomprehensible allusions. It had obviously been written for the priest's eyes only, and in several places it cast doubt on whether the owner of these eyes was in full command of his faculties. But on one score the *Johannes Book* was in a class by itself. Johannes the priest described several people who suffered from various diseases. When it came to knowledge of anatomy, treatment of disease, and surgery, the *Johannes Book* surpassed most of what was available at that time. For the Nordic corner of Europe it was unique, and most scholars were of the opinion that Johannes the priest studied at a university in the southern part of the continent at one time.

Vatten vaguely recalled thinking that Gunn Brita Dahle had read this book more thoroughly than most, and that she discovered something she didn't want to disclose. But before he could question her in depth about this, she started talking about something else. She said it was sad that the two of them hadn't gotten better acquainted, and that made her feel even worse that she was leaving.

As she talked, he drained the last drop of wine from the mug that said "World's Best Mom." Both of them concluded that he was tolerating the wine fairly well and that the experiment had been a success. To celebrate she divided the rest of the bottle between the two empty mugs. He managed to take just one more gulp before everything went black.

Afterward he remembered only fragments—unfocused glimpses of the hideous linoleum, something that could have been Gunn Brita's blouse, and hands that were not where they should have been. A few glimpses of what might have been the inside of the book vault also surfaced, even though he hated confined spaces. Finally, there were some fuzzy images of a raised toilet seat and the acrid taste of vomit.

Otherwise there was only this dreadful headache.

He looked at the clock. It was almost eleven, and it was still Saturday. So it was nighttime, not morning. It took him an eternity to get up from the easy chair. When he was finally on his feet, he staggered, feeling nauseated. With a sense of anxiety bordering on panic he went to the elevator and took it down to the second floor. He went straight to the offices. To his great relief he found that everything looked normal. Someone, probably Gunn Brita, had removed the wine bottle and the mugs. Any spilled wine had also been cleaned up. He made sure that the book vault was closed and locked, but didn't know if he should be relieved or worried. Unfortunately, he couldn't open the vault to check, because that required two different pass codes, and he had only one of them. The second code was held by his boss, Hornemann, as well as by a trusted librarian. Gunn Brita had been that person until now. Since she was leaving, the plan was to change the code on Monday. All he could do was hope that everything was as it should be. Most of all, he hoped that his memory of being inside had nothing to do with reality.

Vatten began breathing a little easier. He went into his office and sat down in front of the computer, which was connected to the closed-circuit cameras. It was turned off. Next to the monitor was a DVD burner that had stored the images that had been taken. He removed the DVD and put in a new one. He put the old DVD in the pocket of his raincoat. There was even a surveillance camera in the book vault itself. He didn't really want to know what had happened in there; this anxious sensation, like a tough coating on his skin, was bad enough.

He found his bike and rode off into the boisterous, drunken Saturday night. Hadn't Gunn Brita promised to accompany him home? Wasn't it a bit odd that she'd just evaporated? One of the last things he could recall from earlier in the evening was that she had been to the Poe Museum in Richmond. That wasn't exactly a destination for Norwegian tourists. Perhaps it was the almost improbable nature of this coincidence that made him forget to tell her that he'd been to that very same museum last summer.

On the way across the old city bridge he stopped abruptly, took the DVD out of his pocket, and tossed it in the river. Then he rode his bike home to a neatly made bed.

6

Richmond, August 2010

Felicia Stone stared dully at her new iPhone. She had bought it two days before, and already she hated it. Homicide investigators pretty much hated anything that woke them in the middle of the night, or like now, way too early in the morning. It usually meant only one thing: a new crime scene, a new stiff in the early stages of decomposition, a life destroyed, and a new hunt for yet another lost fucker. Luckily, before all that, there was time for coffee.

She slipped out of the bed where she always slept alone. She answered the phone on the way to the coffeemaker, which was on the counter that divided the kitchen from the living room. It was Patterson, and she expected to get the usual overlong report full of assumptions and observations that were totally beside the point. Not that it really mattered. She put the phone on speaker, spooned coffee into the filter, and filled the coffeemaker with water. Soon the familiar chuffing sound served as the background for Patterson's narrative.

When he finished talking, she let the details sink in. This was something beyond the normal jealousy, greed, or drugs. Even though it was early, she was awake enough to realize that she had caught her first really big case since being assigned to the homicide division. It was a once-in-a-lifetime case, and she had no idea if she was ready for it.

Before she hung up, she made her only contribution to the conversation:

"I'll be at the museum in twenty minutes."

She went to the bathroom and splashed some water on her face. She'd recently passed thirty, but she still looked young. Early in the morning she could see incipient bags under her eyes, but they were so small that they didn't bother her much. Her dark hair was still shiny, and she kept herself in shape. She put on her clothes from the day before: blouse, jacket, and loose, light slacks with her police badge on her belt. Formal and unsexy. That was how a female homicide inspector should dress, neater than a male inspector, but not too much. On the job she was sexless. Maybe not in private either, she sometimes thought. She fastened her shoulder holster and service weapon under her jacket. Then she left the cramped apartment without taking a shower or putting on any makeup.

In the car she thought of the lessons in poetry she'd had in high school. Her teacher had been a big fan of Edgar Allan Poe, so Felicia Stone knew more about him than most of the other poets she was familiar with. But she'd never imagined she'd have much use for this knowledge in her job as a police officer. At least not until today.

What fascinated her most about Poe was the mysterious way he died.

Edgar Allan Poe spent much of his childhood with foster parents in Richmond, Virginia. He then studied at the University of Virginia in Charlottesville for a while before he enlisted in the military. Oddly enough, it was in Richmond that he last enjoyed the full use of his mental faculties.

On September 27, 1849, he left Richmond, where he had given a speech. The peripatetic author was supposed to continue on to Philadelphia to edit the poetry collection *Wayside Flowers*, by the lesser known American poet Marguerite St. Leon Loud. After several years of adversity, which included a tremendous consumption of alcohol, Poe was reportedly in the midst of a good period, and no one had seen him take a drink in more than six months.

As Felicia Stone passed the Main Street Station, the elegant old railroad station in Richmond that was shut down in the 1970s and renovated in 2003, she tuned the radio to a classical music station. Music to think to. Listening to Beethoven, her mind went back to Poe.

After he got on the train to Philadelphia, almost a week went by before anyone saw him again. When he finally resurfaced, he was not in Philadelphia, but in Baltimore, Maryland. Poe was in terrible shape, and Dr. Joseph E. Snodgrass was summoned. He knew Poe and noticed that his clothes were not the right size. Taken to Washington College Hospital in Baltimore, Poe was delirious. He wasn't clearheaded and alert long enough for him to give the slightest hint of what had happened to him. On his fourth night at the hospital he began shouting in a shrill voice for someone named Mr. Reynolds. Were these screams nothing more than the final convulsions of a feverish mind? Or was this person the key to understanding Poe's condition? No one ever found out who Mr. Reynolds was. The police officer in Felicia Stone was convinced that he didn't exist, but the poetry lover in her wasn't so sure.

Early in the morning of the seventh of October Dr. Snodgrass heard Poe's last prayer: "May the Lord have mercy on my miserable soul." On the death certificate Dr. Snodgrass listed the cause of death as inflammation of the brain. Edgar Allan Poe, the father of the crime novel, was buried two days later without an autopsy.

In 1921, seventy years after Poe's death, a small group of the author's growing number of fans met in Richmond. The meeting took place in a garden behind the old Stone House, one of the city's oldest buildings, though it had no direct connection to Poe. They named the garden The Enchanted Garden and dedicated a memorial to the author there.

When Felicia Stone entered this enchanted garden at 7:30 A.M. for the first time in a professional capacity, it had existed for eighty-nine years. The garden belonged to what was now the Poe Museum, and it wouldn't open for another hour and a half.

She had been here before in her free time and vividly remembered her last visit. Was it three years ago now? She was working in Narcotics back then. A girlfriend from her school days, Holly LeVold, had rented the garden for her wedding. Felicia could even remember what it said on the wedding invitation: "Everyone goes to the altar with a little anxiety in the pit of their stomach. We choose to make use of it! The master of the burlesque and macabre is the host for our wedding." That was Holly's sort of humor; nothing was sacred.

It had been a lovely wedding. The garden was in full bloom and the pastor had read Poe's poem "To One in Paradise." Felicia remembered that she had had to pee, so she hadn't managed to concentrate on the words of the poem. From her English class in high school she remembered that Poe preferred short poems, because he thought literature should be taken in without being interrupted by impressions from the reader's surroundings. But nature's call takes precedence over art, doesn't it? Before the reading was over she had run off to the bathroom. But the rest of the ceremony was beautiful, and she had almost—but only almost—felt like getting married herself. Still, she had known the way it would end for her friend. Holly was divorced after two years.

Felicia Stone said hello to Patterson. He was a big man, six foot four and as wide as a truck. She was surprised at how tired he looked, since he had described the killing to her less than an hour before. Her thoughts went back to Poe. The master of the burlesque and macabre strikes again, she thought grimly.

She asked Patterson, "Who's here?"

"Morris is in charge. He was inside, but went back to the station," Patterson replied. "Then there's Reynolds; he went back with Morris. Laubach is here and has started work."

"Laubach. That's good to hear. We might need a technician of his caliber if it's as bad as you said."

"Come and see for yourself," he said, lighting a cigarette.

They walked in silence to the end of the Enchanted Garden. Most of Felicia Stone's colleagues had seen far more dead bodies than she had, but even though she'd spent seven years on active duty and two brief years as a homicide inspector, she had seen her share. However, the corpse that was tied to the bust of Edgar Allan Poe didn't look like any she'd ever seen before. Usually there was something peaceful about people, even if they were dispatched by the most brutal methods. But this corpse seemed . . . what could she say? It sounded melodramatic, especially in these surroundings, but it didn't seem that the corpse had found peace. Presumably this was because the corpse had no skin, or maybe it was because the body was standing upright without a head. She had a strange feeling of unreality, as if she were looking at a ghost. She was immediately nauseous, a feeling she thought she'd left behind over the course of her career. The feeling scared her, because below the nausea something darker and more dangerous was lurking. The monster she had fought with back when her childhood had come to an end. Somewhere deep in her stomach she noticed the sinking sensation that she wouldn't allow herself to feel.

Laubach and a coroner whose name she couldn't remember were preparing to untie the corpse from the pillar. They stopped working when she and Patterson came over to them.

"What have you found so far?" Stone asked, noticing that the churning in her stomach stopped as soon as she began talking shop. Laubach was confidence personified, and old enough to be her father. Tall, half African American, his well-groomed hair starting to go gray, he had a sense of calm about him that came from the Deep South, but his mind was still quick. This combination of outer calm and sharp thinking made him a fount of laconic remarks. But today he had put aside any witticisms.

"Well, I'll tell you this—our friend here didn't have a simple or quick death. He was tied to the pillar with steel wire around his arms, feet, and waist. He still has skin in some places. The marks from the steel wire show signs of swelling and bleeding, which tells us that he was alive when he was tied up."

"So his throat was slit and he was flayed as he hung here?" she asked, trying not to let the images take shape in her head.

"Not exactly. Well, at least not in that order. All the skin on his upper torso between his neck, shoulders, and navel was removed, also on his back. It wouldn't be possible to do that while he was hanging the way he is now. The skin was most likely taken off before he was tied up."

"And you said that he was still alive when he was tied up there. So in other words, he was . . ."

"Skinned alive, yes," said Laubach, completing her sentence.

"Jesus Christ!" said Patterson. "But his head was upstairs in the office. Wouldn't it be more logical that the murderer killed him up there, flayed him, and then dragged him down here to tie him up?"

"There's a good deal here that isn't logical. His head was beaten severely before he died. There was blood and signs of a struggle in the office, but we don't have a full picture yet. The cleaning woman made a mess up there, which makes our job even harder. We think he was knocked unconscious with a blunt instrument up in the office, but that he didn't die from it. Then he was dragged down here and flayed, most likely on the lawn over there, where there's quite a lot of blood." Laubach pointed to a spot over by the fountain. "Then he was probably tied up and his throat cut, apparently with a small ax or a very heavy knife—possibly with more than one instrument. It took several hacks to get the head off. Finally he carried it back up to the office and put it in the wastebasket."

"Why do you think he did that?" Felicia asked. "It doesn't make any sense."

"Does any of it make sense?" replied Laubach. "But I know what you mean. It seems unnecessary to take the head back upstairs. Maybe he did it to confuse us. I have no idea what the intent was. Maybe the killer was trying to tell us something."

"You've been watching too much TV," said Patterson.

"This might be one of those rare instances when reality is stranger than fiction," said Laubach.

They stood in silence for a moment, mulling over what he had said. Then Patterson voiced what they were all thinking.

"Does this mean we're looking at a serial killer?"

"Based on the crime scene alone, I would venture to say that the perpetrator has killed before," Laubach said. "What do you think, Stone?"

She knew why he had asked. Last year she had taken part in a three-month-long course on serial killers, at the FBI in Washington, D.C.

"I'd say that you're right, Laubach. Even just looking at the crime scene. But at the same time . . ."

"At the same time what?" asked Patterson. Felicia couldn't help thinking that he often acted like an impatient little boy, even though he was older than she was, and more experienced. But she also knew that it was precisely this impatience that made him the talented investigator he was.

"At the same time I think we can say with certainty that he has never killed quite like this before," Felicia replied.

"How can you tell?" asked Patterson.

"It's too extreme, too conspicuous—almost theatrical, as if the killer wants to be noticed. If there had been other murders like this before, we would remember. We would have studied them. They would have been required curriculum. Flayed alive, tied up, and throat sliced? I haven't read about anything like that."

"There is Ed Gein, though," Laubach pointed out.

"Of course, but we're talking about the present," she said. She knew about Ed Gein. The much too real grave robber and killer from the sleepy little town of Plainfield in the 1950s. He didn't just flay his victims; he also skinned the bodies he stole from the local cemetery. But this was different. "There's something about the location of this crime scene," she went on. "The Edgar Allan Poe Museum. I have a feeling the choice was no accident. We don't have a series of killings yet, but maybe it's starting right here."

"Could it be somebody who's killed before, but who has gradually worked his way up to this stage?" Patterson asked.

"And what exactly would be the intermediate stages to a murder like this?" she replied dryly.

Laubach broke in. "What if the perpetrator has killed before in other countries: Mexico, Brazil, Russia? How much do we know about possible serial killers abroad?"

"Actually, the FBI has a surprisingly good overview, better than any other international agency. We discussed several foreign cases in the FBI course I took, including a possibly unsolved case in Europe, but nothing that was anything like this one. Still, there's always a chance. But a foreigner here in Richmond? And why here at the museum?" Felicia once again recalled her friend's wedding invitation and the words "burlesque" and "macabre."

"I'd be surprised if Morris doesn't ask us to cast a wider net, but I have a feeling that there's a connection between the victim, or at least the victim's workplace, and the perpetrator," she said.

At that moment Patterson, Laubach, and Stone all received the same text message:

> You've seen the crime scene. Laubach will put his team to work. Reynolds is coming back to talk to the staff. The rest of us will meet at the station in an hour. War council.

It was from Morris.

7

Trondheim, September 2010

When *Vatten woke up* on Sunday, it was way past breakfast and the usual time for his Sunday walk. He drank his coffee and looked out the window. Then he put on a pair of worn but sturdy hiking boots and rain gear and went out. He walked all the way up to Kuhaugen Hill, sat down on a bench, and looked out over the town and the fjord. The drizzle landed like drops of dew on his face, and he hoped for a moment that the rain would clear his thoughts enough to remember more than just blurry glimpses of what had happened in the library the day before. Or that it would also wash away the unpleasant feeling that he had done something terribly stupid after drinking those two mugs of Spanish red wine. But the rain did nothing but make his face wet.

On the way back he took a detour, and unexpectedly ran into Siri Holm, the new librarian. She was walking in the vicinity of Kvilhaugen with a smug-looking Afghan hound. It was the dog who saw him first.

"Well, if it isn't our security officer," she said with a smile.

"Oh, hi. I almost didn't see you. Lost in my own thoughts," he said apologetically, with a strained smile. He looked at the dog, who was staring haughtily into space.

"Your dog?"

"No, I found her here and caught her with a leash I just so happened to have with me," she said with a teasing laugh. "I'm sure she belongs to the local tribe of Afghan hounds."

"Dumb question. I just didn't picture you as a dog person."

"I'm probably a lot of different things you can't imagine." She smiled and held his gaze so long that he blushed. "If you're out for a Sunday walk, maybe you have time for a cup of tea at my place?"

He hesitated.

"Come on, I promise not to put the moves on you. Not right away, anyway."

Siri Holm was fifteen years younger than Vatten. He didn't know many women her age, but he didn't think that young women had changed much since he was in his early twenties. He realized that she wasn't just young. She was something altogether unique. If he took her at her word and was interpreting her signals correctly—the smile, the way she put her hand on his shoulder when they were talking—then he had to assume that she was flirting with him. Still, he wasn't sure. It was more like she was coming on to the whole world.

"Have you got any coffee?" he asked.

She didn't, but he followed her to her place anyway. She lived in a two-room apartment in a wooden building at the top of Rosenborg, with a view over the whole town and the fjord. She told him that she'd gotten the apartment from her father, who, according to her, had made a bit too much money a bit too easily.

Vatten knew how places could get messy. Several rooms in his house were filled with old books, magazines, newspapers, and other useless items he didn't have the energy to clean up. But at least he had some kind of order; things were in boxes or stacked up. Siri Holm's apartment, on the other hand, was utter chaos—he'd never seen a messier place. Apart from a bookcase along one wall of the living room, where the books stood in surprisingly neat rows, everything looked like it was out of place. There were clothes on the floor and dirty dishes everywhere: on the coffee table, on the rug, under the couch. There was a hodgepodge of antiques and stuffed animals scattered over the floor and piled on the tables. On one of the wide windowsills lay a trumpet, one of the few objects not covered with a layer of dust. In the middle of the room stood a mannequin wearing a tae kwon do outfit. Around its waist was an ominous black belt.

The dog ignored the mess completely, sauntering across the living-room floor without stepping on anything, and lay down with a lethargic expression on a pillow near the door to the kitchen. Vatten watched Siri through the doorway as she fixed the tea. She had to fish out the teapot from underneath a pile of mail and old newspapers.

"Welcome to my cabinet of curiosities," she said when she entered the living room carrying two cups. She set them down on two bare spots on the coffee table that he hadn't noticed at first. Then she cleared off some books and magazines from the couch and invited him to have a seat.

When he sat down a bit hesitantly on the sofa, she came and sat down right next to him, so close that he could feel her thigh against his own. It was firmer than his was.

"When I get my first paycheck I'm going to hire a cleaning service. I hate housework. It's such a waste of time, don't you think?"

"I thought you were a librarian," he said laconically.

"I keep my thoughts organized, and my books," she said, pointing at the bookcase. "All the rest are just things in the way." She laughed. "I think I have to get myself a boyfriend who's a neat freak.

At least for long enough so he could set up a couple of big cabinets for me that I could put everything in." Then she put her hand on his knee. "Maybe you'd like the job?"

"May I take a look at your books?" he asked, getting up and smoothing out his slacks.

"That's not all you need to ask a lady to take a look at," she said. "Go for it."

The bookcase covered the whole wall across from the windows, and to Vatten's great surprise, it contained only one genre.

"I see you like mysteries."

"It's more of a mania than a real fondness, I'm afraid." She had left the couch and was standing next to him. "I collect solutions."

"Solutions?"

"Yes. Look here." She took out a book with no lettering on the spine. It was a thick, leather-bound diary, obviously expensive. When she opened it he saw that it was filled with short, handwritten entries. Each of them began with what was evidently the title of a mystery novel. Then there was a name—under the heading Murderer. After that was a page reference.

"Here I've written down the names of all the murderers in the novels I've read and on which page I figured it out. It's one of my specialties. I once had a boyfriend who claimed that it was my biggest talent: figuring out the murderer in a mystery novel. But he didn't know me very well. And now that I think of it, I never gave him a decent blow job."

Vatten blushed.

"Agatha Christie is the easiest. Lots of people think she's hard, but I think she's easy," Siri went on. "But every author has his own pattern. That's why the first book you read by a new author is always the hardest. How does this author think? How does she construct her books? Figuring out the murderer in a book isn't the same thing as doing it in reality. The biggest mistake people make is that they try to stick to the facts of the case, but that doesn't matter at all. It's about the narrative flow, the way the story is laid out, what function the various characters have in the story, things like that."

"Interesting," he said, and meant it. "Can you give me an example? I always get fooled." The erection he had been trying to get rid of since he left the sofa was beginning to subside.

"The rule of thirds," she said.

"The rule of thirds? And what's that?"

"The murderer is usually most visible in the first third of the book. That's when the author dares to show a glimpse of him or her. The rest of the book is spent trying to present that character as being unimportant, irrelevant, while other possible suspects are put forward instead."

"And then the murderer is pulled out of the hat again at the end?"

"Exactly. But as usual, knowing a rule isn't enough. There are a lot of other signs you have to look for and keep track of. It's a matter of experience." She smiled, clearly aware of the curious and somewhat absurd nature of such insight.

"You read Poe, I see." Vatten took out a volume of collected works translated to Swedish from the bookcase and felt a rather alarming tingling in his body. This was the second time this weekend he had ended up talking about Poe with a woman, though he couldn't remember how it had turned out the first time.

"Sure, but I don't really like him. I don't like any sort of fantastic literature: horror or fantasy or science fiction. I don't see the point of it. It's just too easy for the author when he can make up whatever he wants. It's sort of the same with Poe as a mystery writer. The solution of 'The Murders in the Rue Morgue' is just a gimmick. I mean, an ape as the murderer? You have to give the reader a chance. If you don't, it's not a crime novel, the way I see it."

She paused. "Have I disappointed you? You like Poe, don't you? I can see it in your face. Not everything he wrote is bad. I like the one with the police officers who can't find the letter."

" 'The Purloined Letter,' " said Vatten.

"Yes, that's the one."

She leaned forward unexpectedly and kissed him on the cheek. She took the book he was holding and put it back on the shelf. He watched with fascination as she lined it up perfectly with the other books, so that it didn't stick out or get pushed in too far. Then she took his hand and leaned toward him again. This time she kissed him on the lips.

"Something has happened in your life," she said. "Either you're grieving over something, or you have a great secret, or maybe both."

Then she slipped her face down along his body, until she was squatting with her head even with his hips. She opened his fly and took him quickly into her mouth. His eyes swept over the spines of the books on the shelves, and then fled out the window on the other side of the room, out across the town and the fjord. At last he focused his gaze on the isle of Munkholmen covered by a drifting mist. When was the last time he was out there? It was before, when life was still normal. Back when he used to receive pleasures like this from his wife.

Then he came. He felt her swallow, and then she wiped her hand playfully across her mouth, and laughed.

"Oi, and here I promised not to come on to you."

"I think I'd better be getting home," said Vatten.

"Okay," she said and went back to the sofa to sit down.

I never learn, Siri Holm thought after Vatten had left. But I'm sure that something good will come of this. The man is completely tied up in knots. He'll relax more the next time we meet.

She went into the cramped bathroom, which was just as messy as the rest of her apartment, found her toothbrush, which had fallen on the floor, and brushed her teeth. Then she got out her trumpet and stood in the living room playing a tune from Miles Davis's *Kind of Blue*.

The last thing she thought before her head was filled with music was this: She had heard all about what had happened to Vatten several years ago. But like everyone else, she wanted to know the answer to the question she had hinted at earlier. The solution to the puzzle that was Vatten. Was he in mourning, or was he harboring a secret that not even the police had managed to discover?

8

Near Trondheim Fjord, September 1528

It *was from the* beard-cutter himself that he had learned the art of making vellum. It was tedious work. The dried calfskin was first softened in water, stretched on a frame, and then scraped until it had the proper pliable writing surface. Calf was considered the best, but the beard-cutter also taught him how to use other types of skin to produce writing material with different qualities. As he sat working with this skin, which was definitely not calf, he noticed what an excellent material it was, and he could not help but think back on the first time he had met the beard-cutter.

Trondheim, 1512–14

The boy was holding the cat by the tail, listening to the screeches that were so similar to those of a tiny, hungry baby.

"Crybaby," he said to the animal, watching it writhe to get loose.

The hairs on the cat's back were standing up. It was trying to scratch him, but he held it at arm's length.

"You are just a little crybaby."

It was Nils, the son of Erik the smith, who had told him that cats always land on their feet no matter how you drop them. To see if that was true, he was going to throw the cat in the river. Then it would land softly, and it could swim. He knew that. He did not want to kill the cat. With one hand he gripped its tail, with the other he held the cat's neck. Then he turned the animal over so its back faced the water below. The distance was at least the height of two men from the edge of the wharf where he was standing, alone in the shadows between two warehouses.

"Don't worry, it'll be fine," he said. And then he let go.

He saw the cat turn in midair, just as Nils had said. Its paws were now pointing straight down, the skin under its front legs spread out, almost as if it had wings. An angel. Then the cat hit the water and disappeared in a swirl of bubbles and foam. When it surfaced, the little head looked even smaller out there in the current, which caught the cat and swept it along. He ran after it but could not keep to the edge of the wharf the whole way. In some places the warehouses stood at the very edge, and he had to run around them. He lost sight of the cat several times, but always managed to locate it again. The little head, the bravely struggling paws. The cat kept itself afloat but was being pulled farther and farther away from him. Where the wharf ended, a path ran along the river toward the fjord. He followed the cat the whole way but could do nothing to save it. All he could do was watch it being swept along by the current. When he reached the mouth of the river, he saw the animal for the last time, before it vanished into the white foam where the seawater met the river. Then the cat was gone. He sat down in the grass by the riverbank. He was seven summers old. He would no longer have the cat to sleep with at night, no one to lie awake with as he listened to the bellowing men who visited his mother in the bed right next to his, the ones who left money to put food on the table. There was no longer anyone to share his food with, or to rub against his leg when he came home after a long day on the streets or in the smithy with Johan, his mother's friend. The smith never shared his mother's bed, but he gave the boy work to do on the days when it was busy.

"That was a stupid thing to do," he said out loud to himself, but he did not cry.

"I saw you," said a voice behind him. "I saw you in-between the warehouses back in town."

He gave a start and abruptly turned around. He hated surprises. They made him feel so small. A man with a big, dark beard and clear green eyes stood behind him wearing a blue woolen cloak. Under it he was dressed in fine, clean linen. The clasp on his cloak showed that he had money. The man looked tired, as if that was a constant condition for him.

"That didn't go the way you thought it would, did it?" said the man.

The boy shook his head slowly, then looked out over the fjord. It was dark today. Maybe it was going to rain.

"You'll see the cat again in heaven," said the man.

"Do animals go to heaven?" asked the boy, looking the man in the eye for the first time. He did not usually look men in the eye. Not even the smith. What he really wanted to ask was, Will I go to heaven?

"Animals that are loved do," said the man. He leaned over and put his hand on the boy's head.

"Did I love the cat?"

"Didn't you?"

"I don't know." The boy looked out toward the fjord again, at

58

the cloister on the island. He saw it every day from the smith's window, but it belonged to a different and more peaceful world than his.

"I think you did," said the man. "And I think you've learned something from this. Remember that the way you treat animals says a lot about what sort of man you are."

The boy understood that the man with the fine cloak regarded him not as a boy, like his mother and the smith did, but as a man. He had waited a long time for someone to realize that. He was a man.

"Come with me," said the man, "and I'll buy you a beer."

The beard-cutter stayed in Trondheim for two winters. He made some attempts to get himself a cabin where he could carry out his work, but he could not find one for a good price, nor could he find a widow to marry. But he was not trying very hard. He had plenty of money after selling a house in Bergen, and could spend his time as he liked. Mostly that meant reading the books at the school, where he got along well with the headmaster, buying beer and food for the boys from the Latin school, and going on fishing trips up the river. He lived with his guild brother, and as time went on, he became better and better friends with the boy's mother. Gradually more food appeared on the table, and the first autumn he was in the town, the beard-cutter managed to get the boy admitted to the Latin school. His mother no longer had to entertain the little group of craftsmen who had kept them alive until then. After a while they were able to move in with Ingierd Mattsdatter, the widow of Odmund the carpenter, a hot-tempered fellow who people had simply called Odmund the Hammer. Few missed him, least of all Ingierd.

After two years had passed, there were no more books for the beard-cutter to read, either at the school or at Archbishop Erik's estate, and he began to feel restless. The boy was the first to notice, but his mother mentioned it one evening when the beard-cutter came to supper. The boy was sitting on the bed he shared with his mother, now that she was no longer sharing it with other men. His mother spoke softly, afraid that he might hear, but he heard it anyway.

"Are you leaving soon?" she said.

"I'm afraid so. There's not much for me to do in this town. There never was."

"Then why did you stay so long?"

"I don't know. There were things I had to put behind me. But now I'm ready to move on."

"I want you to take the boy with you," she said.

"You can't mean that," said the beard-cutter, but the boy could hear from where he was sitting that he was not surprised.

"You can give him what I cannot. The boy has a good head on his shoulders. I've always known that, but I've never understood him. I can never seem to reach him. It's as if a little demon lives inside, locking him away from me." His mother sighed. "Maybe it's just because he's a boy."

"I'm traveling far this time. I'm seeking happiness. But no matter whether I find happiness or misfortune, you will never see the boy again."

"Then it will have to be happiness," said his mother.

9

Trondheim, September 2010

P*er Ottar Hornemann was* an impulsive boss. Siri Holm had known that the moment he hired her. She had seen the applicant list for the position, and there was no good reason why she should have gotten the job other than that she was young and knew how to charm head librarians pushing seventy.

Still, she stared in astonishment at the pudgy little man with the curly and surprisingly thick gray hair. He sat in his office, glasses perched on the tip of his nose, giving her a sharp glance in an attempt to fool her into believing that he wasn't as amenable as he actually was. Still, she had never imagined that he would be quite this impulsive.

"But there are plenty of other people who've been here much longer than I have, people you know better."

"That may be, but I'm giving it to you, starting today. You're right out of school. Statistically that means you will stay here longer than all the rest of us. It's important not to change the code for the vault too often. That's why you'll be in charge of it from now on."

"How can you tell that I'll stay here for a long time?" she asked with a sly smile.

"Of course, we can never know anything for certain, but people tend to stay here. For a librarian there's no better place than the Gunnerus Library. It's that simple. So now you have an office, and you've been given the code to the book vault. It's time to get to work. I won't keep you any longer."

Siri Holm gave Hornemann a flirtatious smile, without knowing whether such things had any effect on him, and she took a look around. The library, particularly the special collections, contained many treasures: first editions of all the great Norwegian authors; antique maps; a heraldic globe; telescopes from the 1700s. A boss who was a bit more pompous than Hornemann might have taken the liberty of decorating his office with some of these things. But not him. He just sat there with his glasses on the end of his nose, in an utterly bare room, and did his best to look stern.

From the boss's office she went to Jon Vatten's door and knocked. It took several seconds before he answered and asked her to come in. He was eating lunch and actually smiled when he saw her.

We're making progress, she thought. Incredible what a little trumpet playing can achieve.

"Guess who was given the second code to the book vault?" she said. "What do you say we open it tonight and make off with the most valuable treasures? A life of luxury in Bermuda awaits."

"I hear it's a great place to disappear, both for ships and hidden fortunes," he said with a laugh. "So, the new girl is entrusted with the code; not atypical of Hornemann, I'm afraid."

"I wouldn't mind taking a tour through the book vault. Not a bad idea to find out what's inside. Since I've become its guardian and all, I mean. I'm looking forward to seeing the diary of Johannes the priest. Did you know that I wrote my thesis on it in college, without ever touching it? It's a strange book."

"We could go right now," said Vatten, stuffing the last piece of sandwich into his mouth with an eagerness that was unlike him.

"Gunn Brita, your predecessor, was also quite intrigued by Johannes the priest's book," Vatten said, as he punched in the code on the control panel of the book vault, after Siri Holm had done the same. They heard a click from the lock, and he slowly pulled open the door.

A horrible stench washed over them.

"What the hell?" Vatten said.

Siri turned away, holding her nose.

"What the hell?" he repeated. He opened the vault door all the way and took a step inside.

Siri forced herself to look, peering over his back as he leaned forward, clutching his stomach. Inside the vault, in the middle of the floor between the shelves, lay a body. It was clothed from the waist down, but the torso was not only naked, it was without skin. And the head had been chopped off. But she knew at once who it was. She recognized the pants from Saturday. They belonged to Gunn Brita Dahle.

What struck Siri was how unexpectedly slim Gunn Brita looked. The killer had not merely removed the skin, but also the layers of fat to reveal the muscles underneath.

10

Jesus Christ, is that what was in his stomach?" Felicia Stone stared openmouthed at a tumor the size of a grapefruit, which the forensic pathologist had just cut out of Efrahim Bond's dead and flayed body.

"Yep. The good Mr. Bond was a very sick man."

"So if he hadn't been murdered . . ." she began hesitantly.

"Then this would have done the job," he concluded, holding the tumor up to the light of the work lamp and examining it as if it were a crystal ball with the answers to many of life's riddles. Then he dropped it into a container next to the dissection bench.

"Do you think he knew he had cancer?"

"Impossible to say. He must have had symptoms: constipation, night sweats, things like that, but it's incredible what people choose to ignore."

"I don't know which is worse," she said with a sigh. "Dying abruptly and brutally like this or being slowly eaten up from inside by cancer."

"Well, this is what gave him the big headlines." The pathologist smiled laconically and nodded at the flayed corpse. He was the one who had picked up the body from the Enchanted Garden. Felicia Stone was still trying to remember his name. He was roughly her age and had worked in the investigative division about as long as she'd been with homicide. He was good-looking, tall, with dark hair and blue eyes. The type of guy who might make her feel embarrassed, even a bit dizzy and sick to her stomach in that dangerously churning way, if she'd met him in a bar and not on the job. She hadn't had a lot to do with him for precisely that reason, but she had spoken to him enough times that it was too late to ask him his name without seeming dim-witted. She would have to look him up online when she got a little time to herself. Until then she had to be careful to avoid revealing that she didn't know his name.

"He certainly did get headlines," she said, thinking of all the commotion in the past twenty-four hours. The morning had barely started before the case had been snatched up by the national press; it had been the top story for several hours on Fox News and the biggest Web sites. The bloggers had immediately started writing about the latest serial killer in the States, despite the fact that there hadn't been a similar murder anywhere else. Loads of theories had already been presented. Most of them naturally drew connections to Edgar Allan Poe's literary world, but also discussed as possible sources of inspiration for the murderer were American Indian ritual killings, Roman execution methods, and animal slaughter. The press conference at police headquarters didn't seem to put a damper on the public imagination. And this in spite of the fact that both the police chief, Ottis Toole, District Attorney Henry Lucas, and investigative team leader Elijah Morris did their best to present the murder as an isolated event that would be investigated the same as any other homicide case in the city.

This had been Morris's main point at the so-called war council in a stuffy meeting room with bad air-conditioning, where Patterson, Laubach, and Stone were present.

"We can handle this," he'd said. "We can't get sidetracked by all the blood and butchery in this case. This is a homicide like any other, and we know how to investigate homicides."

Morris was a tall, middle-aged man. His hair was close-cropped to camouflage the deep inroads in his hairline. He had a big furrow in his forehead that never went away, not even on calm days, when he could doze off in his desk chair. He was a sensible man, a practical man, somebody who didn't lose his head even if the murder victim did. After talking for fifteen minutes he had managed to convince the others that the Poe murder, as the media had begun calling it, was a case that could be solved, and that the solution would presumably be found where it usually was—somewhere in the life of the victim.

"It would definitely surprise me," Morris said, "if the perp hadn't been in contact with Efrahim Bond somehow. As in all homicide cases, first we have to look at the immediate family, then at any love affairs and colleagues."

After this speech by Morris, the investigative work almost felt routine. Felicia Stone now stood next to the autopsy table waiting to get a verbal and very preliminary report. She'd done this several times before, and she knew exactly what to ask.

First things first. The deceased had been hit on the head with a blunt instrument, possibly a crowbar or a metal pipe. He had survived these blows but was probably knocked unconscious. Then the killer had flayed the skin off his torso before tying him to the Poe monument and cutting off his head. This sequence of events was fairly certain. Death occurred sometime during the night.

"Can you say anything about the decapitation?" she asked the coroner, thinking she might have gazed too long into his blue eyes. She wondered how she would have felt about him if he weren't

66

always standing next to a corpse when she talked to him. Imagine if he were the kind of man she had once hoped to meet? Someone who could hold her so that it felt good all over her body, even in the pit of her stomach.

"This is not a model decapitation, if you can say that," he replied.

"Amateurish, in other words."

"Yes, I might say that, but there aren't many professional de-capitators left nowadays, are there?" Again that sardonic smile.

"You know what I mean," she said, not amused. "Has he done it before?"

"It's hard to say, but if you force me to give an opinion, I'd say no. If his intention was to separate the head from the body quickly and efficiently, then this killer didn't know what he was doing. He used the wrong tool—an ax that was much too small, I think, and a very sharp knife that still wasn't sharp enough. He also used the wrong technique. It looks like he used the knife to hack at the neck instead of slicing."

"So the killer had no idea how to decapitate a person before he arrived at the scene. Is that what you're saying?"

"Either that, or he wanted to take a long time cutting off the head. There's a certain pattern to all the cuts and chops. As if he were en-joying it."

"But what about the flaying?"

"There was nothing precise about that either. He probably used the same knife he used for the neck. In many places he cut a little too deeply into the flesh. But the fact that he managed to flay a man's torso while leaving the skin on the arms and legs indicates that he must have had some sort of experience. Maybe we're dealing with a hunter, or someone who worked as a butcher. A doctor is also a possibility."

"So in general you don't think he got this experience from ear-lier murders?"

"I'll leave that sort of conclusion to you experts."

Stone nodded.

"Can you put a rush on the autopsy report?" she asked.

"Today I'm eating lunch in the office," he replied. "But promise me that you won't tell anybody." He did a rather good imitation of a mad scientist, both in voice and expression. He looked like a character in an old horror movie.

She laughed. And it struck her that it was probably the first time she had laughed in that room.

On the way out the door she also remembered his name. Knut Jensen. Scandinavian, she surmised. A rarity in the South.

The press conference was over, the first interviews of the staff at the Edgar Allan Poe Museum were finished, and the crime scene investigation was well under way. The verbal autopsy report told them nothing new. Even though the city news desks were jumping, the Internet was overflowing with sensational reports, and her stomach was churning with an inexplicable nausea that came and went, things were getting back to normal at the police station. It was time for a lengthier, more in-depth meeting. They needed to map out the long-term plans for an investigation that could potentially become extensive. Besides Stone, Morris, Reynolds, Laubach, and Patterson were at the meeting. The five of them made up a special investigative team. For the time being this case would be handled locally, and Morris would wait to seek reinforcements from the FBI, at least until something new turned up. Stone knew that meant it wouldn't happen anytime soon. Morris didn't like outsiders.

The meeting started where the last one ended, with one important change: A janitor had finally fixed the air-conditioning, so now it was possible to think without sweat running down their temples. Morris had already touched on the important issues. They would start with the assumption that the victim was not chosen at random. There had to be some sort of connection between Efrahim Bond and his killer; it was crucial to find out what that connection might be.

"I don't really think it's any of the museum staff," said Morris. "What do the rest of you think?"

"Nobody stands out as a hyperviolent killer among the ladies on staff," said Reynolds. True to form he didn't look directly at anyone, and he chewed gum as he spoke. Reynolds was a methodical guy, indispensable because of his precision, but not a great thinker. The big breakthroughs in a case seldom came as a result of anything he had deduced, although they might emerge from the basic work he had laid down. It was Reynolds who'd been assigned to talk to the people at the museum this morning. By "the ladies" Reynolds was referring to the fact that all the museum employees except for Efrahim Bond and one external conservator were women between the ages of twenty-four and sixty-three. He had spoken with all of them. There weren't that many: two ticket sellers, who worked alternate shifts; one person who worked in the gift shop; three docents (all master's students in English, who worked there part-time); Bond's secretary; and the curator, who actually worked at the University of Richmond but came in one morning a month to tend to the collection of books, furniture, and rarities.

"But doesn't it tell us something about Bond, that he hired only women?" said Stone, keeping her tone neutral.

"Sure, it shows he was a man," said Patterson with a laugh. "And that he had business sense," he added a moment later. He tilted his chair back and gave her a boyish grin.

"Naturally I asked all of them what sort of relationship they had with Bond," Reynolds went on, "and the whole bunch said that it was good, but professional. It seems like he was a fair and knowledgeable boss, but slightly reserved. Of course, one of them could be covering something up. There might have been some other type of relationship going on. But I don't think all of them would lie, and he wasn't exactly the Casanova type. In fact, one of the employees . . . I think it was the one who works in the gift shop," said Reynolds, as he paged through a notebook. "Yes, it was Julia Wilde. She claimed that Bond seemed to have no further interest in women after he and his wife were divorced years ago."

"No interest in women? If you ask me, that just raises suspicion that he was hiding something," Patterson sneered.

It irritated Stone that he felt it necessary to behave like a jerk. But she did think he might be on to something. As a rule, a controlled exterior concealed something underneath.

"I believe we can make more progress by starting close to the bone," said Morris. This was one of those rather oracular statements he came up with from time to time.

"You mean closer to the victim than his workplace?" Stone asked.

"Precisely. The man had a family. It's the natural place to start."

"The problem is that everybody I've talked with so far claims that Efrahim Bond no longer had any contact with his family. His parents are dead, he had no siblings, and his kids all live in other parts of the country and didn't visit him even on Thanksgiving. His ex-wife moved out of state long ago to live closer to her grandchildren up north somewhere."

"So we have to do some digging. No man can completely escape his family," said Morris.

Stone groaned. Everyone in the room looked at her as if she had something important on her mind.

"We're starting with a rather empty slate here," she said. Then she turned to Reynolds. "Didn't anything concrete come out of your morning at the museum? Has anything special happened in the past few days?"

"Zip. Things have been absolutely normal. The only thing is that the secretary and the cleaning woman both thought that Bond was a tad more introverted than usual. The cleaning woman described him as secretive. And there could be something else. Bond's secretary got a message to send a piece of leather from one of the book bindings to the university for examination. I didn't write down which book. He wanted to know what sort of animal the leather came from. I think she found it a rather strange request, and that's probably why she mentioned it. But I have no idea if it has to do with our case."

"I'll look into it," Stone said, casting a glance at Morris. She would do anything to get out of flying north for a series of depressing interviews with long-lost relatives. She also had a hunch. From the beginning she thought that this murder had some connection to the museum: not necessarily to the people who worked there, but to the museum itself, to the objects it contained, or to Poe's work. She didn't know whether it was odd to take samples from a book binding to determine what sort of animal the leather came from, but since the secretary had bothered mentioning it, she felt it shouldn't be ignored. It might be important.

"Okay," said Morris. "We'll concentrate on the family first. Reynolds and Patterson will track down the whole clan, make contact with the police where they live, and prepare to take some trips. Stone, you follow up on what we have locally. Ask the museum people for more details. Find out what you can about that piece of leather. Laubach, before we adjourn, can we have a report from you and your team?"

"At present we're still gathering information. The murder scene was spread over a relatively wide area, and it'll take time to comb through all of it. Three sets of fingerprints were found in Bond's office, but I'd bet anything they belong to the secretary, the cleaning woman, and Bond himself. We haven't received the final analyses yet. Otherwise, plenty of people have touched the marble bust of Poe, which is a sort of relic for the most faithful fans. There are no complete sets of prints on it. I doubt that the perp would have left any. I think we're dealing with a very careful man."

"Why do you say 'man'?" asked Stone suddenly. "Don't you think it could have been a woman?"

"Sure, technically it could have been. The killer wouldn't need to have more than average strength. After he, and I'll continue to say he, struck the first blow, Bond would have been out cold and offering no resistance. But this murder is about as far from arsenic in the tea as you could get."

"That's overkill, but it's a man," Patterson interjected.

Stone saw no reason to argue with them.

"There are plenty of organic traces. Lots of blood and bodily fluids. We've started the analyses, but nothing has been nailed down yet. I'm guessing most of it came from the victim. You'll get a report when we have something more," Laubach concluded.

"Don't forget the book," said Stone.

"The book?" Laubach asked.

"If leather from a book binding was sent for analysis, there must be a book missing a piece."

"That's certainly logical," said Laubach with a smile. "We'll track it down."

11

The homicide division of the Richmond Police Department was housed in a massive brick building painted a cement gray. It was oppressive, and Felicia Stone often felt that she had to get out of there to be able to think clearly. She was now standing in the Jefferson Street parking lot across from the imposing structure, wondering whether it had been designed by some criminal mastermind, to make the detectives locked inside sluggish in their thinking. A huge metallic head hung on the bulky gray surface of the wall facing the parking lot where she was leaning against a patrol car and sucking on her first cigarette since New Year's Eve. It was supposed to be a man wearing a police cap. A blue band ran down the center of the face. In order to emphasize the feeling that this whole building had been erected to mock the police, the officer in the sculpture had two big holes where the eyes should have been. Underneath the sculpture was a narrow door leading to the offices that were the domain of the city's detectives. "The dungeon of the blind detectives," she called it. Only Laubach got the joke. All the others were proud of their workplace and were offended whenever she criticized it. That's why she'd stopped making the snide remarks aloud.

She tossed away the butt, which had tasted worse than she'd hoped, but still not half bad. It hadn't helped her nausea any; she was afraid there was only one cure for that. A cure she'd tried once before, that hellish summer after high school, one she could never try again. Felicia Stone got into the patrol car she'd been leaning against. There *is* one other cure, she thought. They could solve this fucking case. That would relax her.

Felicia took a right up West Grace Street. She started thinking about serial killers. More precisely, she started to consider why she was thinking about serial killers. About a follow-up course she'd taken in Oslo, mostly because she'd wanted a break from the job. The instructor had said something she couldn't forget. As a child, a serial killer may have been a bed wetter, an animal torturer, or a pyromaniac. But this is far from always the case. He doesn't even need to have been a very difficult child or subjected to any sort of abuse. There's really only one thing that all serial killers have in common: As children they had a rich fantasy world, a world they could retreat into when reality proved too much for them. And gradually this fantasy world became a dark and dismal place, with violence, oppression, and bestial deeds. But it would always remain a place where they were in control. When these children later develop into serial killers, it's their attempt to realize these fantasies that leads to the act of murder.

The instructor had said something else that really stuck in her mind: "Maybe that's why serial killers are such good material for filmmakers and writers. The actions of serial killers are fiction gruesomely brought to life." The murder they were investigating had the air of fiction about it, as if it had been imagined beforehand.

She turned left a few blocks farther along, and then right at the traffic circle around the Robert E. Lee monument. From there she followed Monument Street out of the downtown core. She liked Monument Street. It reminded her that Richmond had once had ambitions to be a city of significance.

The secretary at the Edgar Allan Poe Museum was named Megan Price. Her address on Canterbury Road out by Windsor Farms told Felicia that the salary from her job wasn't the only income at her disposal. Presumably she was married to a doctor or lawyer who made enough to support them both, and she probably viewed her job at the museum as a good alternative to charity work. Felicia turned onto Lafayette toward Windsor Farms. Most people would have chosen Malvern Avenue, but she never drove down that street unless she had to. It would mean having to pass the house where her life had been split in two.

She hadn't called Megan Price in advance. When you were investigating a homicide, it was seldom a good idea to give people time for reflection. She trusted that Mrs. Price had followed Reynolds's orders for all museum staff to go home and wait for the police to contact them. Naturally the cops didn't call right away, and sooner or later most people would leave their homes and take up their normal, everyday activities. But it was significant to find out how long someone would wait and what he did when he got tired of waiting for something to happen. With a little luck, that knowledge might give the police a new lead.

Before Felicia left police headquarters, she got a brief description of Megan Price. For the time being there was no reason to suspect that she had anything to do with the murder, but Stone had a rule: At the start of a case, suspect everyone. Once, when she was out with her colleagues, drinking cola while they drank beer, she said, "An investigator needs to follow a rule opposite to the one used by the courts. Everyone is guilty until proven innocent. Even then they're exempt only from those specific allegations that have been dropped. They still have to be considered guilty of everything else." As far as she could remember, Laubach was the only one who had laughed with the same heartiness and cynicism. But humor with a hint of truth to it was one thing; letting rules of thumb overrule common sense was another. Megan Price had an absolutely airtight alibi for the night of the murder. She was at home asleep with her husband, and earlier in the evening, she'd had dinner guests who didn't leave till midnight. According to Reynolds, she was a petite lady of sixty-three. They hadn't worked out any profile of the perp yet, but Stone doubted it would fit Mrs. Price very well.

Stone was really only interested in asking Megan Price about one thing: the piece of leather from the bookbinding that they still hadn't tracked down. She parked outside a Victorian brick house with four chimneys, as big and magnificent as she had imagined. There was plenty of room in the driveway for at least ten police cars, but she always got a better impression of a house and its owners if she approached on foot. On her way to the dark front door—was it mahogany?—surrounded by heavy white molding, she ascertained that she had been right about the Price family: They didn't live on only what the wife earned at the museum. Parked in the driveway was a Jaguar, which Patterson could no doubt tell her a lot about. To Felicia it was nothing more than an unnecessary, expensive tin box on wheels. The garden was well kept, and the scent of magnolia blossoms hinted at a hired gardener. The house itself was immaculate, with new windows and freshly painted trim. It was over a hundred years old, and would stand for another hundred if the Price family continued to take care of it with equal parts love and craftsmen from south of the border.

The doorbell had a deep, worthy resonance, followed by a silence that almost swallowed the sound of the light traffic in the residential neighborhood behind Stone. She noticed that she was clenching her fists involuntarily. She was so eager to get started that even an unimportant witness felt significant.

After a moment, the door opened.

Megan Price's hair had undoubtedly turned gray long ago, but she dyed it a reddish hue that set off her rust-brown eyes. It looked as though she'd had some work done, a few wrinkles removed here and there, but it had been carefully and discreetly done, so it wasn't obvious. Not even when she smiled a bit uncertainly, as she did after opening the door and seeing Felicia Stone, who was quite obviously a cop. Stone held out her ID without saying a word.

"That was quick," said Mrs. Price. She was wearing casual, loose-fitting clothes that still looked elegant. Her expression changed from uncertain to serious. "Good to see that you're giving high priority to this terrible case. Who would do a thing like that to poor Bond? He was such a good and cautious man."

"My condolences," said Stone. "And if we knew who did it, I can promise you I wouldn't be standing here right now."

"No, of course not. But do come in." Mrs. Price opened the door wider and stepped aside to let her into a hallway the size of Stone's apartment.

"You can keep your shoes on. I'm expecting the cleaning lady this afternoon," said Megan Price, leading the way into the kitchen. It was oak-paneled, had stone flooring, and all the appliances were black. Mrs. Price asked her to have a seat on a stool at the kitchen island and went to get two flowered Wedgwood cups and saucers from one of the many cupboards.

A phone rang. She pulled out a cell phone from the big floral-patterned pocket of her off-white jacket. She listened for a moment, then spoke. Her voice was businesslike.

"Tell me, Mr. . . . excuse me, what was your name again? Gary Ridgeway, yes. Tell me, Mr. Ridgeway, how much are we paying you for this job? I understand. And why can't you finish tomorrow? Well, I'll have to tell my husband." She sighed and ended the call. "Workmen!" she said, throwing out her arms in resignation.

"Was there something important that had to be done?"

"No, just repainting my car. I have a little VW Beetle. It's taken more than a few days, and I hate driving the Jaguar."

Felicia Stone nodded and registered vaguely that Mrs. Price had mentioned her husband, although the call had concerned her car. They always had to drag their husbands into it, these housewives from the rich suburbs, as if the man was the center of the universe.

"I've just made some tea," said Mrs. Price. "Green. It's supposed to be so healthy. I don't know about you, but I'm too restless to drink coffee."

"Green tea is supposed to be excellent for the digestion," said Felicia with a smile. That was exactly what she needed.

The tea was served in a pot from the same china set as the cups. Mrs. Price also served madeleines, home baked, but perhaps not by her.

"I'll get right to the point," she said, after tasting the shell-shaped French pastry. "You mentioned in an earlier interview that Efrahim Bond had sent a leather sample to the university. Was it the University of Richmond or VCU?"

"VCU. My husband is the head of the Philips Institute. They conduct research into diseases and genetics; you'll have to ask Frederick about that. They're mostly concerned with the head, jaw, and throat region at the institute, but my husband said he knew where to send the leather to have it tested, so I gave it to him. Is it important? Do you think it has something to do with the case?"

"For the moment we're just checking into every possible connection."

"I could call Frederick," said Mrs. Price.

She took out her phone and dialed the number without waiting for an answer from Stone. Mrs. Price explained what she was calling about. Then she said "yes" a few times, almost as though she were bored. Stone got the feeling that she was often bored when talking to her husband on the phone.

She ended the call. "He says that the test results are ready and were supposed to be sent to the museum today. But he held them back for the time being, in view of what happened. If you like, you can pick them up at his office."

"How long will he be there?" Stone asked.

"He said he'd wait until you get there," said Mrs. Price.

Stone stood up. On the way out she stopped and looked at some photos on a table in the hall. They were mostly of Mr. and Mrs. Price. In some of the pictures, which all looked like they were taken by amateurs with expensive equipment, they were standing with a boy who had dark hair and a self-assured smile. In other pictures the boy was alone. He was playing baseball or sitting in a sailboat. Some of the snapshots could have been taken at a summer house, probably on the Chesapeake Bay. Felicia noticed that the boy was no older than ten in any of the pictures; there were no photos on the table of a young man with a family, or of any grandchildren. That might explain the unpleasant feeling of emptiness she'd had since entering the Price home.

She turned away from the pictures and looked at Mrs. Price, who was following her to say good-bye. Felicia thought she looked so frail and thin. She asked: "By the way, do you happen to know anything else about that scrap of leather? Which book it came from?"

Megan Price looked at her and thought.

"Bond wouldn't tell me," she said. "But I think I know. A few weeks ago I noticed that the leather had been removed from the spine of one of the books in Poe's private collection. Those are the volumes in the bookcase in Bond's office: first editions of Poe's own works, and a number of other books Poe himself owned, or belonged to his family when he died. I saw a book lying open on Bond's desk when I dropped off his mail the other day. He wasn't in the office, so I peeked to see which book it was. I know all the books well and had never seen any of them with leather removed from the spine. It was a first edition of *Childe Harold's Pilgrimage* by Lord Byron. We don't know much about it. Some people think that Poe bought it from a European immigrant in New York, along with a number of other books, but there are no reliable sources to confirm that theory."

"Why do you think Bond had removed leather from that book? He must have been the one who did it, right?"

"I'm sure he did, but it was in good condition, so I can't think why. The only reason I can think of would be that Bond had discovered something written on it."

"What do you mean?"

"That book was apparently bound sometime in the eighteenth century. Parchment is made of calfskin and calfskin was hard to come by. People often reused sheets of parchment from old books that were considered obsolete. That's why even today we can find fragments of unrelated texts inside the spines of old books. Sometimes they are important historical or literary sources. And to make it all even more complicated, occasionally these parchments turn out to have several layers of texts, written on top of each other. In the Middle Ages it was not unusual to wash a parchment that had a text written on it, and then use it again. It's known as a palimpsest. Today, using modern techniques, we can often decipher what was in the underlying text. *Scripta inferiori,* it's called."

Stone nodded, rather impressed at Mrs. Price's extensive knowledge.

"And you think that Bond may have made such a discovery?"

"I don't know. I'm just speculating. But maybe that's why he was so secretive in recent weeks."

"But you mentioned calfskin. Do you have any idea why Bond would want to have a piece of it tested? Can books be bound, or for that matter can parchment be made, from anything besides calfskin?"

"Calfskin was considered the best, but parchment was also quite often made from the skins of goats and pigs."

"But why do you think it was important for Bond to find out exactly what kind of skin had been used on that book?"

"I have absolutely no idea," said Mrs. Price with a deep sigh.

Felicia Stone thanked her and left.

The Philips Institute was located on North Eleventh Street, right in the heart of Richmond, not far from the Capitol District and the city's venerable old buildings and monuments. Right here in this city the Founding Fathers had reeled off mighty pearls of wisdom such as "Give me liberty or give me death!"

Today's concept of freedom was more along the lines of being able to choose what flavor syrup to have in your caffé latte or what logo to have on your jogging suit. Regardless of the logo, however, it had been sewn by a Chinese worker who wasn't free. Still, Felicia liked to be reminded that freedom actually meant something, and that in her own way she was working to preserve it. She always took the opportunity to roam about the Capitol District whenever she could. She parked a few blocks away, walked through the park with the Virginia Civil Rights Memorial, and from there headed toward the institute.

Frederick Price was a broad-shouldered, gray-haired man with a few touches of black still left in his eyebrows. He was friendly but businesslike.

"I have the results of the tests here," he said as soon as she had introduced herself, and sat down on the chair in front of his big modern beechwood desk. He held up a sealed envelope. "If you like, I can open it and read it for you. It can be a bit difficult to understand the scientific language."

She felt like saying that she wasn't stupid, and many people on the force could read "scientific language" as competently as the head of the Philips Institute. Instead she nodded, smiled, and let him read the report. It was a good investigative tactic to let people do as much as possible on their own initiative.

He opened the envelope and read the report in silence. Then he said: "I don't know what sort of answer you were expecting from this analysis, and I don't know where the leather sample came from." Frederick Price leaned over the desk, planted his elbows on the desktop, and looked sincerely concerned. "But I think you may be surprised by this."

Then he explained the contents of the report. The moment he told her the results she realized that the little piece of skin was not a minor detail of no consequence. It was absolutely crucial to the case. The analysis showed that it was a scrap of human skin. And it was five hundred years old.

12

Trondheim, 1528

The mendicant monk had reached the city where he was born. It did not take him long to ascertain that his mother was no longer living. But he was told that the smith had made sure she was buried in the churchyard next to the hospital.

Her grave was not marked—that was the custom of only the rich—but she had been laid to rest in consecrated ground. It was raining when the monk visited the cemetery grove one afternoon, and he stood there for almost an hour. As a boy he had often wondered why she had let him go. He no longer asked that question, but he would have liked to see her again one last time.

On the way out of the cemetery, he decided to pay a visit to the archbishop. He wanted to settle down here in Norway. Having made that decision, he could think back with a certain calm to the years that had passed since he last walked among the muddy streets and alleys of Trondheim.

Venice, 1516

It was three days since they had arrived in this city floating on the water and taken lodging at an inn, where they shared a cramped room. Two years of wandering had passed since they left the cold of the north. In a town in Germany the beard-cutter had worked one long summer as an executioner. He chopped the heads off murderers and drunken witches. Otherwise they kept moving, slowly using up most of the funds the beard-cutter had saved.

They had not yet found the happiness they sought. But the beard-cutter had promised that it was here in Venice, the city he called the greatest in the world, even though the boy had heard that there were even bigger cities in the lands with which Venice traded.

The beard-cutter had even shown the boy the house where Lady Fortuna lived, although she had taken a man's form. It was situated on a peaceful canal not far from Piazza San Marco, where the enormous campanile stood. That was where Master Alessandro lived. It was said that he had traveled around the Mediterranean collecting books. He had found many treasures in places like the knights' lovely island of Rhodes and in the lands of the infidels farther east. He had one of the largest collections in the city of works by the old masters, people said. They also said that the famed printer Teobaldo Manucci owed him a debt of gratitude. Master Teobaldo's unusual series of books featuring ancient Greek and Roman works had acquired a great deal of material from Master Alessandro's extensive library. Naturally this did not detract in the least from the honor Teobaldo had won for inventing the strange little books that a reader could easily carry under his arm.

But it was not because of the books or Alessandro's reputation as a book collector that the beard-cutter had set his sights on the famous physician. Master Alessandro was known for one other thing: He opened corpses. Rumor had it that he saw things inside the bodies that no one had ever seen before.

Nonetheless the beard-cutter's plan did include one of Teobaldo's famous books—not any one in particular, but one chosen at random. In brief, whatever book Master Alessandro had chosen to take along on his morning walk.

As the boy and the beard-cutter lay in bed at the inn, before the sun had risen and only the craziest roosters in the city had begun to crow, they knew that he would take a book with him on his customary morning walk. He always took these walks after breakfast, and every time he took a book with him. He would hold it carefully, as if he were walking hand in hand with a young girl, said one of the greengrocer wives.

The beard-cutter had already found a young lad to do the job. His own boy could not do it, because he wanted the boy to continue on with him. They were bound together by an invisible bond, as he often told the boy. The two of them had to stay together, at least until they found their happiness.

That is why the beard-cutter had struck up a conversation with one of the beggar lads who cadged money from visitors to Piazza San Marco. The lads were not the only charlatans in Venice. Visitors to the city were swindled out of money at every turn: by the merchants, the barbers, and the innkeepers. But the little boys who begged and searched with their nimble fingers in coat pockets and bags were still the ones who did the least for the money. They were more reviled than the Jews, that tormented people who were locked up behind walls in the cannon foundry, Ghetto Nuovo, at night. The beard-cutter liked to talk to the beggar lads. It had not taken him long, nor did he have to spend many small coins, before he had talked one of them into helping him.

"So you really want me to do it so that he sees me and follows me?" the lad asked after the beard-cutter had explained the task.

"Yes," the beard-cutter replied, giving him an extra coin. "I hope you're fast on your feet."

"Fast enough," said the lad, taking the coin.

"Tell me again what's inside of us," said the boy, as they ate a break-fast of olives, cheese, and sour bread. He still remembered that night in Germany. They had stayed in a little hut on the outskirts of town, and one evening the beard-cutter came back dragging a dead witch he'd thrown into the river at dawn. He fished her out of the water himself. That was his job. But this time he hadn't taken her away from town to bury her outside the churchyard. He hid her in the woods all day, and in the evening he brought the witch back to their hut. If anyone saw him, he was risking being drowned himself, or maybe even burned alive. Then he sent the boy to bed, while in the light from only two tallow candles, he worked on the dead body all night long. The boy could not see much from the bed, where he was pretending to be asleep, but he heard and smelled everything in the room—the stench that grew worse with each incision and the crunching sound of knives cutting through bone. The boy had never felt so alive. The next day, when the witch was finally buried behind the church, where the path to hell was the shortest, he asked the beard-cutter why he had done it. Why had he risked his life to look inside a human being. But he already knew the answer.

"I simply had to see it with my own eyes," replied the beard-cutter. "There's a whole world in there."

But the beard-cutter had not buried all of the witch. He had kept her skin, preparing it and placing it at the bottom of his sack.

Now, as they sat in the dawn light in their lodgings in Venice, the beard-cutter chewed his bread slowly. The boy noticed the first gray hairs in the man's coal-black beard. His eyes were still clear, while the rest of his face had a heavy, fatigued look that vanished only when he was most excited, as he was the morning after examining the witch.

"There's a lot of blood," the beard-cutter snapped, the way he did when he didn't want to talk.

"And the blood is stored in the liver, isn't it?" said the boy.

The beard-cutter nodded.

"And from there it rises up to the brain?"

Again the beard-cutter nodded without a word.

"And the heart is where the soul resides, right? Is that where God lives?"

"God lives everywhere," said the beard-cutter. Finally the boy had made him want to talk. "God lives in all the body's four humors, even in melancholia, the black gall. God lives in the liver and the kidneys and the heart. But people say that the blood is the life force itself. When a wounded soldier dies on the battlefield it's because the life force seeps out of him. But it doesn't mean that he will be abandoned by God."

The liver, the kidneys, the heart. The boy listened to these words as though they were the names of angels, living beings he had never seen. But he knew that they also belonged to this world, that they were inside everyone and gave life in ways that were still not understood.

"I think that human beings should understand the works of the Creator. Only then can we truly understand ourselves," said the beard-cutter. And when he talked like that, the boy knew that he had been lucky. One of the smartest men of his time had taken him under his wing. He would learn much, and one day he would also see for himself. Then he might understand more than what he could read in a book. Wasn't that exactly what the beard-cutter had said? The reason they had sought out Master Alessandro was that this physician knew more than could be found in books. In any case, that was what was rumored. A rumor that could be dangerous for a man who lived outside the Republic of Venice, which included the city of Padua, with its famous school and its many doctors. In Venice and Padua the city air was freer than in most other places. The beard-cutter explained that autopsies here were regulated by law, and that each year male and female bodies were taken down from the gallows so that the most learned doctors could increase their knowledge of the internal organs of human beings. Venice was not afraid of the pope's wrath. The city had felt it before and feared it no longer.

"Now," said the beard-cutter, putting the last bite of bread in his mouth, "it's time for us to get moving. The sun has reached the rooftops on the other side of the canal. It won't be long before our good doctor goes out for his walk. Today we don't want to miss that walk for anything in the world."

The street urchin met them as they had previously agreed, by the bridge where they could see the front door of Master Alessandro's house from across the canal. The plan was simple: When they saw him come out the door, the lad would run across the bridge toward the doctor while the beard-cutter and the boy would walk along the canal on the opposite bank toward the next bridge. There they hoped to meet again, and change the path of destiny.

Master Alessandro let his forefinger glide slowly and tenderly along the spines of the books he kept on the little shelf just inside the door of his library. The little shelf was reserved for Teobaldo's handy little volumes. The rest of the library was filled with parchment rolls and large tomes that he had collected on his travels.

His finger stopped on a work by Plato, which, somewhat indelicately, had been dedicated to Pope Leo. But that might fit now-adays, he thought with black humor, letting his mind drift back to the house in Padua and the corpse that was supposed to be awaiting him there. If that laggard Pietro had done his job at the grave site outside town. But he could not count on it. He had long pondered finding a replacement for his servant Pietro. He made mistakes far too often. Pietro never got used to handling dead people and made mistakes, such as forgetting to tie them down on the cart. Eventually they would fall into the ditch and lose limbs during the transport. Or else he let himself be scared off by the watchmen in the cemetery and came back empty-handed the night after an execution. And he was no good with a knife, so he wasn't much help during the dissections.

Master Alessandro tucked the book under his arm and left the library. For a moment he placed the book on a table by the door while he put on a voluminous burgundy velvet cape. It kept him warm in this autumn weather. Then he picked up the book to take along on his walk.

Even though the sun was shining, there was a cold wind coming off the sea, the type that felt like it was blowing right through you. Master Alessandro greeted the woman selling vegetables and asked whether there had been frost in the night. She told him that it had not yet arrived, and if they were lucky they might be able to save the whole harvest this year. Alessandro blessed her and promised to buy some turnips from her the next time he came by.

He was taking his usual route along the canal and over the bridge to Piazza San Marco. But he had not even come to the bridge when it happened. A little street urchin who barely came up to the belt on his cloak popped out of nowhere. Alessandro had no time to tighten his grip before the lad grabbed the book out of his hands. Then something odd happened. Instead of turning and vanishing in the crowd, the lad stood still in front of him for a couple of seconds. Alessandro was just about to reach out and grab him when he took off at a run.

Master Alessandro was beside himself. One of these little scamps had made off with his coin purse more than once. Here in Venice he never carried more in his purse than he could afford to lose. But this was a book he had lost, and that was quite a different matter. A book, even one of Manutius's small ones with the velour spines, was irreplaceable, even sacrosanct. One did not steal a book.

Alessandro was not used to running, but now he ran. He set off after the lad as though a wild beast had been awakened inside him. At the same time he bellowed, "Stop thief!"

A couple of men who were fishing in the canal reacted, but too late. The lad slipped away as they reached out to seize him. Soon he was across the bridge.

On the other side of the canal two people were walking along. A tall man with a big black beard in an expensive but well-worn cloak and a boy of about eleven or twelve. As the man spied the urchin who came running and heard Master Alessandro's wild howls, he lunged and grabbed the thief by the arm. Then he pulled the book from his hands. The little devil wriggled from the beard-cutter's grip and got away. But the man was left holding the book. Master Alessandro thought that the lad had escaped rather easily, but he thought no more about it as he went jogging across the bridge to thank the man. The most important thing was that the book was in good hands.

"I presume that this belongs to you?" said the man as Alessandro approached. "Allow me to introduce myself. I am Olav the beard-cutter. I come from a land far to the north, and I am a master with my knives. The boy here is named Johannes. He is my apprentice.

And to whom do I have the pleasure of offering my hand on this fine, sunny day?"

"Alessandro," replied the physician, curious. "Tell me, Olav the beard-cutter, you have clearly left your own beard alone, but can you cut other things than beards?"

"There are many ways I can use my knives," replied the beard-cutter.

PART II

Palimpsest

The center of the universe is everywhere and its circumference nowhere.

—Johannes the Priest, ca. 1550

13

Trondheim, September 2010

Each morning was like waking up after an operation. At first everything was a fog. Or maybe like a viscous sea, where everything was white and still. The landscape of death. Then things grew a little sharper. The lamp with the floral shade, hanging from the ceiling but not switched on, the nightstand with a stack of *Missing Persons* magazines and a nonfiction book written by a Swedish police officer. On top of the stack lay the cell phone. Odd Singsaker hated it, just as he did everything on which he was dependent. But when it lay quite still and motionless, as it did now, it didn't bother him much.

Before the brain tumor, he always used to start his day with a shot of Rød Aalborg aquavit. It had to be at room temperature to get the most out of the spicy flavoring. After the operation, when he was declared healthy again, he had increased his morning dose to two shots. He still liked to drink his aquavit the Danish way, with herring and rye bread. Singsaker thought it was an excellent way to start the day. The water of life and the silver of the sea. Today he was supposed to return to his job as chief inspector at Trondheim police headquarters. But the bottle of aquavit was empty, the last pieces of herring were resting dully at the bottom of the jar, and the rye bread had gone stale. If he were still on sick leave, it would have been time to go shopping. But now he would have to begin the day on an empty stomach. Not a good start for what would turn out to be a crash landing in reality.

On his way out the front door he glimpsed the neighbor who lived across the street, who came out of the portal riding a very expensive but dilapidated Cervelo racing bike. Who would let such a costly bike fall into disrepair like that? Singsaker wondered. Perhaps something had happened to his neighbor, some sort of crisis in the man's life, something so devastating that he had become indifferent to things he once cared about.

Singsaker didn't really know him, although they had met long before the brain tumor, before his memory went bad. The neighbor didn't glance in his direction; he just rode off, lost in his own world, and heading toward Asylbakken.

On the short stretch from the apartment to Bakkegate, Singsaker walked past another neighbor, Jens Dahle, who was washing his car in the autumn sunshine. Dahle was the only person he ever talked to along this stretch. They had never talked about anything personal. Just small talk. He hadn't told Dahle that he was newly divorced. Or that his wife, Anniken, whom he had regarded his whole life as the better person, told him that she had found someone else—two weeks before he went in for surgery. It was an operation in which the chances were fifty-fifty. The surgeons would either be able to remove the whole tumor or they might kill him in the attempt.

Anniken told him that she'd been seeing a master mason from Klæbu for a long time, and that she didn't want to keep it a secret any longer. Odd had no choice but to accept her feelings. Most likely the brain tumor had been affecting his personality for more than two years. Though it wasn't the only thing to blame, it had contributed to making him peevish and difficult to live with. Thinking about the way he had treated his wife then, it was a wonder she hadn't left him earlier. Instead she had taken a lover, a mason, and Odd Singsaker would be the first to admit that she deserved every one of the mortar-moist caresses the man had given her.

Anniken hadn't intended to leave him. Instead she had broken things off with the mason. She said she wanted to save their marriage. Her somewhat faulty logic probably went something like this: Honesty would destroy the tumor infecting their marriage. Then the two of them would fight the real tumor, the one growing in his brain. And eventually, not too long from now, everything would be fine again. He didn't believe it. She couldn't save him. Nor was she to blame for what had happened. He never believed that the tumor in his head was anything but a manifestation of cells going berserk. It was not a result of dishonesty or an ailing marriage, nor could it be cured by a good one. He understood why Anniken had been unfaithful, and maybe even halfway forgave her, but it wasn't possible for him to get beyond her confession. It merely made him see clearly what had been sneaking up on him ever since he heard the diagnosis months earlier. He had to get through this headache by himself. It was simply a matter of directing his forces where they were needed most. He would have to move out and live alone.

So that was what he did. But now, after a successful operation, he wasn't sure that it had made any difference. The tumor had been cut out of his head by surgeons whose hands didn't shake. Anniken had visited him several times after the operation. She had brought flowers and tea, and aquavit the last time, a sure sign that she counted on him coming back to her soon.

Jens Dahle knew nothing about this. Odd Singsaker talked to him about the weather, the Rosenborg Ballklub team, and car wash detergent. The last topic seemed to interest Dahle the most. No wonder, considering he washed his car at least once a week, always doing a careful job. It could take him hours. Sometimes Singsaker would go downtown while Dahle was at it and return before he was done. As a policeman he felt that this type of knowledge— what he knew about a neighbor's car-washing habits—was often more revealing than the most intimate details about a person.

Today Dahle remarked that his car was extra dirty. Singsaker had stopped, mostly so as not to seem unfriendly, although he really didn't have time to chat. Dahle had been away at his cabin with the kids all weekend and hadn't come home until after his wife had left for work in the morning. As far as Singsaker could recall, his wife worked at the Gunnerus Library.

"The narrow cart path that leads from the highway to the cabin turns into a big mud bath in the fall. It's better when the frost sets in and there's some snow on it," Jens Dahle said with a smile.

Singsaker looked up to catch his eye. Dahle was over six foot seven and particular about his appearance, always wearing a shirt and tie, even when he washed the car. Singsaker knew that he was an archaeologist, and it amazed him that somebody so tall and fond of nice clothes would choose such a profession. He couldn't imagine him kneeling in a fire pit from the Stone Age, picking out remnants of charcoal. But that probably wasn't what he did, anyway. Jens Dahle had a position at the Science Museum, where he sat safely ensconced behind a desk. Singsaker assumed that with a job like that he could easily take Monday morning off to wash his car. As he said good-bye, without mentioning where he was off to, it occurred to him that he knew a great deal more about Jens Dahle than the archaeologist knew about him. Singsaker didn't think he'd even told him that he was a cop.

Moving faster and taking longer strides than he had for the past few months, he walked down Bakkegate and across the bridge to the center of town. He was wearing a parka with a black turtleneck underneath, and jeans. After a weekend of rain, it was a clear day. On the other side of the bridge he turned right, taking the sidewalk on the same side as Olavshallen, then continued across the Brattør canal to arrive at police headquarters. It looked the same as it had when he left it on a cold day last December. The headquarters had been designed in the same quasi-maritime style as most of the buildings around Beddingen, a sort of conglomerate of oil-drilling platforms, shipyards, and the big ferries to Denmark. In the midst of everything stood a gray concrete tower with the word POLICE written on it in huge, bold type. This was the new battleship of the Trondheim police. He had never felt at home here. But he'd never felt at home in the old building either, so it didn't really matter. He was out of breath when he stepped inside the service entrance, and he felt a faint prickling just above his hairline at the site of the surgery scar.

The day before he had talked to Gro Brattberg on the phone. She was the leader of the violent crimes and vice team, and his boss. Brattberg told him that his old office was still waiting for him. It seemed strangely quiet in the corridors. He tried to remember if it was always that quiet, and was shocked to realize how little he actually remembered from the last time he was here. But maybe that wasn't so strange, when he thought about it. The whole year before he was diagnosed and went on sick leave, he had felt lethargic and suffered from bouts of dizziness, foggy vision, brightly colored hallucinations, and a constant buzzing sensation behind his eyes that not even a whole bottle of Rød Aalborg could cure.

It wasn't until he reached the administrative wing that he realized things might be worse than he feared. It was as quiet as a murder scene. All the offices on the way to his own were empty. The whole wing seemed deserted. When he opened the door to his office, he stopped and gaped. Then he forced himself to smile. How could he have run out of aquavit on a day like this? He had feared a welcoming committee. What he got was a whole convention.

Everyone in violent crimes and vice had squeezed into his office; even people who weren't on duty had dropped by to say hello. As he stood in the doorway, people from other departments crowded around in the corridor, including crime scene technicians and officers from the traffic police. The only one missing was the police chief herself, Dagmar Øverbye, but hardly anyone ever saw her. Witty tongues had begun to call her "The Phantom Ghost." But thanks to people like Gro Brattberg, this leadership model functioned all right. Actually, Singsaker doubted there would have been room for Øverbye if she'd decided to show up. She was a solidly built woman, and the hallway behind him was crowded. People had somehow figured out how to sneak up on him from behind, and he stood there wondering whether an experienced policeman like himself should be embarrassed at being caught unawares like this. But the worst thing had to be that he felt so touched. Somewhere in all the crap he'd been through with the operation, weeks of hospital smells, gallons of sweat on the sheets, nice nurses, and dreams about his own corpse, the control he used to have over his emotions had disappeared. Odd Singsaker was now easily moved. The tiniest thing could make him break down in tears; even silly sitcoms could make him laugh like a kid.

He stood there looking at all the friendly faces, the banner saying WELCOME BACK hanging from the front of his desk, the flowers on the shelf by the wall, and Gro Brattberg, who stood fumbling with a piece of paper on which she had obviously scribbled some words of welcome. He knew there was really no way out. His Adam's apple swelled like a mushroom in water, and the tears began running down his cheeks. This was the first time any of the people in the room had seen him cry, and many of them had known him for over thirty years. Several of them came over and gave him a hug, also something new and untried, and it did nothing to quell his tears. Thorvald Jensen came over and placed a hand on his shoulder to lean over and give him a manly hug with no actual skin contact. That was when Singsaker understood that his job would never be the same as it had been when he left with a tumor the size of a golf ball inside his head. Chief Inspector Odd Singsaker, the laconic, pensive investigator with the cynical comments, was gone. No one in the room knew who would replace his old persona. All they knew was that things were not going to be like they were before. And maybe that was just as well.

Fortunately, things got back to normal fairly quickly. Gro Brattberg gave her speech. Singsaker received a gift, a Moleskine notebook (he had almost forgotten that he swore by these legendary notebooks). Everybody had a piece of cake. Then there were more hugs before they all went into the conference room and started work with a brief report on a quiet night. Most of the team members had assignments they were working on: a serious domestic dispute; a suspicion of sexual abuse in a church congregation; a teenage gang that had beaten up a boy the same age, or "happy slapping," as they called it. Odd was going to spend the day getting organized and making phone calls. Brattberg, who was aware that Singsaker wasn't satisfied unless he was working on a specific case, promised that she'd update him on the church case if it turned out there was anything to it.

Finally alone in his office, Singsaker sat down and leafed through the notebook he'd received, wondering what differentiated a Moleskine from other notebooks. Had these books ever made him a better detective? From the advertising material included with the book, it appeared that great writers such as Hemingway had used them. Something told him that he had known this, but now it was forgotten and no longer made any difference. He did need a notebook, however, so it would do. That was when he started to think about his neighbor with the dilapidated Cervelo bicycle. The two of us just stopped caring, he thought.

After paging through the empty notebook, he went to the canteen and bought a dry rusk, a hard, twice-baked biscuit, with ham and cheese. Back in his office, he ate it slowly as he thought about herring, rye bread, and aquavit. Then the phone rang. It was Brattberg.

"Hey, I promised you something to work on," she said, pausing for effect. "But what sort of shape are you in?"

"I've been declared fit to work," he said. "I'm here to do my job."

"I could send Jensen, but he's still with the pastor."

"Just get to the point," he replied. "I'm here to work."

"A few minutes ago Operations received a report of a murder. At the Gunnerus Library."

"Jesus, inside the library itself?"

"Yes, in the book vault, as a matter of fact."

"Has it been confirmed?"

"We have people on their way over there to secure the scene. I'll have confirmation soon."

"Who reported the killing?"

"A man named Hornemann, head of the library."

"And the victim?"

Brattberg hesitated before she answered. He could hear her shuffling through her papers.

"Gunn Brita Dahle," she said at last.

He sat there without saying anything. Gunn Brita Dahle was the wife of Jens Dahle. He had just talked to him this morning on the way to work. The man had shown no sign of grief as he washed his car, believing that his wife had gone to work before he came home from the cabin. Or? Right away the detective in him took charge. How carefree had Jens Dahle actually been? Wasn't it a little odd that he hadn't called his wife to tell her that he was home? But maybe he had. Maybe she'd unplugged her phone, the way people occasionally do at work. It was too early to jump to conclusions. He was in the unusual situation of having unknowingly spoken with the victim's husband after the crime was committed. It gave him the opportunity to evaluate Dahle with the eyes of an impartial witness. And his impression this morning had not been that he was talking with a killer. Jens Dahle had seemed like a relaxed and content family man with plenty of time to wash his car.

"Are you there, Singsaker?" said Brattberg from somewhere far away.

"I'm here," he said. "I'll take it."

"Are you sure you're ready for something like this?"

"What I'm not ready for is to sit here staring at the wall," he replied.

Brattberg suggested he take Mona Gran with him, a rookie officer who had started just before he got sick; he barely remembered her.

Wasn't she the one who had danced wildly with Thorvald on the table at the Christmas party the night before he collapsed and was taken to St. Olav's Hospital? In any case, she seemed sharp.

The Christmas party was not a topic of conversation on their way through the downtown area.

"A murder in the library! It's almost like an Agatha Christie story."

Mona Gran was excited, and Singsaker wondered how many murder scenes she had been to.

"This will be real enough, I promise you," he said. "But I agree that it certainly does sound incredible," he added, thinking that he had assumed a much too stern tone. They were met outside the Gunnerus Library by two uniforms, who gave them a brief rundown of what they'd found; a dead body inside the book vault.

"The victim has been flayed. And it's the most horrific thing I've ever seen," one of the officers whispered to Singsaker. From his confidential tone, Odd assumed that they'd known each other before the operation.

As they talked, an elderly gentleman came outside to join them. The officer introduced the man as Per Ottar Hornemann, head of the library. They followed him up to the public area on the second floor.

"We have gathered the whole staff in Knudtzon Hall," said Hornemann. "No one has been admitted to the offices or the book vault since we made the discovery. Jon Vatten here is in charge of security. He can show you the way, if you like." He pointed at the security chief. It was Singsaker's neighbor, who rode the dilapidated bike.

Another neighbor, and the case has hardly begun, he thought ironically. He instinctively had a desire to greet Vatten as an acquaintance but realized that he'd only seen him from a distance a few times. The man probably wasn't aware that they had recently become neighbors. He extended his hand.

To his great surprise, Vatten said, "We meet again."

Only three words and nothing more. Enough to catch him completely off guard. What the hell did he mean by that?

It occurred to him that he wasn't really ready to start back to work. Jon Vatten recognized him. It even seemed that they knew each other fairly well. He hadn't just seen him from his window.

The two of them had spoken on some occasion, perhaps several times. And the way Vatten had said "we meet again" told him unequivocally that the security man did not find the encounter pleasant. So they must have met before in a professional capacity. People he met on the job were not always glad to see him again. It came with the territory. It was also part of his job to remember these people. Now he stood there wondering how many memories of acquaintances he might have left on the operating table.

"Yes, we meet again," he said flatly, hoping to hide his confusion.

"What would you like to see first?" Vatten asked, obviously not wanting to elaborate on their previous contact.

"I think we should go straight to the crime scene," said Chief Inspector Singsaker, relieved to escape the awkward situation.

Gunn Brita Dahle was lying on her stomach. Her head was missing. The skin had been flayed off the body above the waist. Next to the victim were two big plastic bags. Singsaker opened one to see what was inside. Fat. From under the skin. She must have had a lot of it. The bulk of the rest of her body indicated as much. The stench was unbearable. Mona Gran, who had accompanied him into the book vault, had turned away and taken a few steps back. He was pretty sure she was looking for a toilet, or at least a wastebasket, where she could throw up. The entire floor inside the vault was covered in blood, apart from a small area by the door where Singsaker was standing, blue plastic booties over his shoes. He turned to Jon Vatten, who was standing right behind him and staring dejectedly at the floor.

"Did you find her here like this?" he asked, glancing again at the grotesque corpse, blood vessels and muscles exposed.

"We haven't touched anything in here," replied Vatten.

"All right, then. I want you to return to the others. Knudtzon Hall, you called it?" he asked, knowing quite well that it was.

"Yes, that's the showpiece of the building, re-creating Knudtzon's personal library of rare books and art," Vatten explained.

"Knudtzon's personal library. I see," said Singsaker. "Go there, and I'll be down soon." He thought hard. "One thing before you leave. Have you noticed if anything is missing from the vault?"

"I haven't had time to think about that, to tell the truth," said Vatten.

"Could you take a quick look? You know what's supposed to be in here, right?" He studied him carefully.

"Yes, I do," said Vatten firmly.

Singsaker watched as Vatten inspected the shelves. He was very thorough. Not once did he stop and look down at the body. Finally, he said: "No, everything seems to be in its place."

"I see," said Singsaker. "There's one more thing," he added, and was just about to ask him where in the hell they'd met before. "As head of security, do you oversee who opens and closes the vault?"

"I have one of two codes to the vault, so anyone who wants to go inside has to talk to me. The second code is kept by one of the librarians. Gunn Brita was actually the one who knew what it was. The codes are secret and aren't given to anyone else. The only person who can enter without telling me is Hornemann. He knows both of the codes."

"So the big question is," said the chief inspector, examining Vatten closely, "How did the victim and the murderer get into the vault without help from you or Hornemann?"

Vatten stared him straight in the eye and answered, "I've been wondering that myself."

Singsaker couldn't interpret his expression. He could be a good liar, but he could also be completely innocent.

"How long do you think she might have been in here?" he asked.

"I was here with Gunn Brita on Saturday morning. And she had no plans to come back. She was supposed to start a new job today."

"I see. But in theory she could have come back anytime after that, correct? Maybe she forgot something and came to get it, let's say on Sunday. Is it possible she knew the other code? Do you ever stand close enough when you open the vault that she might have seen you enter the code and memorized it?"

"That's possible, sure, but I'm careful about shielding the keypad when I type it in," said Vatten. "As far as I know, she hadn't turned in her card key yet, so she might have come back here on Sunday. If she used a card key in any of the outside doors to the library, we'll see it in the log."

"When did people arrive this morning?"

"I was here at seven," said Vatten. "Most people show up between seven and nine."

"And the body was found just before you called the police at ten thirty?"

"That's correct."

"And it's quite certain that the body was here for several hours without anyone noticing the smell?"

"The book vault is climate-controlled and sealed to maintain optimum humidity for the books. Not a drop of moisture or, for that matter, a molecule of odor could escape through this door."

"I understand," said Singsaker, surprised at the security man's academic mode of speaking. There was also something about his slouching, washed-out appearance that indicated Vatten had more education than security training.

"Let's say that she was lying in here from Saturday morning until early Monday morning. Don't you think it's odd that no one reported her missing? Didn't she have any family?" he asked, playing dumb.

"A husband and children. But they were apparently at their cabin all weekend."

"In that case they should have reacted when they came home Sunday evening," said Singsaker.

"Well, that's something you'll have to ask them about."

"I'll do that."

"Her husband is an archaeologist. He works at the Science Museum in the building next door. His name's Jens Dahle," said Vatten, stepping out of the book vault.

Maybe it was being in the same room with a stinking and decomposing corpse for so long that did it, but Vatten seemed shaken.

Singsaker thanked Vatten for his cooperation. He didn't regret detaining the man in the same room as the body, even though it was beyond the limit of responsible police work. So he let Vatten return to the others.

Then he was alone. He was never enthusiastic about murder scenes. Although he had taught himself to switch off his emotions and not think about the fact that a human life had ended in this very spot, he never managed to escape the sense that there was something insistent about every murder. Murder was a form of human expression that humanity could do without. It was always messy, foul smelling, and disgusting. When he saw a dead body, he always thought about the murderer and asked: Jesus Christ, you motherfucker, couldn't you have told us this some other way?

Only the gods knew what the killer was trying to tell them with the murder of Gunn Brita Dahle. This murder didn't resemble any he had seen before. He thought about TV crime shows and psychotic murderers, serial killers, people who killed for the hell of it, people who didn't think that death itself was enough but who somehow had to make a drama out of the act of murder. This looked like a murder in which the act was the actual motive. But above all it made him think of hunting.

His colleague Thorvald Jensen usually enticed him to go hunting with him in the fall. Singsaker was no hunting enthusiast, but Jensen was good at convincing him, and aquavit tasted especially good in the autumn woods. That's why he went along. He had seen carcasses of deer and moose hanging from thick branches, skinned and ready to be butchered. What surprised him was how much a human body resembled an animal once the head was removed and the skin flayed off. Gunn Brita Dahle looked like a hunting kill lying there, except that she hadn't been hung up and there was no moss or heather for the blood to seep into. She lay in a pool of blood that covered every square inch of the floor inside the book vault except right where Singsaker was standing.

His phone rang. He was too lost in his own thoughts to look and see who it was before answering. He assumed it was one of his colleagues at the station.

"It's Lars," said a voice that should have been more familiar.

"Lars?" he repeated blankly.

"Yes, Lars, your son." An indignant silence followed.

"Oh! I was out of it. First day back on the job."

"Is everything all right?" Lars asked, trying to sound cheerful.

"If you're asking about the tumor, then yes. If you mean the rest of my life, I'm not so sure."

He sensed that Lars wanted to say that his life would have been much better if Odd had managed to have a minimum of contact with his immediate family. But he was too cautious to say that. That was how he'd always been: plenty to complain about, but few complaints actually voiced. Many times Odd thought that Lars let him get away with things too easily. If his son had demanded more, he would have received more. But Odd knew that it was wrong to put the blame on him.

He turned away from the body and peered into the waiting room outside the book vault. An image of Lars as a little boy appeared in his mind. He was lying in bed, asleep. Singsaker had come home too late to tell him a good-night story; he'd always made up these stories as he went along, but they both enjoyed them tremendously. He knew that Lars lay awake as long as he could the nights he was gone, because their good-night stories were the best times they had together. Whenever he pictured Lars as a little boy, he was always sleeping, but with his face turned toward the door, as if he had fallen asleep while staring at it. As the years passed, the worst thing about this image was that this was the way he still thought of his son. As a little boy who had fallen asleep waiting for his father to come home. He had grown up. He had studied to be an engineer, got married, had kids. But none of that had really sunk in for Singsaker. Lars's life was something he heard about on the phone. In his mind his son was still a little boy who had missed his good-night story.

"I'm calling because we're planning the christening." It dawned on him that Lars and his wife had had another boy, at just about the same time Singsaker had gone under the knife.

"I see," he said.

"We really want you to come this time," said Lars.

"When is it?" he asked, turning back toward the corpse. He had no idea if this case would allow him to get away for a whole weekend to go to Oslo, where Lars and his family lived.

"That's why I'm calling. Before we decide, we wanted to check with you. You're usually the one with the tightest schedule."

"No, you shouldn't worry about that. Schedule the christening whenever it suits you."

"All right, but we really hope you can come," said Lars faintly and without much hope.

"I'll come," he said. Then they hung up.

Singsaker went to look for Mona Gran, who had left the immediate crime scene. As he walked, he took out his phone and called Brattberg. He got her voice mail. That must mean she was on the toilet, which might take a while. Some things he did remember from before. Thorvald Jensen, on the other hand, picked up after the first ring.

"Are you at the station?" Singsaker asked.

"I just got in. I don't think there's much in the rumors about that pastor. How about you? I heard you went to the library. Is it big?"

"It's big. We need more people, a whole bunch of techs, everybody who's on duty."

"That big a case, huh?" replied Jensen.

"We also need people to do interviews."

"We'll be there soon."

"Great. One more thing. Find out everything you can about a man named Jon Vatten."

There was a pause. Then Jensen said, "You're pulling my leg, right?"

Singsaker groaned before replying. This was Thorvald. It would be hard to fake his way out of this.

"I know him, don't I?" he said.

"I think they must have dug out more than a tumor from your head," said Jensen, as brutally honest as only a real friend can be.

"Sometimes I'm afraid of that, Thorvald," he said.

"Don't take it so hard. Things like this take time. We had Jon Vatten in for an interview about five years ago. Many lengthy interviews. You and I handled it together. He was suspected of killing his wife and young son. But we never found the bodies, and Vatten had a solid alibi. The case is still open, but only as a missing persons case. To this day we still don't know whether or not a crime was actually committed. But we've had our suspicions. Damn, you're lucky that you can forget such things. By the way, Vatten was a very promising academic before this happened. Afterward he had sort of a breakdown. He was committed in the Østmarka psychiatric hospital for a while before he started as security officer at the library. I thought of him as soon as I heard about this case today."

"In other words, he's a guy who's not easy to forget."

"You could say that."

"I wonder if he has something to do with this murder?"

"You tell me. You're the one who's there."

"All I can say is that whoever is behind this could definitely use a trip to a more secure psychiatric hospital than Østmarka."

"I see. We should get over there then," said Jensen.

"ASAP," said Singsaker and hung up.

He found Mona Gran on the sidewalk outside the main entrance.

"I didn't think it would be that horrible," she said. She looked pale but didn't look like she'd thrown up.

"No, no one expected that," he replied. He took out a pack of Fisherman's Friend lozenges that he happened to have in his pocket and offered her one. She had barely popped it in her mouth when his phone rang again. A name he remembered with a vague sense of dread appeared on the display. Vlado Taneski. A reporter at *Adresseavisen*. Who the hell had tipped off the press? Singsaker wondered. He remembered that he and Thorvald had both had suspicions about leaks, but he could no longer recall any names. He refused the call by pressing the button so hard that it left a mark on the tip of his thumb.

Then he and Gran just stood there, sucking on their lozenges in silence.

In 1864, Broder Lysholm Knudtzon died at the age of seventy-six in Trondheim. He was a merchant's son who hated business and dedicated his life to science, art, and literature, although he himself produced nothing of consequence. It's uncertain whether he had any literary talent. He burned his papers, including most of his personal letters and notes before he died. The bonfire of documents included a number of letters Knudtzon had received from around Norway and abroad. Among them were several from Lord Byron, a dear friend of Knudtzon's. But fortunately the childless bookworm did not burn his books. Instead, he left his entire library, including two bas-reliefs and three busts by the great Danish sculptor Bertel Thorvaldsen to the Royal Norwegian Scientific Society. A condition of the will was that a special room be established for preservation of the books and artworks "in which, however, with a View to the Preservation of the Items, the Smoking of Tobacco must not be permitted." This was probably the first smoking ban ever issued in Norway.

In the Knudtzon Hall, inside what is now the Gunnerus Library, the books are arranged on mahogany shelves with carved palmettes. The bas-reliefs *Night* and *Day* by Thorvaldsen, as well as Jacob Munch's oil painting of the young Knudtzon, hang on the walls. From the ceiling hangs a crystal chandelier. The book collection does not impress with its number of titles, which is around two thousand, but by its quality. The library left by Knudtzon contains a number of first editions of classic works in French, English (especially by Lord Byron), German, Italian, and Danish, as well as travel accounts. Some of the books are great rarities printed on parchment, calfskin, or bound in Moroccan leather. After Knudtzon's death, many large, whole skins were found that he had purchased to use for bookbindings.

When he entered Knudtzon Hall to speak with the staff, Chief Inspector Singsaker could barely remember the last time he had been inside, or how he had acquired all that useless knowledge about Knudtzon. But that was how things were lately. He could remember the most trivial details he had read long ago, while big, important events from his life were gone. But he knew that he had been in the Knudtzon Hall several times before with his wife, attending various lectures back when they enjoyed sharing cultural experiences together. He also had a vague recollection that this made them feel more connected.

The entire library staff was seated around a long table on art nouveau chairs when the chief inspector came in. On the floor were hand-knotted Persian rugs. The walls behind the bookshelves were painted with green enamel, and the ceiling was high and white. He had an odd feeling of entering a fictional world and remembered Mona Gran's comment about Agatha Christie. *The Body in the Library* might be a suitable title, he thought. And here we have all the suspects gathered in the Knudtzon Hall as the detective steps into the room. He clasped his arms behind his back and moved slowly along the table as he introduced himself. Then his phone rang. Again. It was Brattberg. Singsaker excused himself and went back out into the corridor. His boss had a simple, clear message.

"Bring Jon Vatten to the station when Jensen shows up."

"Okay," he said, and glanced up. "As a matter of fact, Jensen is here now." He ended the call. Thorvald Jensen had a round face with friendly but sharp eyes. He had just walked into the corridor, along with three crime scene techs dressed in white.

"The whole bunch is sitting inside," said Singsaker to Jensen, pointing at the door to the Knudtzon Hall. "They're all yours. It would probably be easiest to call them for interviews one at a time in another room and then send them home. Wait on Vatten. I'll come and get him after I show the boys in white where they have to work." He gestured toward the techs and discovered too late that two of them were women. They gave him a resigned stare, pegging him for the old fool he was. The third tech was Grongstad. A proper old bloodhound. He smiled wryly.

"Long time no see," he said in English.

"Good to see you again," replied Singsaker, and he meant it. Grongstad was a Trondheimer in the best sense of the word— jovial, laid-back, exacting, and the best in his field in all of Norway.

"So the boss wants Vatten downtown?" Jensen asked. "He's certainly been there before."

"Not a bad idea to refresh his memory. Mine too," said Singsaker.

After getting the evidence team started in the book vault and greeting the medical examiner, who had come straight from a lecture at the university hospital, Singsaker went back to Knudtzon Hall. The employees were still sitting nervously on either side of the long table. Only Hornemann was standing when Singsaker came back in. Singsaker asked whether Jensen had begun taking people away for interviews, and learned that he had. Then he assured everyone that this wouldn't take all day. The police just wanted to get a general idea of what had happened in the library over the weekend and during the morning hours. Then they could all go home. He knew that this was very stressful for them, but if the police were going to find out who was responsible for this murder, it was important that everyone cooperate. His brief speech was met with muttered agreement from the group, and he realized that Jensen had already told them much the same thing. Then he turned to Jon Vatten, who was sitting in the chair closest to the door.

"Do you have time to accompany me to the station? We'd like to speak with you in more detail."

As soon as he said this, he realized that he should have been more discreet. Everyone in the room looked at Vatten. Naturally they all knew about his past. Most of them might have pushed it aside in their daily work or archived it somewhere in the back of their memory. In the years since then, Vatten had slowly but surely become a reserved but reliable security man, with nothing but a tragic story in his background. The suspicions that had clung to him back then had apparently been laid to rest through hours of peaceful cooperation at work. Even so, a small, nagging doubt had survived. And now this. Most of the people in the room probably knew that Vatten might have been the last person to see Gunn Brita Dahle alive. There were not many people who could have unlocked the book vault and gone inside with her. Suddenly the group around the table resembled a jury that had just agreed on a guilty verdict. All except for a young woman with blond hair and a faint sprinkling of freckles over her nose. She sat at the far end of the table and looked at Vatten with something that seemed to be a mixture of affection and concern.

She'll be the next one I'll talk to, Singsaker thought, putting a hand on Vatten's shoulder and walking out of the room with him. The memory of their previous meeting gradually began to return.

14

Trondheim, September 2010

Vatten was thinking about the video surveillance system. From experience he knew that the police would examine everything in minute detail. It wouldn't be long before they found out he'd changed the DVD on Saturday. Then he thought about that afternoon and his vague recollections that he had had some sort of intimate contact with Gunn Brita. The conclusion to be drawn from all this, he thought, was unequivocal. If Gunn Brita had actually been killed that Saturday after he got drunk and his brain switched off, then he was going to have a lot of explaining to do. He had gone along voluntarily to the police station, but right now he felt like a prisoner, just as he'd felt the last time he was questioned there.

The interview back then had taken place in the old police headquarters on Kalvskinnet, not far from where he now worked, and the rooms had seemed closer and clammier. Still, memories were stirred up as he sat on a hard chair in an equally sterile room.

Trondheim, May 2005

Severin Blom was a professor at the Department of History and Classical Studies at NTNU in Dragvoll. He was one of very few, if there were indeed any others, professors in the department who had read almost all of the books in his office. It was a spacious and bright corner office, with a view of the athletics building, and it was close to the library. He was also one of the few, if not the only, lecturer who still dared to have a clandestine cigarette in his office. He might even offer one to people he knew well. Always with the windows wide open, of course, because of the smoke alarm.

The young, up-and-coming Jon Vatten thus took it as a compliment when the professor opened a pack of Marlboros and offered him a cigarette. They had smoked together outside the main doors, as everyone else did by then, but never inside the office in conspiratorial peace and quiet. Vatten took this as a good sign, said thank you, and offered to open the windows to the mild spring air outside. Then he told an anecdote he'd heard about two Japanese researchers who had visited the university some years before. When asked what they thought of the facilities, they had replied that they thought everything was fine, except for all the prostitutes hanging around out front.

Severin Blom, who had apparently heard this old story before, laughed loudly, and said that it was much better to take his cigarette break here in his office. Then he lit his cigarette, inhaled like a walrus before it dives, and gave Vatten a friendly look.

"Nothing is decided yet. But I wouldn't bet against you."

Vatten knew at once what he was talking about: it was the first associate professor position he had applied for. He also knew that what Professor Blom had said meant he'd gotten the job. The pretext for this meeting with Blom had been to discuss a linguistic detail in Plato, which he was working on at the moment, but his actual intention was to try to finagle some news about the open position. Now he was relieved that the professor had read him just as fast as he read books, and that he was so forthcoming. It made everything easier, also with regard to the future.

"This means that we'll be working even more closely with each other, and we'll have time to discuss Plato's linguistic caprices another time. I propose instead that we have a glass of whisky."

The professor opened the door of a cabinet under his desk and took out a bottle of an excellent old single malt and two glasses.

Vatten stared at the glasses and his temples began to sweat. Could he handle a little glass?

During the questioning that followed in the days after what was supposed to have been an innocent glass of whiskey shared by two colleagues, Jon Vatten was unable to explain what he had done in the hours after he put the whisky glass down on Professor Blom's desk. Feeling dizzy, he had thanked him for the talk but had only one thought in his mind: to get home before he passed out. He didn't recall falling asleep on the Number 36 bus and riding the entire route three times between the city and Dragvoll before the driver's shift ended and he noticed Vatten. He had left Dragvoll around 3:00 P.M., and he was thrown off the bus on Munkegata downtown sometime after 7:00 P.M. This four-hour-long bus trip would later serve as his alibi.

On the way home he had sobered up. So he was disappointed at first that Hedda and Edvard weren't home. He wanted to tell them about his bright prospects for the future.

He and Hedda had been arguing lately, nothing serious, just a little more sarcasm in their everyday bickering, a little longer interval between caresses. He assumed that this was normal. He was convinced that a piece of good news, such as this job, was just what they needed. He was fond of Hedda, but he was also well aware that she was the type of woman who occasionally needed to admire her man. It didn't have to be a big deal, but few things turned her on as much as a published article or a pay raise.

After spending an hour at home alone, he began to worry. First he sent a humorous little text message to Hedda, so it wouldn't sound like he was fretting, but after twenty minutes had passed with no reply, he called her up. Her cell was off. Then he got seriously worried. He called Hedda's parents to ask if she was there or whether they were babysitting Edvard that evening. But they said they weren't.

"I talked to Hedda yesterday," her mother said in that unintentionally prim voice that always irritated him. "And she said that she'd be home today sewing a costume for Edvard for the school concert next week."

"That's odd," said Vatten. "That's exactly what I thought she'd be doing."

After calling a few of Hedda's friends and work colleagues, he was convinced that something serious had happened. At 9:30 he called the police. It was an hour past Edvard's bedtime, and there was no sign of Hedda and Edvard.

At the station the police explained that they usually didn't initiate an investigation for someone missing such a short time. These types of cases almost always solved themselves when the missing person turned up a little later than expected, offering some explanation—either plausible or not—for what had happened. But since a child was involved, and since Vatten was adamant that this was not normal, the police agreed to put an officer on the case.

The officer arrived just after ten. He seemed surprised when Vatten told him that he had still not heard from Hedda and Edvard.

They sat down in the kitchen and went through all the available information. The officer got Vatten to call all the places where Hedda and Edvard might be. Then he called places he had called earlier to check whether they may have shown up in the meantime. Nothing panned out, which Vatten could have predicted. Then the officer got up.

"We'll put out an APB," he said. "I believe the situation will resolve itself, but we're still going to take it seriously. If they haven't turned up by tomorrow morning, I'll send over a tech to secure any evidence here at the house, in the event that a crime might have been committed. The best thing you can do until then is try to get some sleep."

Vatten stood there wondering how the officer thought he'd be able to do that.

Trondheim, September 2010

"The Vatten case didn't resolve itself," said Odd Singsaker with a glance at Gro Brattberg, who was sitting at her desk filing her nails.

Five years after being the prime suspect in an investigation, Vatten was once again in the police spotlight. The officer who had conducted the majority of the interviews back then, and the lengthiest ones, had undergone a long convalescence after brain surgery, and his thoughts had been far removed from police work.

"You'll have to refresh my memory a bit," he added, without revealing to his boss how utterly he had forgotten all about it.

"You're right," said Brattberg, putting down her nail file. "The case did not resolve itself. We were sure that the poor bastard was going to break down and confess to everything. But it never happened, and then we had nothing more to go on. If there's any case where the expression 'vanished without a trace' applies, it was the

Vatten case. Hedda Vatten and that boy, what was his name, Edvard, I think it was, never showed up again. Our techs came and went without finding anything that helped us in the least. There was no sign that the two had been taken from the house against their will, and no indication of violence. After a neighbor saw them come home a little after four P.M., no one saw them leave the house or spotted them anywhere else. They seemed to have been swallowed up by the earth."

While Gro Brattberg was talking, several memories surfaced in his mind.

Trondheim, 2005

After a few days, the interrogation of Vatten got tougher. He was often asked to come down to the station to talk there rather than at home, and after a week he was officially a "suspect." The police didn't have enough evidence to hold him in the case but anticipated that they eventually would. That was when Chief Inspector Singsaker took over the questioning.

There were several problems with the Vatten case. First, the strange alibi. How could Vatten have slept so soundly on the bus? The bus driver didn't notice him except when he got on the bus, and then four hours later, when he threw Vatten off. Several other passengers had come forward and testified that they had seen him sleeping in one of the seats. But there wasn't enough testimony to verify that he'd been on the bus the whole time in question. He could have hopped off, gone home and done whatever he had done, and then gotten back on the bus. That scenario would have given him about an hour to act, but maybe not enough time to kill his family and then get rid of the bodies somewhere where they were now impossible to find. Then there was the fact that Vatten himself was the one to report his wife and son missing. The missing persons report was filed with the police two and a half hours after Vatten had been thrown off the bus at 7:00 P.M. Only Vatten himself could tell them what had happened between then and the time he called the police. It was quite possible that Hedda and the boy were in the house when he came home, and that's when something happened. The problem with this explanation was that two neighbors saw Vatten when he arrived home a little before 7:30. One of them sat on his balcony until close to 9:00 P.M., which was after Vatten texted his wife, and then tried to call her, and finally talked to his mother-in-law on the phone. All of this was confirmed by the telephone company's log. The neighbor on the balcony had been enjoying the mild spring evening in Trondheim to the fullest, and had gone inside only a couple of times to use the bathroom. He was positive that nobody had come out of Vatten's front door, which he could see clearly from his third-floor balcony. The Vatten family car had also remained parked in front of the house the whole time. Jon Vatten's alibi might not have been rock solid, but it was still unshakable.

The question of a motive was even more problematic. No matter how much the police searched and how many questions they asked, they were unable to turn up anything suspicious. As the case dragged on, it became more and more evident that their suspicions were based on little more than the old rule of thumb that the husband or boyfriend is usually to blame. But all police officers know that, while this assumption is an excellent starting point for an investigation, eventually it has to be confirmed by concrete evidence. Simply being the husband isn't a strong enough motive for murder. They have to be able to uncover other circumstantial evidence, such as previous violent episodes, witness testimony about loud arguments, jealousy, money problems, or the like. But in the Vatten case such things seemed to be absent. The couple had certainly had their arguments, like most couples. There had been minor quarrels, irritation, and frustrations, but nothing serious enough to warrant a murder investigation. And as one wit on the police force joked, "If your marriage can be examined for weeks by the Trondheim police without a motive for murder turning up on either side, then it's a very solid marriage." Finally, the police had no choice but to release Vatten. But they did it with an uncomfortable feeling that there was something odd about him. A feeling that was reinforced by the fact that they had no other leads.

Quite a bit of time was spent examining Hedda Vatten's extramarital life. But the closest they ever came to finding a clue was when a woman friend claimed she'd always had a feeling that Hedda had a secret she wasn't telling anyone. She was the sort of straightforward and open woman who believed that good friends talked to each other about everything. Once she had even asked Hedda straight out if she had a lover, but Hedda's denial had been quite believable. And there was no other lead in the case pointing to the fact that Hedda Vatten might have had a relationship outside her marriage. But that didn't mean it was impossible. She might have been very good at concealing it. They found no one in the rest of Hedda's circle of friends with good reason to wish her dead. One by one they were all ruled out. They all had solid alibis—her parents, siblings, and friends of both sexes. The Vatten case remained an unsolved mystery.

Vatten came to this realization when the police hadn't contacted him for a couple of months. By that time he'd stopped talking to anyone but the police, so when the long arm of the law relaxed its grip, his loneliness was complete. Then one day, he couldn't recall when, he got a letter saying that ultimately he'd been third in line for the position of associate professor, and not the number-one choice, as Professor Blom had intimated. The rumor that he might have killed his family had apparently reached the hiring committee. He never heard from any of his colleagues at Dragvoll. Most of his university friends lived in Oslo, where he'd gotten his master's degree before he moved to Trondheim for his doctorate. His best friends called now and then, but he avoided them, saying he wasn't in the mood to talk, so the phone calls grew less and less frequent. Vatten was an only child, and both his parents were dead. The intervals between days when he talked to anyone but himself became longer and longer as the summer wore on.

Vatten was naked when he opened the outer door of the apartment. He didn't feel the early fall chill that had moved in from the north over the course of the day, didn't smell the clear air. It was as if he were moving in a fog that came from inside himself.

He staggered a few steps into the driveway and had to lean against the car that had stood there unused for several weeks. It was wet from a light shower that had passed through, although he hadn't noticed it. With one hand on the hood, he stood there swaying back and forth briefly before he continued. Slowly, like a sleepwalker, he moved over to the gate and opened it. Then he took a few steps out into Kirkegata. There he stopped again. Swayed back and forth a few times. Looked up at the gray sky, and finally fell flat on his face. He lay there in the middle of the street until a car came along.

The driver of the car was a neighbor on his way home from work. Actually, he was in a hurry, because he wanted to catch the soccer game between Rosenborg and Brann at Lerkendal stadium. But when he saw the man lying in the street, naked, and recognized him as his unhappy neighbor, he knew right away that the game would be played without him in the grandstand. He stopped his car and went over to the motionless body. He could see that

Vatten had thrown up. Vomit had flowed out onto the asphalt and formed a pool around his face. He felt for a pulse. It was very weak. Then he called an ambulance. While he waited, he turned Vatten onto his side, as he had learned to do a long time ago in the military. Then he noticed the pill bottle in Vatten's hand. He took it from him and read the label. It said, NITRAZEPAM. As far as he knew, it was some sort of sleeping pill.

Trondheim, September 2010

Maybe it would have been best if they hadn't been able to revive me back then, Vatten thought, as he sat staring at the wall, waiting. It was a thought he'd had less frequently lately, and after his trip to the States this summer, he thought it had vanished for good. But now it suddenly seemed more pressing than ever.

He just couldn't handle this. He thought about the things that the police didn't know. They didn't know about the DVD he had switched. They didn't know what he and Gunn Brita had done. He hardly knew that himself. The question was: What was he going to tell the police? And what should he let them find out on their own?

Then there was the secret he'd been keeping since the suicide attempt. If anyone had known what he knew and had asked him why he didn't go to the police with what was possibly the only explanation for the disappearance of his wife and son, he wouldn't have known how to reply.

Maybe he could say that he'd lost confidence in the police. Most likely he was afraid they wouldn't believe him, suspecting instead that he'd written the letter himself. Or maybe it was just the fact that it was all he could do to fight his way out of the dark hole he was in, with the nightmares, night sweats, and hallucinations. Post-traumatic stress syndrome, they called it at Østmarka Hospital.

But in fact there was an even grimmer reason why he never went to the police. Because the day he got the letter in the mail, all hope was lost. Since they were gone forever, what difference did it make whether the police knew about it or not?

The letter was written on parchment. But it wasn't old and antiquarian; it was fresh. A small piece. Small enough to fit into a normal-sized Norwegian envelope. There was only one sentence written on the parchment. Vatten had never doubted that it was sent by the man who had killed his wife and son. Nor had he wondered where the killer had gotten the skin to make the parchment. Vatten burned it in the wood stove the same day. He scattered the ashes to the wind from the veranda above the Møllenbergs' roof. Then he went and swallowed a whole bottle of sleeping pills. It wasn't his intention to ever wake again.

But he did wake up, and now here he sat, five years later. Once again involved in a murder. Once again he knew things he didn't dare tell the police. And maybe most important of all: This time too, the murderer had taken skin from the victim. But now Vatten was worried that the police were going to find traces that linked him to the victim. Neither sleeping pills nor the Østmarka Hospital could save him from that.

So he sat there staring at the confining white walls. He saw himself in a silk-lined coffin with a lid that slowly slid shut. He closed his eyes and could feel the rocking and shaking as the coffin was lowered into an open grave. Then the sound of the earth falling on the coffin lid.

When Chief Inspector Singsaker came into the room with his boss, Vatten's throat had begun to constrict, and he was breathing heavily. Through sheer force of will he managed to push away the fantasy that threatened to engulf him.

15

Interview of Jon Vatten

PRESENT:

Gro Brattberg, *leader of the Violent Crimes and Vice Team at Trondheim police headquarters*
Odd Singsaker, *police investigator*
Jon Vatten, *suspected of murder for the second time*

The scene is an interview room at police headquarters in Trondheim. The walls are white. On one wall there is a one-way mirror, which gives the impression that someone is always standing on the other side looking into the room, unless someone closes the Venetian blinds in front of the mirror, as Singsaker does before he sits down with Brattberg. Vatten is facing them, seated at the table, which has a white laminated top. He looks stressed. A digital voice recorder, Olympus brand, is switched on. Before the interview begins, Chief Inspector Singsaker receives two phone calls in quick succession. One is from his son Lars. The other is from Vlado Taneski at Adresseavisen. The detective declines to answer both calls and turns off his cell phone (which he should have done before the interview). The scene begins in silence following these interruptions.

Singsaker: *Interview of Jon Vatten, September 5, 2010. The purpose of the interview is to discuss the death of Gunn Brita Dahle. Vatten has the status of witness. [Looks at Vatten.] Just had to get through the formalities. Are you ready?*

Vatten: *Yes.*

Singsaker: *This is Gro Brattberg, my boss. She will be sitting in with us for parts of this interview.*

Vatten: *Interview?*

Singsaker: *Interrogation, if you like. But I remind you that for the time being you are considered only a witness. Naturally you have the right to decline to speak to us and to demand that an attorney assist you during the questioning. Do you think that's necessary?*

Vatten: *I have nothing to hide.*

Singsaker: *Fine. We know each other from before, Vatten. Wouldn't you say so?*

Vatten: *You have questioned me before, yes.*

Singsaker: *Do you have any objection to going back a bit in time, to that previous case?*

Vatten: *I can't see what that has to do with the present investigation.*

Singsaker: *I think that it's relevant, although not directly. But let's not play to the gallery, here. This is the second time you have been involved in a serious case. The last time it was a disappearance. Now it's a murder. I assume you realize that it's important for the police to clarify whether there is some connection here or not. For your own sake, it's also good to remove any misunderstandings.*

Vatten: *I see. It's just that I've made an effort to put that matter behind me.*

Singsaker: *And have you managed to do that?*

Vatten: *No, I certainly have not.*

Singsaker: *Some things never lose their grip, I presume. I'd like to talk a bit about your bicycle.*

Vatten: *My bicycle?*

Singsaker: Yes, that's right. The day you got on the bus from Dragvoll five years ago and came home to find your wife and son missing. You rode your bicycle to work that morning, didn't you?

Vatten: Yes, I suppose I did.

Singsaker: You did. I looked it up in the case file. What I don't remember was whether we ever asked you specifically about why you didn't ride it back.

Vatten: I was drunk.

Singsaker: Precisely. You got drunk after one glass of whisky. You're hypersensitive to alcohol, isn't that so?

Vatten: Yes, that's correct.

Singsaker: So tell me, How does that work? Hypersensitive to alcohol. It's not something you hear about every day. Teenage girls who get drunk after a bottle of beer, sure. But hypersensitive? Is that a medical diagnosis?

Vatten: Not that I know of. But I've asked doctors about it, and there is a medical explanation. Or perhaps several.

Singsaker: And what are they?

Vatten: Apparently I lack one or more enzymes in my intestines. These enzymes prevent alcohol from being assimilated by the intestines. This makes most people react more to the third or fourth drink than they do to the first two. If you don't have these enzymes, the alcohol goes straight into the bloodstream, starting with the very first drop. You mentioned teenage girls. Well, it's been shown that women have fewer of these enzymes than men. So that's why they get drunk faster. Teenage girls also tend to have a lower body weight than their older sisters.

Singsaker: Vatten, you're not a large man, but you're certainly no teenage girl.

Vatten: That's true. In me it's apparently the lack of these enzymes, combined with a number of other factors.

Singsaker: Such as what?

Vatten: Such as various physiological conditions. The biology of the brain. I honestly don't know.

Singsaker: So the fact that you get drunk after one glass of whisky is not something you can prove medically. Am I right?

Vatten: If you want to take it to its logical conclusion, then yes. But don't you think it's odd that I would make up a story like that? It would have been easier for me to say that I'd had more than one glass and got drunk in the usual way.

Singsaker: That's something we can investigate, as you know perfectly well. If that's what you claimed, where did you get the other glasses of whisky from? Your colleague? Or did you go and buy beer at the canteen in Dragvoll? We could have had those things checked.

Vatten: I'm sure you could. But it would have been a lie. And I didn't lie. You also found out back then that it wasn't so important why I was sitting on that bus; the fact was that I was on the bus, and you never managed to disprove it.

Singsaker: Are you saying that there was proof to the contrary?

Vatten (sighs heavily): No, that's not what I'm saying. I was sitting on that bus. Now I've voluntarily come in for an interview about a totally different matter. Maybe we should start talking about that instead.

Brattberg: Yes, let's do that. So it's true that you were the one who found Gunn Brita Dahle dead in the book vault?

Vatten: That's correct. I found her, along with a colleague.

Brattberg: And who was this colleague?

Vatten: Siri Holm. A newly hired librarian.

Singsaker: Why did the two of you go to the vault?

Vatten (after a brief pause): We wanted to try out Siri's new code.

Singsaker: Siri's new code?

Vatten: Yes. As I told you at the scene, two codes are necessary to open the book vault. I have one and the librarians have the other.

Brattberg: All the librarians?

Vatten: No, just one trusted librarian.

Singsaker: And this Siri Holm had just received such a code? She took it over after Gunn Brita Dahle? Dahle had already quit her job, isn't that right?

Vatten: That's correct.

Singsaker: But you said that Siri Holm was just hired. Was she supposed to take over from Dahle?

Vatten: That's also true.

Singsaker: So that means it was her first day on the job?

Vatten: Yes, officially.

Singsaker: But perhaps she had been inside the library earlier?

Vatten: I met her on Saturday.

Singsaker: On Saturday. Wasn't that also when you saw Gunn Brita Dahle?

Vatten: That's right; they were there together. Gunn Brita was giving her an orientation.

Singsaker: I see. Is it normal for a newly hired employee such as Siri Holm to be entrusted with the code to the book vault?

Vatten: No, it's not. I don't know why Hornemann gave it to her. But you never know what he's going to do.

Singsaker: Do you know exactly when Hornemann gave Siri Holm the code to the book vault?

Vatten: I think it was Monday morning. Just before we opened it.

Singsaker: This past Saturday, was that the first time you met Siri Holm?

Vatten: Yes. She just graduated from library school in Oslo. She's from eastern Norway.

Singsaker: And you didn't see her again until Monday morning?

Vatten: Is that relevant?

Brattberg: It's important for us to map all movements throughout the weekend. We don't yet know when the murder occurred.

Vatten: I met her by chance on Sunday, when she was walking her dog on Kuhaugen. It turned out that she lived nearby, and she invited me home for tea.

Singsaker: What time on Sunday was that?

Vatten: In the morning. Maybe around twelve. I didn't stay long.

Singsaker: Why not, wasn't the tea good?

Vatten: There was nothing wrong with the tea. It was green tea.

Singsaker: They say it's supposed to be so healthy. Has a cleansing effect on the body. But back to Saturday. Did you drink anything that day?

Vatten: Tea, then too. Tea and coffee.

Singsaker: No, I mean, did you drink any alcohol?

Vatten: I haven't touched alcohol since that day five years ago.

Singsaker: So when our technicians have combed through your office, they won't find a drop of alcohol there, no empty bottles, no old spills on the floor?

Vatten: I'm sure of it.

Singsaker: And other places in the library, would it be possible to find any there?

Vatten: Alcohol? I can't answer that. It's not common to drink on the job at the Gunnerus Library, but we don't keep track of everything that people do.

Singsaker: If I told you that we've just received a preliminary analysis of some red spots under the table outside the book vault, and that they proved to be red wine, what would you say?

Vatten: I have nothing to say about that.

Singsaker: Precisely. Just as I thought. There are surveillance cameras in the Gunnerus Library. Isn't that so?

Vatten: That's correct. There are five cameras: one inside the book vault; one in the office wing; and one in Knudtzon Hall. Then there's one in the reading room and one outside the main entrance.

Singsaker: And your job is to monitor these cameras?

Vatten: I'm in charge of the system. It doesn't mean that I sit there and watch everything that happens. It's recorded and stored on DVD. Then transferred to hard drives. We retain the recordings for six months *before they have to be erased. The idea is that we should be able to refer to the recordings if anything illegal occurs.*

Singsaker: *Such as now?*

Vatten: *Yes, such as now.*

Singsaker: *So when we're finished here, would you accompany me to the library and help me gain access to these recordings?*

Vatten: *Of course. But I'm afraid there won't be any recordings from parts of the weekend.*

Singsaker: *And why not?*

Vatten: *Saturday I discovered that I'd forgotten to insert a new DVD when I removed the old one on Friday. So the system recorded nothing between Friday and Saturday evening.*

Singsaker: *Saturday evening. Didn't you say you were in the library on Saturday morning?*

Vatten: *I stayed there until evening. Sometimes I sit and read for a while.*

Singsaker: *And when were you planning to tell us about this? You're saying that you were in the library during a large period of the time when the murder may have been committed?*

Vatten: *I was sitting in a completely different part of the library. I couldn't have seen anything that happened in the administrative wing.*

Singsaker: *Where were you sitting?*

Vatten: *Up in the stacks.*

Singsaker: *In the stacks?*

Vatten: *Where the books are stored. I like to read. That's how I spend my afternoons. I'm a single man. Is there anything wrong with that?*

Singsaker: *Not really. But why didn't you mention it the first time I spoke with you?*

Vatten: *It was a short conversation. I just told you where I'd last seen Gunn Brita.*

Singsaker: *What did you do after you left the stacks?*

Vatten: *I went home.*

Singsaker: *But you didn't stop by your office first?*

Vatten: *Yes, I did.*

Singsaker: *What about the room outside the book vault?*

Vatten: *Just my office.*

Singsaker: *And then you put in a new DVD?*

Vatten: *That's right.*

Brattberg: *Which means that if the murder occurred after you met Dahle in the morning, and before you stopped by your office in the evening, there would be no recording of what happened?*

Vatten: *That's correct.*

Singsaker: *How convenient for the murderer.*

Vatten: *I'm sorry about that, of course. But mistakes do happen.*

Singsaker: *Mistakes such as someone being murdered in the book vault at the library?*

Vatten: *I had nothing to do with the murder. I can assure you of that.*

Singsaker: *Why is this giving me a feeling of déjà vu?*

Brattberg: *We're not going to get any further now. Singsaker, will you take Vatten with you to the library and go through the recordings? Check the new DVD that was inserted on Saturday evening. If the body is visible on the recordings in the book vault, then we'll know more about when the murder was committed. If it's not there, we might have the perpetrator on film. At least if what Vatten here is telling us is true.*

Singsaker: *Yes, and that's a big "if."*

16

They *drove through town,* creeping along during the afternoon rush hour back to the Gunnerus Library. They went up to Vatten's office without speaking to anyone. He turned on his computer and logged into the program that controlled the surveillance system.

"Why don't you record directly to the hard drive?" Chief Inspector Singsaker asked, looking around the office.

"The system is a bit out of date. But we do record on DVDs and transfers to a hard drive are done regularly. And the resolution is good," said Vatten.

A DVD drive began to hum next to the monitor. Singsaker stood there thinking about what they were doing. Maybe they would see a recording of the murder itself, which was undoubtedly the most bestial murder he'd ever investigated. Maybe they were about to see what happened. And this was only his first day back on the job after his long sick leave.

"Saturday, 10:21 P.M.," said Vatten, and clicked the mouse. The hum died down, and the video started playing. The vault appeared on the monitor. It was the same view Singsaker was familiar with: Gunn Brita Dahle's mutilated body lying on the floor. And that left only one possible conclusion: "This means that she was killed before 10:21 P.M. on Saturday, when you put in the disk, right?"

"Yes, that's right."

"So while you were still in the library?"

"Yes, so it seems." Vatten looked resigned.

"The images that were recorded by this camera, can they also be viewed on this monitor?"

"Sure. I can sit here in my office and follow along if I want to. But that's not the point. The primary objective with the surveillance is to document what goes on."

"So Saturday night when you changed the DVD, the monitor wasn't on?"

"Of course not. Then I would have seen the body in the vault," said Vatten.

"I think it would be best if you come with me back to the station," said Singsaker, placing a hand cautiously on Vatten's shoulder.

He sighed heavily, then ran one hand through his disheveled hair. But he said nothing.

He's five years older, Singsaker thought. But his hair is still just as thick, and he sighs as heavily as he did last time.

Brattberg, Jensen, and Singsaker had a brief meeting with police attorney Knutsen and they upgraded Vatten's status to "suspect." But they still didn't have any tangible evidence against him. Even though his explanation rang false, they couldn't put a finger on any falsehoods in what he'd said. So far all they had was that he'd been in the library during the period when Gunn Brita Dahle was killed, that he was one of very few who could have been with her inside the book vault, and that he had previously been involved in a possible murder case. One thing they could present at a court hearing was the fact that he was responsible for the surveillance system, and that there hadn't been a DVD connected to the camera in the vault when the murder took place. The question was whether it was an honest mistake or had been done on purpose. For prosecutor Knutsen, a meticulous man who was even closer to retirement than Singsaker, the evidence wasn't substantial enough to proceed.

"So he'll have to stay home from work for a day or two," said Brattberg. "And we'll have to ask him to give us a saliva sample before he leaves."

"I think we have one from the last time he was detained," said Jensen. He had a laptop on the table in front of him, and he was frowning as he moved the mouse uncertainly.

"Well, we're going to get what we need from him. Complete DNA, fingerprints, and everything," Jensen asserted.

"Fine! We just heard a rumor from St. Olav's that there are biological traces," said Brattberg.

"Which means what?"

"Sexual contact," she said. Her tone of voice belied what she actually felt: scorn for the sexual act as well as sympathy, sorrow, and a deeper insight into human fallibility. And Singsaker thought that this was what he liked best about his boss. The dry and matter-of-fact style that concealed a wisdom and humanity that surpassed that of most other people.

"But it'll take some time before we get a final autopsy report. The body arrived at Pathology less than an hour ago. A DNA analysis will take days, maybe weeks. But we can use what we have already in the next interview, to pressure him a little. At the same time we have to follow up on a number of other potential leads. Primarily the husband, Jens Dahle. And I think this Siri Holm could be interesting. She was also in the library just before the murder. But if she's a new hire from Oslo, she's probably not a hot lead. Jensen, you continue interviewing the staff. Try to direct the conversations so they focus on Vatten.

"By the way, that bluff of yours, Singsaker, that the tiny red spots that Grongstad found were wine, seemed to make an impression on Vatten. And it actually turned out not to be a bluff. We got the analysis, and it really is wine. Very fresh spots, too. Could well be from Saturday. But we'll wait on this until the techs have had more time to work. In addition, some fingerprints were found inside the book vault. It won't be long before we have more concrete finds to put on the table. Until then, Singsaker, you take the husband and the new librarian."

"Aye aye, sir," he said in English.

"You mean, aye aye, *madam*," Gro Brattberg corrected him with a smile.

"What are we going to do about the press?" Thorvald Jensen asked. "It's the top story on all the news sites, and somebody even found out that we've been interrogating Vatten. I doubt it's been difficult to get the others in the library to talk."

"We're saying as little as possible to the media. They'll have to wait until tomorrow's press conference. By then we may be able to give them something more about Vatten, if we're lucky," she replied.

"One more thing," said Singsaker.

Everybody looked at him.

"Are there any experts on serial killers here in Norway?"

"Why do you ask?" Brattberg snapped back. "We only have one murder."

"True enough," he said. "But I'm thinking about the way the murder was committed. And of course, there's the old Vatten case."

"We do have that cop in Oslo. I don't remember his name," said Jensen. "He solved a serial case in Australia in the nineties. I heard he's turned into a drunk since then."

"Doesn't sound that reliable, does he?"

"It's worth a try," said Jensen, with his usual understated optimism.

"No, it's not worth a try," said Brattberg. "It's only on American cop shows that the police call in experts on serial killers after only one murder. That's not how we conduct our investigations here in the real world."

Singsaker had known Gro Brattberg long enough to realize that the topic was not only closed, it was dead and buried. Too bad, really. He'd been looking forward to meeting the drunken detective.

The meeting broke up. When Brattberg went out the door, Jensen turned to Singsaker.

"It's OK by me that Brattberg isn't enthusiastic about perp profiles, but there's still one thing I'd like to find out."

"What's that?" asked Singsaker.

"What the hell does the killer intend to do with her skin?" Jensen threw out his arms in resignation before he followed their boss out the door.

Singsaker remained standing there, thinking about what he'd said. Something told him that Thorvald's question was important.

After the meeting, Singsaker called one of the officers who'd been assigned to inform Jens Dahle about the murder. They had found him at home, just about to leave for work. He was alone in the house. The news of his wife's brutal murder seemed to have made a strong impression on Dahle. According to the officers, he told them he was going to stay home until the police contacted him again.

Before visiting Jens Dahle, Singsaker decided to Google him. The result clearly showed that he really was a scientist. Apart from the obligatory hits in various telephone databases and meaningless information about Dahle's ranking in the big tax assessment race, which was quite high, all the hits dealt with various scientific publications, seminars, conferences, and lectures. A few feature articles in the daily press also turned up. Most of the material was incredibly turgid, especially for Singsaker, who had not yet had his daily shot of aquavit. This had also been his toughest workday on the Trondheim police force—at least as far as he could remember.

One article interested him more than the others. It was written in English and was part of a database that, with typical academic stinginess, published only the first page for the curious public. The rest of the article required a subscription that only cultural snobs and public institutions could afford. For Singsaker the title was enough: "Forensics of Time." And from the introduction alone he knew that he now had something to talk about with Jens Dahle.

The article turned out, despite its fancy title, to deal with an excavation on the Fosen peninsula carried out about twenty years ago. The excavation was done in an old graveyard from the late Middle Ages. In the introduction Dahle intimated, although with a large dose of academic caution, that examinations made of many of the skeletons at the site indicated they might have been victims of murder. There were stab marks and other signs of external violence on the old bone fragments. This was nothing unusual for grave sites from that era, which according to Dahle was a violent age, when murder was a common cause of death. But what was special here, he hinted, still with a scientist's caution, was that much of the bone damage exhibited conspicuous similarities. But it was the last sentence in the free portion of the article that particularly piqued the interest of Chief Inspector Singsaker.

It read, "Could we be dealing here with an unknown serial killer from the past?"

In the late afternoon, Jens Dahle's car was still parked in the driveway, shiny and newly washed. All traces of the weekend trip to the cabin were gone.

Singsaker rang the doorbell. As he waited, his thoughts returned to the conversation earlier that morning. Jens Dahle had looked so healthy and content, and he couldn't recall ever seeing him look any other way. The few times he had spoken with him he'd always given the impression of being extremely fit. A well-dressed sort, always with a woolen undershirt. A guy who could metamorphose from a desk jockey to an outdoors type during a quick trip to his cabin.

It took almost a minute before he heard any sound on the other side of the door. Had he been sleeping? The door was unlocked and opened slowly. Singsaker looked for some sign of surprise on Dahle's face. Until now they had known each other only as passing acquaintances. But his expression showed no such reaction.

Jens Dahle looked shattered. Even in broad daylight his face seemed poorly lit; all his wrinkles and furrows cast shadows across his face. He's older than I imagined, thought Singsaker. Jens Dahle was the father of two schoolchildren, but this was the first time it occurred to Singsaker that he had to be relatively old for a father. An old and now sad father. And even though the inspector had encountered murderers before among fathers and husbands, who were equally sad at the loss of their victims, he didn't think he was looking at a murderer.

"I'm sorry it took me so long to answer the door," said Jens Dahle. "Is there something I can help you with?"

"No," said Singsaker. "I'm the one who's come to help you."

"I see. What's this regarding?"

"I don't know if I ever told you very much about myself," he said, "but I'm a police officer, and I've come to talk to you about your wife and what happened." He studied Dahle as he said this. It surprised him how little his neighbor's expression altered. It remained morose and mournful.

"So you're a police officer?" he asked in a monotone.

"That's right. Do you have time to talk?"

Jens Dahle opened the door all the way and stepped aside.

"Come in," he said.

Inside they stood looking at each other in an entryway that was being renovated, with unvarnished pine paneling and missing floorboards. The remodeling project was obviously something that Dahle was doing himself. Something that probably wouldn't be finished before his kids were grown. Under normal circumstances this might have been the icebreaker for a conversation. They could have talked about the dimensions of various types of panels and such things. But now was not the time for that.

"My condolences," said Singsaker. "You must be in shock."

Jens Dahle stared at the inspector, his eyes doleful.

"I don't know what to say," he said. "To tell the truth, there's still part of me that expects her to come home from work at any minute. When you rang I was asleep on the couch. I dreamed that I was cooking dinner for her. Fish soup. She loves fish soup, and I made it for her, even though I knew the kids wouldn't like it. It's been a long time since I've had a dream about daily life."

Singsaker was afraid that Dahle was more out of it than he'd first believed, and to make sure that they fully understood each other, he said, "This is a bit strange, because we've spoken several times before, but now it's important for you to realize that I'm Chief Inspector Singsaker. And that I've come from the Trondheim police to talk to you about the murder of your wife, Gunn Brita Dahle."

Jens Dahle seemed to wake up a bit.

"I may be in shock, but I haven't lost my mind. I know very well who you are."

"And are you prepared to answer some difficult questions?" Sing-saker asked, adding, "This could wait. But the sooner you're ready to help us, the faster we'll be able to solve this case."

"I'm happy to answer your questions right now," said Dahle. "Shall we sit down?"

Dahle showed him into the kitchen, which had recently been remodeled. Oak and white laminate. Very tasteful. Clearly the work of professional craftsmen, which told him that Dahle could afford it, and that he seemed to know something about carpentry.

They sat down at the heavy oak table that took up most of the space on the parquet floor.

"Coffee?" Dahle offered politely.

"Only if you feel the need for some."

"I don't know what I need," he said, going over to a built-in coffeemaker that looked expensive. "Espresso?" he asked.

Singsaker considered the question absolutely absurd under the circumstances. A discussion he'd once had with Anniken popped into his head. In his opinion, "espresso" ought to be pro-nounced "expresso" in Norwegian, like explicit and express train, since all these words come from the Latin verb *expressare,* which means to express something or press something through. Annik-en's completely plausible argument was that espresso was an Ital-ian word and should be pronounced in Italian and not Latin. But she agreed that at any rate he had a sophisticated argument for pronouncing the word "espresso" in a lowbrow way. Now he sat there wondering why Jens Dahle, who pronounced the word in resounding Italian, would bother to serve anything but black Norwegian-style coffee. Still, Singsaker did say yes to an espresso. Dahle brewed the inspector a double, prompting a lot of gurgling and coughing from the machine. He poured himself a glass of wa-ter, and then came to sit down.

Singsaker looked at him for a moment before they started. By now Dahle had taken off the shirt and tie he'd been wearing that morning and put on a loose, thin wool sweater with a crew neck. A bit strange to wash the car wearing a shirt and tie, and then change. When he'd met Dahle this morning, he was dressed to go to work after taking time to give his car a quick wash. When going to work was no longer an option, he had changed his clothes. But who goes and changes clothes the minute he hears that his wife has been killed? Singsaker wondered. At the same time he knew there was seldom a logical explanation. There could be no pat answer to what a man might do after being told that his wife had been murdered.

"Let's get the most important things out of the way first. We know that Gunn Brita Dahle, your wife, was killed before ten P.M. on Saturday."

"You do?"

"There's a video from the surveillance camera inside the book vault."

"Did you get the murder on video?" Dahle looked downright terror stricken.

"No, not the murder itself. That would have made it easier for us, of course. But we do have pictures showing that her body was lying in the book vault at ten o'clock Saturday night. Possibly before then as well. So I have to ask you if you can confirm where you were from Saturday morning until Saturday night."

"As I told you this morning, I was at the cabin. You don't think that *I* did it, do you?"

"At this point we have no specific theories about the case. We're just gathering information. If you don't feel like answering questions right now, it can wait."

"No, that's fine. I'm just a little out of it. That's all."

"I understand," said Singsaker calmly, and went on. "Could anyone else testify that you were at the cabin during that time?"

"Only my kids. We were at the cabin all day. I was in and out, of course. The kids were playing with their LEGO and Nintendo. We went to bed early."

"I see. And your children, how old are they?"

"I have a ten year-old girl and an eight year-old boy," Dahle said dully.

"All right. Where are they now?"

"I sent them to stay with friends when they got home from school. So far they haven't been told."

"OK. This cabin—where is it?"

"The cabin is out on Fosen, not far from Brekstad."

"Would you say that it's isolated, or can other people see the cabin?"

"It's in a grove between two low, rocky crags. We're quite secluded there. It's probably about a kilometer to the neighboring farm. The couple at the farm, Isak and Elin Krangsås, can certainly confirm when we arrived and left. They usually keep an eye on the road. But they'd have a hard time saying whether we were at the cabin the whole weekend, I'm afraid."

"From Brekstad, how long would you say it takes to drive to Trondheim?"

"There's a ferry from Brekstad to Vallset on the other side of the fjord. It's also possible to drive to Rørvik and take the ferry to Flakk. With either route it's about two hours by car to Trondheim, including the ferry ride if you know the departure schedule."

"Two hours, and both ferries are hooked up to the electronic AutoPASS system, I suppose?"

"No, only the ferry between Rørvik and Flakk."

"So if you take the ferry to Vallset, it's possible to travel to or from Trondheim without leaving an electronic record anywhere. Is that right?" He stared intently at Jens Dahle. He was a man in mourning. There was no reason to suspect him of murder, but there was something in him that enjoyed seeing Dahle sweat. But Jens Dahle wasn't sweating nearly as much as he would have expected.

"You can pay cash on the ferry and otherwise avoid traffic cameras, but you still have the toll stations around Trondheim. It's not easy."

Of course Singsaker knew about the toll required to enter Trondheim by car. What interested him was the fact that Jens Dahle had thought of it, too. He was definitely a man who kept a clear head. Somebody at the station would have to go through all the toll stations, speed traps, and ferry crossings and search for his license number, credit card, or other possible traces he might have left. But the search would most likely just confirm his alibi. Dahle wasn't an easy man to read. If Singsaker had been a gambling man, he would have bet that Dahle actually was on Fosen all weekend, a bet that probably wouldn't have high odds.

"We just have to check everything," he said.

"I understand." Jens Dahle picked up his glass of water and drank half of it in one gulp.

"You're an archaeologist, right?"

"That's right."

"And you work at the Science Museum?"

"Yes, I do."

"So you worked next door to your wife? Then you probably know your way around the Gunnerus Library fairly well, don't you?"

"Sort of. Actually, we were careful not to visit each other too often. We chose to live separate lives at work. The reason I know people at the library is mainly because I had to deal with them in my job. The two institutions cooperate a great deal. I often needed material for my work."

"So you're a frequent borrower?"

"Yes, you could say that."

"But based on what you know, would you say that your wife had a closer relationship with some of her colleagues than with others?"

"Not really. Gunn Brita gets, I mean got, along well with all of her colleagues, but none of them were close friends of hers."

"And there was no one who harbored animosity toward her?"

"Not that I know of."

"So you don't think that anyone at her workplace would have wanted to kill her?"

Dahle gave him a defeated look and said, "To tell the truth, I have no idea who could have wanted to do that, either at the library or anywhere else."

"No, I guess not." Here Singsaker paused to sip the espresso that Dahle had made for him. Even though it had cooled off, it was perfectly brewed. The espresso machine that the Dahle family had had installed was no toy. He sat there wondering which of them had insisted on buying this marvel. But now wasn't the time to ask about that sort of thing.

"Exactly what is your job at the museum?" he asked.

"At the moment I have a research position. That is, I'm in charge of a number of excavations, I do some teaching, and I write articles."

"But you don't do any of the digging?"

"No, only seldom. The excavation work is usually done by students on summer jobs and archaeologists hired as temps. It's a pretty crappy profession, really. We really push the boundaries when it comes to complying with workplace regulations," he said with an ironic smile.

"By the way, the other day I came across an article that you wrote a long time ago," said Singsaker.

"Oh, really? Which one?"

" 'Forensics of Time.' "

Jens Dahle looked like he was trying to remember it. Then he smiled and said, "Oh, that one. I'd hardly call that a scientific article. I wrote it many years ago, back when I was working on my doctorate, if I'm not mistaken. How did you come across it?"

"It was on the Internet, in a database."

"Well, yes, there's no controlling one's digital life, is there? But I assume the journal that published it has the rights in order."

"I only had time to read the first page," Singsaker said. "What's the rest of it about?"

"It deals with a find we made out on Fosen back then, at the Krangsås farm. Actually, not that far from where my cabin is located. There was a chapel there in the Middle Ages with an old cemetery. When I set out to write about it, I made a big deal out of the fact that many of the skeletons we found exhibited striking signs of injuries. We could see that many of the bodies may have been killed in the same way. But as an archaeologist it's obviously not possible to determine a definite cause of death from five-hundred-year-old bone fragments. The whole thing was rather speculative. But the article did create a stir, as I recall. The most interesting thing about that dig was probably that we found the *Johannes Book*."

"The *Johannes Book*?"

"Yes, it's one of the most important sources of the medieval history of the Trondheim area. It's a book handwritten on parchment from an age when paper was becoming more and more common. It was written by a priest in Fosen just after the Reformation. A rare treasure. It's particularly known for its surprisingly good medical knowledge. And for its aphorisms."

"Aphorisms?"

"Yes, wise sayings. Such as: 'The center of the universe is everywhere and its circumference is nowhere.' For scholars the aphorisms in the *Johannes Book* raise a lot of questions. For instance, why does Johannes the priest write about the universe and not about God? Has he lost his faith? Is he a Nordic representative of the growing scientific currents in the Renaissance? Where did this Johannes come from? Had he studied at a university? The aphorism I mentioned is of particular interest for several reasons. As early as 200 B.C. it appeared in a book we call the *Corpus Hermeticum*, which belongs to the writings of the Gnostics: 'God is a comprehensible sphere whose center is everywhere and circumference nowhere.' And around the year 1200 the French theologian and poet Alain de Lille wrote exactly the same words in one of his texts. Almost five hundred years later, in 1584, the mystic Giordano Bruno in Italy wrote: 'The center of the universe is everywhere and its circumference nowhere.' The interesting thing is that this was written several decades after the *Johannes Book,* which was created around the middle of the fifteen hundreds. But it doesn't end there. A hundred years later the mathematician and philosopher Pascal wrote: 'Nature is an infinite sphere in which the center is everywhere and the circumference nowhere.' This quotation, which keeps cropping up, was also mentioned by the Argentine author Jorge Luis Borges in *Ficciones,* which came out in 1944. It's an example of how we constantly repeat ourselves, and how few ideas are actually original. But Borges wrote about this before we found the *Johannes Book,* so naturally he was not quoting from that source. But it's coincidences like this that contribute to the mystique surrounding this strange text, which continues to confound scholars. Was Johannes the priest a mystic or a sort of gnostic, or was he merely a freethinker who had lost his belief in God as a unifying force?" Jens Dahle fell silent. When he talked about his work, he seemed to be in his own world.

"This book must have been quite a find. How did you come across it in a graveyard?" Singsaker asked.

"We didn't find it in the graveyard. The couple at the farm had it on their bookshelf, with no idea what it was worth or what it meant. The book had been at the farm since the nineteenth century. I noticed it one evening when they invited us over for coffee. The farmer told me a peculiar story about how the book had come to be owned by his family. It was his great-great-grandfather who acquired it."

"Acquired it?"

"Yes, one day more than a hundred and fifty years ago an elegant gentleman from the city suddenly showed up at his farm. The man introduced himself as a book collector, and he wanted to give the book to the people who lived on the farm. Naturally the farmer's great-great-grandfather asked him why. He replied that this book belonged there. Apparently he also claimed that there was a curse on the book, and that the only place it could find peace was on that very farm. The book collector intimated that the book had been written by a murderer before he left the farm, never to return. In the farmer's family this had always been a good story that they told with a gleam in their eye. But they had never noticed any sign of a curse. One of us remarked on the statement that the book was supposed to find peace out there. The farmer reiterated that this was what the book collector had claimed, and he couldn't vouch for what might happen if anyone took the book away from the farm.

"That same evening I borrowed the book to read in bed, and by the next morning I understood what a treasure I was holding."

"So what happened to the book?"

"It was handed over to the Gunnerus Library. It's still in their collection." Here Dahle stopped, and Singsaker could see by his eyes that he was now back in the present.

"Does anyone have an idea who this book collector was?" he asked, to keep the conversation going.

"No, it's a mystery. Of course, many people have tried to find out. But no one has been successful. Most of the speculation, though, has leaned toward Broder Lysholm Knudtzon."

"The one Knudtzon Hall was dedicated to?"

"Yes, precisely. He was a well-known book collector. But there isn't much else to connect him to this mysterious person on Fosen. What is certain is that the man who delivered the book didn't want anyone to know that he'd been there. He came, presented the book with that rather odd explanation, and then vanished from the story."

"And do we know that the book was written by a priest and not a murderer?"

"It's evident from the content that it was written by a priest. He states as much himself. Some of his ideas, as I mentioned, go beyond commonly held Lutheran teachings. There's nothing in the text that alludes to the fact that he may have been a murderer. But it is a fact that some of the parchment pages in the book are missing. There are signs that they were torn out. Naturally it's impossible to say who was responsible. I recall that we joked a bit that the alleged murderous author might have been the same person who had killed the victims whose remains we'd found in the graveyard in the meadow behind the farm."

Dahle fell silent once again. Did it feel good for him to get his mind off what had recently happened? Was that why he could go on talking about this book for so long? Singsaker was trying to get a handle on him. Also, he had a hunch that this had something to do with the case, but he didn't know what.

"The pages that were torn out of the book—do you have any opinion about who might have done that, or when it was done?"

"No, nobody knows. But it definitely occurred before the book arrived at the farm where I found it. You have to remember that the pages of the book, which were made of parchment, were valuable in and of themselves. Starting in the twelfth century, paper came into use, and as the centuries passed, parchment became scarcer and scarcer. But parchment has been used all the way to our day, for such things as deluxe editions. A book collector may have torn out the parchment pages in order to sell them individually. They may also have been used as bindings for other books. They simply could have fallen out because the book was not taken care of properly."

"I should think this *Johannes Book* would be worth a lot of money."

"It's probably impossible to put a price on a book like that. It's absolutely unique. Nothing like it has ever been sold on the open market here in Norway. Or in any other country, for that matter," said Dahle. "As a stolen object I'd think it would be impossible to sell unless you found the right eccentric millionaire," he added.

"And that's probably true of many of the other books in the vault as well, isn't it?" Singsaker asked.

"Absolutely. But you don't think that theft was the motive, do you?"

"As of right now, we can't rule out anything," he said.

But when Singsaker pondered the way the murder had been committed, he realized that homicide with intent to steal was not a credible theory. In any case, not if someone was stealing for money. But there might possibly be other and less rational motives for a theft. Then it dawned on him that so far they had only Vatten's word that nothing had been taken from the book vault. They would have to confirm that as soon as possible.

After some small talk and some consoling words that sounded hollow, he took his leave of Jens Dahle. But as they got up from the table, he thought of one more thing he wanted to say.

"I'd like to ask a favor of you. It won't be easy," he said, placing his hand on Dahle's shoulder.

"What would that be?" said Dahle, looking exhausted.

"You need to tell your children what happened. The police will have to talk to them. Not that there's any hurry. But if you could do it sometime today, that would be best. Better that they hear it from you than from somebody else. It's impossible to keep it from them forever."

Jens Dahle nodded, and looked as though he realized Singsaker was right.

17

O*dd Singsaker headed in* the direction of his apartment. But instead of going straight home, he went over to the intersection of Nonnegata and Kirkegata, where Bjørn's Video was still clinging to the past. He went up Nonnegata toward Rosenborg middle school. On the way he took out his cell phone and punched in the number of the police station. He asked to speak to Mona Gran, but she'd already gone home. It suddenly occurred to him that he should have done that long ago himself. This was his first day back at work. But oddly he didn't feel worn out.

He asked to speak with someone else. Whoever was on duty in the violent crimes and vice teams would do. He was patched over to an officer he didn't know.

"Could you find me the address of a woman named Siri Holm? She's a new employee at the Gunnerus Library," Singsaker said.

"Is that all you know about her?" the officer asked.

"At the moment, yes."

"Let me call you back."

Singsaker ended the call and kept walking toward the recently constructed middle school. From there he went into the neighborhood of Rosenborg Park. It was almost as new as the school and consisted of a park area and apartment buildings with a world-class disparity between price and square footage. Yet the park itself was one of the biggest urban design successes in Trondheim. Festningsparken, the old Rosenborg soccer field, and Kuhaugen had been linked into one large green zone.

Here he found a bench and sat down to wait for his phone to ring. He sat there gazing at a pond with a group of lanky, Gaudí-inspired metal figures, among them a fish and a ballerina. Common to all the figures was the water running or spouting from them. What bothered him about the whole tableau was that the fish—which was the only sculpture that spouted water in a high, vertical jet—was placed at the very edge of the fountain design. This gave the whole thing an asymmetrical look. He could swear that it had been done on purpose, but as a cop it bothered him. He had a strained relationship with anything that was not symmetrical.

As he sat there he began to think about the *Johannes Book* and the tale of the collector. It had all the ingredients of a good ghost story: old graveyards, curses, a book filled with mysterious aphorisms. It almost seemed that the book collector had been right about the curse. True enough, the book had been taken from the farm almost twenty years ago, but maybe the curse had just now been activated. He noticed that he was smiling grimly as he thought of these things. A little aquavit would have hit the spot right now.

He looked at his watch and saw that it was too late to make it to the liquor store. His breakfast had been spoiled this morning, too. This case was really getting to him. There was something irrational about it. Why Gunn Brita Dahle? Why had her body been flayed? And why in the book vault, of all places? He tried to tell himself that murder was murder, and an investigation always started out the same way. They gathered evidence, they analyzed it, they talked to witnesses and possible suspects, they put together all the pieces of the puzzle, and in the end they developed a clear picture. But this time there was an overabundance of pieces. They had a suspect who had previously been suspected of killing both his wife and his young son, and who was present near the scene of this crime, when the murder was presumably committed. But why would a perp, who had previously proven to be a master at covering up his tracks, now leave behind such a messy scene? This time they had organic evidence and fingerprints. In the case of his missing wife and son, Vatten had presented an alibi that the police never managed to crack. But this time he had definitely been present at the scene, even after the murder was committed, and could not come up with anything remotely resembling a good explanation. Objectively speaking, there was little to indicate that the two crimes to which Vatten was linked had been committed by the same perpetrator. The MOs were totally different. And what could be Vatten's motive?

Then there was Jens Dahle. They couldn't rule out the husband, even though his alibi seemed strong. The fact that husbands do murder their wives is well-known, but what husband would feel the need to flay her afterward? No, a book with a curse attached to it almost seemed the more reasonable place to start. His thoughts were interrupted when the young officer called back. He told Singsaker that Siri Holm lived on Asbjørnsens Gate, only a five-minute walk from where he was.

Siri Holm opened the door wrapped in a towel from breasts to the tops of her thighs. Her blond hair was wet, and she had drops of water on her shoulders and legs. Two sharp eyes stared at him, amused.

"Oh, excuse me. I didn't know it was the police at the door," she said, after she noticed the rather surprised expression on his face. "Or I would have gotten dressed first. I was in the shower."

"My name is Odd Singsaker. I assume you saw me at the library this morning. Were you expecting someone else?" he asked in embarrassment.

"Not really. I was on my way to work out."

"So you take a shower before you work out?" he asked.

"Tae kwon do. There's quite a bit of close contact. Might as well smell good. Don't worry, I take a shower afterward, too. But do come in. I assume you're here for some reason other than to check on my personal hygiene."

He tried not to laugh. She showed him into an apartment with a fantastic view over the fjord. It was also possibly the messiest apartment he'd ever seen. For a moment he stood there, fascinated by all the things that were strewn about.

"I see you collect antiques," he said at last, picking up something from the floor that looked like an old compass.

"Most of this stuff is from Mamma. She died a year ago. I inherited a bunch of stuff that Pappa didn't want. Unfortunately, I also inherited an aversion to throwing anything out."

He bent down, set the compass on the floor, and picked up a knife. It had a beautiful handle of carved bone depicting a man in a long cloak. The blade was small, sharp, and thin, almost like a modern-day scalpel. The knife looked old, too. The iron was dark with patches where rust had been burnished away.

"You have good taste," said Siri Holm. "That's the jewel in my collection. The only object I could actually sell for plenty of kroner if Pappa ever stopped sending me money. The knife belonged to a famous Italian surgeon who lived in the early 1500s. Alessandro Benedetti."

"Never heard of him," said Singsaker.

"You should have," she said sternly. "He was the world's first plastic surgeon. Benedetti was known for performing the first nose job in history. He took skin from the arm and reconstructed a nose. But above all he was an anatomist. A man who was keenly interested in the structure of the human body."

"Do you have a keen interest in the human body?" he asked, as he continued studying the knife.

"Only when it's alive," she replied with a laugh. She was laughing a lot for someone who'd found a corpse earlier in the day. "To be honest, no."

"What about knives? Are you interested in them too?" he asked.

"The bread knife is the only one I use often. But the one you're holding in your hand, as I said, is a form of life insurance."

"How do you know it's genuine?"

"Mamma bought it from a reputable antique dealer at San Maurizio in Venice. It came with a certificate. She spent half of her inheritance from my grandfather on that knife—not a small sum. I also had it appraised by an expert in Oslo. If the knife didn't belong to Benedetti, it did belong to some other anatomist or surgeon in Venice or Padua at around the same time. That doesn't decrease the value appreciably. I like that the knife may have been used to fix the nose of some Venetian in the 1500s. It reminds me that progress doesn't proceed as fast as we'd like."

As she was talking, she began without embarrassment to dry herself off with the towel. Then she tossed it onto a sofa that was covered with everything from laundry to balls of yarn and an old sewing machine. Stark naked she reached for a tae kwon do uniform that hung on an old mannequin in the middle of the room. Singsaker turned to look at the view over the fjord, studying a sailboat gliding past Munkholmen while she put on the outfit.

"All right, you can look now," she said.

He turned around and watched her tighten a black belt around her waist. For a moment he stood there wondering if he should comment on what he'd just seen, but decided not to.

"I came to ask you some questions about the murder in the library," he said.

"Yes, I gathered that," she said, removing some dirty dishes from the sofa and sitting down. She also put the sewing machine on the floor so that there was room for him, too. He remained standing.

"Do you have time to answer them before you go to your work-out?"

"Of course. I'm not in that big a rush."

"You were one of the first to discover the body, right?"

"Yes, Jon and I found her."

It was a little odd to hear someone refer to Vatten by his first name.

"How did that make you feel?" Singsaker asked.

"It was gruesome. I'd been with Gunn Brita all Saturday morning and had gotten to know her. She was a pleasant woman, a bit stern. Meticulous, the way a librarian should be. I can't imagine anyone doing something like that to her. Or in that place."

"You were with Jon Vatten. How did he react?"

"I know that you suspect him. But you're wrong about that," said Siri Holm, as if confirming a generally accepted truth.

"And how can you be so sure?" he asked.

"I just know," she said. "The same way I know that you're divorced and that you recently went through a crisis in your life and that you were just pretending you were completely unaffected when I was naked."

He tried to hide his astonishment. But was he really surprised? Siri Holm wasn't the only one in the room who could read people. He'd known that there was something unique about this young woman from the first time he saw her at the library.

"Knowledge is always based on something," he said. "Provided it's not just speculation, or in your case, a lucky guess."

"Do you read crime novels?" she asked.

"Do doctors read doctor novels?"

"If you read crime novels, you'd know that there are two main types of investigators," she said. "There's the rational, methodical kind who collects evidence and finds the solution by putting together all the clues in the case. Then there's the less systematic type, who follows his intuition and searches for the decisive clue. Most investigators are probably a mixture of both types. The thing is, both the systematic and the unsystematic investigator are really doing the same thing. They evaluate the evidence. It's just that some investigators think and make associations more rapidly than others. Sherlock Holmes, for instance. What seems like superior intuition is actually only an extremely rapid and systematic processing of data."

"And you think this is relevant to reality?"

"Certainly. Take yourself. Since you came in here, you've scratched your head about fifteen times in a particular spot just above your forehead. That could be a bad habit, of course, but people who habitually scratch their heads rarely scratch in exactly the same spot. Which could mean that you actually scratch there because of something other than an old habit. The same is true of the way you scratch. You do it quickly, as you look away. It's obvious that you don't want other people to notice that you're scratching. So what you're scratching must be something you don't want to talk about. I think it's probably a scar from an operation. And I think that most people with a scar on their forehead have been through some form of life crisis."

"And the divorce?"

"That's easy. You got divorced last summer. You still have a mark from your wedding ring on your finger. So you continued to wear it during the summer, long enough to get a little tan on your hands before you took it off. Of course, you may have just left it at home today. But if we put that together with the way you behaved, there's really no doubt."

"And how am I behaving?"

"Like someone who wants to be in control. Not in control of other people, because then you wouldn't have let me talk as freely as I have. But in control of yourself. The way you looked away when I was naked, even though you didn't want to; the way you examined the room. I'm guessing that you had a very serious illness that made you feel like you'd lost control over your life. And in an unsuccessful attempt to win back that control, you've fled from yourself."

"Impressive," he said. "But what about the other thing you said about me?"

"You mean about pretending not to desire me? If you hadn't wanted me, you would have come over and sat next to me on the sofa long ago," she said, patting the place next to her. "There aren't many other places to sit in this room, are there?"

He couldn't help laughing. Nor could he help being entertained by Siri Holm. It was rare to meet someone with so few inhibitions, especially in his profession. Someone who was so outspoken, and also such an accurate judge of character. Surprised at himself, he went over and sat down beside her. Her hair was still wet.

"Let's return to the matter at hand," he said. "You said you didn't think Vatten had anything to do with the murder."

"I didn't say that he didn't have anything to do with it. I said that he isn't the murderer. You're all suspicious of the wrong person."

"And what do you base that on?"

"Tell me, Singsaker, are you asking me to do your job for you?"

"No, I'm not, but if you have information about the case, I have to ask you to tell me."

"The only information I have about the case is that I consider Jon to be absolutely incapable of cutting someone's throat and then flaying them. The rest is up to you to figure out."

He sighed in resignation but knew that he wasn't going to get any further this way.

"You obviously have keen powers of observation," he said. "When you were in the book vault and the two of you discovered the body, did you notice anything else?"

"Like what?"

"Like a book missing?"

"I wouldn't have known that since it was the first time I was inside the vault."

"True enough."

"Did you have a specific book in mind?"

"Not really. But have you ever heard of the *Johannes Book*?"

"Of course I've heard of it."

"Why 'of course'?"

"If you're a newly hired librarian at the Gunnerus Library, you have to know about it. The *Johannes Book* is something of a celebrity among the book crowd. As for me, I know it better than most people. I wrote a thesis on it when I was studying to be a librarian."

"Interesting," he said. "And had you heard that there's supposed to be a curse on the book?"

"Of course," she replied, and laughed as she looked at him. "But honestly, Singsaker, you don't think . . . I must say, you surprise me."

"No, I don't believe in the curse, and I don't think it's suddenly been awakened to life," he said firmly. "I just thought that other people might."

"You scared me for a minute there. I also think we could be dealing with an irrational murderer," she said. The affected way she was talking suited her in an odd way, as if she had stepped right out of one of the crime novels on her shelves. Then she added, "But I believe this might be something much worse."

"Which is what?"

"An ice-cold killer who's trying to appear irrational," said Siri Holm.

"I think you've read too many mysteries," he said, nodding toward her bookcases.

"You don't learn to solve real-life murder cases by reading mysteries. There's something quite different going on in a fictional investigation. Many people think that the point is to reveal the murderer, while what's actually important is to reveal the author."

"That's an interesting way to look at it," said Singsaker.

"What determines how fast the reader learns the identity of the murderer in a mystery is how well or how badly the author succeeds in hiding him. From the author's point of view, the difficulty is obviously that the murderer has to be included in the story in some way. The most common way is to make him one of several suspects. A common mistake is to try to portray the murderer as less suspicious than the other characters. That makes it easy. But it can be done in an elegant way. Agatha Christie was for many people the master of hiding the murderer. She wrote novels in which a child is the murderer, or the narrator is the murderer, or in which all the suspects are the murderer, and even a story in which the murderer is apparently one of the victims. There are a number of books in which the detective himself is the murderer. It could be a detective who somehow suffered a blackout or amnesia, and so he's investigating himself without knowing he committed the murders."

As she said this, she put her hand on Singsaker's knee and kept it there. He could feel himself flushing. He noticed that he wasn't paying attention to what she was saying. All he was thinking about was that it had been a long, long time, and that a young woman had her hand on his knee, and that she had known he was divorced just by looking at him.

"I really have to go work out soon," she said. "One way or another." Her hand moved from his knee to his cheek.

After the first kiss he was lost. A lost policeman.

Siri Holm opened her eyes. She fell asleep after Singsaker crept out of her apartment. Now she was lying on the sofa with sweet memories. She still had her black tae kwon do belt around her waist. The rest of her outfit lay on the coffee table next to the sofa. She sat up and stuck both thumbs under the belt as she smiled. Black belt in love, she thought, as she slipped the belt down over her hips and let it drop to the floor. Then she went to the bathroom and took a shower. Siri Holm was careful about her hygiene.

Afterward she put on jeans without panties, a colorful blouse, and a red raincoat. She looked at an antique wall clock next to the kitchen door and saw that it was already late in the evening. Then she went out.

Yep, my policeman was right. I do have sharp powers of observation, thought Siri Holm, as she punched in the code she had seen Vatten use on the lock of the book vault in the Gunnerus Library. Her own code was already entered. The vault door gave a good-natured click, and she was able to open it. Inside she stood looking at the surveillance camera up by the ceiling. The system was turned off; she'd already checked that in Vatten's office, which for some reason was unlocked.

Nobody is more sloppy about security than the police, she thought. When a crime has occurred, no one expects another one to be committed in the same place. She sniffed at the air. The police had taken away everything but the stench of death. But that didn't make much difference. She wouldn't be in here for long. She went straight over to the bookshelf where there was a thin little leather-bound book. She took it from the shelf and paged through it. She inspected each page carefully. Then she looked at the cover.

"Just as I thought," she murmured to herself. Then she slipped the book inside a plastic bag she'd brought along and put it in her raincoat pocket. Siri Holm left the Gunnerus Library at thirteen minutes past midnight. No surveillance cameras recorded her arrival or departure. Since she was using a passkey while waiting for her own key card, no one would be able to track her electronically.

18

Richmond, June 1996

Shaun Nevins? *Are you* sure?" Susan laughed.

"What's wrong with him?" Felicia wanted to know. "Besides, it has to be somebody. The plan was to lose our virginity before graduating from high school."

"But Shaun Nevins? That daddy's boy? If his parents didn't have so much money, everyone would see what an idiot he is."

"Ah! Are you calling my date an idiot?"

"He is, and you know it."

"Well, I like him, and he's good-looking," Holly broke in.

"Thank you, Holly," Felicia said, and had to laugh at the whole conversation.

"We can agree that he's good-looking," said Susan, taking a big hit. "And all three of us know that we're not going to marry them. It's just a matter of getting it over with. You're the only one left, Felicia. Are you sure you don't want a toke?" She held out the joint, which was smoked down to the roach.

Felicia shook her head and held up the regular cigarette she had between her fingers.

"Virginia's finest. Don't you think it's a lot healthier?" she said dryly. "Besides, I want to have a clear head."

They were sitting by the bank of the James River. Susan Maddox, Holly LeVold, and Felicia Stone. Three best friends who shared everything. Even the most private things. Things Felicia didn't really want to share but reluctantly agreed to talk about, such as the fact that she would soon be graduating from high school and was still a virgin. Susan had a simple view of the matter.

"The objective, first of all, is to get laid, and if it can be done in a halfway civilized manner, that's a plus," she said.

"Jeez, he at least has to try and seduce you first. If not, forget about it," said Holly.

"I don't need to be in love, that's not it, but I think I have to know that I *could* fall in love with him," said Felicia.

"Seriously," said Susan. "Are you getting married, or are you getting laid?"

If Felicia were honest about it, she'd admit that she'd rather avoid both. Though lately she had been getting excited about the thought of losing her virginity, not just to get it over with, but because she was also almost eighteen and felt ready for it. It felt like the right time. She had managed to wait so long that she actually felt like doing it. Susan was right. Falling in love would have to wait for a more important occasion. But one thing was still important: He had to be good-looking.

She looked at Susan in the glow of the roach as she took one last hit and flicked it toward the riverbank. Behind them, at the end of a path that led up toward River Drive, they could hear the roar of Brian Anderson's party; they were just taking a short break. The noise level was reaching new heights. Felicia knew it wouldn't be long before the cops arrived and told them to break it up. If she was going to get Shaun to come with her without first having to talk to a few of her father's colleagues, she ought to go back to the party and drag him away. But how was she going to do that without seeming desperate? Because she was determined to hold on to some vestige of dignity.

They walked back through the blossoming cherry trees at the bottom of the Andersons' yard. It smelled so good. Felicia thought about something she'd read in English class, about the poet Basho who lived in the 1600s. He would gather his friends together each year when the cherry trees bloomed in the spring. They would lie next to each other under the trees and write long linking poems, called *renga*. One haiku would take over where the last one ended. One long improvisation. It was a sort of jazz, using only words.

"Old lady, a frog jumps, the sound of water," Felicia said suddenly.

Susan looked at her and instantly started to giggle, stoned as she was. But Holly was in the same poetry class with Felicia, and she recognized the words.

"Haiku," she said.

"Basho," Felicia clarified.

"Haiku is good, Felicia. Empty your head of thoughts and just let things be what they are. Let the frog jump." Holly smiled.

"But what about the sound of the water? What does the frog think about that?" asked Felicia, more to the cherry trees than to Holly.

Felicia didn't have to drag Shaun away against his will. She found him standing with a beer in his hand together with the guys from the soccer team. They drove Volkswagens or BMWs, depending on how much money their parents had, wore Topsiders and shirts with a polo player on the breast pocket, and listened to weird British bands like the Smiths. Shaun despised everything that was vulgar and what he called "redneck." Some people might say that Shaun was the vulgar one, or at least a bit full of himself, but he did have a sense of humor. He was in the poetry class with Felicia, and many of the things he said during class were well formulated and smart. But for tonight the most important thing was that he looked good. When he caught sight of Felicia, he left his pals and came over to her.

"Hey, how's my date doing?"

"Pretty good," said Felicia, in a tone of voice designed to tell him that she'd probably have just as good a time somewhere else. Shaun caught on. He was good at those kinds of subtle hints.

"Actually, this party is pretty tame. What do you say we go for a ride?"

"Haven't you had too much to drink?" she asked.

Shaun downed the rest of the bottle and tossed it on the grass.

"Just a bottle or two," he said.

Felicia laughed.

"Well, please drive carefully. I have no plans of saying hi to my dad at work tonight," she said.

"I always drive carefully, you know that," said Shaun.

First they drove a long way up the river and out of the city. Shaun drove a BMW. It was an older model, probably because his parents didn't want to spoil him, though they certainly could afford to. They stopped in an isolated spot under a railroad bridge. Down the slope they could make out a dark section of the James River. As soon as the engine was turned off they started to make out. Shaun tried to feel her up right away, and she let him. But when his hand moved down she pushed it away. He refused to be stopped, and made a new attempt to reach between her thighs and under her short skirt. Then she twisted away from him.

"I want to do it, but not in the car," she said. Felicia could see that he was aroused as he sat straightening his collar, which she'd been grabbing a minute ago. Suddenly she wasn't sure how good he really looked.

"Okay," he said. "We can go back to my house. My parents are at their summer house and won't be back till tomorrow."

Her chest tightened. She felt something that resembled the sound of the river below them as it surged past, like a somber melody in the landscape. But in a strange way, she still wanted him.

Shaun drove slowly along the meandering road toward town. There was nothing to see but the beams of the headlights and the dark of the night. It almost looked like the lights were pulling them forward. On the radio Chris Isaak was singing his hypnotic song "Wicked Game." As they started seeing houses again, and the song ended with the depressing words "Nobody loves no one," Felicia realized that she no longer had control over the situation. She should have asked Shaun to drive her home at once. Why she hadn't done that, she had no idea.

At half past eleven they parked in the garage at the Nevinses' house next to an empty spot and a small Japanese car. They went straight up to Shaun's room. It was big, with a corner window and a view over a yard full of trees that shielded the room from the neighbors but apparently not from the sunshine during the day. There was a double bed in the middle of the room, and it reminded Felicia of her parents' bedroom. All except the temperature.

While the rest of the Nevinses' house had been air-conditioned, it was hot in Shaun's room. The AC was turned off in here, and the window stood open so that the heavy, humid air came in from outside.

"I sleep best when it's hot," said Shaun.

Felicia smiled.

"If you think it's too warm in here, we could take off some of these clothes."

Felicia gulped. Then she said, "You'd better turn off the light."

Nothing felt right anymore. They undressed in the dark. Shaun quickly and efficiently, as if getting ready to go to bed for the night. Felicia slowly and hesitantly. She fumbled with her bra. She felt stressed, and for a moment was afraid that Shaun, who was already naked and lying beside her in the double bed, would try to help her. If he had she would have panicked. But he just lay there, as motionless as a shadow in the dark, and she couldn't see whether he was looking at her or had closed his eyes. Finally she got the bra off, but she kept her panties on. Then she lay down next to him and leaned over to kiss him. He didn't kiss her back. Instead he grabbed the elastic of her panties on one side and pulled until it snapped.

"That's better," he said, and she didn't recognize his voice. He yanked at her panties a couple more times, until he got them all the way off. Then he laughed and tossed the torn panties on the floor. All at once she felt the drops of sweat on her skin turn ice cold.

"No, I don't want to," she said, sitting up in the bed.

"What is it with you, anyway? All girls like sex a little rough, don't they?"

"No, we don't," said Felicia, feeling her voice quaver. She didn't sound as confident as she would have liked.

"Don't tell me you're leaving?" said Shaun. "I've heard that you're a regular prick teaser. But you know what? You're not gonna tease me."

She couldn't believe what she was hearing. Couldn't believe that she really had intended to go to bed with this idiot lying next to her. She turned over to go. But before she could get out of bed, he sat up and grabbed her hair with one hand. He quickly stuck his other hand between her thighs and shoved a couple of fingers into her vagina. A searing pain filled her whole abdomen. He hurried to pull them out again.

"Goddamn, you're as dry as toilet paper. But if you don't want to screw, then you'd better give me a decent blow job." He turned her around by her hair.

She screamed. It was rage and fear. But she thought she sounded like a kid. Then she said, "Damn it, stop pulling my hair. I'll do it, all right?"

"That's better. Fucking skank."

Felicia was shaking with anger, but she held back her tears. That fucker wasn't going to see her cry. Now she just had to do it, and then she could go home.

She bent down and opened her mouth. He put his dick in. His thrusts were rhythmic and hard, and every time he was pulling out it seemed that he was sucking something out of her. He moaned each time. Then he came. She wanted to turn away, but he held her head and made her take it all in her mouth. But she didn't swallow. When he was emptied, he released her, and she fell back on the bed. She got up as fast as she could. Grabbed her dress off the floor and pulled it over her head. Then she put on her shoes. Shaun was lying on the bed with his hands clasped behind his head.

"I hope it was as good for you as it was for me," he said with a laugh.

She still had the semen in her mouth. She spit it out and hit him square in the face.

"Fucking piece of shit," she said, calm and cool. Then she turned and ran out of the house. She was relieved that he didn't come after her.

19

Felicia *walked all the* way home to Monument Avenue Park. She was shivering all over despite the warm night, alternating between rage and an almost paralyzing feeling of emptiness, which several times made her stop short. A question kept surfacing, over and over: How could she have been so wrong about a person? Nice eyes, sort of. But a sick asshole. And she had just let him do it. What did that make her?

When she entered her family's apartment on the second floor, she saw that a light was on in the living room. Her father had come home from the swing shift. He was a policeman and sitting right there, but there was no way she was going to tell him that she'd almost been raped. She just couldn't. It suddenly dawned on her that Shaun knew that too. He knew she would never go to the police. He knew she'd never tell her own father about it. This thought made her feel even more nauseated. She sneaked past the living room archway and into the bathroom. There she stuck a finger down her throat and threw up, trying to do it quietly, so her father wouldn't hear. She wasn't worried about her mother. She always fell asleep with sleeping pills in her bloodstream. After throwing up, Felicia brushed her teeth. She rinsed her mouth and spit out the water at least twenty times before she slipped out of the bathroom and into her own room. Dad is going to think I came home drunk, she thought. But what does it matter now?

That night she lay awake, staring at the ceiling, sweating and freezing at the same time. She thought everything was ruined. Soon she'd be eighteen, and she was supposed to graduate from high school in a few weeks. But now she wasn't sure she'd be able to go back to school. The thought of seeing Shaun Nevins again was intolerable, of course, but she didn't know if she could look her friends in the eye either. Not after this. A strange mixture of shame and rage filled her when she thought about Susan and Holly. In a way, she'd retained her virginity but had lost everything else. She was due to start college in the fall, meet new friends, maybe find a new boyfriend, and travel. But how was she going to face all that now?

At five in the morning she crept into the bathroom and stole two of her mother's sleeping pills. She fell asleep soon afterward and slept until late morning. Neither of her parents woke her.

A rushing sound noise had settled in her ears. It reminded her of the sound you hear in big conch shells, which people say is the roaring of the sea. The trembling in her hands had subsided to a sort of numbness. The nausea came and went, and each time she tried to get up from the bed she felt dizzy. Like a hangover in reverse, it got worse as the day progressed. When Felicia still hadn't emerged from her room for Sunday dinner, her mother came in and sat on the edge of the bed and stroked her hair. Her hand felt ice cold.

"Are you sick, Felicia?" she asked, genuinely concerned. She must have noticed that there was no sign of drunkenness in her daughter's room.

"I just don't feel good," replied Felicia, hoping her mother would stop stroking her hair before she burst into tears.

"Do you want me to bring your dinner up here? We're having roast veal."

"No, I have an upset stomach. But a glass of water would be nice," she said.

Her mother came back with the water and let her stay in bed for the rest of the day.

She stayed home sick from school for three days. She stole pills from her mother to get to sleep at night. By the fourth day some of the vertigo was gone, but not the numbness. She had begun to appreciate the numb sensation, and wanted more of it. She wanted it to seep from her fingertips and the outer layer of her skin all the way into her nervous system, so she wouldn't feel anything. Right before she fell asleep, after taking a sleeping pill, she felt like she was floating away. That was how she wanted to feel. On the fourth day she pretended to be well and went off to catch the school bus. But she was planning to meet her neighbor, Brad Davis, the pothead.

As usual, he stood waiting for the bus as he did some small deals with teenagers who needed something to fortify themselves on an early Thursday morning. Felicia gave him a friendly hello for old times' sake. Oddly enough, he was the first boy who had kissed her. Or maybe she had stolen the kiss from him, since he was too shy to do anything like that. It happened in the tree house in the Davises' backyard, when they were around eight years old. The kiss had felt wet and nice and Brad had been so happy with the kiss she had stolen from him that he gave her a lollipop the next day. They had never kissed again, but they stayed friends. Until they were around thirteen, that is, and Brad got zits and started smoking weed, while Felicia got her tiny boobs that never got any bigger and started reading poetry. But they still said hi to each other every morning at the bus.

Now Felicia went right up to Brad. The decision had been made in advance. He gave her a surprised look when she handed him twenty bucks. Their hands hadn't been close to each other in years.

"I need something to calm me down," she said.

"Got the jitters about finals?" he said.

Felicia gave him a confused look. She'd completely forgotten that final exams were next week. And the week after that was the graduation ceremony, where they would get their diplomas and stand there wearing a gown and a cap with a tassel, and Holly would give the commencement speech in front of all the parents.

"The strongest you can get hold of," was all she said.

"It's going to take some time," said Brad.

"I'll come back tomorrow morning." Then she went back to her brick apartment building. But she didn't go up to the apartment on the second floor. Instead, she went down into the basement. She made her way to a room at the end of a corridor. On the door into the room, childish letters were painted in bright colors: "Secret club! Admission only to Holly, Susan, and Felicia!" Felicia still remembered when she painted those words eight years ago. Inside the walls were painted with princesses and horses and stars and planets. There was a table in the middle of the room with a candle burned all the way down in a bottle covered by hardened drips of wax. Along one wall was a sofa beneath a basement window that allowed daylight to seep through a gap in the flowered curtain. Felicia Stone, soon to be eighteen, lay down on the sofa and stared at the ceiling without the slightest hope that she could fall asleep. At noon she heard her mother leave the house to go to her part-time job at the branch library. Then she sneaked up and stole more pills. She took three pills, realizing that it was only a matter of time until her mother noticed something.

Brad would have to come through.

He did.

Valium has an anesthetic effect on most people, and if you take more than the recommended dose, your emotional life can really be paralyzed. Felicia got enough Valium from Brad to get her through finals and the graduation ceremony. She lied to her girlfriends and told them everything was fine, and that nothing had happened between her and Shaun Nevins, even though he had probably blabbed to the whole school about it. She told her friends that she no longer cared about sex, and wanted to wait until the time was right. In her own mind she thought that would be never.

Luckily she wasn't in the same room as Shaun during finals, and she got a seat far enough away from him at graduation that she wouldn't ever have to look him in the eye again. He eventually disappeared on a Eurail vacation, then to some Ivy League college in New England, and she stayed behind in Richmond with her pills.

In the weeks that followed, the anesthetizing effect that had helped her get through the last terrible days started to diminish, and she began taking the pills with beer or bourbon. She spent hours in the basement, half wasted from pills and alcohol, while her parents thought she was at Holly's house, and Holly thought she was at Susan's, and Susan thought she was at home.

But the numbness would occasionally leave her, and then she could almost taste Shaun's dick shoving into her mouth. A rank, ammonia-like smell. The gag reflex when the head of his dick pressed against the back of her throat and the suction when it pulled back for a new lunge. She could remember how she wanted to bite it, clamp down on it as hard as she could when he was all the way in, and maybe bite off the whole fucking thing. But she hadn't dared. Once in a while she would lay there thinking about it for hours, not noticing that she was grinding her teeth or tensing her jaw muscles so tight that they started to ache. Then she would realize that she needed more pills or beer or booze. In the beginning she only drank in the morning, so the smell would be gone by the time her parents got home from work. Then she would manage to get through the rest of the evening with pills. There was no problem getting a ready supply. Brad was helpful. Felicia got them so cheap that even she realized that Brad was taking a loss for her sake. But he never mentioned it. He must have concluded long ago that she was worrying about something bigger than finals. Still, it was obvious that Brad thought he was helping her. And he was.

Eventually she stopped caring. She would drink all day long and try to avoid her parents in the evenings. Either she stayed in her room or pretended that she was out late, and she made sure to come home when her father was at work and her mother had gone to bed. But it was only a matter of time before someone noticed something. She was getting less and less able to hide her situation. Even through the haze, she was aware of that. But as the summer progressed she grew increasingly indifferent, and escaped more and more from real life. Luckily, both her girlfriends went off on vacation before they managed to grow too suspicious. This was something she didn't mention to her parents, so that she could still use her friends as alibis. But even her parents were going to find out soon. She knew that, and she also knew what they would do when they found out. She'd be sent to rehab. What Felicia feared most of all was that there might still be hope for her. That somebody could actually help her escape from this world of fog she was living in now, which meant she would have to live with the taste of Shaun Nevins's prick in her mouth for the rest of her life. At last she realized that there was only one way out.

One morning in early August she opened the mail her mother had left for her on the kitchen table. It was an answer from the university in Richmond. Felicia had been accepted to the bachelor's program in English literature. She crumpled up the acceptance letter and stuffed it in her pocket without feeling a thing. Then she went out. She went next door and rang the doorbell at the Davises' house. As she had hoped, Brad opened the door.

"Did you run out again?" he asked. He invited her in.

"No, this won't take long," said Felicia. "I'm not here to get pills this time."

"No?"

"No, I came to ask if you could get hold of something else for me."

"What would that be?"

"Heroin," she said flatly.

Brad gave her a long look, his pupils tiny.

"Heroin? Are you trying to kill yourself?" he asked.

"I don't know," replied Felicia, realizing that that was exactly what she was thinking of doing, but the slow way.

20

September looked like it was going to be as hot as August, the air heavy with humidity. After the police got the results on the five-hundred-year-old piece of human skin that Efrahim Bond had sent to VCU for analysis, the investigation of the murder took a new turn. The volume that Mrs. Price had observed without a leather spine came into focus, and both the book and the binding were quickly located by Laubach in one of the desk drawers in Bond's office.

"A book bound in human skin. Have you ever heard of something like this?" Felicia Stone asked her boss, shaking her head. They were sitting alone in her boss's office, and Morris was loudly eating a carrot.

"Actually, I have. I've even seen one," said Morris, a bit smug about the answer. She gave him an expectant look. She had long ago given up being surprised by Morris's vast store of knowledge.

"The book is in the anatomy museum at Edinburgh University.

My wife and I went there on our honeymoon a long time ago. That museum is unforgettable."

"Really? What poor soul did the skin come from?"

"Not a poor soul—William Burke, a serial killer. One of the first we know of. You've studied serial killers—haven't you heard of William Burke and William Hare?"

"Yes, that does ring a bell. They were grave robbers in Scotland in the nineteenth century, weren't they? They sold corpses to anatomists."

"That's right. In Great Britain back then they could only perform dissections on people who'd been executed. But that couldn't meet the increasing demand for corpses from a medical field that was rapidly expanding. So anatomists bought corpses from grave robbers to use in their studies and lectures. The authorities turned a blind eye to this practice. The problem with Burke and Hare was that they gradually switched from stealing corpses to producing their own. Altogether they killed at least seventeen people, and they sold the corpses to a doctor named Robert Knox. To this day we don't know whether or not Knox knew where the bodies came from."

"But how did Burke's skin wind up on the spine of a book?"

"Well, the law finally caught up with Burke and Hare, and they were executed. Since they'd been sentenced to death, their bodies were legally available for dissection, ironically enough. During the dissection of Burke's body, his skin was stolen. It resurfaced some weeks later as decorations on a number of objects, among them the notebook that I saw."

"I have goose bumps!" said Felicia, looking at her arm. Her thoughts shifted to Ed Gein, the murderer Laubach had mentioned the first time they saw the body of Efrahim Bond. She recalled that after Gein was caught, they found a whole bunch of things at his home that had been made of human skin. Among them was a woman's dress that Gein used to put on to play his dead mother, but also lamp shades and chair upholstery.

"Pretty creepy," said Morris. "But Burke was probably not the only one in history that had happened to. The museum guide told us that there was a famous anatomical atlas written by an Italian Renaissance anatomist, Vesalius or some such name, and the nineteenth-century edition was bound in human skin. There's also supposed to be memoirs by a noted robber named James Walton, also known as The Highwayman. The memoirs were apparently bound in his own skin."

"Please tell me that you looked this up right before I got here, and that you don't remember all this from your honeymoon," she said.

"A policeman has to have a good memory, you know. It was a fine trip, otherwise. And now we've got another example of this macabre form of bookbinding. I think we ought to have a talk with the curator of the Poe Museum ASAP," Morris said. "The first priority should be to find out more about the Lord Byron book with the missing spine, and the human skin that was attached to it. The big question, after all, is why Efrahim Bond removed the spine from the book."

"Where do I find the curator, and what's his name?"

"Just a minute," said Morris, rotating a half-chewed mass of carrot in his mouth as he searched through one of the big notepads he used to record his notes. Only an investigator who rarely left his office for fieldwork would take notes in such an impractical way.

"John S. Nevins," he said eventually. "His office is in the Boatwright Memorial Library on the campus of the University of Richmond."

Felicia Stone had a sudden feeling of weightlessness. She was not only dizzy, but she was also trembling. A feeling she thought she had learned to control was about to get the upper hand.

"John Shaun Nevins," she said dully, mostly to herself.

"Yes, I think the 'S' is for Shaun. Curator, professor, and something of a book collector, I noted here. Fifty-nine years old. That's all we've got. Do you know him?"

"I knew his son, Shaun," she replied.

"I see. He must be about your age, right?" said Morris, apparently in the mood for some small talk.

"Yes, unfortunately," she said, her voice ice cold. She was not in the mood to chat.

"Not a pleasant acquaintance, in other words," he said. "But I hope you won't mind talking to his father. You'd be the best person to follow up this lead. Since you pointed us in this direction."

She thought about it and felt her vertigo begin to subside.

"I'll do it," she said and got up, surprised that her knees didn't buckle. "Have you transferred your notes on Nevins to the case file?"

"We haven't started a separate file on him, if that's what you mean," replied Morris. "He's hardly a central figure in the investigation. For the time being I thought we'd regard him as a specialist. For consultation purposes."

"OK," she said.

"Do you think he's involved?"

"I have no idea. It's just an uneasy feeling."

"This case is wide open, so why not?" said Morris. "I mean, human skin that's five hundred years old. What does that make you think of?"

"That two people were flayed by two different sick fucks," she said firmly. "There are five hundred years between the cases. But I'm thinking that we shouldn't view this type of sadistic murder as a purely modern phenomenon. Europe in the fifteen hundreds was a much more violent place. There were vicious, wacko criminals back then, too. But I can't see the connection between the cases."

"A phantom from the past," said Morris with a smile, taking another bite of carrot. "It's almost in the spirit of Edgar Allan Poe. A psychotic killer is reanimated from the spine of a book."

"The flayer returns," she laughed with gallows humor. "But to be serious, we have to consider the distinct possibility that the murderer knew about this book and was somehow inspired by it. And if there's anyone who ought to be familiar with the books in the museum and the material they were bound with, it's definitely the curator."

"True enough. But for the moment, let's consider it merely a hypothesis. I want to have the curator on our side, at least to start with."

"Certainly. A woman is entitled to voice her opinions, that's all," said Felicia Stone, and she left.

Naturally, it was more than merely opinions. She was actually thinking that a man with a shithead for a son is probably a sick bastard himself. Such thoughts ought to have convinced her to leave the interview to someone else. But this was precisely why she wanted to do it herself. This investigation would eventually lead them to a pitiful sociopath. And she had gotten wind of one. If only she could follow the trail.

Boatwright Memorial Library was a big, redbrick building that overlooked the small Westhampton Lake located at the heart of the university campus. Like most of the other buildings, the library was built in the neo-Gothic style. For many Americans this style symbolized the height of old, venerable academe. The building itself was erected in the 1950s to organize a book collection that was about to get out of control. So even though the building was venerable, it wasn't particularly old. Felicia also knew that the big, ostentatious bell tower was equipped with a digital carillon that entertained students and teachers in deep concentration with music twice a day.

She parked in the lot closest to the lake and took the path past the bell tower and into the library. On the third floor she found the office of Nevins Sr. She knocked on the door and was invited in by a deep bass voice.

Nevins's office obviously belonged to someone who used books as a status symbol as much as a source of knowledge. All the walls were covered with floor-to-ceiling bookcases. Nevins stood in front of a large, heavy desk and held out his hand. To Felicia's great surprise, he looked friendly. He was dressed informally in a short-sleeved shirt with the top button undone and beige chinos. His hair was completely gray but still thick. The furrows in his brow and the bags under his eyes made him look peaceful and grandfatherly. He looked like a man who would be utterly incapable of raising a crowbar to strike someone, let alone flay someone alive. She shook his hand and noticed that he had a pleasantly firm grip. She reluctantly had to admit that she had a good first impression of him.

Reynolds had interviewed Nevins earlier, so they didn't need to go through the formal details. Felicia Stone had also called in advance to tell him what she wanted to discuss.

"The book by Byron that Poe owned, well, that was actually a bit of a mystery. Nobody knows where he got it from. It's a valuable treasure, of course. A first edition of *Childe Harold's Pilgrimage* is a rarity under any circumstance. But this one had several things about it that were especially interesting. First of all, there's the spine. I always thought that it had a unique quality about it; look at the color, almost grayish white. But human skin? That's horrible. A few months ago we discovered that the spine is most probably a palimpsest."

"And by that you mean that something was written on it

earlier?" she asked, proud of what she'd learned recently. At the same time she was annoyed that she felt she had something to prove to Shaun Nevins's father.

"That's right," said Nevins, impressed. "Do you have it with you?"

She opened a briefcase she'd been carrying as a shoulder bag and took out a clear plastic bag containing the book spine made of human skin. She also took out the book itself and placed both of them on Nevins's desk.

"May I?" he asked politely, picking up the bag to remove the spine.

"Do you have gloves?"

"Of course, that's basic equipment for a curator," he said with a smile, taking a pair of white silk gloves from a desk drawer. He put them on, and then took the spine out of the plastic bag.

"Come over here," he said, going over to a high white table in one corner of the room. He placed the spine on the table and smoothed it out. Then he turned on the work lamp and picked up a magnifying glass. He held it over the skin and let her look through it. It was possible to see letters, as if printed on the skin. But she couldn't decipher any of the words.

"It's in Latin," said Nevins. "But I'm afraid that this palimpsest hasn't resulted in great interest among scholars yet. It was newly discovered, and no one has begun any systematic work to interpret it. Most likely because it was viewed for so long as a rarity in Poe's collection and not a possible historical source."

"But is it possible to read the words?"

"Yes, probably. There are various techniques to discern this type of text, such as X-rays or photographs exposed in different light spectra to amplify the contrast in the washed-out ink. That's what made it possible to read eighty percent of the underlying text on the famous Archimedes palimpsest at Johns Hopkins University. The subtext in that case turned out to be an unknown text by the Greek scientist Archimedes."

"The one who said 'Eureka!'?"

"Precisely. And did you know that *Eureka* was the title of Edgar Allan Poe's only scientific work?"

"No, I didn't."

"It doesn't have much of anything to do with the present matter, but it's an obvious example of what a literary scholar would call 'transtextuality.' The idea that text can move from one work to another, and that old bits of text remain as a kind of subtext in new texts."

"So when we say a text is deep, it only means that it contains things that were written before?" she asked.

"That's one way to look at it," said Nevins with a hearty laugh. "The concept of a palimpsest can be viewed as a prime example of that very idea. The fact that all texts are in a sense written over their predecessors. But to get back to your question: At present, the Archimedes palimpsest is kept at the Walters Arts Museum. There they used fluorescent X-ray photography to try and read the rest of the palimpsest. But on our palimpsest, I think there are indications that the skin has been written on more than twice, maybe as many as four or five times. That will make it more difficult to interpret the text, of course. But not impossible."

"Haven't you ever considered getting it analyzed?" Felicia Stone asked.

"I don't have the authority. The book is the property of the museum, after all. It was Bond who made the discovery of the palimpsest this past spring. I got the impression that he initiated some investigations, but I don't know much about it. But I did enter the new information about the book in the relevant databases. I also informed several appropriate scholars. I even mentioned the spine of the book at a conference I attended. But as I said, no one has taken the bait yet. That's what often happens in academia. You wouldn't believe how many discoveries have yet to be made. People no longer invest their time or risk their prestige on anything that might not pan out. Most likely it's just some nonsense from the Middle Ages that's written on the spine. Something for a master's thesis, possibly."

"But it could also be an important historical source, right?"

"Perhaps. In this instance it's a problem that we don't know where the spine of the book came from. But there happens to be a good clue that someone could follow up on if they were interested. There's a name on the title page of the book."

Nevins went back to his desk and held up the interior of the Byron book. She saw something written on the title page but thought it was illegible.

"I don't know how this name is pronounced," said Nevins. "I'll write it down for you." He wrote something on a Post-It note and gave it to her.

It said: "Broder Lysholm Knudtzon."

"I'd guess it's Scandinavian," said Nevins.

"You're something of a book collector yourself, Mr. Nevins," she said, putting the note in her briefcase.

"I am, yes," Nevins replied.

She looked around the room.

"The books in here, are they yours, or do they belong to the library?"

"Most of them are mine," he said. "But they're not as valuable as they might appear. These are books that I use in my work."

"But you do own valuable books, too?"

"Yes, I do."

"And where do you keep them?"

"At home," said Nevins, noticeably more laconic.

"Is that safe?" she wanted to know.

"I have an alarm system. Tell me, is this relevant to the matter at hand?"

"No, I'm sorry, I was just making small talk." But she thought to herself that she had somehow struck a nerve. Although she didn't know what it might mean.

"You don't have a safe where you keep your most valuable books, do you?" she asked.

"Why do you ask?"

"I've read about collectors who lock up their most valuable treasures, and I've always wondered what the point was in collecting something if you're just going to hide it away from the rest of the world."

"Yes, you might well ask," Nevins chuckled. Felicia wondered if he sounded tense?

"You probably know a great deal about other book collections besides your own, I would think," Felicia went on, trying for a more innocent tone.

"Yes, that's true," he said, apparently relaxing a bit now that the conversation had turned away from himself.

"Would you say that you're familiar with collections abroad?"

"Yes, I go to Europe frequently."

"And you go there to buy books for your personal collection?"

"Yes, if I'm not there for a conference related to my job, which does happen sometimes. I also take occasional assignments doing appraisals for insurance companies."

"So if someone like you doesn't know who this Broder Lysholm Knudtzon is, that must mean that Knudtzon doesn't or didn't have a particularly important book collection. Would you agree?"

She studied his face. She'd struck a nerve. He hesitated. Then he said, "I wouldn't say that. The book world is huge, and I really don't know that much about Scandinavian collections," he said at last.

"I see," she said. "But I assume you wouldn't object to finding out more about it. Something tells me that you could work a lot faster regarding this matter than we could. The police need to find out as much as possible about this book, both about the spine and the text inside."

"I'll do my best." Nevins thought for a moment. Then he said, "Actually, I'm taking a trip to Europe next week."

"Really? Where are you going?"

"Frankfurt," he said.

"Isn't there a book fair there every year?" she asked, surprised at her own knowledge.

"There is, but I'm not going to a fair. I'm going to appraise a private book collection. The owner wants to insure it with an American company, and the company is sending me over to evaluate it."

"I see."

"I'll also be meeting with some German colleagues over there. They may be able to help us with this Knudtzon."

Felicia took the book spine and put it back in the plastic bag, which she placed in her briefcase. Then she thanked Nevins. As she was on her way out of the office, he suddenly said: "Felicia Stone. I think I've heard that name before. Tell me, weren't you in the same class as my son, Shaun Nevins? In high school?"

She gave a start.

"I think you're right," she said, and felt like adding: You don't forget somebody who's raped you in the mouth. Instead, she said, "How is Shaun doing?" She wished she could say that she wasn't the least bit interested in the answer to that question. But even though she'd spent her whole adult life trying not to think about it, or him, he'd gotten under her skin, and it would have made her happy to hear that things weren't going well for him. She knew there was little chance of that.

"Shaun is married and has two sweet little girls. He's a corporate attorney in New York," said Nevins.

What did she expect?

"Good for him," she remarked, then closed the door behind her and left.

On her way out of the library she thought to herself, Didn't he seem a little too restrained about that book spine? Wouldn't a newly discovered palimpsest be for a book curator what an undiscovered city is for an archaeologist? No matter if it's some nonsense from the Middle Ages? Was the good Mr. Nevins holding something back?

When she got to her car, she took out her iPhone before she climbed in, and called Laubach. He picked up at once.

"What is it, sweetheart?" he asked.

"When you found that book," said Stone, getting right to the point, "how much other paperwork did you get a chance to look through in Bond's office?"

"Most of it, really, but just superficially. We were mostly looking for that book. Otherwise we gave priority to technical finds. You tacticians get to take the reading material after we've gone over it with our magnifying glasses. You know the drill."

"Yes, I do. But do you know if anyone noticed any photographs, or even X-rays, in Bond's office?"

Laubach answered at once. "No, not that I know of."

"All right then," she said, disappointed.

"Should there have been something like that there?" he asked. "Would that have made things fall into place for you?"

"I don't know. Right now, it feels like the more I find out, the less it makes sense."

"I know what you mean. But since you're younger than me you should remember one thing."

"What's that?"

"Most photos these days aren't lying around on paper."

"No, of course not. But I was thinking of big X-ray negatives, the kind they hang up on a light box."

"You've been watching too many doctor shows on TV."

"Could be. Has your team gone through Bond's cell phone and PC?" she asked.

"His cell was an archaic model without a lot of storage. He was old. Many people his age don't even have a cell phone. He had a PC in his office, but none at home. Preliminary examinations of the PC showed that nothing was encrypted or password-protected. We haven't studied the individual files yet."

"Could you put somebody on it? I think it's important. Look for photos or X-ray pictures with text—possibly fuzzy, erased text."

"X-rays of text? Are we looking for a hidden message here?" Laubach joked.

"You might say that," she said, and ended the call.

Felicia Stone got into her car and turned on the ignition. The radio came on. And there was Chris Isaak, like a ghost from the past. Before she could turn it off, the song had crept under her skin. Yes, that's how it felt. Literally. As if the lyrics were etched into her skin word for word. Like ink on parchment. She sat there paralyzed, listening until the song faded out. Then she looked down at her arm. Was something written there, under her skin? Wasn't there an almost illegible impression of words? "Nobody loves no one." She was having a hard time breathing. I've been working too hard, she thought. It's only a reaction from having met the father of that pig. And then this song. What a creepy coincidence. She looked at her arm again. Inspected her skin. Veins were all she saw. Naturally there was nothing written there. Then came the dangerous thought: I need a drink. And after that the even more dangerous rationalization: It wasn't alcohol I was dependent on. It was pills. I can handle a drink.

She turned off the engine, and the radio was quiet before the DJ introduced the next song. Then she got out of the car. Dizzy, she stood there looking out over the calm lake. She recalled that once it had been her dream to attend this university. She was going to study literature and history, try to answer the big questions in life. She knew that each year the students who graduated would gather around this lake in the evening with candles lit in a beautiful farewell ceremony. At one time she was hoping to experience that herself. Instead her life had taken her to detox and rehab. Alaska, and then the police academy. Did she have regrets? She felt that her path was not of her own choosing. So how could she regret it?

Slowly she walked down to the shore of the lake. There she bent down and filled her hands with water and washed her face. It's not a drink I need, she thought suddenly with a clear head. I need to go home.

By home she meant the apartment in Monument Avenue Park where her father still lived after her mother had died several years ago.

She parked on the sidewalk outside Brad Davis's house. She knew that he still lived there, too, even though she hadn't seen him in years. Sometime after she left home, he had stopped dealing. Most likely because his clientele had never included anyone but his friends in high school, and most of them went off to college. Evidently at some point he also cut back on smoking weed. He got married, at any rate. Got through college somehow and became an advertising executive. He had two kids, a boy and a girl, who played in the yard sometimes. Felicia could see that he had helped the kids to rehabilitate the tree house where she once upon a time had experienced her first, wet kiss. She'd never met Brad's wife. This morning the Davis family's house stood empty.

She fished out the key she still had and let herself into the stairwell leading to her father's apartment. When she got inside she stopped and stared at the basement door. She looked at it whenever she came here, but she could never bring herself to go downstairs—not since that last time. She was breathing hard.

Slowly she went over to the basement door, opened it, and went down the stairs. The clammy smell was still there. She walked calmly down the hall to the room where she had once had a secret club with her two best girlfriends. She wasn't surprised to see that the childish letters were still on the door. She opened it cautiously and stepped inside. Nothing had changed. The candle was still on the table. She was shocked to see that a glass was there, too. It was the same one she had used back then. Nobody has been here since, she thought. But that wasn't quite right. The pill bottles, the empty liquor bottles, and the syringe were gone. Someone had removed what had to be removed, but otherwise the room was left undisturbed.

She stood there looking around, and she thought back to when this had been their secret club room. The most vivid memory was of the time they painted the walls. All the discussions they'd had about the choice of designs, all the plans for the club. She didn't remember very well what they had actually done down here once the club room was finished. The planning had been the best part. And she remembered their dreams. The thought of being alone, just three friends with no grown-ups around. To be able to have a place where they decided everything. Unbridled freedom in a tiny, closed-off room.

She lay down on the sofa. Here she had lain a whole summer, until one day, when she almost died of an overdose. And it wasn't very comfortable either, she thought. She got up. Inhaled the musty basement smell deep into her lungs. The desire for a drink was gone.

From the basement she went up to her father's apartment and let herself in without knocking. Her father lay dozing on the sofa.

"So the retired guy just lies here taking it easy," she said in a loud voice.

He opened his eyes and looked at her, sat up, and began clearing off the table. An empty beer bottle vanished among rolled-up newspapers, and he took everything with him into the kitchen. When he came back he said, "I wasn't expecting to see you for at least a few weeks. A hell of a case you've got on your hands."

"You can say that again," she said, glad that her father was still keeping up with what happened at the station. Lately she'd been thinking more about the age difference between them. Her father had been over forty when she was born. When she was going to school and he was working, it had seemed perfectly normal. Now the age gap felt like an eternity, as if her father had suddenly turned into her grandfather. She didn't know how long she would still have him around, and she was often afraid he would lose his capacity for clear thinking.

"But I didn't come here to talk about the case."

Her father seemed disappointed, and that made her happy. The cop was still in there.

She sank onto the recliner where he always sat when he watched a game. That was the only thing he watched on TV. Always baseball, never anything else.

"I came to ask you about that time," she said.

A shadow passed over his face. Was it surprise, fear, or relief?

She thought it was relief. This was something she had been waiting to talk about, and she had known for a while now that she shouldn't wait too long. Her father wasn't getting any younger.

He sat motionless for a moment. Then he did something that surprised her. Maybe it surprised both of them. He stood up, went to the kitchen, and opened a can of beer. He had never done that in front of her since that summer. He came back into the living room and set the beer on the coffee table after he took a sip.

"I think you've made enough progress by now that this shouldn't bother you," he said.

"It doesn't bother me. As long as you don't have too many," she said in the motherly tone she'd involuntarily adopted after her father ended up living alone.

"Don't worry about me. I've turned into an old man and can finally do what I want," he said with a smile. Then he began his account without waiting for any more urging.

"It was Holly who found you. Your first shot of heroin was an overdose. It was one of God's miracles that Holly came home from vacation on that very day and was determined to find you. She'd spent her vacation thinking about you and had realized that something was wrong. She refused to stop until she found you. She interrogated us and went around to all your friends. Finally she called up the neighbor boy, Brad. It turned out that he'd already saved your life the week before. You'd asked him for a dose of heroin, and he'd refused. He thought he'd talked you out of it, but you were harder to save than that. You'd gone across town and bought what you thought you needed. But it was Brad who mentioned the secret club room in the basement. He thought that's where you might be. It's strange that none of us had thought of it. I have no idea how much he knew and how much he was guessing. And I don't want to know about how much he was involved in getting you the pills you'd been taking all summer without our knowledge." Here he paused and took another swallow of beer before he continued.

"You were lying on the sofa, unconscious, with a syringe on the floor next to you. Holly ran upstairs to get us to call an ambulance. I remember that your mother was terribly pale. She couldn't believe what had happened. We went with you to the hospital but had to sit in the waiting room until they managed to revive you. Your mother didn't say a word the whole time. Then they let us in to see you, and you were lying there with a little more color in your face, but still pale. That's when the tears came. Your mother cried like I'd never seen her cry before."

Felicia sat looking at her father. She'd never heard him tell this story. She could hardly remember what happened herself. The whole thing was like a muddled haze. She remembered that detox was hell, and that they drove her to a rehabilitation center in West Virginia. She remembered that she was lucky to be there, and that it had really helped. And then her father came and got her, and they moved to Alaska, where her father had taken a job as a sheriff in a small town. That was what saved her. It was almost a symbolic action. A year on ice. A year away from the world. A new start. In Alaska she got to work as her father's assistant at the sheriff's office. To her amazement, she liked police work. At the end of the year her parents decided that they couldn't protect her up there away from the world forever. So they moved back to Richmond, and she started at the police academy.

But she hadn't actually come here to listen to her father's account of what happened. She was the one with the secrets. Her parents had never asked her why she changed from being a happy high school graduate to shooting heroin in two short months. She knew that this must have tormented them. But for some reason they'd let her keep that secret, no doubt hoping that one day she'd find the strength to tell them.

"We've never talked about this before," she said.

"No," said her father, chugging the rest of his beer.

"It's good that we've started."

"Yeah."

Next time it's my turn to say something, she thought. Next time.

"I have to get back to the investigation. You know how it is," she said, getting up.

Her father nodded. He knew very well how it was.

"What you need to ask yourself . . ." he said, as she was on her way out the door.

She stopped.

". . . is what he's doing with the skin."

She nodded thoughtfully, then left the apartment. She was glad that she'd taken this detour home.

On the way down the stairs her thoughts turned again to Ed Gein. He's real, she told herself. Killers who flay their victims do exist. At the same time she realized that one of the biggest challenges she had to deal with during the remainder of the case was going to be the strange feeling of unreality. And she didn't know how much it would help to think about Ed Gein. He was the inspiration for movies like *Psycho, Texas Chainsaw Massacre,* and *The Silence of the Lambs.* Just like the murderer she was hunting, Gein was a figure from another world. He had danced around his dead mother's untouched bedroom wearing a suit he had sewn from the skin of dead people.

You need to ask yourself what he's doing with the skin, her father had said. But how could she find a rational answer to that question? Rational people don't do anything at all with human skin. But she already knew the answer. He writes on it, she thought, closing the front door of her father's building behind her.

Back at the police station, Felicia sat down at her desk in one of the cubicles that made up the homicide division. She had a laptop in front of her. The techs had already examined Bond's PC and extracted the files from it, including what they could retrieve from the deleted folders. It turned out that Bond only used his work e-mail for work-related purposes, and even then not often, pretty much just to answer inquiries that he couldn't ignore. The curator may have used a Web-based service, such as Gmail, for his private e-mail.

But nobody other than people with whom he'd had a purely professional relationship could recall being given the solitary old man's e-mail address.

She copied the files on Bond's PC to a folder on her own machine, and started searching for image files. To her great disappointment, she didn't find what she was looking for. She found only pictures of the inventory of the museum, a few unsuccessful snapshots of Bond's colleagues, all taken on the job, and otherwise very little. One picture piqued her curiosity more than the others. It was of a very fat lady with red hair. Felicia didn't recognize her. Someone in his family, she guessed. Maybe Bond's daughter. But what interested her about this particular picture was that it wasn't taken inside the Poe Museum, like all the other images were. It was taken outdoors, and she recognized the lake in the background. It was Westhampton Lake, on the university campus. She started to wonder who might have taken this picture but couldn't come up with anyone. In frustration, she closed the laptop and phoned Laubach.

"Where are you?" she asked.

"Here," said Laubach, putting his cell phone down on her desk.

"Good grief, I didn't even hear your phone ring," she said, and had to laugh.

"On vibrate," he explained. "Useful for when you have to sneak up on somebody from behind."

"Good job. But listen. I'm not finding out anything at all from Bond's PC."

"All right, but how do you know these pictures you're looking for really exist?"

"I don't. It's just a hunch. A lot of stuff would fall into place if they did."

"So it's really just something you're wishing for."

"Yeah, I guess so." She sighed heavily.

"It's usually best to work with the evidence we have and not the evidence we wish we had," said Laubach.

Felicia Stone gave him a wan smile.

21

The rest of that week and the next were spent on fruitless interviews and an endless examination of Bond's papers and effects. No new pictures were found. Reynolds and Patterson visited Bond's relatives, without result. But Patterson was able to rule out the red-haired woman in the picture on Bond's PC as a family member. "Only dark-haired, skin-and-bone types in that family," he reported. This made the image of the fat, red-haired woman far more interesting to Felicia. Since Bond didn't have his own camera, not even one on his phone, and hadn't received the picture through his work e-mail—which was the case with the other pictures—there was a good deal of discussion about where the picture might have come from. Patterson thought it could mean that Bond had an e-mail address they didn't know about, and that he had downloaded it from there. But there were many other ways an image could end up on a computer. So it remained a mystery.

Patterson learned that Efrahim Bond hadn't been much of a family man. His children didn't have anything directly negative to say about him. They actually seemed to have warm feelings for him, but they had given up on him taking an active role in the family. He never called or took it upon himself to contact them. As the years went by, he had just slipped further and further away from all of them.

Reynolds added that they all had good alibis, and none of them seemed to have a motive for killing their father, particularly in such a bestial way.

The case had come to a standstill. What had seemed a promising start had led them nowhere.

Several days later Felicia Stone decided to Google "curator Nevins." Not that she hadn't done it already. They had checked him out in detail, through vigorous searches on the Web and in various databases, but she also knew that the more times you Google someone and cross-Googled one or more names, the greater the chance of finding unexpected connections.

Apparently a quarterback in college football named John Stuart Nevins had had a good season. There were more hits for him than for the curator. Still, she didn't want to type in the middle name Shaun in the search box for fear that it might lead to more hits on Nevins Jr. than she wanted. So she sat there scrolling through the list, and some of the hits were for the correct Nevins after all. Several were from Web sites for the library and the university. And then there were some from local newspapers, mostly rather old, in which Nevins commented on some anniversary celebration honoring a writer at which a first edition was displayed from the library's collection. Nevins's name also popped up as the author of a number of scientific articles, and as a participant at various conferences all over the country. None of this seemed to have anything to do with the case, though.

Felicia chewed on her pencil and stared blankly at a photo of Nevins she'd stumbled upon. There he stood, wearing elegant white gloves, holding out an old book. The picture was from the *Richmond Times-Dispatch*. The headline on the accompanying article read: LOCAL COLLECTOR BUYS VALUABLE BOOK COLLECTION.

The article recounted how Nevins had bought a number of valuable books from the estate of an elderly widow from one of Richmond's old, well-to-do tobacco families. And how Nevins bought and collected old books privately, which Felicia already knew. But suddenly she noticed the title of the book that Nevins was holding up. *Peer Gynt*. Henrik Ibsen. The letters were stamped in gold on red cloth. There's something familiar about that, she thought. Henrik Ibsen. Wasn't he Swedish? At any rate, he was from somewhere in Scandinavia. Nevins claimed that he didn't know much of anything about Scandinavian book collecting. Sure, she thought. And yet here he stands holding a book by Henrik Ibsen. She realized that of course it could be pure coincidence. The book Nevins was holding in the photo was not from a foreign collection. It had been bought here in Virginia. But why had Nevins chosen to hold up this particular volume for the photographer?

She had an idea. On Google's search page she clicked on search settings. A number of choices came up for the category of search language. She clicked on Swedish, Norwegian, and Danish. This time she searched for the full name: John Shaun Nevins. A single hit was all she got. It was an article on a site called adressa.no. It was probably a newspaper.

Nevins did in fact have a point. He hadn't made himself very well known in Scandinavia. But here he is, she thought triumphantly. Her eyes fell on the photo accompanying the brief article. It showed a room that looked like it was furnished sometime in the nineteenth century, with books lining the walls, completely in Nevins's style. A group of people posed, all smiling. In the middle was Nevins. The only place in the article where his name was mentioned was in the caption. It was obvious that the curator from Virginia was not the most important person in the room. But what was he doing in the picture?

She had no idea what language the article was written in,

although from the domain name she guessed it was from Norway. But maybe the photo wasn't even taken in Scandinavia? The article could be a Norwegian report of something that had taken place in the States, for all she knew. She sat there and stared at the caption again. Most of the other names seemed foreign, but she couldn't say if they were all Scandinavian. Then she noticed the words at the beginning of the caption. *"I Knudtzonsalen,"* it said. She opened a desk drawer and took out a piece of paper. It was the note that Nevins had written for her. Broder Lysholm Knudtzon, she read. Knudtzon. *Knudtzonsalen.*

She looked up the Web site of the university in Richmond, hoping to find somebody there who could translate from the Scandinavian languages. But before she could scroll down the whole list of faculty, she had a sudden brain wave. She closed the laptop, grabbed the phone, and dialed an internal number for the morgue basement.

"Knut Jensen," said a voice from the depths of the building. Talk about luck. Just the guy she wanted.

"This is Felicia Stone upstairs. I have kind of an unusual question for you."

"I've got an unusual job, so shoot," replied Jensen.

"Do you happen to have Scandinavian ancestors, by any chance?"

"Jeez, is it that obvious? What gave me away? My name or my blue eyes?"

"Both," she said with a laugh.

"Well, I confess. My father was born in Norway. He came here when he was fifteen with his parents. So what's my punishment?"

"That depends. Did your father ever teach you Norwegian?"

"My dad insisted on us being American. We always spoke English at home."

"That's too bad."

"Yeah, basically. But it didn't stop my grandmother from speaking

Norwegian to us. She taught me to read a little, so I'd be able to read the newspaper to her when she got old, she said. Relatives sent the *Bergens Tidende* newspaper to her every month. Grandma never ended up with bad eyesight, so I didn't get much of a chance to read out loud. But I can stumble my way through simple Norwegian."

"In that case, you're sentenced to half an hour hard labor in my office right this minute," she said with a laugh.

"Accused and convicted in the same phone call. Is this is a police state or what?" Knut Jensen quipped.

"No, but it *is* a police station," she said, wondering if they were flirting.

"I'll be right up," he said.

Knut Jensen spent a long time studying the article.

"This is typical local news. The Web site is operated by a newspaper in Trondheim, the third-largest city in Norway. It's really just a small town, but they do have a university. The photo here is from the university library. There was some sort of conference dealing with Norwegian manuscripts and transcriptions of documents from the Middle Ages. The article emphasizes that there are very few such manuscripts in the country, but that those that do exist are extremely interesting. The book by a certain Johannes the priest is said to be especially exciting." Jensen looked up at Felicia Stone. "Does this really have something to do with the case?"

"No idea. But there, underneath the photo, what does that say?"

"It only says that the picture was taken in the Knudtzonsalen, which is probably a room named after somebody called Knudtzon. And then the names of the people in the picture. Participants at the conference, I would guess."

"What would you say if I told you that one of these men told me that he doesn't know anything about Scandinavian book collections?"

"I'd probably say that was pretty strange. I don't think he just stumbled into this photograph."

"That's what I think, too. But when is this article from?"

"Let's see, here's the date. They write dates the other way around in Norway. It was published in April this year."

"Do a search on this room, this Knudtzonsalen," she said.

Jensen searched for it, and he got a number of hits. He clicked on the first one and read: "The room was named after a guy named Broder Lysholm Knudtzon," he said, after reading for a while on what looked like the home page of some institution, maybe a library or university. "He was apparently a big-time book collector."

"I knew it," Felicia Stone muttered.

Jensen clicked onto another article. She saw that this one was from *Adresseavisen*, too. The article was quite recent. It was actually from today.

Knut Jensen sat there in silence, reading.

"I don't get this," he said after a while.

"Problems with the Norwegian?"

"No, the language is understandable enough. It's the content that's baffling. The mention of Knudtzonsalen refers to the fact that all the employees in a certain department of the university library in Trondheim were assembled there today during a police investigation. And the case that was being investigated . . . Well, that's amazing. This changes nearly everything, I should think. Either you're a genius, or you're the luckiest detective I know."

"Tell me what the hell you're talking about!" She almost felt like grabbing Knut Jensen by the collar and shaking him.

"Exactly twelve hours ago a woman was found murdered in the book vault at the university library in Trondheim."

"All right, that's a strange coincidence."

"Right, but here's the really strange thing. The woman was found with her throat cut and her body flayed."

Felicia just stared at him. This is where the case cracks wide open, she thought. She might have felt even better if they hadn't simply stumbled on this information by accident. But what difference did it make? It was moments like this that a detective lived for. A breakthrough in the case. Finally!

Then she stared at an image on the screen. It was a picture of a red-haired, full-figured woman. And she knew right away that she'd seen her before. It was the woman from Bond's mysterious photograph.

"Who's that a picture of?" she asked, pointing, even though she already knew the answer.

"That's the woman who was murdered."

She gave Jensen a long look, wondering whether she ought to hug him. She made do with putting a hand on his shoulder.

"Jensen, we need a written translation of this article as soon as possible. I'm calling an urgent meeting for the whole team, and I want you to be there."

An hour later the team was assembled in the conference room. They began with the pathologist reading aloud his translation of the article from *Adresseavisen*. He had also spent time before the meeting surfing other major Norwegian online papers and told them that the case was big news all over Norway, and the police already had a suspect in custody. To that, Reynolds replied, as he chewed a big wad of gum, "If the press over there is anything like ours, we can take it all with a grain of salt. We also have a probable suspect."

"Well, do we really?" said Felicia Stone, who'd had time to go over a number of things in her mind after the initial intoxication over the breakthrough had subsided. "How likely is it that Nevins is actually in Norway?"

"Theoretically, Nevins could be in Norway," said Reynolds. "He left for Europe three days ago."

"He went to Germany," she pointed out. "He mentioned that trip to me last week."

"In the meantime I've checked his alibi for the day Bond was killed. He was meeting with a book dealer in Louisville. I talked to the guy as well as people at the hotel he was staying the night of the murder. There's no reason to doubt that he was there."

"We don't have anything concrete on him at the moment," said Morris, who until now had been sitting silently at the head of the table. "But just because he didn't personally commit the murder, it doesn't mean we can rule him out as a suspect. We shouldn't forget the most important discovery. Today we learned that there were two murders instead of one. And no matter how much Nevins seems to be the link, it looks as though the victims actually knew each other. Bond had a photo of this Norwegian woman, Gunn Brita Dahle, on his PC."

"Well, there's one more connection. Old books," said Felicia. "I think we have to focus on that. It's got something to do with books and bindings made of human skin."

"The main thing now is to confirm that these two cases are as similar as they seem. Jensen, what did you say the inspector's name was? The one handling the library case in Norway?" Morris asked.

"I didn't say," said Jensen, leaning close to his PC. "Let me see. His name is Odd Singsaker."

"Odd? That's an odd sort of name," Patterson said with a chuckle. Felicia just rolled her eyes.

"Stone, get him on the phone so you two can compare notes. Maybe you ought to start thinking about packing an overnight bag."

"Yes, sir. Not to be difficult, but is that the way it's done?"

"What do you mean?"

"We're talking about a foreign case here. Aren't there certain procedures that have to be followed? Don't we have to go through a higher authority?"

"Not before we know more. For the time being we have a case we're working on, and they do, too. All we want is to exchange information. And I'll bet they're just as interested in talking to us as we are in talking to them."

"Great. But isn't it better for Jensen to do the talking, since he knows the lingo?"

"Jensen's not a cop. No hard feelings, Jensen," said Morris.

"Morris is right," Jensen said. "Besides, they're good at languages over there. I was in Norway on vacation two years ago. As they heard my accent, they switched right into English."

"So Norwegians who've lived in Norway all their lives speak better English than you speak Norwegian?" Patterson asked.

"Yep, you could put it that way," Jensen said with a smile.

"So how can we trust your translation then?" asked Patterson. Everybody looked at him in surprise. Patterson shrugged.

"Just a joke," he said, with a sheepish grin.

One hour and several discoveries later, Felicia Stone sat with the telephone in her hand and a swarm of butterflies in her stomach that were very restless, even for butterflies. Despite Jensen's assurances that Norwegians spoke excellent English, she was worried that they wouldn't understand her. A friendly woman at overseas information had found her the number of police headquarters in Trondheim. When she called and introduced herself in English, a pleasant woman there switched to her language, with a lilting accent that was nevertheless easy to understand.

Then she was patched through to Odd Singsaker.

22

Padua, 1518

Monkeys!" *The word sprayed* out of Master Alessandro's mouth as if he were spitting at them. "Monkeys!"

The boy and the beard-cutter were sitting on the bench at the back of the room where they had eaten breakfast, which consisted of dark bread and salt-cured ham. The master was pacing the floor in front of them. He had just come home from his morning walk. As usual his head was full of thoughts that he needed to air before he could calm down. Some days they were the most elevated ideas and insights, other days they were reproaches and protests. The latter were seldom directed at Galen of Pergamon, that great scholar of the human body. But today it was his turn to be criticized. The master had not even taken off his new ocher-yellow velvet cloak, which had flowered embroidery on the chest and ermine collar. The cloak was supposed to be worn only on his morning walks and when he stood at the lectern. Now it was flapping around him like a whirl of autumn leaves in the wind. They could do nothing but listen without comment. The topic of Galen and the interior of the human body always made the master's cheeks flush and the words spray from his mouth, but as a rule not in anger.

"Good Lord my Creator! Monkeys!"

The boy had never seen a monkey before. The kids on the street never tired of talking about the merchant who had brought three monkeys with him to the marketplace the summer before they arrived in Padua. The merchant had sewn hats for them, and the monkeys performed a trick in which they imitated crafts-men using various tools. He was banned from the marketplace after one of the monkeys hit a margrave on the head with a hammer. The margrave was saved only by the tall hat that he had purchased that very day. Oddly enough it was the same nobleman, a student from somewhere in North Germany, who bought the monkeys after the merchant was unable to perform with them any longer. It was because of what he had done with them that Master Alessandro was now getting all worked up.

Even though the boy never got to see the monkeys, he'd seen many of the drawings the other kids had made of them on the walls of neighborhood houses. They looked like people with long arms. But in one of the master's books from the Orient he had also seen a picture drawn by a more skilled artist. In it he could clearly see that the monkeys were animals with fur and big, stupid eyes. And that was exactly what the master was talking about as he circled the room, waving a quill pen, as if he were writing something in the air.

"Dumb animals, with no resemblance to human beings whatsoever. What can they teach us about the secrets of the human body?"

The secrets of the human body. That was something he was always going on about; the boy knew that he loved this phrase, perhaps because he knew more about these secrets than anyone else. In short, it was a matter of secrets to which he had been made privy.

What he actually was thinking about now, as he paced and his cheeks flushed red, was that he knew things about which Galen had never had the slightest idea.

Galen's renowned anatomical knowledge had been elevated to the required curriculum, not only at Galen's own academy—consecrated to the god Asclepius on the outskirts of the magnificent city of Pergamon long ago—but in all later studies of human anatomy. It was true at the medical school in Salerno, at the universities, and not least here in Padua, where Master Alessandro himself was a teacher.

Many times the boy had heard him lecture on the teachings of Galen. From the lectern the master called the end of the intestine the rectum, without winking, and made a point of mentioning that a man's rectum was not straight, but curved—all because this was what Galen had taught. But then these monkeys had shown up on Alessandro's table. The vengeful North German margrave had bought the monkeys and then kept them captive in his study for almost a year before giving them to the medical faculty at the university. There they ended up under the expert knives of the beard-cutter and Alessandro. No public dissection, but a long examination at night of the monkeys' anatomy.

The boy had not been allowed to attend that evening. He was disappointed, because it was his last chance to see the monkeys. But it was during this dissection that the master had a sudden epiphany. It was well-known that Galen had performed his dissections on animals. Yet on that night the master had realized that monkeys had a completely different anatomy from us. They could not be used as a model for understanding human beings. This was the insight that occurred to him. The boy saw the change in him; he saw that the master sometimes wanted to shout it from the lectern. "It's monkeys that have rectums, not humans." But he did not say it. He continued to develop his ideas in secret, sharing them only with a close circle, which included colleagues, students he trusted implicitly, and the beard-cutter. The boy also heard him speak of these ideas a few times. In the biggest medical schools in the Christian world, students were being taught that the human body was like that of an ape. At a number of universities it was considered sacrilege, yes, even pure heresy, to present any theories other than Galen's. His teachings about the anatomy of a human being were the only accepted ones. Anyone who attempted to obtain tangible proof of other ideas might find himself burned at the stake for heresy.

That is not how things were in Padua, which was under the wise protection of Venice. The laws of the mighty trading city stipulated, on the contrary, that every active physician was duty-bound to attend the autopsy of at least one executed prisoner annually. In Padua at least two anatomical presentations were given each year. Master Alessandro lectured at many of them, and at the last of these autopsies, which took place at the home of a nobleman, it was the beard-cutter, the master's new, trusted assistant, who had wielded the knives.

During these public dissections the master kept a good distance from the corpse. His role was to stand at the lectern and expound his ideas. The boy knew that it was precisely this situation that had created the deep schism in the master's mind. Because at the lectern it was Galen who was the expert, while at the corpse it was the eyes of the witness. The beard-cutter could freely see what Galen had never seen, while the master's eyes were locked solidly on the old physician's writings, like a captive held imprisoned by the text.

But for every public dissection, at least five unofficial ones were performed. The boy had personally witnessed some of them in Master Alessandro's loft, with body parts he had personally helped to procure. It was during these dissections that the master could allow himself to wield the scalpel. It was here he had begun to see with his own eyes, feel with his own fingers, smell with his own nose, discover how infinitely little we knew about ourselves.

His suspicion that there were serious errors in Galen's teachings had slowly become a certainty. So when he finally dissected the three rabid monkeys, he understood what the biggest mistake was. Compared to animals, human beings are superior not only by virtue of their merits or their spirits. Human organs are also superior. Certain aspects of the human body were beyond anything that could be learned from dissecting an ape.

Tomorrow it was going to happen—what the master wanted, but had not dared. He had invited only those closest to him, and for the first time he was going to wield the knives himself during a dissection with an audience. This was no officially sanctioned dissection. They would have to obtain the corpse themselves.

The anatomical theater was his own invention. He had long yearned for a stage like this. The solution had come to him gradually, conjuring up images, small sketches, in his mind. Eventually he was able to draw the whole thing on paper and take his drawings to Alfonso, the master builder.

He had had the theater built in the backyard of his house in Padua. It consisted of three rows of benches in a round amphitheater. The rows were built at a steep angle above one another, in order to make the line of sight as short as possible, even from the top row. The theater was built without a roof, so that daylight could enhance the view. In the middle was a rotary table, where the corpse would be placed. The whole structure was built out of wood. But as the master said, "A structure like this should be built out of stone. It should be erected on the best site in the city and should accommodate hundreds of viewers. An anatomical theater should not be hidden away in a backyard."

Alessandro took off his cloak and looked at the beard-cutter and the boy. Peace had returned to his countenance. His intelligent eyes were once again the way the boy remembered them.

"Alfonso finished his work last night," he said. "Now all we need is a corpse. We'll have it at sundown."

Located outside the city walls of Padua, a short distance along the road to Venice, was what the local populace called with dark ambivalence "the cemetery of the innocents." This was no ordinary cemetery but a piece of land surrounded by a stone wall. This was the final resting place for the poor souls who succumbed to the plague in the years when it so ravaged the land that the churchyards closer to town could not hold all the victims. Here were also buried those who had been executed and committed suicide, as well as others whose souls, for some reason, had been condemned to eternal perdition.

For anyone who needed a human corpse, this was the place to look. The graves here were shallow, the guards negligent, and the markers only sporadic. The boy had been out here before with the beard-cutter. Master Alessandro owed much of his knowledge to this place.

They were not always lucky enough to find a whole body. But the master's thirst for learning was great and could be satisfied by bones devoid of flesh, connected only by sinews, perhaps with a muscle or two still in place. The beard-cutter and the boy had rocked parts of skeletons loose from corpses in various stages of decay, and once they got hold of a shoulder blade, an arm, and a hand missing the fingers, as well as a foot. When the master saw this, they were sent back to secure the thorax. The next day they carted the skeleton piece by piece back to Alessandro via various detours to the city, so that the master at last had an almost intact skeleton.

The two of them sat on the wall that surrounded the graveyard of the innocents, as the sun slipped down behind them, each with a spade dangling alongside their legs. The beard-cutter was whistling a tune they had learned in Germany, about a ne'er-do-well who fell asleep out of indolence, only to awaken and find himself buried alive. The boy was listening to the sounds of the night.

Then they heard the cart come clattering up to the gate at one corner of the wall. They saw the hasps of the gate move. Both of them hopped down outside the wall and stood there. As the sun disappeared completely and darkness fell, they heard the people who were working inside. They were talking about the execution.

A serving girl had been convicted of murdering her own child, conceived out of wedlock. The rumors said that the son of her master, a rich local merchant, had gotten her pregnant. True or not, she had been hanged from the gallows in the market square that afternoon, and now two grave diggers stood chatting over her corpse as they dug a grave that matched the shallowness of their work ethic. It did not take them long, and the last part of their conversation revolved mostly around the wife of one of the grave diggers, who had apparently purchased an excellent rooster at the market. The question now was whether to employ it for cockfighting or stud service.

When the diggers finally ended their chatter and their gloomy work, the two outside the wall heard the gate close and the cart drive off into the dark of the night.

The wall had not been made to keep grave robbers out; it was barely taller than the beard-cutter. Its purpose was to ensure that people outside wouldn't have to see inside. The two climbed over the wall easily and found the spot where the two diggers had covered over the corpse. They knew they would not have to dig very deep to find what they were looking for, and after only a dozen spadefuls, they struck firm flesh.

The beard-cutter commanded the boy to kneel down and do the rest of the job with his bare hands. He began at the end where he thought the head would be. After pushing away the loose dirt, a chalk-white face appeared. The open eyes were filled with black earth. The skin was smooth and cold. The hair was black and merged with the surrounding darkness. The boy put a hand under the neck of the corpse and raised her head. He sat for a while holding the head in his hands, as if wanting to say something to the girl. He stared at the pale blue lips for a long time. Suddenly he was filled with a sorrow he had never before felt in the presence of a corpse.

"What are you doing? Keep digging." The beard-cutter's voice behind him was impatient.

The boy did as he was told. He removed the dirt from the chest, stomach, pelvis, and legs. Then they lifted her out of the grave.

To get the body over the wall, the beard-cutter stood on the outside and pulled on a rope fastened under her arms, while the boy pushed at her feet. They finally got her over the wall and into the cart. They tied her firmly in place. Before they whipped the donkey into motion, they placed a cloth over the corpse. As the beard-cutter covered her face, the boy noticed something. She looked like his mother up in Trondheim. He stopped, wondering if the beard-cutter had noticed this, too.

The next morning the boy took a bath in Master Alessandro's tub and rubbed his skin with the best olive oil. After he had dried himself off and put on clean clothes, he was allowed to enter Master Alessandro's studio. They sat down in two soft chairs with a table between them. The boy was still thinking of the merchant's monkeys, and remembered that Alessandro had several stories about monkeys.

"Could you tell me about the monkey in Alexandria?" He leaned forward to take an apple.

"Ah, the monkey in Alexandria," said the master, rubbing his hand over his clean-shaven chin. The beard-cutter had done a good job that morning, and the master had no more beard than the boy. The master took a dried fig and studied it closely before he put it in his mouth. The boy watched him with silent admiration. Everything the master did looked so profound, as if the slightest hand gesture expressed thoughts that the boy could not begin to understand. But one day I will, he thought. One day I'll be able to think such thoughts myself. He admired the master. Not that he didn't look up to the beard-cutter, but the beard-cutter frightened him. He had seen his temper flare many times in the German taverns. The beard-cutter excused himself by explaining that he had too much yellow bile in his body, and sometimes he would go on a cure consisting of white bread and herbs to combat these sudden attacks of rage. But even that didn't help. The weekend after such a diet he would have another outburst. But he had never laid a hand on the boy.

It was not only the beard-cutter's brutality the boy feared. He had also seen him with other boys his age. Sometimes they had taken two rooms in the inn, so that the boy had a room to himself, while the beard-cutter took another boy to his own room. The beard-cutter had never touched the boy; he was the beard-cutter's lucky charm. They both knew that. But what would happen after they found their fortune? Would he still be able to trust him? He didn't know.

He knew that he could trust Master Alessandro. But it was not the master's heart that he trusted, even though he believed the doctor had warm feelings for him. It was his mind. Someone who let his mind be master of the other organs in his body was a reliable person. He could trust Master Alessandro the way he could trust an argument he knew was valid.

"You like that story about the monkey in Alexandria, don't you?" The boy nodded.

"You're right to do so," said the master. "There's a strange sort of wisdom in that story. I met that monkey myself. The monkey in Alexandria. The monkey who could write all the letters of the Greek alphabet. I'd probably been staying a week or so in the faded grandeur of that city. The city that had once housed all the knowledge in the world. I had spoken with the city's doctors, who excelled in many fields and spoke excellent Greek, even though they were all Arabs and Jews. It was from one of them that I heard about a first-class craftsman and merchant who was called Kinshar the Scribe. He was originally from Baghdad but lived in Alexandria. This scribe was said to own books that had come from the time before the fire destroyed the famous ancient library. And you know me," said the master, in a way that made the boy feel proud. He did know him.

"I simply had to meet this scribe. I got a messenger to set up a meeting with him a few days later. Unfortunately, the books turned out to be a disappointment. They were all newer copies, none of them older than a couple of decades. But I did buy some fine copies of Archimedes that I didn't own, and which I thought might at least contain some of Archimedes' own words. The visit to the merchant was not time wasted, however. He showed me around his scriptorium, which was one of the finest I've ever seen in all my long journeys. A dozen men worked there, and they produced just as many books as my friend Manutius, the printer in the city."

The boy knew that "the city" Master Alessandro referred to was Venice.

"But the only reason why I will never forget my visit to Kinshar the Scribe was his foremost scribe, a monkey they called Alexander."

"A monkey?" the boy said with a laugh, as if he had not heard the story ten times before.

"Yes, precisely, a monkey," said Alessandro, popping another fig into his own laughing mouth. He went on, "This monkey was not just any old monkey. This monkey could write. The animal could hold a pen, and on large sheets of paper, he could write heavy, ugly letters one after the other in a row. He knew all the letters in the Greek alphabet, and he put them down on paper as if they were words and sentences. Yes, he had even learned to put spaces in between the words now and then. He didn't know punctuation, so there was some distance between periods and commas. As for Manutius's brilliant new invention, the semicolon, even the scribes down there had not yet heard of it. Nevertheless, that monkey could write. But because he was an animal, even a drunk dock worker from Genoa could think more clearly than he could, and he had no idea what he was writing. He simply put down one letter after another in a wild and random order. Still, he sat there every day writing, serving almost as a model for the other scribes. One day a miracle occurred. Or at least it was what Kinshar the Scribe convinced me must inevitably happen, for, as he said, if you set enough monkeys to writing a sequence of letters long enough, sooner or later one of them will write something that makes sense. If you have an infinite number of monkeys writing down an infinite number of letters, then at some point in the insanity you will end up with a reproduction of the works of Plato or Horace. A dizzying thought.

"What the monkey had written was only one sentence that made sense. But since then I've realized that it was a very good sentence. It has settled inside me. Actually, it has become something of a motto for life."

"What did the monkey write?" asked the boy excitedly, happy to be hearing these mysterious words again.

" 'The center of the universe is everywhere and its circumference nowhere,' " Master Alessandro recited in sonorous Greek. "Those were the monkey's words. The scribe let me see them with my own eyes. He had hung the sheet of paper on the wall above the writing desk so everyone could see it. I had already seen the monkey write, and there was no doubt that it was in the monkey's handwriting."

They both sat in silence for a while.

"That's my favorite story," said the boy at last. Whether or not it was true, he added to himself.

The boy did not want to play that afternoon, even though the other boys outside had made a ball from a pig's stomach and invited him to join their game. The winner would get a cup of raisins.

Instead he went off by himself to think. He wandered through the streets all the way to the market square, where rubbish still remained from yesterday's execution. What he thought was this: Why had his mother sent him off with the beard-cutter? A devil was living inside him, she had said. Was that true? And what did it mean? Was there a devil living inside the beard-cutter too? Could the two of them ever find their fortune?

The corpse they had stolen the day before had already been placed on the rotating table inside the anatomical theater. The beard-cutter and Master Alessandro had discussed the matter for a long time and decided that the body was fresh enough to lie on the same cloth overnight. The master had had bad experiences with older corpses that had begun to decay. Large amounts of sticky corpse exudation, probably a mixture of the body's four fluids, soured by the heat, had filled the room with a stench that made any lecture impossible.

The boy still believed that the sun glided across the sky, even though the master had taught him that it was otherwise.

"It is we who glide past the sun, and not the other way around," said Alessandro, and he always added: "One day soon I'm sure that somebody will dare to write that in a book. But don't tell it to a priest if you value your life."

Yet the boy could not imagine that people would ever come to view it that way, no matter how wise they became. Sometimes our wisdom is greater than ourselves, he thought.

After the sun glided across the sky that day, the boy felt more and more drawn to the theater. He knew that it was locked with one of Angelo the smith's unbreakable locks. But he also knew where the key was kept. It was in the fruit bowl in the master's workroom.

After six hours had passed, he could not stand it any longer. He just had to look at her. There was actually nothing odd about him coming home at that hour. It was the time when even busy academics preferred to eat dinner, so there was usually food on the table. But today the servants had not prepared a meal. They told him that Alessandro and the beard-cutter were eating at a tavern in town, along with those who were going to attend today's dissection. They would all go to the theater while the sun was still high enough in the sky to provide good light. The servants had left the boy some boiled eggs, along with smoked meat and a bowl of raw vegetables.

After eating he sneaked into the workroom and found the key in the expected hiding place. He took it with him to the backyard. None of the servants in the house paid any notice, because the boy often played down there. Sometimes he sat by the pond and gazed at the water lilies. He thought that the leaves floating on the water looked like hearts. And the carp that stuck their mouths out of the water tried to catch these hearts and tear them apart. Now he passed by the pond and walked around the new anatomical theater. The fresh lumber glistened yellow in the sun. He went over to the lock on the door. Nobody could see him from the house, because the door faced some olive trees and the red brick wall at the back of the yard. The key slipped in easily and turned.

After opening the door he paused for a moment. He stared at the damp clay ground. The stench of decay reached him all the way out here. Then he went inside and was impressed by the way the sunlight filled the whole room.

She lay on the table, illuminated by the sun, almost like a vision. He felt like he was looking at his mother. And as if enchanted, guided by powers that neither God nor the Devil controlled, he went over to the table. Her face was paler than paper. Like snow, he thought, and remembered the winters up north. White as the snow that covered the town, that dark and angular human world, every winter. That was how his mother's face looked. Cold as winter itself was her skin. He put his hand on her cheek. Let his fingers slip down over the dry, ice-cold skin, down her neck, between her breasts and over her stomach. Below the hair was black as night, like the spaces between the trees in a forest. He stopped and stood there breathing hard. He thought about the people who had come to his mother's bed before the beard-cutter came. Had they continued to come after he left, or was it for the sake of her son that she had welcomed them?

The shadow behind him seemed to slip into his thoughts, like mud into clear, cold water. He had not heard a sound, but suddenly he was aware of this shadow coming from all directions at once.

Then the beard-cutter's hand landed on his shoulder like a

hunting falcon. The boy snatched his hand away from the corpse and looked up. The beard-cutter was staring at him with an expression he had never used before. Not even when he looked at an enemy across the table in a tavern after many beers. His eyes were filled with a malevolence that the boy had never seen before, except in his dreams. It was the look of a devil.

The beard-cutter grabbed him by the scruff of the neck and squeezed hard. Holding on tight, he ushered the boy out of the theater. Outside, he let him go.

"This is not over," he said, and slammed the door behind him.

The boy dropped to the ground, not knowing how he should feel. He thought that the beard-cutter's ominous gaze had not surprised him as much as it should have.

After getting back onto his feet, he went and sat on the bench by the pond. Soon Master Alessandro came through the gate up by the house and walked past him. He was followed by a whole parade of students, doctors, and noblemen who wanted to watch. The master greeted the boy with a tight smile as they passed. The boy nodded, but did not smile back.

Soon everyone was inside the theater.

Alessandro's property was bountiful with his own vegetable garden, a chicken yard, and a small orchard that produced olives and peaches. The house at the end of the yard was whitewashed, and between the house and the carp pond was a shed where the servants stored their tools. It took a lot of tools to keep the house and garden in order. Among other things, a tall ladder was required.

After Alessandro and his excited entourage had vanished inside the anatomical theater, the boy went to the shed and got the ladder. The ladder was big and heavy, while the boy was small and light, and it was hard to drag it along the path all the way down to the theater. It was even harder to raise the ladder and lean it against the wall of the building. But whoever wants something badly enough will get what he wants, as the beard-cutter had told the boy many times. No matter how heavy the ladder was, it had to go up. The beard-cutter's expression may have scared him, but not enough to stop him from climbing up the ladder.

When he reached the top rung and stood on tiptoe, he was just high enough to be able to peer over the edge of the wall. He had a clear view inside.

The presentation was already under way. The boy saw at once that it was proceeding differently from other presentations he had witnessed. This time it was the doctor who wielded the knives. Alessandro himself stood leaning over the corpse and was just about to cut open the abdomen. Every successful dissection began with an incision in the belly. The master called this point just be-low the navel "the center of the skin."

The boy gazed at the beard-cutter standing beside the master. He still wore a dark expression, but the boy doubted that he was thinking about what had just occurred between them. The boy had lived with him for two years now, and he knew him well. He knew what the problem was. Pride. What bothered the beard-cutter was that he had had to lend his knives to someone else. The boy saw them lying there, sharp and glistening, placed neatly and systematically on a little table covered in a white cloth, just behind the corpse. The beard-cutter's only task today was to hand the master the knives when he asked for them. He had been reduced from a surgeon to an assistant. He got to follow the whole autopsy at close range, but the boy understood that for the beard-cutter, a dissection was not a visual experience. For him it was the feeling of cutting, the incisions, the cracking of bones. It was a tactile jour-ney of discovery. A performance with the knives. It was the cutting into the body that actually meant something, not what was found inside. Wounded pride and envy. That was what the boy saw in the beard-cutter's eyes as he stood obediently behind his teacher.

The dissection lasted five hours, until darkness fell. The boy had climbed down when they started in on the head and the eyes. He did not want to watch that face being destroyed. He fell asleep, dreaming of a stench that filled his nostrils.

When the door to his room was torn open that evening, it took a few moments before he grasped the reality that had descended upon him. The beard-cutter used this confusion to seize the upper hand. He bounded forward and clamped his hand over the boy's mouth.

"What were you doing with the corpse, you little cur?" he whispered.

He could not reply. The beard-cutter was pressing his hand too tightly over his mouth.

"You've ruined everything. The corpse is for the knives. It is always just for the knives. You can't touch it the way you did. What's gotten into you? Your mother could see there's a devil living inside you. I thought it was a guardian angel, but it turns out that your mother was right."

The beard-cutter wrapped his free hand around the boy's throat. The boy's eyes grew wide, and in the dim moonlight coming through the window, he could clearly see a tear running down the beard-cutter's cheek as his hand began to squeeze. The dizziness came first. The night filled with light before it turned blacker than ever before.

"Fortune has abandoned me again," said the beard-cutter, somewhere in the dark.

The boy felt a rocking and a shaking that came and went. I am on the road to hell, he thought. Then his eyelids began to flutter. He blinked uncontrollably. When he finally stopped blinking, he lay still and was able to see. He was lying in a cart. In front of him sat the beard-cutter, holding the reins to the donkey. So we are going to hell together, he thought. But then he began to look around the dark landscape. They were riding along a cart path he recognized. This was not the road to perdition. Not exactly.

His only hope was to lie completely still and breathe as slowly and as quietly as he could. He lay like that until the cart rounded the wall at the graveyard of the innocents and swung around to the back. He remained lying there quietly while the beard-cutter dug a grave for him outside the wall. When it was deep enough, he came over to the cart and grabbed the boy by the hair. The boy clenched his teeth so he would not scream as the strong man yanked him by the hair from the cart, as if he were unloading a slaughtered animal. Then the beard-cutter's boots rolled him along the ground, until he fell into the grave. There he lay on his back with an arm over his face. The beard-cutter was in a hurry, and began at once to shovel dirt over him. The boy counted himself lucky that it was dark, so that he could put his hand over his mouth and make a little pocket of air. Soon everything went black, and there was a terrible weight on his chest. The boy remained lying there until he heard the last shovelful of dirt land on top of him. He, too, had been given a shallow grave. He could hear the beard-cutter get into the cart and whip the donkey into motion.

When everything was quiet, the boy moved the hand covering his mouth and began to relieve some of the weight pressing down on him. He started to dig. As he did so the dirt fell in and covered his whole face. Sudden panic struck him. He was breathing in a little dirt every time he inhaled, and the mound over him was weighing more and more heavily on his chest, as if trying to squeeze the life out of him.

But he did not stop moving his hands. Panic made him dig

faster and with greater frenzy. Luckily the dirt was loose and not very deep.

First he got one hand into the air, then the other, so he could dig a tunnel as he pressed his face toward the starry sky above. As fresh air came in, he could not help coughing. Bits of dirt and gravel sprayed out of his mouth, and his lungs filled greedily with fresh air with each breath he took. The prickling and numbness vanished from his limbs, and the dizziness was gone. For the first time since he had climbed down from the ladder to go to bed, he felt fully awake.

Was it all just a dream he had awakened from? Was it not dirt but Master Alessandro's heavy wool blankets lying on top of him? He felt with his hands. No, it was dirt. This had really happened. And so unexpectedly, the way everything happened with the beard-cutter. He had fallen into disgrace, and without warning the beard-cutter had tried to kill him. The boy lay there wondering what he had done with the corpse earlier in the day that had aroused such violent wrath. He could not understand it. He had only touched the body, nothing more. He had imagined that it was his own mother, and that he might bring her back to life. If the beard-cutter had known that he missed his mother so much, maybe he would not have flown into such a rage. Or would he? The yellow bile must be to blame, the boy thought. It could not be anything else.

It had not rained much that fall, which meant the earth was dry and loose. That was what had saved him from a gruesome death. He kept digging with his hands. It took a long time to get his whole torso free, but as soon as that was done, it took hardly any time to get his legs loose. The boy who had been buried alive arose from the grave. He thought of the song the beard-cutter had been whistling the last time they were here. Was it a premonition that neither of them had registered or had the beard-cutter been planning to kill him all along?

The boy stood there for a while looking down at the grave. Then he turned and walked toward the road. When he reached it, he continued in the direction leading away from Padua. He walked all night. At a crossroads he chose not to take the road to Venice but instead headed into the countryside. Not until daybreak did he lie down in a ditch to sleep. There he slept until late in the day, when a man in a gray cape woke him. The boy had seen mendicant monks like this along the road before, and knew what sort of men they were.

"You look like you're a long way from home," said the grayfriar, peering at the boy with eyes that showed concern but were merry at the same time.

PART III

Scalpel

The center of the universe is everywhere and its circumference nowhere.

—Giordano Bruno, 1584

23

Trondheim, September 2010

O*dd Singsaker had just* come back to his office after meeting with Siri Holm when Felicia Stone phoned him.

On his way upstairs he hadn't spoken to anyone, only nodded and murmured hello when necessary. But his mind was in turmoil. He had just broken an unwritten but unalterable rule for a detective: Never get personally involved with a person of interest, no matter how innocent you think she is. He didn't know how many times he had cursed himself on the way back. But he was more surprised than angry. The whole thing had happened so fast, and without warning. Siri Holm had obviously been right. Normally he had enough self-control to avoid what could be career suicide, especially of the magnitude involved here. But he had simply let go and allowed himself to be seduced. Odd Singsaker, the stoic detective and faithful husband for several decades, who until now hadn't slept with any woman other than his own wife and a girlfriend he once had in his youth. Yet suddenly he'd let his dick take over.

How could he have let that happen? Worst of all was that it had felt so good. Siri had taken control of him in such a thoughtful and tender way, as if she'd always known what he liked, better than his wife ever did. At the same time there had been something oddly impersonal about the whole thing. He had no idea why she had seduced him so wildly on the red sofa. There was nothing to indicate that she even liked him better than any other man. Most of all it felt as though she'd done it as a kind of service. As if she'd seen that he needed a fuck and viewed it as her duty to be helpful. A sort of adult girl scout's good deed. He had to laugh. There was something liberating in that. Siri Holm was a remarkable woman in many ways, and he sensed that the next time they met she would act as if nothing had happened. As a witness she would most likely be just as objective. And she might turn out to be a very important witness. But she was no suspect. Or was she? Was he reasoning with the wrong organ now?

Right before the phone rang he thought about how they'd parted. On the way out of the apartment, as she lay on the sofa with only a black belt around her waist, he'd asked her what sort of detective she thought he was, the systematic or the unsystematic type?

"Detectives like that are only found in books," she'd said with a laugh. "You're a human being, Odd Singsaker. So you can be whoever you want to be. By the way, I don't think you'd be very good as the hero of a crime novel. You're too nice. You make compromises. I doubt that you have conflicts with your superiors very often, and if you drink, you don't drink enough."

"A shot of aquavit, Rød Aalborg, every morning," he told her.

"Ah, at least you have a favorite drink. And you make obvious mistakes, like going to bed with one of the witnesses. Maybe there's hope for you after all."

He had laughed on the way out the door. A laugh that despite self-recrimination and regret had kept on resonating until now.

"Chief Inspector Odd Singsaker," he answered the phone, wondering if it was cheerfulness he heard in his voice.

"My name is Felicia Stone, and I'm calling from Richmond, Virginia," said a woman in English on the other end. She spoke with an accent, American and from the South, both rural and sophisticated at the same time. Her voice was deep, and he had the mistaken impression that she might be a jazz singer. But she quickly introduced herself as a homicide detective. She didn't beat around the bush as she continued, "I think the two of us are investigating the same case."

"Excuse me, but you will have to explain that some more," he said in English that was not as fluent as he'd like.

And so she explained. She told him about the corpse they had found in a museum dedicated to Edgar Allan Poe, and about a book that had been bound with five-hundred-year-old human skin. And even though Singsaker's heart was almost pumping out of his chest, he replied calmly, "What makes you certain that these two cases are connected?"

"We found a photo of your murder victim on the PC belonging to our murder victim," said Felicia Stone in the straightforward way that he'd already begun to appreciate. "I don't know what that tells you."

"It tells me two things," he said. "First, that the two cases are connected, as you say. We are most probably looking at one and the same murderer. Second, now that we can demonstrate that our perpetrator has murdered before, we can abandon the notion that we are dealing with a serial killer."

He'd expected a bit of puzzlement at the other end of the line. Instead, she said, "You seem to know a good deal about serial killers. I was actually thinking the same thing. A serial killer usually kills victims chosen at random. They can be selected based on various criteria; the killer may have studied them for a while and planned the murders for a long time. But only rarely does a serial killer know any of his victims well. I've almost never heard of victims who knew each other across such long distances. There must be some connection that we're not seeing. A motive that goes beyond the act of murder."

"And what do you think this connection might be?"

"I don't know, but it has something to do with books, I think."

"Books. I've never heard of anyone who killed because of books," said Singsaker.

"True enough. The motive is probably something else. But I think that the connection between Efrahim Bond and Gunn Brita Dahle is this Byron book I mentioned. And I also think that the killer must have something to do with that book."

"So perhaps we are dealing with a serial killer after all. One who is obsessed with an old book bound with human skin, and who kills random people who have anything to do with it. But the question here is what connection Gunn Brita Dahle had to this Byron book." Singsaker felt that they were talking in circles.

"Have you ever heard of a man named Broder Lysholm Knudtzon?" Felicia Stone asked.

He had to ask her to repeat the name several times before he understood what she was saying in her thick accent.

"Ah, Lysholm Knudtzon," he finally realized. "Of course I've heard of him. There's a room called the Knudtzon Hall at the Gunnerus Library, where Gunn Brita Dahle worked and was found murdered."

"Well, there's our connection. The Byron book originally came from this Knudtzon's book collection."

"I think you are on to something, but it's still not much to go on." Singsaker sat there thinking. So far he'd been playing along just to hear what the Richmond police had discovered. Now it was time for him to give something back. "Have you come across other Norwegians in your investigation?" he asked.

"Like who?"

"A Jon Vatten, perhaps?"

"John Watson? Isn't he from Sherlock Holmes?"

He chuckled.

"No, Jon Vatten," he said with a distinct Trondheim accent. "But actually his work colleagues do call him Doctor Vatten."

"No, he hasn't shown up in our case."

"That's too bad. Vatten is someone we are looking at here. Very closely, actually. He was at the scene at the time of the murder, he gave unclear and doubtful information when interviewed, and he was previously a suspect in a missing persons case. We are only waiting for the analysis of the biological traces."

"Biological traces?"

"Semen."

"Why didn't you mention this before? That's an important deviation from our homicide. In ours there was extreme violence but no sign of sexual activity."

"And what do you think that means?"

"I have no idea. That Gunn Brita Dahle was a woman, and that our murderer prefers women to old, dried-up men, perhaps," said Felicia Stone, but she didn't laugh.

"Anyway, the most important thing is Vatten," he said a bit impatiently. "I suggest that you put all your effort over there into finding out if he has visited the USA recently. Then we will do some investigations here."

"No problem. We can check on such things with a few keystrokes."

"Stroke away," he said, getting ready to end the conversation.

"As a matter of fact," she said, "I'll have to get someone else to do the computer work. I'm getting on a plane in three hours. And

I've got to make it through rush-hour traffic to pick up my suitcase first."

"Are you about to leave?" he said with trepidation, as he looked at the clock. It was afternoon in Virginia. But in Trondheim it was almost eleven at night. This had been the longest day of his life.

"I'm coming to Norway," she replied. "This case is too big for us to discuss everything we need to know over the phone. We need to compare notes in more detail."

"That may be true. But I don't know how such things are done. Shouldn't your boss speak with my boss first?"

"While we've been talking, those exalted gentlemen, our bosses, have been e-mailing each other. Everything is already arranged. The proper papers have been signed and faxed over. I'm looking at the printouts now."

"My boss is a woman, not a gentleman," he said.

"Really? Norway is a land after my own heart," she chuckled, and for the first time in the course of their conversation she sounded really American.

"Don't jump to hasty conclusions," he said.

Felicia Stone concluded the call with a snort of laughter that suited her.

When Singsaker put down the phone, his boss was standing in the doorway.

"You're going to pick her up at the airport tomorrow," said Brattberg.

"What should I do until then?" he asked.

"We'll proceed as before. Honestly, it looks like you could use some sleep. The only thing I ask is that you drop by and see Jens Dahle on your way home. We have to find out if his wife has been in Virginia recently."

"Fine," he said, rubbing his eyes. "You won't hear from me unless something interesting turns up. I think I need more than a normal night's sleep. A twelve-hour coma should do it."

Both of them laughed, though it sounded a bit strained.

He had just fallen asleep when the phone woke him. He sat up with a jolt. He noticed that he'd forgotten to turn off the light, and the magazine *Missing* had slipped to the floor next to the bed, open to an article about a detective somewhere in eastern Norway. It was an old issue.

He picked up his cell, pressed the button with the green stripe, and cleared his throat a couple of times before answering. It was Gro Brattberg. He looked at the clock. Quarter past midnight. Only a little over an hour since he spoke with her last.

"I hope I reached you before you sank into your coma," she said.

"I was just about there," he said.

"I'm calling to tell you that Knutsen has arranged a search warrant for Vatten's place. We're going over there tomorrow morning at eight. You can meet us there."

"Great," he said, annoyed that she hadn't bothered to tell him this an hour ago.

"I assume Jens Dahle had nothing of interest to tell you, since I didn't hear from you," she went on with poorly concealed zeal.

He swore to himself. Jens Dahle *had* told him something interesting. He'd debated whether to call Brattberg before he went to bed, but then made the mistake of lying down before he dialed her number.

"Actually, I was just about to call you," he lied. "Jens Dahle was awake and told me that his wife attended a library conference last spring, probably something about old manuscripts. And guess where the conference was held."

"Not in Richmond, Virginia, by any chance?"

"That's right. At the university in Richmond, in the Boatwright Memorial Library, to be precise."

"So we have even more to talk about with our American friend tomorrow."

"It seems so. But now you'll have to excuse me. I've got an appointment somewhere in dreamland."

"I didn't think people dreamed when they were in a coma," Brattberg said with a laugh.

"Don't I wish," he said, and he wasn't laughing.

24

Odd Singsaker hadn't been alone in dreamland. Siri Holm was there, too. She was naked, and she had talked to him in a deep Southern accent. It had sounded like a long lecture about Edgar Allan Poe. Yet it wasn't what she said but what she did with him as she talked that he remembered afterward. For the first time in ages his dreams had been sweet, and he had woken up feeling almost refreshed. He could only think that he'd be paying for it in some way during the course of the day.

In Trondheim, September is without question an autumn month. But on rare occasions a day would come along that people living south of the Dovre Mountains would call summerlike, no matter what the date. After a long period of rain showers and overcast weather, it now looked like they were going to get another one of those days. Even before eight in the morning the thermometer in the kitchen window read 64°F. He found a dry crust of bread and a little orange marmalade and ate breakfast. The humidity was unusually high, and as he was eating he could feel the sweat forming on his temples. He was wearing a long-sleeved woolen shirt, and realized that was a mistake. He went to change as he chewed the last bite of his breakfast.

Singsaker hated sweating. That had been the first symptom of everything that had followed; he began sweating on cold nights last autumn. Then came the headaches, the bad moods, and the feeling that the world wasn't real. Before he finally collapsed the day after Christmas, he'd already started to hallucinate. No pink elephants or castles in the sky. Just small things, like hearing Anniken's voice when she wasn't there, or the feeling of having his wallet in his hand when he'd actually left it at home. He remembered one time, when he pulled out his Visa card to pay for something. He stood swiping it through the device again and again before the cashier told him that he didn't have a card in his hand. He didn't think he was afraid of death anymore. If you've cheated it once, it's not as scary. What he couldn't face was the thought of everything else happening all over again. The growing tension. The breakdown. The feeling of losing his grip. The intolerable, slow drama of cancer.

He put on a thin, light-blue, silk shirt. It was a gift from some friends who'd been in Thailand many years ago. He didn't wear it often but more often than he saw those friends. It was great on hot days, he told himself, and it was the truth, that he was sweating because it was warm, that he was healthy. The tumor in his brain had become an empty wound. Before the tumor, he could remember things that hadn't happened, but now he forgot things that really had. Hallucinations had turned into loss of memory—the supernova into a black hole.

On the short walk across the street to Vatten's house, he tried to organize the events of the day before, but couldn't do it chronologically. The order was fuzzy. Had he spoken with Jens Dahle before or after he visited Siri Holm? And when had the interview with Vatten taken place? He paused on the sidewalk outside the house and thought about something she had said yesterday, or was that from the dream he'd had last night? There were books in which the killer was a detective with amnesia who was investigating himself.

This is no mystery novel, he told himself, almost wishing that it were. He didn't need to check his alibi. Not yet.

Two police cars were parked outside Vatten's house. Singsaker went in through the courtyard gate and noticed Vatten's Cervelo bicycle leaning against a fence. The old Volvo was parked in the driveway, as always.

Inside, the house bustled with activity. Members of the white-clad team were scuttling about everywhere. The other officers, who could wear whatever they liked but oddly enough often chose similar attire, were in the minority. Actually, he saw only the lower part of the denim pant legs of a detective at the top of the stairs leading to the second floor. Mona Gran was standing right inside the door, smiling.

He looked at her. Only now did he notice that she was really very good-looking. Dark blond hair and blue eyes. A nose that was just big enough to attract attention but not so large that it ruined the overall impression.

"What have we found?" he asked.

"You should probably ask the evidence techs. Anyway, we didn't find what we were looking for."

"You mean he'd already left for work?"

"No, not according to our colleagues who checked with the Gunnerus Library."

He stood there staring at her, thoughts churning through his slightly mangled brain.

"So where is he then?"

"I wish we knew."

"Damn," he said. He might not remember everything he should

about the Vatten case, but he was sure of one thing: Jon Vatten was not the type to run. "Did he take off?" he asked, almost to himself.

In the meantime, the detective in jeans had come downstairs. Thorvald Jensen shrugged in resignation. Behind him came Gro Brattberg.

"This bird has flown," said Jensen. "But look what we found."

He held out a notebook and turned to a specific page. On it was sketched a picture of a little brick house that looked like an English country cottage. But larger buildings could be made out behind it, which indicated that it most likely was located in a city.

"What's this?" Singsaker asked.

"Look at the sign next to the house," said Jensen.

Singsaker studied the sign on the sidewalk: The Museum of Edgar Allan Poe.

"What sort of book is this?" he asked.

"It's a notebook," said Jensen dryly. "Looks as though Vatten used it as a sort of diary. He has a whole stack of them on the kitchen table. He wrote a bunch of strange stuff in this one. Little sketches and thoughts, some philosophical observations, some factual stuff, including things about Edgar Allan Poe. Did you know that he married his cousin, Virginia, when she was only thirteen years old? If you did anything like that today, it'd be a case for the police. But most of the things in this notebook are pure nonsense. And then he glued in this picture. Based on what he wrote, it seems that he visited the museum some time this summer."

"Oh, shit. But nothing really happened there this summer, did it? We're more interested in finding out whether he was there about a week ago."

"True enough. Did we actually check out his alibi for the time of the murder in Richmond?"

"No, that didn't come up until we talked to the States last night," said Singsaker. They stood looking at each other, thinking.

"You know what bothers me the most?" said Jensen after a moment. "That fucker took off, and we thought that was the last thing he'd do. Aren't we supposed to be the best judges of people?"

"Vatten isn't the world's easiest person to get a handle on," said Singsaker.

The thing was, Jon Vatten—the somewhat modest, diffident Vatten, the man who never went anywhere and who rode his bike to work at the same time every day—didn't seem like an insane murderer who would flay his victims and steal their heads. But if he really was the perpetrator—and the investigation was pointing more and more in that direction—it also meant that nobody had the slightest idea who the real Vatten was. Nobody had managed to see behind the mask that hid the insanity.

"Have we put out an APB?" asked Singsaker.

"All over the country," said Brattberg.

He stared at her. She looked worn out. Dead tired. He felt like asking her what time she'd gone to bed last night, but he wasn't used to expressing concern for his boss.

"What about the press conference?" he asked.

"Without a suspect in custody there really is no point," said Brattberg dully. "We'll make a simple announcement. 'No developments in the case.' That'll have to do."

"So the fact that a suspected murderer is running from the police isn't something the public needs to know?"

"That's correct, Singsaker. What can the public do with information like that except panic?" she snapped.

He shrugged and asked, "So, what now?"

"We continue investigating at the Gunnerus Library. Everyone has to be questioned again. Focus on Vatten, and find out whether anyone has any idea where he might be hiding. Does he have a cabin? Does he ever take trips outside the country, and if so, where? Things like that."

It struck Singsaker that she had left out one possibility.

"We also shouldn't forget that Vatten tried to commit suicide the last time we had him under investigation," he said.

"We haven't forgotten any of that," Brattberg said sharply. "No matter what, the main thing is that we have to find him."

Odd Singsaker got into one of the police cars and immediately drove to the Gunnerus Library. Before he got there, Per Ottar Horne-mann called him. His tone was sharp, like that of a director under a lot of stress.

"It's gone," he said.

"What's gone?" said Singsaker, as he held the cell phone to his ear while maneuvering through the heavy traffic. He stopped at a red light and was finally able to concentrate on what Hornemann was saying. A woman in the car next to him gave him a dirty look for talking on his cell while driving. It didn't look good to be break-ing the law while sitting in a police car, but he had no time to waste. So he just shrugged apologetically.

"The *Johannes Book*," Hornemann said. "The *Johannes Book* is gone. It disappeared sometime after Gunn Brita was picked up by the morgue and after we locked the book vault yesterday after-noon. I locked it myself, so I know that the *Johannes Book* was still there."

"How could that have happened? Are there any signs of a break-in at the vault?"

"No. Whoever was in here must have had both codes. And I'm the only one who's supposed to have them both. What's even stranger is that we changed the code on Monday morning, when Siri Holm took over one of the codes."

"If I understand correctly, only you, Siri Holm, and Jon Vatten have the codes to the book vault. Nobody else?"

"That's right. Only I have both of them."

"And Vatten hasn't shown up for work today, as far as I know. What about Siri Holm? Is she at work?"

"No, and that's what worries me. She isn't here either. She and Vatten are the only ones who didn't come to the meeting we set up for eight o'clock this morning. We were supposed to discuss a strategy for the difficult situation we find ourselves in."

The light changed to green, and Singsaker started off.

"Just stay where you are," he said. "I'll be there in ten minutes." He stomped on the gas, noting that the fact that Siri Holm hadn't shown up for work made him feel more distressed than was appropriate.

Hornemann was pale and looked like Singsaker felt. As if he should have retired long ago. He was sitting in his ascetic office gazing at Singsaker. Singsaker had sat down, wondering what it was about book people. Hornemann seemed more distraught today, after losing his valuable book, than he had the day before, when one of his employees was found murdered. But perhaps the sum of all these events had begun to take its toll on him. Singsaker took out the Moleskine notebook from his back pocket. He still hadn't written anything in it, and he probably wasn't going to do so now, but he'd noticed that a notebook had a calming effect on some interviewees. He decided to get straight to the point.

"When did you discover that the *Johannes Book* was missing, before or after this morning meeting?" he asked.

Hornemann's eyes became more focused as he began to talk.

"It was afterward. I went there at about a quarter to nine, straight from the meeting. Fifteen minutes later I called you."

"OK," he said, paging a little farther in the notebook's blank pages. "But what was it that made you go into the book vault at all?

Didn't my colleagues tell you that the area is off-limits for the time being?"

"Yes, but I'm the director here. I feel a certain responsibility. I discovered that the surveillance cameras hadn't been turned on, and that they'd been off since you were here together with Vatten yesterday. I just wanted to check that everything was in order."

"That nobody had taken anything?"

"Precisely."

"Did you think that seemed like a logical possibility? Given who had access? What I'm asking you is, Did you have any reason to suspect that somebody had been inside the vault?"

"No, not from a rational standpoint; it was more of a hunch. I've always felt a great responsibility for our book collection. The *Johannes Book* is a national treasure. It's only here because the farmer who donated it stipulated that it had to be kept here, and not at the National Library in Oslo. So when something happens, like yesterday, I'm extra vigilant."

"Yes, of course, that's only natural," said Singsaker, studying the head of the library. There was nothing to indicate that he was holding anything back. But it was difficult to determine that with certainty.

"Why did you call me first?" he wanted to know.

"You're the only one who gave me a card."

Singsaker tried to remember when he'd done that.

"This *Johannes Book*. Is it ever removed from the vault for legitimate reasons?" he asked.

"We've loaned it out a few times this year. Our conservator and bookbinder, Silvia Freud—she's German—has done a little work with it, but mainly she has been working on a copy of the book."

"A copy? Why is that?" He pretended to take notes.

"It's going to be used in an exhibition about the Norwegian Middle Ages that we're planning for the Science Museum in the fall. But the security at such an exhibition isn't good enough to warrant displaying the original source material. You should see the copies that Silvia makes. She's a master. I can't even tell the difference from the original. For the *Johannes Book* she used calfskin that we've had in storage ever since the days of Broder Lysholm Knudtzon. Besides all the books, he left a good deal of whole calfskins and remnants. Some of these remnants are of the same quality as the rare parchment in the *Johannes Book*. Naturally we discussed to what extent the skins themselves needed to be preserved but agreed that we could use some of the remnants for such purposes. Of course, we won't use the whole calfskin."

Hornemann had livened up now, as if talking about books was enough to make him forget the situation.

"Where can I meet this Silvia Jung?" asked Singsaker.

"Freud," Hornemann corrected him. "She has an office in the basement. I can take you there."

On the way downstairs Singsaker asked the head of the library whether he had tried to call Siri Holm. He said that he hadn't. It was normal for people who called in sick to do so later in the morning.

"We generally work quite independently here," he said.

Hornemann's reply didn't reassure him, so Singsaker asked for Siri Holm's number. He got it, put it in his pocket, and promised to call her after he spoke with Silvia Freud. Then he called Brattberg and informed her about the missing book.

He said good-bye to Hornemann outside the conservator's office. Silvia Freud's door was big and white and had no nameplate. He never would have found it by himself. He knocked on the door and was invited in by a voice with a German accent. The book conservator was a sun-tanned woman younger than forty. She demolished all his preconceived notions about book conservators by not even wearing glasses. She was dressed in tight designer jeans and a colorful, form-fitting top. Silvia Freud was sitting at a slanted work-table in the middle of a large, windowless basement office, with a work lamp above it that would make any dentist jealous. A faint murmur could be heard from the ventilation pipes below the ceiling.

They shook hands, and she told him how upset she was about what had happened in the library the day before. It struck him that she didn't look as upset as she claimed. When he told her about the *Johannes Book,* on the other hand, she turned deathly pale. She sat motionless for a minute or two. But she didn't look at him. Her gaze flitted restlessly, as if not sure where to settle.

"What do you mean by 'gone'?" she said at last, and he could almost hear a quaver in her voice.

"It's no longer in the vault," he said.

"You mean it's been stolen?" she asked, and her expression changed. Her voice also became more steady, but he had a feeling that she was straining to control herself.

"I doubt that it left on its own accord," he said.

"But that's just terrible! A treasure like that. Do you think that the murderer took it?"

"I don't know. But it would be helpful if you could answer a few questions."

"Naturally," she said. Now she was just as composed as when he'd arrived.

"When was the last time the book was out of the vault?"

"That was about two weeks ago."

"Was that when you were finishing the copy for the exhibition?"

"Yes, did Hornemann tell you about that?"

"That's right. Where is this copy kept?"

"I have it here." She pointed to a tall, white cabinet against the wall. It had a lock on it.

"Could I see it?"

"Of course," said Silvia Freud. Had some of the quavering returned to her voice, or was he just imagining it? She opened the cabinet quickly, removed a book, and closed it so fast that he couldn't see anything clearly. But he got the impression that there were two rather similar-looking books inside.

She handed him the book.

"May I look through it?" he asked.

"Do what you like, it's only a copy. But keep in mind that I put a lot of work into it."

He paged rapidly through the book. He had no idea what the original *Johannes Book* looked like, but he had no doubt that Silvia Freud was an expert in her profession. The book looked ancient. When he reached the final pages, he noticed that she had done such a thorough job that she even included remnants of the pages that had been torn out, just like in the original. The pages that Siri Holm had told him about.

"What can you tell me about the pages that were removed?" he asked.

Silvia Freud smiled.

"In the copy, of course, they were not really torn out. I just replicated what the remnants of those pages looked like. There are so many rumors about the *Johannes Book*. Most of them come from the family at the farm where it was discovered. The family used to tell stories to each other. One of the stories says that the last pages in the book were torn out by a previous owner because they revealed why there was a curse on the book. A more credible rumor, one circulating here at the library, says that the book once belonged to Broder Lysholm Knudtzon, and that he tore out the pages at the end in order to bind another book. Apparently the text on those pages made no sense. Those pages were said to have been written on and erased several times, and what remained was almost illegible. Knudtzon probably thought it was a good idea to reuse them, but he was also said to have believed in the book's curse, and as he got older, this belief grew stronger. I don't know if something in particular happened, but apparently he was the one who went to this farm in Fosen and returned the book so that it could find its proper resting place. But he forgot to give back the book that he had bound with the last pages of the *Johannes Book*. Some people think that book was among the five or six books he later sold to a hatter who emigrated to America. But we don't know anything for certain. Not even if Knudtzon was really the one who owned the *Johannes Book*."

"Isn't it incredible that such a famous book could have so many gaps in its provenance?" Singsaker asked.

"Yes, it is. We know very little for certain about the *Johannes Book*."

He thanked her for her time and left, closing the door behind him. On his way toward the stairs he remembered something that he should have asked, went back, and opened the door without knocking. The conservator, holding a cell phone in her hand when he came back in, gave a start. He apologized.

"I just have to ask you, How well do you know Jon Vatten?"

Her face relaxed a bit.

"I don't know him well. I usually only talk to him when I need books from the vault."

"And he never talks to you about his life outside work?"

"I don't think he has any life outside work."

"Do you know if he's been here every day for the past three weeks?"

"I'm quite sure that he has, though I don't see him every day, since I'm down here in the basement. You'd have to ask Hornemann."

Singsaker thanked her, realizing that he should have done that already. Damn that hole in his brain! Then he left. But he didn't go up to the second floor. Instead he took up a position under the stairway by the wall, where he couldn't be seen from the corridor. It wasn't even five minutes before his suspicion was confirmed. Silvia Freud came hurrying along the corridor and headed up the stairs above him.

He followed and caught a glimpse of her as she vanished out the back door to the parking lot by the Suhm building. He watched from inside until she got into a little green Nissan Micra. As she backed out of the lot, he ran through the building to his police car, which was parked on the other side of the library. He jumped in and just managed to turn the corner at the Erling Skakkes gate in time to catch sight of the little green car as it signaled a left turn near the theater. The squad car wasn't the best vehicle to tail someone in, and there was at least one traffic light between him and Silvia Freud. She turned down Prinsens gate and disappeared. He'd need a lot of luck to catch up with her again.

When he reached the intersection, he had to stop for a red light. He sat there looking down the street in the direction the Nissan had gone but saw no trace of the green car. He cursed to himself. There was no point in calling for backup. All he had was a vague feeling that something was fishy here. It was a big leap from there to claiming that she had something to do with the murder, and he was well aware that tailing the library's conservator just because she behaved a bit strangely was a detour that Brattberg wouldn't appreciate. He'd have to go solo.

Without much hope of making progress, Singsaker turned into traffic and followed everyone else down toward Kongens gate. A good detective always needs a bit of luck, and for a mediocre one like me, it's an absolute necessity, he thought. When he reached the next intersection, he stopped again and looked around. He spied the car parked outside the Prinsen Hotel. He parked on the other side of Kongens gate and walked across the street.

The Prinsen was one of the city's better three-star hotels and a popular choice both for business travelers and tourists with urbane taste. One time he'd picked up Lars from a school dance there— his son had been half drunk, with his mouth full of peppermint gum—but otherwise Singsaker only went to the basement bar that had an entrance in the back. The Kjeglekroa bar was said to be the oldest watering hole in Trondheim, but its status as a local dive was always being jeopardized by the well-dressed hotel guests who frequented the place. Sometimes he and Thorvald would hang out there on evenings when they weren't working, but now, at ten o'clock in the morning, Kjeglekroa was closed. He decided to try the Egon restaurant instead.

The restaurant was only half full, with latecomers from the hotel who were busy eating breakfast. The waiters went from table to table cleaning up, taking their time. At a window table farthest from the door, Silvia Freud sat with her back turned, carrying on a heated conversation with an elderly gentleman. He was dressed like an academic, in a turtleneck sweater and tweed jacket. If not for the nonsmoking ordinance, he would probably have been sucking on a pipe. His face was furrowed with concern as he listened to what she was telling him. Singsaker moved as close to them as he could while the conservator was turned away. He fished out his cell phone and surreptitiously took a series of photos. Then he slipped the phone back into his pocket and left. Outside he looked at the photos he'd taken and was pleased to see he'd made a good choice when he bought this new phone. The camera was excellent. He'd captured the whole face of the unknown man, sharp and clear. He still didn't know what he was going to use the pictures for, or what the meeting between those two was about, but something told him that the photos would come in handy.

When he got back in his car, he noticed that he'd developed

sweat rings under his arms. On the dashboard he could see that the temperature had risen to seventy-two. We must be approaching some kind of record high for September, he thought.

At the police station, Brattberg wanted to talk.

Singsaker told her about his conversations with Hornemann and Freud but left out the part about tailing the conservator.

Gro Brattberg was impatient.

"But still nothing more about Vatten?"

"Honestly, I don't think anyone knows him very well," he said. "But the theft of the *Johannes Book* has given me so much to do that I haven't had a chance to talk to many people. It'd probably be best to send down another detective. But oddly enough, I got the impression that this new librarian, Siri Holm, knows more about Vatten than the people who've worked with him for years."

"So why haven't you talked to her?"

"She wasn't at work yet. I was going to call her."

"All right, we'll look into that," she said. "But first I want you to talk to the coroner. They're almost finished with the autopsy and should be able to give us an oral report.

"And one more thing. We've gone over all the AutoPASS records, including the one between Flakk and Rørvik, and we got no hits on Jens Dahle on either Saturday or Sunday. However, his car was registered on the ferry Friday afternoon and Monday morning, as he told us. Mona Gran also went to talk to his kids at their grandparents' house. They've been told what happened. The only sensible thing she got out of them was that their father was at the cabin all day Saturday."

"So we can rule out the husband," said Singsaker.

"The husband is never ruled out of any case," said Brattberg cynically. "But all the focus has shifted to Vatten. What's he up to? Is he the one who took the damned book? Is that how he's going to finance his escape?" She was bubbling over with questions.

For a moment he stood there wondering whether to say anything about Silvia Freud and the pompous academic at the Prinsen Hotel. But again he rejected the idea. His boss was right, of course. Now it was all about Vatten.

25

Kittelsen, the coroner at St. Olav's Hospital, was an old, stooped doctor with an eye for detail. He never made jokes, always got straight to the point, and never had time for small talk. He was a medical examiner after Chief Inspector Singsaker's own heart. It wasn't often that he went to Kittelsen's office for an oral report; usually they just received written ones. Kittelsen never said more or less than he wrote in his reports, so there wasn't much to be gained by asking him questions. But this was no ordinary case. So much damage had been done to the corpse that he was sure Kittelsen could have written a whole book about it.

"Give me the main points, Kittelsen," he said, sitting down. The office was located in the new lab in the department of pathology and medical genetics. Kittelsen didn't fit in with the modern furnishings, and the heart-shaped desk offered a sharp contrast to his blunt manner. In order to feel more at home, he'd brought with him the most important items from the rundown office he'd had before. A skeleton stood evaluating Singsaker skeptically from the darkest corner of the office. Yellowed anatomical charts covered part of the newly painted walls. Singsaker's gaze fixed involuntarily on the poster just behind Kittelsen. It was an anatomical depiction in black and white. He couldn't tell when it had been printed, but it wasn't this century. The image showed a female cadaver tied into a sitting position by a rope around her neck. The spine was straight, and you could see one thigh bent forward in what would be a natural, possibly somewhat provocative position for a live young woman. On this corpse all the skin was flayed off, while along the hips the subcutaneous fat hung down over the rear section, like a blanket that had been partially removed. Was this a morbid kind of striptease? The muscles on the flayed back were numbered, as if to emphasize that this had been done in the service of science. It struck him as downright unseemly for Kittelsen to have a picture of a flayed human being on the wall, especially considering the present case, but the doctor must have had the poster for so long that he no longer noticed it.

"The main points," said Kittelsen, pausing to smack his lips but only as long as his efficient nature would permit. "The reports on the semen residue already came in. My findings show that the semen had been inside the victim for a good while before she was killed."

"How long is 'a good while'?"

"Based on where the semen was located in the vagina and how much had been absorbed through the vaginal wall and such, I would say an hour or two. Maybe more."

"So that means that the person who had sex with the victim wasn't necessarily the same one who killed her?" he asked without understanding why that made him feel so elated.

"I leave that sort of conclusion to you," said Kittelsen dryly. "I'm only presenting our findings. I can tell you that the person who killed, cut the throat, and flayed Gunn Brita Dahle could possibly have done this before. But I wouldn't describe this person as skilled. The incisions are too rough and irregular to have been made by a surgeon. The skin and most of the head were removed after the victim died."

Scalpel

"Most of the head?"

"Yes, the cause of death was most likely the fact that the throat was cut first. While the victim was dying from the first cut, the perpetrator continued slicing at the neck. To sever the spine a small ax or a very sharp knife was used. But the murderer obviously tried various different tools. You asked for the main points, and this is probably the major one," said Kittelsen, fishing out a dark piece of metal from an aluminum bowl on his desk.

"And that is what?" asked Singsaker, as he felt his pulse quicken.

"It's a piece of metal."

"You'll have to give me more than that."

"I found it between two of the cervical vertebrae that were still attached to the corpse. It's my guess that one of the tools used in the attempt to cut through the spine broke, and a piece got stuck. The killer then took another tool and finished the job a little higher up the neck."

"So this is a piece of one of the knives that the killer used?"

"That's my theory, yes."

"Can you say any more about it?"

"No," said Kittelsen. "It will have to be analyzed by experts." The doctor took out a transparent bag, placed the metal piece in it, sealed it, and handed it to him. "If I could make a suggestion," he said as Singsaker got up, "an archaeologist should take a look at it."

"Why?" asked Singsaker.

"Because it's not exactly stainless steel," said the pathologist laconically.

"Based on the quality of the steel and the little I can evaluate from the shape, I'd say it's from at least the seventeen hundreds. It was most likely oiled and maintained almost continuously, since it's in astoundingly good condition. If special care was taken, the knife

261

could be even older, but probably not much older than five hundred years." Jens Dahle raised his head from the microscope and straightened to his full height in front of Chief Inspector Singsaker.

Gunn Brita Dahle's husband had agreed to meet him at the office in the Science Museum. Singsaker had told him on the phone why he wanted to see him, assuring Dahle that someone else could do the evaluation, but adding that there were a couple of other questions he'd like to ask him. When the detective arrived at the museum, Dahle was already in his office, waiting to receive him. He was unshaven and had beads of sweat on his forehead. It was close to one o'clock, and the temperature outside had gone up to seventy-five degrees. Jens Dahle raised his eyebrows when he saw the knife point that Singsaker handed him.

"The fragment is definitely steel, which is actually no different than iron but with a higher carbon content. But steel has been produced by different methods since ancient times. So that in itself tells us a little about its age. A closer analysis of the alloy could tell us more. For instance, any modern tool made of steel would contain some mineral, to give the steel different properties. The element chromium is used to make the steel stainless. In so-called surgical stainless steel we find a minimum of eleven percent chromium, as well as nickel. I can definitely state that this is not the case with this fragment. But if you want to know the exact age, it would have to be carbon-dated. I can arrange that for you, but it will take time."

"A test like that will probably have to go through our own technicians," said Singsaker. "Right now I just want to get a quick preliminary evaluation. But you don't have any idea where a knife like this might come from?"

"This fragment isn't big enough to tell us what sort of knife it's from. It could be a hunting knife or a butcher's knife. It's from a time when pretty much every man wore a knife on his belt. Since it's so pointed, I would guess that it's not a barber's knife, though it may well have belonged to a barber."

"What makes you say that?"

"In the period we're talking about, barbers owned the widest selection of knives, sawing implements, and drills. They did more than just cut beards. A barber often functioned as both a local surgeon and executioner. They were experts with blades of all types. At some of the universities on the southern part of the Continent, it gradually became more accepted to dissect human bodies, starting in the fourteen hundreds. Then it was usually a barber-surgeon who performed the dissection itself, while the professor stood at a lectern above the dissection table and lectured from his notes. Often the actual findings that the barber-surgeon made did not agree with the lecturer's manuscript, which was frequently copied out from much older sources. If there was any doubt, the professor was always right, of course." Jens Dahle chuckled.

Singsaker wondered if this was something Dahle had talked about so many times before that he managed to forget his grief for a moment. Even Dahle's laughter was programmed into the subject matter.

"In any case that's how it was until the renowned anatomist Vesalius began his series of dissections in the fifteen hundreds in Padua. Vesalius dissected the corpses himself. He became famous for doing that and, in some places, infamous. In Pisa he was called a barber surgeon. Vesalius was one of the first to prove that the great authority in the field of anatomy until then, the Roman doctor Galen of Pergamon, had built most of his knowledge about the human body by dissecting apes and other animals. Vesalius came to this conclusion because he himself dissected animals as well as humans. But some of Galen's erroneous conclusions are still retained in anatomical terminology. The terminus of the human intestine, for example, is curved rather than straight, as the term 'rectum' indicates. In apes, the rectum is straight."

For an archaeologist, Dahle knew a surprising amount about medical history. Singsaker couldn't rid himself of the thought that this subject matter was somehow relevant to the murders. The corpse of Gunn Brita Dahle bore a remarkable similarity to the charts on the medical examiner's wall. The murderer must have shared Jens Dahle's fascination with anatomy, but in a way that was far more perverse than scientific.

"Did this Vesalius make drawings and charts?" he asked.

"Not personally, but he had one or more unknown illustrators," said Dahle. "Vesalius published what is considered the first serious anatomical atlas, *De humani corporis fabrica*. That book consists of eighty-five detailed illustrations of the human body, in which the various anatomical details were revealed layer by layer."

Almost like a striptease, Singsaker thought gloomily. Then he described the illustration in Kittelsen's office.

"That's probably not Vesalius. It sounds like a copperplate engraving by a famous anatomical illustrator from the sixteen hundreds. Now what was his name? Gerard de Lairesse, I think it was."

"You seem to know a lot about this topic."

"If you've dug up grave sites and studied enough bones, you begin to take an interest in the subject. But everyone ought to know more about it. Understanding one's body is to understand oneself." Here he stopped, and his expression turned somber. For the first time it seemed as though he was looking at himself from the outside, and he may have noticed the chasm between the scientific way he was speaking and the emotional chaos he found in himself.

But Singsaker wanted to push him further.

"Do you know anything about the anatomist Alessandro

Benedetti?" he asked, finally getting to what he really wanted to know.

"Yes. But we don't know as much about him as we do about Vesalius. Benedetti lived in Venice and Padua before Vesalius began working there. He's one of several doctors who laid the groundwork for Vesalius, you might say. He presumably performed a number of dissections, possibly doing some of them with his own hands, and it's conceivable that he already knew about many of the things that Vesalius is famous for having discovered. Like Vesalius, he stole a number of corpses from graveyards, but no doubt he also performed public dissections, which were legal and regulated in Venice starting in the fourteen hundreds. Alessandro Benedetti was the first to describe an anatomical theater."

"An anatomical theater?"

"Correct. The first anatomical theater that we know of was built in Padua. There is still one in Padua today, and tourists can visit it. But several smaller and temporary theaters were presumably built earlier, perhaps according to Benedetti's instructions. We don't know for certain. The theater was supposed to be a place where public dissections could be held for many onlookers. The main point was that people who came to watch—students, doctors, and other spectators—could see what was actually revealed during the dissection. According to Benedetti, the theater had to ensure a good view, a large, well-illuminated dissection table; good ventilation; and a security staff. He also thought it was a good idea to charge an entrance fee. From Padua the concept spread from one university to the next in the fifteen and sixteen hundreds. Soon there were anatomical theaters everywhere. The northernmost one was built at the university in Uppsala, Sweden, in the mid–sixteen hundreds. This theater is actually one of only three that have been preserved from that period. I recommend paying a visit to it."

"Maybe when this case has been solved," said Singsaker, and once again the shadows returned to Dahle's eyes.

"To get back to the matter at hand," Dahle said, more bluntly, "the knife you are looking for could be one that was used for such dissections. It's thin and very sharp, and the edge has a slight curve like a modern scalpel. No autopsies were performed in Norway during the period we're talking about, so if the knife is Norwegian, it's more likely that it was used for other medical purposes, such as amputations."

"I see. But you don't think the knife might be from Venice or Padua?" Singsaker asked.

"No, why should I? But if it was used for dissections, anything is possible, of course."

"Who might be thought to own such a knife today?"

"Not many people. Maybe a collector, a farmer with far too much old junk in his barn, I don't know. Most objects of this type are probably kept in storerooms at institutions like this." The archaeologist threw out his arms.

"And if this knife turned out to be from the fifteen hundreds and privately owned, would you say that it was valuable?"

"It would be extremely valuable, because of the quality and condition of the metal. But of course it depends on the provenance. For example, if it could be linked to historical personages, the price would climb considerably in the private collectors' market. And this one is in remarkably good condition, judging by the small fragment we have."

The image in Singsaker's mind was now crystal clear. The ancient scalpel he held in Siri Holm's apartment as she dried herself off with a towel. He had only studied the shaft of the knife and hadn't noticed whether the point of the blade was missing. The first thing I have to do when I leave here is call her, he thought.

"I hope I've been of some help," said Dahle. "When I spoke with you on the phone, you mentioned that there were other things you wanted to ask me about."

"Yes, there are," said Singsaker. "But we'll have to get to them later."

26

Odd *Singsaker swore on* his way out of the Science Museum. He was supposed to be hunting for Vatten, but every new clue he found pointed in a different direction. This case had turned into a labyrinth, no, a cabinet of curiosities, he thought, imagining a museum storeroom full of cartons and file boxes with no catalog or labels, so it was impossible to know what might be hidden in the next box.

He dialed Siri Holm's number. "You have reached the voice mailbox of 555 10 476. Please leave a message after the beep." Singsaker didn't leave a message. His feet were already carrying him toward Rosenborg.

After he had rung Siri Holm's doorbell three times without getting a response, he began to study the locks. One was an ordinary lock that he could probably pick easily. But the deadbolt looked more difficult. It looked recently installed and wouldn't be easy to crack. Even the door was relatively new and seemed solid. Impossible to break it down without causing a lot of damage. He looked at his watch. It was almost three. Just before he got to the apartment he'd called Hornemann to check whether Siri had shown up at work. She hadn't. So she'd been gone almost the whole workday. But he didn't have any indication that criminal activity was behind her disappearance. In other words, he had no legal grounds for breaking into her apartment.

He went outside the fourplex and stood there looking around. The whole building seemed empty. There were no lights on, and no one was moving about. Then he walked around the building to the backyard. There he saw a trampoline, which indicated that there were kids in one of the units. At the top right he could see Siri Holm's balcony. He felt a prickling at the back of his neck when he saw that the balcony door was open. A ladder hung down the wall.

Police officers are never surprised at how easy it is to break into someone's dwelling. They know it's easy. They know that people don't pay close enough attention, especially in broad daylight. Even though anyone could see him if he climbed up the ladder to the balcony, he knew from innumerable witness interviews that few people would think he was doing anything illegal. Most would have seen a workman doing his job, or an unfortunate renter who had locked himself out. Of those who might be suspicious, most would be reluctant to say anything to him. It was incredible the lengths people in Norway would go to in order to avoid bothering strangers, even if they happened to be thieves.

Once inside, he noticed that Siri hadn't cleaned up since the last time he was there. Then he saw the dog, who was lying in the same spot by the door. He tried to recall if it had been there the whole time during his last visit. If it had, that would have been the first time he'd had sex with a dog watching. Now the dog merely raised an eyebrow when he came in. Obviously not a watchdog. That the dog was in the apartment might mean that her disappearance hadn't been planned. The Afghan hound closed both eyes, yawned as if terribly bored, and rested its long snout on one paw. The dog had no objections to him taking a look around. Then he caught sight of a human form standing in the kitchen doorway. The mannequin was naked now, the way Siri Holm had been when he left her. He stood there admiring it. It was beautifully made. The whole mannequin had been carved from wood and polished; was it oak? The limbs were round and could be posed. The proportions were exact, male. And this mannequin was also an antique. He could imagine it in a nineteenth-century Italian tailor's shop. Siri Holm's apartment was an eclectic, disorganized museum.

His looked around the room for something in particular, and in the middle of the floor, about where it had been lying the last time, he found it. Alessandro Benedetti's scalpel. He picked it up and studied the point.

Damn, he thought, when he saw it. He stood there with the knife blade pressed between his right thumb and index finger. It felt warm against his fingertips. Then he threw the scalpel. It spun several times in the air before it struck the oak mannequin over by the door. The arms and one leg shook as if in death spasms. The scalpel protruded from the mannequin's chest. It had gone in right above the heart, with a point that was still intact. Damn, he thought again, but he was relieved. Siri Holm wasn't the killer. But where was she?

He looked around again. It would take too much time to sift through all this junk for clues, if there were any. As he stood there thinking, his cell phone rang. Vlado Taneski again, the reporter. With a mixture of irritation, professional pride, and uncertainty regarding how long he'd be able to hold out in the siege against the warriors of free speech, he pressed the END button. Then his cell rang again. It was Brattberg. This time he took the call.

"Where are you?" she wanted to know.

"I'm outside Siri Holm's apartment," he lied, and gave her a brief report on his visits to Kittelsen and Jens Dahle.

"That is an interesting development," Brattberg said. "But what are you doing at Siri Holm's place? You know we're still looking for Vatten, right?"

He paused to think. Then he told her about the conservator, Silvia Freud.

"That doesn't sound like a very strong lead. She had an appointment with somebody at the Prinsen Hotel. So what?"

"I suppose it's kind of a long shot," he had to admit.

"A very long shot. But there's one thing that makes me not want to discount it entirely. Grongstad just gave me a printout of everyone who used a card key at the library that Saturday. It was Gunn Brita Dahle and Vatten, and also a student who was manning the counter until the library closed, and who did not have access to the office wing. But also this conservator, Silvia Freud. She left the office long before the estimated time of the murder. We also know that Siri Holm was there. But she was probably let in and out with Gunn Brita Dahle's card key. Most likely she also left the scene before the murder. If there were any other people inside, then they must have used a key. For someone who doesn't want to leave evidence behind, that's actually a possibility. Several system keys are in circulation, and I don't think that Hornemann has a complete list of who uses them."

"But this does connect Silvia Freud more closely to the murder than we thought."

"As I said: Both she and Siri Holm left the library early, while the video surveillance system was still on. We have footage from the book vault. I don't know how you're going to link either of them to what happened."

"Me neither. But I've got a hunch."

"Now listen to me, Singsaker. I have great respect for your hunches. I know they've been helpful before. But you've been through a lot, and this has been a brutal way to start back on the job. I want you to go home and lie down for a few hours. This evening you can drive out to Værnes and pick up our friend from the States. That's the only assignment you have for tonight. The rest of us will keep looking for Vatten. He's the one at the center of it all. If this Siri Holm is missing, and if she has something to do with the case, that still doesn't rule out Vatten. Grongstad's people, by the way, also found an empty bottle of Spanish red wine in a trash can outside the library, and guess what?"

"Fingerprints?"

"Not just anybody's."

"Vatten?"

"And Gunn Brita Dahle."

"But what about the semen samples. Do we know any more about them?"

"Singsaker, it's September. It's a little early to start waiting for the fat guy with the big white beard and red suit. You know the way they work at Forensics in Oslo," Brattberg said.

"Kittelsen told me that the semen apparently landed where it did long before the murder occurred," he said.

"I know. I've got the report right here. But now that we found the wine bottle, we know that Vatten lied to us."

"Well, it's not illegal to drink wine. And we don't know when the bottle was tossed in the trash can. But of course you're right, everything does point to Vatten," he said, wondering why he instinctively came to Vatten's defense.

"So let us handle things now. I want you to rest up for tomorrow. We'll send a car to your apartment this afternoon to pick up the knife point. We need to take a look at it as soon as possible," she concluded.

After Brattberg hung up, he thought going home and taking a nap wasn't such a bad idea. Instead, he went into Siri's kitchen. To his surprise he discovered that one of the cupboards was used as a well-stocked liquor cabinet. He perused the bottles. Most of them were unopened liter bottles, apparently bought in the tax-free shop or abroad, or maybe received as gifts. At the back of the cupboard stood a bottle of aquavit. Not Rød Aalborg from Denmark, of course, but domestic Linje. The bottle had been opened and was half full. He pulled out the cork and put the bottle to his lips. The first swallow hit the spot. The next four failed to have quite the same effect. Brattberg was right, he thought, as he replaced the bottle in the cupboard. I could use a rest.

With a leisurely gait he crossed the living room floor, glancing at the sofa where they had made love so passionately. Then he looked at the dog, who was the only one who knew about it. In the bedroom he saw that the only thing on her bed was the tae kwon do outfit. He lay down, breathing in the scent of her. She smelled like eggnog, raspberries, and a hint of mature cheese. Then he fell asleep and slept like an overworked cop who'd had brain surgery, with just the right amount of aquavit in his blood.

The female passport officer gave her a big smile.

"How are you?"

"I'm fine," Felicia Stone lied. It was more than twenty hours since she'd left Richmond via Atlanta, and ever since changing planes she'd been sitting in the same damned seat in front of the emergency exit. For safety reasons the seat could barely be reclined, and her lumbar region had almost collapsed before they reached London. Nothing had improved on the connecting flight to Oslo.

"How long is the flight to Trondheim?" she asked impatiently, as the passport officer tried to get the scanner to read the code in her passport. Couldn't she just look at the picture? Felicia thought.

It's not that hard to see that it's me, is it? Finally the computer beeped, and the officer got the information she needed on her monitor.

"The flight is only forty-five minutes," she said. "But I hear there's a good deal of turbulence because of the wind and the unusually warm weather in the Trondheim region."

Felicia groaned.

"I thought I'd at least escaped the heat," she said, taking her passport and heading off to search for the domestic terminal.

At eight o'clock, the phone rang. Singsaker had been in a dark corner of dreamland for five hours. At one point he had found himself lying on a dissection table in an anatomical theater. He had been unable to move, as if he were anesthetized, but he was still conscious. It was Dr. Kittelsen who was in charge of the dissection. He slowly flayed him. Then he tried to sell the skin to the highest bidder. The dream ended when Singsaker bought the skin himself and wrapped it around his shoulders like a cape. When he woke up he was far from rested.

"Singsaker," he coughed into the phone he'd fished out of his pocket without getting up from the bed.

The officer introduced himself, saying a name he didn't catch.

"We're outside your place and need to pick up a piece of evidence. It's going to the crime lab."

Singsaker sat up slowly and looked around. Outside it was getting dark. Shadows filled the room, but he quickly saw that he was not at home.

"I'm out shopping right now. Tell them I'll bring the object in myself a little later," he replied, and ended the call. He felt sick. Nausea was not good. He hated nausea almost as much as sweating. He gingerly moved his feet off the bed and set them down on a throw rug. He sat there swaying on the edge of the bed. Finally he fixed his eyes on the nightstand. He saw a stack of mysteries. On top of it was a wireless phone, and next to it a yellow note was stuck to the spine of the book on top. It took a few seconds for his eyes to focus on what was written neatly on the note. And it took a little longer for his brain to understand what the words actually meant.

"Egon at the Prinsen Hotel. 10 o'clock. Bring the book," it said.

He grabbed the note and stood up. The deadbolt couldn't be opened from the inside without a key, so he took the ladder back down the way he'd come. From the tenth rung he hopped down onto the lawn. Now there were two kids sitting on the trampoline, a boy and a girl. They were staring at him as if he'd fallen off the roof. He waved to them and calmly went around the corner of the building.

Odd Singsaker called Hornemann at home.

"I need Silvia Freud's phone number," he said.

"I can send her business card to your cell," Hornemann replied politely.

"Do you know what time she left work today?" he asked.

"No, but it must have been early. I didn't see her this afternoon."

"I have one more question," Singsaker said before he hung up. "The copy that Freud made of the *Johannes Book*. It's very good, isn't it?"

"Yes, it is."

"How can you tell it's not the real thing?"

"It's easy if you examine it properly with a loupe, fluorescent light, things like that, but even then you'd need to know a lot about it."

"But if you just looked at the book with the naked eye?"

"You'd have to be very sharp to be able to see any difference from the original."

"How many people at the library would notice that difference without a closer examination?"

"Not many. Probably nobody but Silvia herself, I should think."

"And if someone were to examine a book to see whether it was genuine, who would do that?"

"That would also be Silvia."

"Are the books in the book vault ever loaned out?"

"Some of them are occasionally loaned to researchers. But they are monitored closely."

"I see. What about the *Johannes Book*?"

"It has been sent for inspection to a select few historians. Otherwise the plan was for future borrowers to read Silvia's copy. The genuine book would be kept in the book vault, untouched, indefinitely. It's simply too valuable."

"So it would be almost as if it didn't exist at all?"

"In a way. But the book could be preserved much longer that way."

Singsaker thanked Hornemann for the information and ended the call.

Immediately after that he received the business card on his phone and called Silvia Freud. It sounded like she used the same cell phone company as Siri Holm: "You have reached the voice mailbox of . . ." He looked at the digital business card Hornemann had sent him. It also listed a home address. Silvia Freud lived in Solsiden. Conveniently on the way to police headquarters.

Silvia Freud's apartment building was across the bridge from the shopping district. When he saw the location of her doorbell, he figured that she must live on the second floor, probably squeezed in between two buildings and without the top floor's expensive view of the warehouses on Brattøra, with a glimpse of Munkholmen out in the fjord.

After ringing five times and waiting thirty seconds between them, he realized that she either wasn't home or wasn't going to open the door. He ambled back toward the dock and sat down on a bench facing a row of bars and restaurants. Even though the sun had set, it was still warm. The bars were full of people, and the reflections of the lights and street lamps danced on the puddles that covered the old wharf.

He looked at the photo he had taken that morning. The time stamp on it said 9:53 A.M. Siri Holm must have arrived at Egon's just after he left. And he had no doubt that she'd gone to meet Silvia Freud and the unknown man. But why?

There was one more big question, of course: Did this have anything to do with the murder of Gunn Brita Dahle?

From Solsiden he walked the short distance across to the police station and stuck his nose in his office but saw no one he absolutely had to talk to. Then he checked out a cruiser. He was supposed to be at Værnes at eleven.

When Brattberg called him from Byåsen at ten thirty, he was able to tell her with a certain amount of satisfaction that he'd already passed the electronic checkpoint at Ranheim. She asked him what he'd done with the piece of the knife blade, and he told her it was lying on the desk in his office.

"Great. I'll send Grongstad up to get it right away," she said.

"Jeez, is he working at this time of day?"

"You know Grongstad," she said with a laugh. "Fresh evidence has almost the same effect on him as coca leaves on an Inca messenger."

"Or an Energizer battery on a toy rabbit," he said, laughing too. He instantly realized that this was "fatigue humor," the kind of jokes people laughed at only when they were overworked or had gone to an after party they should have skipped.

PART IV

———◆◆◆———

The Mask of Sanity

Nature is an infinite sphere in which the center is everywhere and the circumference nowhere.

—PASCAL, 1670

27

The *last straw was* the final leg of her flight to Trondheim, when Felicia Stone had to sit beside a mother with a baby obviously in need of a diaper change. The turbulence made it difficult to leave one's seat for almost the entire flight. During the approach she tried to look out the window and see the city of Trondheim, but she saw nothing but dark mountains in the night. Hardly a single light or any other sign of human habitation. She had seen a landscape like this before, during the year she'd lived in Alaska.

Now she stood in the arrival hall of a small airport with no air-conditioning, even though the temperature at eleven o'clock at night was not much cooler than back home in Richmond.

She didn't have a description of the police officer who was supposed to meet her, but she picked him out immediately. Was it the fatigued face, the sweat rings under the sleeves of his shirt, or the way he clung to his cell phone with his right hand, like a gunslinger just before a shoot-out?

Singsaker spotted her just as quickly, even though the deep but odd female voice he'd heard on the phone didn't really fit with her slight figure. Felicia Stone was a woman in her thirties with dark, shoulder-length hair and a pale complexion. She wore no makeup, which instantly struck him as a bit un-American. Her eyes were big and brown. He took an immediate liking to her.

Singsaker pocketed his cell phone, went over, and offered to take her suitcase. She gave it to him and held out her right hand. Instead of putting down the suitcase he took her hand in his left and gave it a squeeze, introducing himself. He thought that the whole scene was a little awkward, as if they both had no idea what to say.

"I'm Felicia Stone," she told him.

"I have a car outside," he said.

They moved toward the exit.

"Some case, huh?" she said, although she didn't sound convinced that her remark would break the ice.

"Some case," he said with a nod.

Singsaker didn't really start a conversation until they drove off. She thought that was typical of men, that they didn't like to talk while they were busy doing something else. Except driving, of course. But she didn't say that out loud.

He told her about everything that had happened since they last spoke.

"Let me see the picture of this academic type with Silvia Freud," she said when he finished bringing her up to date.

He took out his cell and flipped through the photos as he kept half an eye on the road. When he found the right one, he handed her the phone. She recognized the man at once.

"That's him. John Shaun Nevins. He's the suspect in our homicide," she said, adding as if it were an unimportant detail, "Except for the fact that he has an airtight alibi."

"I hate airtight alibis," said Singsaker.

She laughed. It was the same dark laughter from the phone call.

"But it's clear that he has something to do with the case," she said. "I was really hoping that you could tell me something that would unravel a bit of the riddle for us. Instead, it seems like all the threads are weaving together into an even tighter web."

"I agree. This case has turned into a real ball of confusion," he said, unsure if he'd used the right English word. "But tell me about Nevins. He's an academic, right?"

"Actually, he does the same thing Silvia Freud does."

"A bookbinder?"

"Conservator. Nevins works for the university library in Virginia, but he's also known as a big book collector. Some of his fortune was earned buying and selling rare books. His late wife probably contributed most of the funds, though. A tobacco family."

"So he has money? Enough to invest a hefty sum in a book he could never allow to see the light of day?"

"I wouldn't be surprised. He's the type. It might be precisely the feeling of power that cowardly, rich men like him are looking for, combined with a childish need to own something that nobody else has."

Singsaker wondered if she was taking this case a bit too personally.

"What joy would it give him if he can't brag about it?" he asked.

"If you're self-centered enough, you don't need to brag to anyone but yourself." Again that dark laughter.

He noticed that he was just as interested in Felicia Stone herself as he was in their conversation.

"By the way, I have some bad news for you," she added. "I received a message on my way here. There's no record of a Jon Vatten traveling into or out of the United States in recent weeks. He was there earlier in the summer, as you know, but that was long before the murder. The same goes for Gunn Brita Dahle. She was there in the spring."

"I have a couple of other names I'd like you to check," said Singsaker and gave them to her. He wrote them on a pad attached to the dashboard as he glanced at the road. She looked at the names and nodded.

"I'll e-mail my office about them. But we should probably focus on the two most likely candidates. Should we start with my guy or yours?" she asked with a sigh.

"Mine has disappeared," he said.

"And I don't know where mine is at the moment. He's supposed to be in Frankfurt."

"He could be anywhere by now. With or without the *Johannes Book*. I think we'll have to start somewhere else."

"Where's that?"

"It's just an idea. But I think I'll take you out to Fosen to visit a farmer out there."

She nodded wearily. Singsaker guessed she didn't have the slightest clue as to what he was talking about, but he didn't want to inundate her with too much information. She looked jet-lagged.

"We'll start tomorrow," he said.

She looked out the window.

"Isn't there supposed to be a city somewhere in this wilderness?"

He had to laugh. He'd never thought of Malvik as the wilderness. But it was probably all a matter of perspective.

Life is a chain of coincidences, and one of them was that Felicia Stone had booked a room at the Prinsen Hotel. After Singsaker had helped her take the luggage to her room, they went downstairs to the bar, and each had a pilsner. They tried not to talk about the case. He told her a little about Trondheim and the city's history. She was more interested in the odd bowling game in the pub. But to her great surprise, he didn't know the rules. At one o'clock he left to return the police car. There was more than a little alcohol in his bloodstream. Then he went home and fell asleep as soon as his head hit the pillow.

Vatten thought he heard a noise. He looked up at once, listening closely. The pines outside the cabin rustled in the plaintive September wind. A bird called vainly into the night. That was all. He kept listening. Yes, there it was again. Footsteps approaching on the path outside. He could hear them more clearly now. His hands and feet were bound with a stiff rope that scratched his wrists, making the skin burn. He tried not to move. Just lay there listening to the footsteps coming closer. How had he ended up here? When he opened the door at home, the crowbar had struck him instantly. He had no chance to see the kidnapper's face.

Then the door opened. In the dim light he recognized the man who'd come to kill him. Was he surprised? He didn't know. All he knew was that his hatred from the past had returned. And now he had a face to direct it toward.

The man spoke. "On the way up here I was thinking about Edgar Allan Poe. You like Poe, don't you? Weren't you at his museum this summer, in Virginia?"

How does this shithead know that? Vatten thought. Nobody knew about that, did they?

"I've been there myself. The garden has a mysterious air about it, don't you think? I had a chance to see it at sunrise, which most people don't get to do. It's incredible to think that Poe has been immortalized like that. But few have been as dead as he was in his unmarked grave."

The kidnapper stopped talking and looked at Vatten, who was still concentrating on lying quietly.

"Why are you so silent? I thought you'd appreciate the topic. You know, Poe was almost maniacally obsessed with death and bringing the dead back to life. Maybe that's what literature is really about, waking up what is dead and breathing life into a world that's gone?"

The figure in front of him cocked his head. Only now did Vatten notice something he was holding in one hand. It was a rolled up piece of grayish-white skin. A kind of bundle. The odious man moved to the middle of the room, where a table stood. He laid the bundle on the table and unrolled it. Vatten raised his head. Inside the roll of skin were tools. There were knives in many shapes and sizes, scalpels, saws, and drills. It reminded Vatten of an illustration he'd once seen in a book. An old copperplate engraving from the 1500s. The picture showed all the necessary tools a good anatomist might need to perform a dissection. They were the same tools he now saw on the table.

A pair of ominously calm eyes observed him from behind the table.

"I have many excellent tools here. People don't store them like this any longer."

Vatten suppressed a scream.

"But the most interesting thing is the packaging itself."

In the light from the window Vatten could see that the inside of the skin that the knives were packed in had been scraped and prepared to make a smooth writing surface, like a piece of parchment, and that there was something written on it. The letters were big with curlicues, but they had begun to fade, fragile words struggling with encroaching invisibility. This was an old text.

"Do you know what this is?"

Vatten said nothing but knew he was going to get an answer.

"This is the climax of the *Johannes Book*. Scholars have known that some pages were missing. I've heard that they were recently rediscovered in Virginia. These pages reveal that Johannes the priest was himself a murderer who took the lives of victims in his parish, then flayed and dissected them before he buried them. I've known about this for a long time. What no one else knows is that a final page exists. One that was never included in the book yet was also written by Johannes. This parchment was used to pack the priest's knives. He had quite a good selection. On the page I have here, he goes into more detail than anywhere else. Here he describes a vivisection. Tell me, Vatten, do you know what a vivisection is?"

All Vatten knew about vivisection was that it involved being flayed and dissected while you were still alive. In the Renaissance it was occasionally performed on animals. Once he had read about a doctor in ancient times who had done it to a prisoner, but he had never quite believed it. Now it occurred to him what sort of fate had been planned for him. And he was honest enough with himself that he dreaded the pain. At the same time he realized that he'd done nothing but wait for death since Hedda and Edvard disappeared. And no matter how crazy it sounded, he thought that this wasn't the worst way to die. This was the opposite of being buried alive. It was being opened up instead. Letting in the light so that everyone could see.

"We are all books of blood," said Vatten, resigned without knowing where the words came from. "No matter where you open us up, we are red."

"I'm liking you more and more. And that will just make things even more interesting." The sound of the whetstone against the knife edge filled the room.

"Bringing the dead back to life," said Felicia Stone. "That's what we really want to do, isn't it? That's why we're detectives. To create a story that will give meaning to a meaningless death."

"That's one way to look at it," said Singsaker.

"Relax," she said with a laugh. "I just get philosophical in the morning before I have my coffee. I hope it comes soon." She looked around for Egon.

He had guessed that she, as an American, would go for the whole works for breakfast: eggs, bacon, and toast. But she had ordered only toast and coffee.

"While you've been philosophizing, I've done some investigating. Silvia Freud hasn't shown up, either at home or at work, since the last time we spoke. The same is true of Siri Holm. So now we have three people missing, four if you count Nevins, and no good leads. There are plenty of police on the case here in town. So I've decided to expand the investigation a bit outside of Trondheim. We're going to talk to a farmer out on Fosen."

"Who is this farmer?"

"He's the previous owner of the *Johannes Book,* and since it seems that most things are circling around that book, I thought I'd have a talk with him. My boss, though dubious, has given me the green light to follow this lead, since we don't have a single clue that ties directly to Vatten. But she really doesn't want you to be involved. You have no authority on Norwegian territory, she says. Her plan is for me to sit here all morning and go over the case with you, then drive out to Fosen in the afternoon. But I think it's a much better idea for you to come with me, then we can talk while we drive. There'll be less downtime that way."

"Do you make a habit of not doing what your boss tells you?" Felicia Stone asked with a laugh.

"All the time," he lied.

"It's true that I have no jurisdiction here, but I do have a valid passport and can travel wherever I like," she said with a sly smile. And from that moment he was no longer in doubt. He definitely liked her more than he should.

28

Felicia Stone stood on the top deck outside the café on the Fosen ferry. She leaned on the railing above the open deck and looked back toward Rissa and Trondheim, now hidden in the bay behind them. Her black hair danced in the wind and revealed a slim white neck, with skin so thin that the blood vessels were visible underneath. The temperature had dropped overnight, back to a normal level for September. Felicia, who had apparently been prepared for chilly Norway, wore a boyish green all-weather jacket with the hood removed. It looked like something a rather unfashionable hunter might wear.

Singsaker emerged with two cups of black coffee and two small vanilla pancakes.

"Norwegian ferry food," he said, handing her a paper plate with a *svele* on it.

"Thank you, but I've already had breakfast, and I'm not that keen on pancakes, at least not cold ones with no syrup," she said, looking skeptically at the buttered *svele,* which had a thin layer of sugar on top.

"This isn't a pancake, it's a *svele.* It's a traditional Norwegian food," he said, pretending to be offended. "Aren't you curious?"

"Thanks, anyway, I value honesty more than curiosity," she said with a laugh.

"And evidently more than our Norwegian national pride," he said, laughing with her. He put the two *sveler* together to make a double one and took a bite. It was seldom he felt a rapport with anyone as quickly as he had with her. "You're right to give our Norwegian national pride a kick. It's as inflated as a soccer ball," he added.

"You certainly have a way with words," she said with a smile. She took the coffee and gazed at the Trondheim Fjord. "This place reminds me of Alaska. Especially now that the temperature is lower," she went on. "So many mountains and pine forests."

"Have you been to Alaska?"

"Yes, once, a long time ago. I needed to put my life on ice for a while."

"I hope it thawed out afterward."

"In a way it probably has. But you know how it is with thawed goods," she said with a wry smile. "What I think is proving so confusing," she continued, eager to change the subject, "is that we're not searching for a serial killer, yet we are."

"What do you mean?"

"There's something personal about the murders. I think the killer knew both the victims well. Especially Gunn Brita Dahle," said Felicia Stone. "He didn't take the time to knock her unconscious before killing her; he slashed her throat immediately. Apparently while holding her tightly from behind. There's something more intimate about that than hitting somebody with a crowbar or a metal pipe. But I think there's some private motive for killing them both. At the same time, we can't ignore the fact that this is a killer who has made a very big deal about the murders. He likes killing. We're probably dealing with a killer with a deviant personality. A thrill killer. Also, he's killed more than one person. The FBI defines a serial killer as someone who has killed at least three victims with a cooling-off period between each one. In our case we only have two that are confirmed. But Vatten's son and wife could also be victims, which puts us over the magic number."

"Let's set aside the Vatten family and stick with the two murders we have right now. Who in our investigation had a personal relationship with both Gunn Brita Dahle and Efrahim Bond? I'm not as sure as you are that the killer must have had a closer relationship to Dahle than to Bond. The different MOs don't have to mean anything but that it was easier to subdue Dahle, or that the killer felt more confident. I read somewhere that many murderers wish to be as close to the victim as possible at the moment of death. I still think that it has something to do with the book. The personal relationship has to be the killer's relationship to this *Johannes Book*. After all, it's the only link we have between Bond and Dahle."

"I agree that the book is the link," said Felicia, "but I don't know whether it was that *in itself* that made him kill. Something here seems calculated."

"You mean the killer has some rational reason for killing that we're not seeing?"

"I don't know. Are there rational reasons for killing?"

"How long have you been a homicide investigator, Felicia Stone?" he said, unable to keep a fatherly tone out of the question.

"Two years," she replied.

"So, long enough to know that there are unfortunately far too many rational reasons for murder. What keeps the great majority of us from killing anyone is that there are almost always more good reasons not to do it."

"So there's more than one philosophical cop on this ferry," she said with a smile. "I don't know if I agree with your reasoning, but I was coming to a similar conclusion myself."

———

After driving almost two hours from the ferry landing, they turned off the highway toward the farm of Isak and Elin Krangsås. It had started to rain, and the windshield wipers had been going nonstop the whole time. The peninsula of Fosen was a foggy and crepuscular landscape, with shining sheets of glacier-polished rock interspersed with heavy conifers. The buildings on the Krangsås farm looked like big, wet mushrooms standing at the top of a gently sloping green hill.

Singsaker had found the address in the telephone book. The GPS in the police car handled the rest. He had called ahead, saying as little as possible about the murder of Gunn Brita Dahle, although he knew that the couple had already heard about it. All he told them was that he was interested in finding out more about the *Johannes Book*.

Mr. and Mrs. Krangsås met them in the courtyard, both farmers approaching retirement age, he in overalls and she in a comfortable jogging suit.

They were invited into the main house, which faced the courtyard, and it looked like it needed a new coat of whitewash. They saw that the Krangsås family was not unaffected by recent interior design trends. The kitchen was done in stainless steel. The living room had a walnut floor and designer furniture that looked Italian. But although the interior of their house had been updated with a new look, they themselves had not. They no longer matched their own home.

Elin Krangsås had made a big stack of waffles. Singsaker took two and loaded them up with strawberries. Grown on their own farm, he surmised. Felicia Stone helped herself to one heart-shaped waffle. He could see from her expression that she categorized Mrs. Krangsås's offering as "cold pancakes with no syrup."

He went over to a big picture window at the end of the living room. Isak Krangsås came and stood next to him.

"This is quite a view," said Singsaker as he looked out over the rolling countryside of Fosen. In between hillocks and woods he could make out the fjord, a black arc in the distance.

"You get used to it," said Krangsås laconically.

"I understand it was a group of archaeologists who discovered the *Johannes Book*."

"Well, I don't know if I'd say they 'discovered' it. The book was on the shelf here in the living room."

"But one of them realized what a rare book treasure it was, right?"

"Yes, that's true. Jens Dahle, poor man. It's so horrible what happened to Gunn Brita. How is he handling it?"

Singsaker felt bad. He should have offered his condolences long ago. The Dahle family had lived in the cabin next door for a long time.

"He's doing the best he can," he replied, feeling the cliché stick in his throat.

Krangsås stood there a while, staring at the view.

"For us the *Johannes Book* was just another volume on our bookshelf gathering dust."

"What were the archaeologists working on back then?"

"They were going to excavate an old grave site that was apparently located on our property. It dates back hundreds of years, from around the same time as the graveyard at Ørland church. But in the mid–fifteen hundreds all the graves were moved to the main churchyard, and the old grave site became overgrown and eventually ended up belonging to this farm. Now the remnants are under the meadow where the cattle graze. The grass is extremely lush in that pasture." The farmer chuckled.

"How well do you know Jens Dahle?"

"Apart from the fact that his cabin is right next door, you mean? His parents ran a farm out here. Strange folks. But Jens has always been reliable."

"Why did Jens Dahle live here at your farm during the excavation if he has a cabin right nearby?"

"That cabin doesn't belong to him. It comes from Gunn Brita's family. They're from around here, too. At the time they weren't yet married; she was much younger than he was. His parents' farm is a little farther down the road. And I don't think he visited them much in the last years of their lives."

"Where is the cabin located?" asked Singsaker.

"It's just beyond the trees where that green Nissan is parked. Can you see it? The people who own that car are probably guests at the cabin, but they parked up on the road. I'm guessing the path to the cabin is too muddy in this rain. I don't know whose car it is. Gunn Brita and Jens often rent it out to friends and colleagues."

Singsaker was out of the house before Isak Krangsås even finished speaking. On the way he called to Felicia to follow him. When he jumped in the driver's seat he saw her come jogging through the rain toward the car. At the same time he noticed that he was still holding his plate of waffles. The jam was running down his hand.

"Greed is seldom pretty," she remarked dryly as she climbed in with wet hair and fastened her seat belt. Flushed cheeks looked good on her. He tried to scarf down the waffle in three bites, but it took four. Then he licked the jam from his fingers, but not very elegantly.

"Why are you suddenly in such a hurry?" she asked.

"Weren't you listening?"

"All I understood was Elin Krangsås about the embroidery on the tablecloth in ungrammatical English. You were all speaking Norwegian, as far as I could tell."

"Yes, I suppose we were. Sorry. But the thing is, there's a green

Nissan parked on the road outside Jens Dahle's cabin. Silvia Freud drives a green Nissan."

Felicia Stone whistled as he drove off.

"So those two are in it together, Jens Dahle and Silvia Freud?" she asked.

"Not necessarily, although that's an interesting angle. All I know is that Jens Dahle sometimes rents out the cabin."

"Even a few days after his wife was murdered?"

"I agree that something doesn't add up. But it could have been arranged before all this happened. The point is that Silvia Freud is there now."

They followed the road until they were a few hundred yards from where the green car was parked; the cabin was still hidden by the trees. They pulled into a wide turnout and stopped.

"We'll walk from here," he said.

"Have you got your weapon?" she asked.

"Weapon?" he said, baffled. "What weapon? You're not referring to my irresistible charm, are you?" For a moment he wondered where all these jokes were coming from. He'd never been funny before. At least not at work, and he rarely made Anniken laugh.

"Your gun, you big baboon," she said.

They were still talking like they were from two different worlds. He saw that he'd have to explain more clearly.

"You're not in Texas now," he said.

"Virginia," she corrected.

"You're not there either. In Norway the police don't go around playing cowboy."

"So what do you do when you have to arrest psychotic thrill killers?"

"Well," he said. "Either we fill out a form in triplicate and check out something to shoot with, which I neglected to do this time, or else we're damned careful." He got out of the car.

She followed him.

"And what do you think you're doing?" he asked.

"I thought I'd be damned careful, too," said Felicia Stone.

"All right then," he said. "Just remember, this isn't Texas."

This time she didn't correct him. She got the metaphor.

From the road they walked through the woods toward the cabin. They headed up a rise that sloped gently from where they'd parked, and then dropped steeply down toward the cabin on the other side. From the top they could see the cabin through the trees. It turned out to be an old log cabin with a sod roof. Something an archaeologist and a librarian would enjoy living in, Singsaker thought. The cabin seemed well kept. So did the outhouse, which was newer than the cabin and looked like something Jens Dahle might have built himself. The cabin stood in a clearing with tall grass and wildflowers growing all around. The dirt driveway was as muddy as Isak Krangsås said, which was why Silvia Freud had parked out on the road. They hunkered down in the moss to watch. Felicia Stone had plucked a blade of grass and was chewing on it. They were both getting soaked.

Then the cabin door opened. It was a weathered pine door that looked as though somebody long ago had probably had plans to stain it but never got around to it. The door opened slowly, with a suppressed creak. A tall man in a gray jacket and Italian shoes came out onto the thick slate flagstone placed in front of the door. He stretched and looked around, then held out a hand to confirm that it was still raining. She recognized him at once.

"Nevins," she said.

"I assumed he'd already left the country," said Singsaker, look-ing at her lips cautiously sucking on the blade of grass. A raindrop dripped from the end of it onto her wet jogging shoes.

"It's obvious that he still has something to do here," she said.

Nevins moved toward the outhouse. It had two doors. On one hung a big red heart. He opened it and went inside.

"Come on, let's catch him with his pants down," Singsaker said.

Instead of going straight down the steep hill where trees were packed densely together at the bottom, they moved along a ridge down to the rear of the outhouse. Felicia moved as silently as an ermine through the brush. He couldn't say for sure which forest animal he resembled most, but they both reached the rear wall be-fore Nevins emerged from the outhouse. He probably hadn't heard them. They slowly crept around to the front. There they took up position on either side of the door. Singsaker noticed with satisfac-tion that the cabin across the clearing had no windows facing them.

He held up three fingers. Then two. Then only one. When he bent down the last finger to a fist, she took hold of the door handle and pulled. There was a loud bang and a sharp creak as if some-thing were about to break. The door was fastened inside. For two seconds there was silence. Then they heard Nevins inside. He had stood up and was fumbling with his clothes. Felicia grabbed the handle again and yanked on the door. This time the door's bolt yielded and the outhouse door flew open with a crash. Nevins fell toward them with his pants halfway down his thighs. Felicia was quicker than Singsaker and tackled Nevins. She grabbed his right arm and twisted it up to the middle of his back. He lay there gasp-ing, but he didn't yell. Singsaker pulled out his handcuffs and locked them onto Nevins's hands, first one, then the other. It looked like something he'd done many times before.

"Not a sound, Nevins," she said. Then she looked up at Sing-saker. "Maybe you should read him his rights?"

"Here in Norway those things are taken for granted. Besides, strictly speaking we've broken a couple of rules already," he said with a glance at Nevins's naked butt.

She understood what he was hinting at and pulled up Nevins's pants.

"Take him over to the car, would you?" Singsaker said.

She pulled Nevins up by his forearm to a standing position. Only now did he appear to collect himself enough to realize who was arresting him. He stared at her in fright.

"You? Here?"

"You didn't expect that, did you? I can explain in more detail in the police car. Come with me."

"But first, I'd like to know who's in the cabin," said Singsaker. Nevins looked at him as if he'd materialized out of nowhere. There was resignation in his eyes . He was an intelligent man. Smart enough to know when the jig was up.

"Miss Freud is inside. She's . . ."

"I know very well who she is," he said. "Anyone else?"

Nevins stood there silently staring at the Norwegian police officer.

"No, only her," he said.

"Has she got a weapon?"

"No," Nevins replied.

Singsaker saw no reason to believe that he was telling the truth.

Nevins looked down at the ground and submissively allowed Felicia Stone to lead him down the path. His Italian designer shoes squished through the mud.

Silvia Freud stood waiting for him with a crowbar as Singsaker opened the door and burst into the room. The blow struck him on the shoulder, and he dove to the floor as he felt pain shoot down one side of his body. He lay there waiting for the next blow. Instead she stepped over him and disappeared out the door he had just come in.

With a hand on his bruised shoulder he turned to see where she was going. He caught a glimpse of her as she vanished up the road where Felicia Stone and Nevins had been walking just a minute earlier.

He leaped to his feet and tore off after her. The slush sprayed up around his shoes as he ran from the cabin toward the cars. When he reached the road his pants were covered with mud up to his knees. He got there just in time to see Silvia Freud jump into the green Nissan. Fifty yards farther away he saw Felicia Stone leading Nevins to the police car.

Then his phone rang. He grabbed it and looked at the display. It was Lars calling.

"What the hell kind of timing is this!" Singsaker yelled, blocking the call.

At the same moment Freud started her car and spun it around in reverse until the car was pointing toward Stone and Nevins. She stopped and gunned the engine in idle. It looked like she was fumbling to get the car in gear. For a moment he hoped she would kill the engine. Then she floored it. She raced toward Stone, but the American detective was alert. With a firm grip on Nevins's neck she dragged him with her into the ditch just in time, as Silvia Freud raced past and zoomed up the road. Singsaker ran till he reached Stone. She was crawling out of the ditch along with the deathly pale American conservator.

"Take the car and follow her!" she shouted. "I'll go with Nevins up to the farm."

He gave her a thumbs-up and ran to the car. As he got in he saw the green Nissan vanish into a patch of woods in the distance.

"You know what I like best about the *Johannes Book*?" The two loathsome eyes were staring at Vatten.

"It's the story about the curse," he went on. "My theory is that

Broder Lysholm Knudtzon somehow found out what the *Johannes Book* really was—the confessions of a murderer. Maybe it dawned on him that it was written on the victim's own skin. I don't know. The sanctimonious fool wanted to get rid of the book. The tale about the curse was just a pretext. It arose from a strange compulsion that people have to demonize all new ideas. But whether it's nonsense or not, the curse fits in so well with what I've done that I wish I'd thought of it myself. But I'm not a curse. I'm someone who wants to see what he has seen."

Vatten couldn't understand what suddenly came over him. He laughed. A desperate and yet liberating laugh. It occurred to him that he'd only suffered this badly a few times before in his life. Sometime during that evening with Gunn Brita. Once in a bed long ago—he and Hedda. Their first attempt at making love. The only condom he'd brought had ripped the second time he tried to put it on. She suggested a blow job. "Do you want me to suck you until you come?" she'd said. His answer was to laugh recklessly. Strangely enough, they ended up together anyway. Then there was Edvard's birth. And his father's funeral. He had stood before the altar in Horten Church to make a speech. He'd intended to start with a funny story about the time his father had skinny-dipped at Vollane. He didn't manage to get through the story, which ended with two old ladies and a Scotch terrier, before he burst out laughing. He was the only one in the church who laughed, emptying his thundering laughter into the silence. Hedda had finally rescued him and pulled him back to his seat. The pastor somehow managed to make his father's funeral a dignified occasion. And everything was interpreted in the framework of grief, so that Vatten's laughter was regarded as an expression of deep sorrow. That was true, but not entirely.

Now he was laughing like that again. For the last time. When his laughter subsided, it would all be over.

Chief Inspector Singsaker raced along the narrow, winding roads of Ørland in the direction he thought Silvia Freud had gone, until suddenly Austrått Manor came into view. The Renaissance structure was beautifully situated among green meadows that stretched down toward the fjord, with a private marina where most of the boats had been taken in for the winter. Yet the only thing he noticed was a little green car parked in front of the main gate to the castle. He parked next to it.

The entrance to Austrått Manor was a huge, heavy portal made of dark wood, with a smaller door cut into it. The larger door was surrounded by a slate framework in which coats of arms were carved. When he got out of the car he noticed that the smaller door was ajar. He went over to it, pulled it open all the way, and entered the castle. There, in the middle of the courtyard, stood a distinguished middle-aged man with a well-trimmed beard wearing a suit that he certainly hadn't bought at the Dressmann's menswear store. It must have been tailor-made for the man sometime before he acquired that hint of a potbelly that made the suit bulge. Singsaker couldn't take his eyes off the man's bright red bow tie.

"That was some wild driving," said the man, his indignation mixed with a humor that couldn't quite be quelled.

"I'm from the police," Singsaker said, patting his breast pocket without taking out his ID.

"Well, I must say," said the man without entirely losing the gleam in his eye. "Is there a police manhunt under way?"

"Did you see a woman enter the property here?"

"I did," said the man. "But the castle isn't open today. I'm the caretaker here. The name's Gunnar Winsnes. I was careless enough to leave some of the doors unlocked. I just went inside to see to a couple of practical matters."

Singsaker looked at him and couldn't make the adjective "practical" jibe with his appearance.

"Which way did she go?" he asked brusquely.

"She went into the main building. I'm afraid I unlocked that door, too." He pointed up a staircase that led to another one and an entryway with pillars and a red door. "Impertinent woman. I tried to greet her politely."

"She's more than just impertinent, I'm afraid," said Singsaker. "I'll have to ask you to leave the area."

Gunnar Winsnes gave him a shocked look.

"And what are you planning to do?"

"I'm going to do what the police do," he said. "Arrest her."

"Alone?" asked the caretaker.

"You see anyone else around?" he asked, then nodded toward the exit to show that he wanted the man to leave.

The caretaker slunk toward the main gate.

Damn, why didn't I bring my service pistol? Singsaker thought, heading for the stairs. But who could have guessed that a brief interview with a farmer would end in a chase of a suspect?

When he reached the top of the stairs he stopped, breathing hard, and looked at the door uncertainly. He didn't trust Nevins's claim that Silvia Freud was unarmed, but she'd hit him with a crowbar. Would she have used it if she had something more effective on her? In any case, it showed that she was capable of inflicting injury. He pictured the crowbar striking him in the head, maybe right on his surgical scar, flinging his head back, his worries about the brain tumor losing all meaning, and then tumbling down the stairs he had just climbed.

He fumbled his cell phone from his pocket. Brattberg. I need to call her, he thought. She'd probably order backup sent out from the sheriff's office in Brekstad within five minutes. Instead he just stood there studying a row of wooden statues that were carved into the castle wall right beneath him. Allegorical figures from a time when people spoke a different language. He had no idea what they were supposed to represent. Suddenly he felt dizzy. Shit, he thought, I don't need this. Then he turned back toward the door and opened it.

"Do you know what gave you away?" Felicia Stone asked. She was trying not to gloat. She just wanted Nevins to say something, because although they could see the Krangsås farm, it was over half a mile away. And after Singsaker had driven off into the woods, the silence had become overwhelming.

Nevins didn't answer.

"You said you didn't know about Scandinavian book collections. Why did you lie about that? It's always the unnecessary lies that give people away. Or maybe you wanted to get caught. You were the one who showed me the inscription with Knudtzon's name, which is what led us to Norway. Have you been playing some kind of cat-and-mouse game with the police, Nevins?"

Nevins continued to walk in silence beside her, his hands still cuffed behind him. She had a tight grip on his arm, but she wasn't afraid he would try to run. He was as much in unfamiliar territory as she was. They walked a long way before he suddenly decided to break his silence.

"There was one thing you said that almost made me put this whole idiotic purchase on ice."

"Purchase, is that what you call it?"

"Yes, that's my only involvement. I was at a conference here last spring, actually, it was an exchange program, because the university library in Trondheim had sent a delegate to our conference a few weeks before. It just happened to be that librarian who was killed here in Norway, just like Bond was in Richmond. But I didn't have much to do with her. The fact of the matter is that I met Silvia Freud on my first visit to Norway, and she offered me this book. I let myself be tempted. I've always been an obsessive book collector, and I have plenty of money, so it seemed like a perfect opportunity. But you almost changed my mind."

"How?"

"I knew in advance that I could never let the book be seen. That was part of the bargain. But there was something oddly convincing about what you told me in Richmond. About collecting being the same as hiding something from the rest of the world. Still, I couldn't stop myself. Especially not after Bond discovered those palimpsests. I helped him more with interpreting the texts than I let on. Bond probably found out more than I did eventually, but I understood enough. I was sure that the palimpsests had something to do with the *Johannes Book,* and that it had a history that other books I knew about could not compete with. It was almost as though the book were alive, with its own secret life. I wanted to get to know it. Does that sound stupid?"

"Maybe not stupid, but perverse and self-centered."

"When you decide to commit a crime, you open up a space inside yourself that wasn't open before. A space not meant for anyone but yourself. Some people like having an internal space in which the rules are different from those in the rest of the world. Maybe I'm one of them. That's why the thought of keeping the *Johannes Book* to myself was an idea I could live with."

She was astonished by this sudden honesty. It was difficult not to feel a certain sympathy for him. Most likely he was a better man than his son. But just as much a lawbreaker.

"How odd that you would be the one to catch me," he said. "A friend of Shaun's."

"Shaun and I went to school together," said Felicia Stone, "but we weren't friends." She regretted her words the moment she said them. This was the start of a conversation, and she had no idea where it would end. The response she got from Nevins was astounding.

"There are two types of people," he said, looking pensive. "Those who like Shaun and those who don't. It's been that way ever since he was a kid. At first I didn't understand it. I thought that some people just didn't get him. But as time went on, I found out why. There are actually at least two versions of Shaun Nevins. And one of them is not easy to like, not even for a father. And now an accusation has been lodged."

"Accusation?"

"I don't know why I'm telling you this," said Nevins, "but there's probably not much honor left in this family anyways. Sexual harassment. That's what the charge is. A legal secretary at Shaun's office made the most disgusting accusations. A father should always support his son, but I still can't help thinking that her accusations are probably true. Does that make me a bad father?"

Felicia Stone had experienced this before. After a criminal has been exposed, after the person has admitted his crime, he might suddenly decide to bare his soul completely. And it struck her how similar everyone became when they'd been exposed, as Nevins was now. There was no difference between an educated, sophisticated man of letters and a cold-blooded killer or a pimp.

But it was different this time. All those years she had thought that Shaun Nevins had evaded punishment, and that she was the only one who knew what a devil he was behind that slick mask. It turned out that he hadn't managed to conceal it very well after all. Shit stinks. Even his own father could smell it.

She looked up toward the Krangsås farm. They were approaching the gate to the courtyard.

"I have no idea what kind of father you've been, Nevins. But seeing your son for what he is doesn't make you a bad father."

"He's getting divorced. He'll get a suspended sentence, but he'll lose his license to practice law for an indefinite period. I'm not proud of him, although I think I still like him. Strangely enough."

"Maybe it can be a new start for both of you," she said flatly. It felt as though a blood clot had loosened somewhere in her midsection. As if fresh blood had suddenly gained access to new regions in her stomach. Perhaps it was relief. The wish to do Nevins harm had abruptly vanished. Now the police in Norway were in charge. She was done with him.

Lady Inger von Austrått of Austrått Manor was engaged in a personal feud with the mighty archbishop of Nidaros, Olav Engelbrektsson, throughout much of the Reformation in Norway, up until the archbishop fled the country in 1537. But he did not go to the Netherlands empty-handed: He took with him a great deal of church property. On his way down Trondheim Fjord he also made a last raid on his archenemy, the iron lady of Austrått. He plundered the castle of valuable treasures. Today the only object from Lady Inger's era that has been preserved at the castle is the chandelier that hangs in the entry hall of the main building. The chandelier is an exquisite piece of Renaissance craftsmanship, designed to resemble the voluminous sleeves typical of Renaissance attire.

When Chief Inspector Singsaker entered the main wing of Austrått Manor, the first thing he saw was a pair of sandals. They were gold and looked expensive. Could they be Prada? Silvia Freud was a well-dressed woman. When he looked up, he saw what was hanging above the sandals: trousers and a flowered blouse. Around her neck was a rope. The rope was fastened to the chandelier. Silvia

Freud's face was pale, like a well-made-up Renaissance maiden. She had stopped breathing several minutes before Singsaker came in the door. Normally he could tolerate the sight of a dead body. But there was something about this scene that made him feel sick. Maybe it was all the running. He turned and went outside on the steps. There he stopped and leaned over the elegant wrought-iron railing. The contents of his stomach remained in place. His breathing gradually slowed.

Then he went down to the castle courtyard and exited the building. Winsnes was standing outside smoking. Singsaker had never smoked, but he envied him that cigarette.

"Is the hunt over?" asked the caretaker.

"It's over. But don't go back into the main building before the police and an ambulance arrive. A woman hanged herself in there."

Winsnes gasped. Then he nodded and took another drag on his smoke.

Singsaker called Brattberg and told her what had happened.

"I hear what you're saying," she said. "But there are a few things in your explanation that definitely concern me."

"Such as?"

"First of all: What is this American doing with you out there? And second: What were you thinking when you took off by yourself to follow Silvia Freud? The last time I checked, we weren't in America or on some TV cop show."

"Multitasking," he said. "I brought Felicia along to save time."

"Felicia. So you're on a first-name basis now, is that what you're saying?" Brattberg's voice was sharper than usual.

"She's nice," he said, feeling even more sheepish.

"She can be as nice as she wants. But in this country she's a civilian. How could you leave Nevins in her custody? The way things look, he's a key witness—if not a suspect."

"I understand your reaction," he said. "But I trust her. She's a damned good police officer. She's not going to let Nevins get away. What we need now is some people out here to Austrått Castle and a car at the Krangsås farm so that we can formally arrest Nevins."

"And do we have any specific reason to arrest him?"

"What about public indecency? We found him with his pants around his knees," said Singsaker, trying to lighten the mood.

The silence on the other end revealed that he hadn't succeeded.

"Okay, we won't arrest him, we'll just bring him in for questioning, OK?" Singsaker said.

"I'll make a few calls," said Brattberg, and he could tell she'd started to calm down. "Call me if you come up with anything else. And by that I mean before you think up something dumb on your own."

"Okay, boss," he said.

"Trouble with the boss?" The museum caretaker had come over to him. His familiar tone was off-putting.

"Nothing that won't pass," said Singsaker.

"There's a strange sound coming from the green car over there— the one she came in. Can you hear it?"

"What sound?"

At first he heard nothing but the rustling of the wind in the oak trees that surrounded the castle, along with some traffic noise in the distance. Out on the fjord someone had started up a boat. Then he heard it. A thudding noise. As if someone was banging on the inside of the trunk. He walked slowly toward the car as he tried to locate the sound. It was coming from the trunk. Good Lord, there's somebody in there! he thought. When he got over to the car he opened the door on the driver's side and saw that the key was in the ignition. He took it out, then went to open the trunk. The pounding got stronger as he put the key in the lock and turned it. The trunk popped open with a bang. A blond head appeared.

"Siri Holm," he said, taking the gag from her mouth.

"Odd Singsaker," she said. "Shouldn't we be on a first-name basis?" She laughed. She sounded both relieved and a bit shaken. He helped her out of the cramped trunk. Her hands were tied, but not her feet.

"God, it's good to see you," she said, after he removed the rope from her hands. She wrapped her arms around his neck. He held her and cautiously stroked her back.

"How did you get here?" he asked.

"I've been such an idiot," she said.

"I think you'll have to explain in more detail," he said. "But we'll do that at the Krangsås farm." He looked at Winsnes, who'd been watching the whole scene with interest from a distance. "A police car is on the way," Singsaker called. "Hold the fort. Nobody goes in until they get here."

"Easy enough. There's no one here," Winsnes said, throwing out his arms as he stared out over the wet, dark green, and mostly empty landscape that surrounded the castle.

When they got to the Krangsås farm, they met two policewomen who were about to drive off with Nevins. He was no longer handcuffed and seemed a little more confident.

"He's agreed to cooperate," said one of the police officers, a short woman with Persian features. "Trondheim told us to bring him to headquarters for questioning. But I think he's already told the American detective what you need to know." She pointed toward the steps of the Krangsås house, where Felicia stood, gazing at them impatiently.

"Keep an eye on him on the ferry," said Singsaker.

"No ferry," said the Persian one. "Strict orders from Trondheim. We're driving the long way around the fjord."

"So we don't really trust him after all?"

"Apparently not," she replied. Then she put a motherly hand over Nevins's bald spot to get him into the back of the cruiser.

Singsaker and Siri Holm stood there and watched as the car drove out of the courtyard. Felicia Stone came over to them.

"They said he'll probably be charged with receiving stolen property and accessory to grand larceny," she said, pointing after the police car.

"Is that all?" he said.

"Most likely," she said. "That might be enough. I've heard that the prisons in this country are more like resorts anyway."

"You don't seem very enthusiastic about Nevins."

"It's personal."

There was no reason to press her. She'd handled Nevins by the book.

"This is Siri Holm," he said, introducing Siri, who had been listening calmly the whole time. Now she shook hands with Felicia and said it was nice to meet her. She spoke English with a melodious and surprisingly correct American accent.

"Let's go inside," he said. "I assume you two know more about this whole situation than I do."

They sat down in the Krangsås living room in front of a new serving of waffles—Felicia Stone, Siri Holm, and Odd Singsaker.

"Don't people eat any real food out here in the country? I could really use a burger before we get going," Felicia Stone whispered as Elin Krangsås went out to the kitchen for coffee. Singsaker chuckled, gave Siri Holm an embarrassed look. With a nod, he gave her the OK to start talking.

Siri began her story: "On that Saturday, the day of the murder,

I went down to Silvia Freud's office. Gunn Brita had mentioned that she was working. I went there mostly to say hello. I was new on the job and wanted to get to know everyone as quickly as possible. When I got there, she was working on the copy of the *Johannes Book*. She had the real book out and was working off it. I didn't consider that unusual at the time. If anyone would have permission to work directly with the artifact, it would be the conservator. But there were some peculiar details. I had come into the office without knocking. I'm sure you've been down to the basement yourself, Odd. Lots of doors and no names on them. You go knock on all of them until you get an answer. So bam! I burst in and came across her working in her office. She reacted as though my sudden appearance had pushed her stress level to the max. It was something about the tone of her voice, a little too friendly. I didn't really think much about it at the time. I just assumed she was the type who makes a little too much effort in social situations. It was only much later that I began to mull it over. I noticed that the *Johannes Book* was in the vault when we discovered the murder a few days later. So the question was, When did Silvia Freud put the book back?"

"It must have been early on Saturday when you saw her working on the book," said Singsaker. "She could have put it back well before the murder."

"That's true. And that's what I thought at first, too. But I asked Jon Vatten about it when we all gathered in Knudtzon Hall, before you came to get him. He told me that nobody had been inside the book vault after we spoke with each other on that Saturday. He was positive about that, because everyone who enters the vault had to be let in and accompanied by him and Gunn Brita. Besides, he didn't think that the *Johannes Book* had been loaned out to Silvia. Not for at least a week."

"How do you know that Vatten wasn't lying?"

"I didn't know for sure. I did have a feeling that he was holding something back. But why wouldn't he tell me if he had helped the conservator return a book to the vault? And everything became much more interesting if he was telling the truth. Because that would mean that either Silvia Freud was sitting in her office copying a copy, or the book I had seen in the book vault when we discovered Gunn Brita was not the original."

"But who would put a copy in the vault?" he asked.

"Isn't it obvious? Silvia Freud. The plan was simple. In the book vault she puts a copy that is so good that nobody can tell at first glance that it's not genuine. If anyone wanted to have the book checked more closely, she would most likely be assigned the task. The plan for the book was that it would stay in the vault and not be touched. She could arrange a theft of the real copy, that is, the one she was working on when I surprised her, which was supposed to be used in the exhibition. After the exhibition the copy could simply be lost, something that would probably not be investigated very thoroughly, since it was just a copy that could be replaced. If somebody long afterward discovered that the original in the book vault had been switched with a book that wasn't the real thing, no one would know who had switched it, since it would have long since vanished. The police would have no fresh leads to follow; the book would have been sold to some narcissistic book collector with a private safe; and Silvia would have conveniently found another job with a more prestigious book collection on the Continent."

"That might have worked, but don't underestimate the police," said Singsaker.

"I'm not," said Siri Holm. "But the plan was so good that it could have succeeded. So good that two smart people like Silvia Freud and

John Nevins were willing to risk it. No crime is without a certain risk, but the odds were on their side. At least, until the plan was turned upside down by a murder at the worst possible moment."

"But that would mean that Silvia Freud has nothing to do with the murders. Is that what you think?"

"Yes, don't you?"

"Yes, I suppose so," he said.

"And Nevins isn't the murderer either," said Felicia Stone, who had been sitting and listening quietly until now. "He's the narcissistic book collector who was going to buy the book. He's already confessed to that. He first met Silvia Freud when he was in Trondheim at a book conference several months ago. Then, pretending that he was going to Frankfurt, he traveled back to Europe and took the train, which is far more anonymous than a plane, from Germany to Norway to finalize the deal. While he was here, the whole deal fell apart. First because of this murder, and then because you got mixed up in it." She looked at Siri.

"You were the one who took the copy out of the book vault, weren't you?" said Singsaker.

"I did. I sneaked into the vault. It wasn't that difficult, since I had looked over Jon's shoulder when he entered his code the first time we went in there. Jon Vatten is a good man but a poor security chief."

He thought it was fairly cold-blooded of her to have remembered Vatten's code when, just seconds later, they discovered a flayed corpse inside the vault. But he didn't say anything. Siri Holm seemed to be a rare kind: one who could be simultaneously rational and emotional—and not be ashamed of it.

She went on: "It wasn't hard to see that the book was a counterfeit. You could tell from the threads used to bind the book. Silvia had done a good job with almost everything, but she had done a rush job on sewing the binding. The thread was nylon and obviously not old. The plan was to confront her with what I knew. I arranged to meet her at the Egon bar at Prinsen Hotel. When I got there, things didn't go according to plan."

Singsaker sat there thinking of how close he'd been to running into Siri Holm at the Prinsen. Maybe he could have prevented the whole mess there and then.

"Nevins was with her," she went on. "The two of them asked me to go out to the car with them, so we could speak in private. Fool that I was, I agreed. If we hadn't been sitting in the back seat of the cramped Nissan, they never would have been able to overpower me."

Singsaker thought back to the black belt on the tae kwon do outfit Siri had at home.

She went on with her story. "But a blow to the back of my head with something heavy was all it took. When I came to, I was in the trunk of the car, bound and gagged. First they drove a little way out of town. I got a glimpse of the surroundings when they opened the trunk in a deserted parking lot, removed the gag, and talked to me. I think we were somewhere near Trolla. They wanted me to put the copy back in the book vault. I refused, telling them that the plan was already blown, and that there was no going back. Apparently they realized I was right. They shoved me back in the trunk and drove out here. They only opened it twice after that, so I could go to the toilet and drink a little water. You can imagine what it was like to be squeezed into a fetal position for over twenty-four hours. When you caught up with them, they were probably planning some kind of escape. I have no idea what they were going to do with me. But I don't think either of them is a killer."

"And the book?"

"Both books—both the genuine *Johannes Book* that Silvia stole and the copy I took from the book vault—are safely stowed in Jens Dahle's cabin, as far as I know."

"Do you know why they chose that particular cabin?"

"I heard Silvia tell Nevins that she had a key to it. She borrowed it a few weeks ago from Gunn Brita and hadn't given it back. It was probably just a good place to hide out while they planned their next move."

All three of them sat there in silence. Singsaker munched on a waffle and started to share Felicia's craving for a burger.

"But there's one thing I wonder about," he said. "Why the hell didn't you tell me anything about this when I was at your place taking your statement?" The way he said "taking your statement" sounded stiff and awkward in English, and he looked over at Felicia to make sure that she hadn't noticed.

"I did just say that I'd been a fool. I admit it. I've probably read too many mysteries. I thought I'd solved the crime, but I wanted to be sure before I went to the police. But it turns out I'm better at solving fictional cases."

"Obviously. It didn't occur to you that police work depends on experience, among other things?"

"Go ahead, rub it in. But there's one thing we can all learn from this situation," she said with smug confidence. "This case does have one thing in common with many crime novels."

"What's that?"

"Diversion. The case of Silvia Freud and this Nevins guy has nothing to do with the murders. The killer is still out there, and poor Jon is still missing, while we're sitting here talking and wasting time."

"But how can you be so sure that Jon Vatten isn't the killer?" Felicia Stone asked.

"Don't tell me," said Singsaker. "You just know it, right?"

"That's right," said Siri Holm. "I just know it."

He could tell that Felicia liked the young, bold librarian. He wasn't sure whether this was a good thing or not.

His cell phone rang. It was Lars again. This time Singsaker turned the phone all the way off.

29

At *that moment Isak* Krangsås came into the living room. He had been in the cowshed and was standing on the dark-brown hardwood floor in manure-covered boots.

"So, have you made any progress?" he asked in Norwegian.

"We've taken quite a detour," replied Singsaker, also in Norwegian. In a way it seemed absurd to speak English with the sturdy farmer.

"There's one thing I always thought was a little odd about this whole *Johannes Book* matter," Krangsås said. "I've heard some things about the book. I've signed a bunch of papers, and I've received letters of thanks from the Gunnerus Library, the whole deal. But I never heard anything more about the knives."

"The knives?" said Singsaker, straightening up. He noticed that Siri Holm did the same.

"Yes. I had a big leather bundle full of knives, and there were some drills in there, too. According to my father, they apparently belonged with the *Johannes Book*. The gentleman who came here to the farm with the book also brought these knives. They were very old, but many of them were in good condition. I gave them to Jens Dahle when he took the *Johannes Book*. I thought I would hear more about them, too. A book with a bunch of knives as accessories, that's a really good story. But it was like the knives just disappeared."

"Did any of these knives look like a scalpel?" Singsaker asked eagerly.

"Yes. Several of them could have been surgical instruments, but old-fashioned ones. I wouldn't let a doctor use them on me, I'll tell you that."

Several thoughts began whirling around in Singsaker's head.

"This farm that belonged to Jens Dahle's parents," he said, just to start somewhere. "Where is it located?"

"It's down by the fjord. Just keep going down the road that goes past the first cabin, the way you drove before."

"The first cabin?"

"Yes. The second cabin was built where the Dahle farm once was. The whole farm burned down. That's how Jens's parents died. They say it was arson, but they never caught the person who did it. Jens built a cabin on the property several years later. So when Jens Dahle talks about the cabin, it's the place on the old Dahle farm he's talking about. The place that Gunn Brita's family owned they call 'the storehouse' for some reason. Don't ask me why. The family always lived at the storehouse whenever they were out here together. The cabin was Jens's place. Somewhere he could be alone. Gunn Brita said that Jens didn't like her to go there with him. But I don't think it mattered to her. 'A man needs a place to himself,' she said."

"Does that mean that if Jens Dahle's kids say that he was at the cabin, they mean the place down by the water?" asked Singsaker, the pieces beginning to fall into place.

"That's right," said Krangsås.

"Do you know if the couple would ever leave the kids alone in the cabin, I mean, the storehouse?"

"The kids are quite independent. I don't think they would have had any problem being alone for a few hours. They would have just played with those little game machines, I think. Isn't that what kids do these days?"

"Do you know if Jens Dahle has a boat at the second cabin?" Siri Holm broke in.

"Yes, he does. One of those really fast speedboats. He uses it sometimes to go to the city. He says it doesn't take any longer than driving his car."

"In other words: If he wanted to get back and forth to Trondheim in a few hours without being registered electronically anywhere, he could simply take the boat? And if anyone asked the kids where he'd been, they would say that he was at the cabin?"

A text came in with a ping. Felicia Stone took out her iPhone from the pocket of her all-weather jacket, which she hadn't taken off, and read what it said.

"Well, anything's possible, I suppose," Krangsås said. "You don't think that Jens Dahle has anything to do with this case, do you? He's not the type. He's such a calm and rational person."

Felicia cleared her throat.

"I can see that you're in the midst of a serious conversation," she said, in English. "I have no idea what you're talking about, but I think you ought to hear this, Odd."

"OK," he said impatiently.

"The names you asked me to check for entry to the USA around the time of the murder in Richmond," she went on.

"Let me guess. You got a hit on Jens Dahle."

"How did you know?" Felicia asked, looking at him with something that approached admiration but maybe was just surprise.

"If you understood Norwegian, you would have known, too," he said. "Come on, I'll explain in the car." He got up and walked toward the door.

The last thing he said before leaving the room was directed at Siri Holm:

"No, you stay here." It bothered him that he sounded like her father.

"But why me? Isn't this all a mistake?" said Vatten. "Don't you know I'm the prime suspect in the case? If you'd left me alone, I probably would have been arrested, and you'd never be caught."

Jens Dahle had hung Vatten from a roof beam in the cabin. He was hanging by his feet with his head about three feet above the floor. There he hung, looking at his killer upside down. The perspective made Dahle seem somehow supernatural.

"Maybe. But I did make one mistake, and that was not finishing you off," said Dahle, studying the tip of a scalpel. "First of all, you had sex with that fat whore. But you didn't think you could get away with it, did you? Don't you think I noticed the bottle of red wine and the two glasses when I came to the library last Saturday? Who do you think cleaned that up? I got a confession out of her before I cut her throat. Nice of you two to leave the book vault open for me. I was able to do the whole job inside and then lock it afterward. That's how I got such a head start on the police."

"I can't remember, but I think you're right. I did have sex with your wife. But wouldn't a prison sentence for murder have been punishment enough?"

"I thought so, at first. But I'd made a mistake. Do you remember the bit of parchment I sent you after I killed your family? Do you remember what was written on it?"

This is the first time he's openly admitting it, Vatten thought. Ever since he saw Gunn Brita's corpse, he'd known that the same person had killed Hedda and Edvard. But here at last was the confession.

" 'The center of the universe is everywhere and its circumference nowhere,' " Vatten said.

"That's right. I knew you had a good memory. Well, I was sloppy and talked a little too much about that quotation to a detective. That it wasn't very smart of me. I know you didn't tell the police about the parchment. That says a lot about you. But if, at some point, once you no longer saw any way to avoid being convicted of the murders, you might have changed your mind. And if you showed the parchment to the police, I'm afraid this Singsaker might remember our conversation."

"I burned it. It was Hedda's skin," Vatten said.

Dahle was utterly still. Vatten could hardly hear him breathing. The blood was throbbing in his temples. How long can someone hang upside down before he passes out? he wondered.

"Well, it doesn't matter," Dahle said at last. "I really brought you here because I want to finish what I started. When I'm done with you, the rest won't matter. Oh, and the parchment wasn't from your wife. It was a little piece from the boy's back. A first-class specimen. So soft and supple."

Now everything was about to go black for Vatten. Only his rage kept him from fainting.

"You must be wondering why I took them. I don't know if it will be any consolation if I tell you that it was random. I'd seen all of you in the neighborhood many times, and I knew your routines: You often came home late from work; she seldom locked the door. Do you remember all the newspaper articles about how they vanished without a trace? That was just luck. Beginner's luck. It wasn't planned well. That afternoon I opened the gate, went to the front door, and rang the bell. When she opened the door, the boy was standing by her side. I hit her on the head with the crowbar and tossed her right into the trunk of my car. I had to chase the boy through the house. But he thought the way most kids do. I found him under the bed and dragged him out by his hair. A kick to his head was enough to subdue him. Then I put him in the trunk next to his mother and drove off. I remember how amused I was with that eyewitness who claimed he'd been sitting on his balcony all evening. Before I moved in on your place, I sat and watched him. He was drinking beer and went inside every fifteen minutes to get another one. Apparently he stopped to take a leak each time, too. He was inside the apartment almost as much as he was outside on the balcony. Why the police trusted his account, I have no idea. When he went back for his fourth beer, I began, and managed to finish the job before he came back out. To this day I don't know why he told the police he'd been sitting on the balcony the whole time. I'll probably never know. As I said, beginner's luck. It wasn't a sophisticated plan, just a gamble that succeeded."

Vatten was seeing double now. Jens Dahle had two heads. He saw two whetstones and two scalpels. He couldn't tell which one was real and which was the hallucination. For some reason his thoughts turned to Silvia Freud, the bookbinder and conservator at the library. The last time he talked to her she was working on producing a copy of the *Johannes Book*. He recalled that she'd showed it to him, and he couldn't see any difference between the copy and the real book. And now, here was Jens Dahle. But what did it matter that his murders were copies of historical murders? Had that meant anything at all for Hedda and Edvard? Without knowing why, he saw Hedda before him at her sewing machine. She often liked to sit there, sewing. Making clothes for Edvard and him. It occurred to Vatten that she had sewn the pants he was wearing. Corduroy pants. He doesn't take the pants off, he thought, picturing Gunn Brita's corpse, which had been flayed with her pants on. Fortunately he doesn't take our pants off. That was a peculiar form of triumph. His vision was getting hazier. Still, he managed to ask one last question:

"Why?"

"Why?" Jens Dahle emitted a creepy laugh. "You're asking more than is good for you to know, Vatten. You'll never understand me.

You'll never understand the obsession, or the longing for a completely open human being. For muscles, sinews, blood vessels that are still pumping blood, the breath of a person utterly without a mask. And afterward, words on dead skin. But enough chitchat, Vatten. How do you prefer your scalpel: sharp, medium, or dull?"

"Goddamn it to hell!" Singsaker swore in Norwegian, but continued in English. "Amateurs. We've been a bunch of bloody amateurs. What about some control questions? That's standard routine when you're questioning children. Pappa was at the cabin, you say, but were you two at the cabin with him? So fucking sloppy." The car spit gravel as it roared out of the Krangsås courtyard. After turning onto the road down toward the cabins, he stomped on the gas.

"Take it easy," said Felicia. She didn't mean his driving. "Things have moved so fast in this case. It's only been a few days since the first murder and we already know who did it. It's not easy to interrogate kids. You have to be so cautious, especially when they've just lost their mother."

"It's still a huge misunderstanding, and it gave Jens Dahle an alibi for long enough to do God knows what. I should have interviewed the kids myself."

"Could you please forget about the kids?" she said. "Now we know who the killer is. Focus on that."

"That's exactly what I'm doing," he said with sudden insight. "Why do you think I'm so stressed-out?"

She smiled at him. At that moment her phone chirped.

"New report. Things are really happening fast," she said. They had passed the turnoff to the cabin where Silvia Freud and Nevins had been.

"My people back in Richmond found an unknown e-mail address for Efrahim Bond. After a lot of red tape it seems we've gotten access to the account. Bond's inbox contained only one thing: a love letter from Gunn Brita Dahle. It turns out they had an affair during the conference last spring."

"That's a lot of info they sent you in a text message," Singsaker said.

"Laubach had to send it in two pieces," she said with a smile. "I'm guessing it was Gunn Brita Dahle who put Bond on the trail of this palimpsest in the spine of the Byron book. Apparently he'd invited her to his office and showed her the rare books he had in his possession. She had lots of experience with books. Besides, she knew about Knudtzon, so she noticed something that Bond hadn't seen before. After that they not only had an affair, but they also shared a research project. I guess she spent a few exciting days in Richmond."

"That's the last piece of the puzzle. Where there are love letters, there must also be replies. We thought we were searching for a psychopath with some kind of agenda. Now we have a motive. Jens Dahle found the e-mails from Bond on his wife's PC. Then he decided to kill them. But how does a husband kill his unfaithful wife and her lover without attracting the attention of the police? The only way is to make the police believe that they're searching for something far worse than a jealous husband: a serial killer."

"And in a way we're doing just that," said Felicia Stone. "Because Jens Dahle's method shows that he wasn't just blinded by jealousy. He's had a thrill killer inside him for a long time."

Singsaker had slowed down now, as they approached the fjord. Jens Dahle's cabin was around the next curve. He didn't want to go skidding into the driveway, in case Dahle was there.

"Killers like this can be the best actors in the world," Felicia said. Her tone made it sound like she knew what she was talking about.

"They can make you see almost whatever you want in their faces. Large parts of the life of a sociopath are devoted to mimicking normal emotions. But they're only pretending; they don't really have these feelings. I took a course on serial killers, and the teacher called it a mask of sanity. And in many of them, the mask can be so convincing that not even the police suspect them. There are tons of stories about serial killers who were ruled out of individual cases even though the circumstantial evidence pointed to them. They don't usually get caught until they're linked to several murders. Jens Dahle isn't the first thrill killer who's had a wife and children. Often the family is part of their stage set, but sometimes the family ends up among the victims. A sociopath is unpredictable and knows no boundaries. In TV series and movies we often learn that they follow a definite plan, that they have a fixed MO, or leave some signature at the crime scenes. But that's only partly true. A sociopath has no true personality, as we understand it. He continually adapts to the situation. It doesn't take much for him to change things around. Just look at what happens to them in prison. Many of them become model prisoners, as if they would never hurt a fly."

She was talking as if all this information could somehow get them ready for what they were going to find in Jens Dahle's cabin. Singsaker shifted down to second gear. While Felicia was giving her lecture, they had passed a grove of trees and rounded a rocky hill that ended at a bare slope of glacier-polished stone down by a beach. Beyond the beach was a meadow, and the cabin. It looked relatively new. Stained brown and simply designed on a rectangular lot, one story with a pitched roof, with only one small window facing the road. This window was covered by a dark curtain. From the beach, a wharf jutted into the water, and there was a boat tied up at the dock. The engine seemed much too large for the boat, which was hardly fifteen feet long. Singsaker and Stone didn't need to say anything to each other. He pointed and she nodded. He was afraid they'd soon see everything they already knew about sociopathic killers.

"Do you think he's in the cabin?" Felicia asked.

"I doubt it," he said. "Can't see his car. And the boat must have been here since he was here this weekend. He drove the car home on Monday morning."

"How do we get in?"

"Let's hope we can see something through the windows," he said. "In Norway we have something called probable cause. I think you have the same thing."

She nodded.

"We'll only go in if we see signs of something illegal. If not, we'll phone the local sheriff and do everything by the book, with a search warrant and the whole deal. If we see something that looks like Dahle is at the crime scene, we'll retreat immediately. Even in Norway there are some things we don't do unarmed."

He reached into the back seat and found the crowbar he had borrowed from Silvia Freud's car before he left Austrått.

"Just in case the situation requires it," he explained. They parked on the side of the road and walked the last bit over to the cabin. He led the way, holding the crowbar in his right hand.

It was impossible to see anything through the curtains covering the windows facing the road. So they went around to the front. There they found a door and two more windows, also small. The magnificent view of the Trondheims fjord was shut out. Both windows were covered with the same opaque curtains. But the little window in the door wasn't covered.

Singsaker crept up to it carefully and peered inside. What he saw inside made his stomach turn over. He doubled over to catch his breath. He heard Felicia murmur something behind him, but couldn't make out what she said. Then he straightened up and looked through the window again. The front door led straight into the living room. On one wall there were doors into what were probably two bedrooms. The ceiling was open under the roof in the big living room, so that the straw roof and beams were exposed. A floor lamp was on. He could clearly see the whole room. The only furniture consisted of a rough-hewn table, which was more of a workbench with no chairs around it, a plank bed, a bookcase along one wall, and a recliner in a corner. But no furniture in the world could have distracted his gaze from what was hanging from the center roof beam. A corpse dangled there by the legs, wearing brown corduroy trousers. The torso was flayed from the waist to the neck. This time the head had not been removed, and Singsaker recognized Jon Vatten's curly hair.

He grabbed the door handle, found that it was unlocked, and went inside. Only then did he see that it wasn't yet a corpse. Vatten moved. He could see his exposed muscles tighten, his tendons extend as his arm lifted very, very slowly and pointed at him. Was this an accusation? Blood was trickling and dripping. The drops ran down his body to his arms and neck. Then they slid over the skin on his face and got caught in the hair, which was colored a reddish-black. Fat drops fell from Vatten's curls to the floor, where a big red pool had formed. But the blood wasn't gushing. No large blood vessels had been opened. Where the skin ended at the neck, he saw a blood vessel expanding and contracting. A steadily decreasing amount of blood was still circulating through his system.

Vatten dropped his arm back toward the floor. His lips moved. He whispered something that Singsaker couldn't hear. His eyes were dull but were undoubtedly directed at him. Singsaker went closer to Vatten and squatted down so that they were facing each other. He tried to focus only on Vatten's face, where he still had skin. He cautiously put a hand on the back of Vatten's neck. It felt warm and sweaty.

"I'm so sorry," Singsaker said. The words sounded hollow.

"It's his fault, not yours," Vatten whispered. There was a gurgle in his throat. Singsaker was close enough that he could hear what he was saying. Jon Vatten gave a long and rattling cough before he went on.

"Just promise me one thing. Don't make him into a mythical monster. Don't let him become . . . a celebrity. He's just a wreck of a human being. Nothing more. Not worth writing . . . books about. We were simply unlucky to meet him." He spoke slowly, with long pauses, as if each word was the start of a new marathon.

"You and Gunn Brita?"

"Hedda and Edvard and I," Vatten said.

"Your family—he did that, too?" Singsaker asked. He now knew what hadn't felt right all along in the Vatten case. He knew why he had been so uneasy on the way here. Jon Vatten, with all his contradictions and paradoxes, was in a strange way one of the most believable people he'd ever met. He had landed in the police spotlight because of bad luck and coincidences, and still, for some reason Singsaker had trusted Vatten. He wanted to tell him that. But Vatten beat him to it.

"Promise me one more thing," he said.

"What's that?"

Vatten's last wish was surprising, but oddly made sense.

"Take . . . my bike. It was a gift from Hedda, and I should have taken better care of it."

A brief, dull smile slid across his lips. Then he coughed. A rivulet of blood ran down from the corner of his mouth and into his nose. Then he went still.

Singsaker wanted to say something else to him. But what should he say? That his killer had been higher up on his list of suspects? Would that make things better? He doubted it, so he remained silent and looked at Vatten's face. Slowly the last gleam of life faded from his eyes. He stopped breathing. The tiny, almost imperceptible movements that distinguish a person at absolute rest from one who is dead finally ceased.

He could hear Felicia breathing behind him.

"Odd, we have to get out of here," she said quietly. "The door was unlocked when we got here, and you know what that means."

She didn't manage to say any more. He heard three quick footsteps. Then a dull thud. He turned around just as she fell toward him, a knife stuck in her back. Almost simultaneously somebody swung a crowbar against his temple.

"Edgar Allan Poe died in delirium. He was completely out of it," Jens Dahle said with a laugh. Singsaker blinked three times and saw the world come back into focus. Next to him hung the corpse of Jon Vatten. Now the head was gone. A sweet, metallic smell of flesh and blood was in the air. He turned to look at the figure standing in front of him. Dahle had taken off his shirt. He was not only tall, but also muscular and fit. He had pulled a mask over his head. It was the mask of a woman with long blonde hair. Hedda Vatten, Singsaker thought. He'd made a mask out of her skin.

There was no longer any doubt. He was the one they were looking for, but in both cases they had chosen to focus on Vatten. It had cost Vatten not only his academic career, but ultimately his life. If they'd done their job the first time, Gunn Brita Dahle would still be alive. He looked around the room desperately until he caught sight of Felicia, who still lay lifeless on the floor with a knife in her back. Dahle's voice sounded muffled from behind the mask.

"Personally, I belong to the school that believes Poe died of rabies. Not very glamorous or mysterious or honorable for a great author. But few other things are capable of stripping a man so completely from his wits. So I vote rabies. Vatten, on the other hand, he died with dignity. He lived with dignity and he died with dignity. Wouldn't you say that's a good way to sum it up?"

Again that cackling laugh. Today was the first time Singsaker had heard Jens Dahle laugh. If anybody had asked him about it yesterday, he probably would have said that he thought Dahle was a tinder-dry academic incapable of more than a restrained chuckle. He may be masked now, but the mask of sanity is off, thought Singsaker. Then he remembered what Vatten had said: "He's just a wreck of a human being, nothing more."

"The big question now is how *you* will meet your death," said Dahle.

Only now did Singsaker notice the scalpel in Dahle's hand. He realized that he had to keep the man talking.

"You burned down the farm where you grew up," he said.

Dahle laughed. "I know what you're trying to do," he said. "You're searching for an explanation. Where did it start? How did I get like this? Could it be an unhappy childhood? A father who beat me?" He shrugged. He still held the scalpel firmly between his thumb and index finger. His face was covered with sweat. His lips were drawn tight. "But I have no explanation to give you," Dahle went on. Then he came over to Singsaker and placed a hand under his head, searching with his fingertip until he found the scar. He ran his finger over it several times. He smiled. "It's not you who's going to be looking inside me, it's the other way around," he said, holding the scalpel up to Singsaker's eyes and staring at him.

Even now Singsaker thought he noticed something reminiscent of sorrow in the gaze of the insane killer. He knew it was something else but had no idea what else it could be.

The knife was a dagger. It differed from Johannes the priest's other knives in that it didn't serve any hygienic, surgical, or other practical purpose. It was more of a decorative, deadly knife. It had entered Felicia Stone's back between two of her ribs, then it penetrated one of her lungs and punctured it. The dagger had missed hitting her heart by only half an inch, and had not severed any of the major, vital arteries.

When she came to, the first thing she noticed was the knife. She couldn't tell whether it felt ice cold or glowing hot. Then she heard a voice and a heartless laughter. Someone was speaking Norwegian. It was a strangely subdued voice, as if from far away, although other sounds revealed that it must be close: little creaks in the floorboards, a body shifting its weight. Without even raising her head she knew it was the murderer's voice. Don't move any more than is absolutely necessary, Felicia, she told herself.

At first all she could do was move the fingers on her right hand. They slowly moved up her pants leg. Eventually she got her whole hand onto her butt. From there it proceeded at an excruciating pace until her fingers touched the knife. She fumbled with it, concentrating on not making a sound. The voice above suddenly sounded clearer but still turned away from her. The tendons in her arm were burning as she made a heroic effort to get a strong grip on the hilt of the dagger. With a jerk she yanked it out. She knew that doing this could be fatal, that she might sever things that were unharmed, open wounds that the knife had kept closed. But it was nothing compared to what the killer had planned.

She instantly got to her feet, managing to get Jens Dahle in her field of vision before he had turned around all the way. Then she struck. She plunged the knife into the side of his neck. He took a step backward. There he stopped and stared at her, wide-eyed. She studied his gaze, looking for traces of despair, sorrow, and regret, anything that might make him human. But all she saw was a face contracted in pain and rage. She looked at the knife and the blood that ran down his neck, mixing with sweat, and continued down his bare chest. She was starting to have trouble seeing clearly. The hot pain in her back spread over her whole body, even to her head. She wanted to close her eyes, lie down, and go to sleep. But she couldn't. She had to see him fall to know it was over.

Jens Dahle did not fall. Her vision fuzzy, like a movie that was out of focus, she saw him sway back and forth a few times before he slowly raised his left hand and took hold of the hilt of the knife sticking into his neck. With a maniacal howl he yanked it out. For a few brief seconds she could see the gaping wound in his neck. A red torrent was spurting out of it over his left shoulder. She heard his wail become strangled by blood.

Then he came at her, raising the knife. She took a deep breath, seeing nothing but the knife, and knew that she wouldn't be able to withstand another blow.

Her legs must have acted instinctively, because she took a quick step to the side. She felt the air pressure in her ear as the knife slashed past her head. Then she felt the big, crazed monster fall toward her. She released the air she had in her healthy lung without screaming. Then she fell to the floor with Dahle on top of her and almost fainted from the weight of his body squeezing the last breath of air from her.

She was vaguely aware of his arms scrabbling, as if he was trying to get up. She was afraid he was still holding the knife and regaining his strength. But abruptly his arms dropped limply on either side of her body. He went utterly still, having breathed his last.

With a huge effort she managed to roll the lifeless body onto the floor beside her. Then she greedily took a few deep breaths before she got to her feet. She stood there blinking until she regained control of her vision. Finally she could take a proper look at Odd Singsaker. She saw him hanging upside down, with all his clothes on, as well as his skin. Still groggy, she heard him whisper to her, his voice as low and weak, as if he were the one with the knife wound in his lung.

"Thanks," he said. "Thanks, Felicia Stone."

It was over.

She leaned over and put both her arms around his head. She pressed his head between her breasts. And he knew he had found what he'd been searching for ever since that damned operation. A safe place to rest his head.

Odd Singsaker stood on the beach, watching the helicopter fly off. In fifteen minutes Felicia would be at St. Olav's Hospital, and the EMTs had assured him that she was stable enough to handle the flight. Up by the cabin the local police were busy securing the crime scene so that no evidence would be lost before Grongstad and his team arrived. An ambulance turned onto the road and headed away from the cabin. In addition to checking Singsaker's vital signs, the ambulance team on the ground had declared both Jon Vatten and Jens Dahle dead. Now some technical work needed to be done before the bodies could be taken to Dr. Kittelsen's autopsy suite in the city, where they would be subjected to a few more knives.

Before the ambulance left, a car from *Adresseavisen* pulled up in front of the cabin. Probably a reporter from the local office in Botngård. It couldn't possibly be that damned Vlado Taneski, although it didn't really matter. Singsaker was pleased that he'd managed to get through an entire homicide investigation without talking to the press. He shuddered a bit on Gro Brattberg's behalf when he thought of all the questions she would have to answer.

He walked across the beach to the flat rocks, then over to the woods beyond them. At first the woods were quite dense, but after trudging through about forty feet of underbrush, he came out on a little cart path leading down to a boathouse. It must belong to the farm, he thought, because in front of it was Jens Dahle's car. He had been a cautious man. Precise and cautious. If he didn't want to be seen, he wasn't. Singsaker wondered what route he had taken out of Trondheim to avoid being caught by any of the highway cameras, and what alibi he had cooked up for this last act. But it no longer made any difference. Dahle would never need an alibi again.

Singsaker went over to the boathouse and opened the door. Inside he saw an old, dilapidated pram. Fishing nets, fast disintegrating, hung on one wall, and a buoy and some old tires were piled in a corner. Along the other wall stood a workbench. Above the bench hung tools, new and well kept. There were nippers, tweezers, knives, and various scraping tools. In a little tool chest there were needles and thread in many sizes, and next to the chest stood an inkwell. On the floor stood frames of various sizes neatly stacked against the wall. This was the workplace of an orderly man. In the middle of the bench was a frame on which a skin had been stretched. That was the one he'd been working on last. The skin on the frame was undoubtedly human. Singsaker guessed it was from Dahle's wife, Gunn Brita. Next to the workbench stood a mannequin similar to the one in Siri Holm's apartment. Above it hung the prepared skin from what must have been Hedda Vatten's headless body. Another skin, apparently from a child, hung from a hook on the wall. From this skin, a large section was cut out of the back.

There were parchment rolls on a shelf off to the side. Singsaker bent down without touching anything. The first sentences on the outside of one of the rolls were visible.

"One can always count on a murderer having his own imaginative prose style. The boy was already dead when I started on him. Good. He lay still on the workbench. . . ."

He couldn't read more without unrolling the parchment. He didn't want to touch it. Still, these were the confessions they needed. The last piece of evidence.

It was too much for Singsaker. He thought about the mask of sanity. We all wear them. Right now he could no longer keep his police mask on. He couldn't take it anymore. Chief Inspector Odd Singsaker stumbled out of the boathouse and threw up in earnest. Waffles and rage. Sorrow and drip coffee. It all came out in front of the gleaming, shiny car of Jens Dahle.

Goddamn, what a job I've got, he thought, lying down in the wet heather next to the cart path. He lay there for several minutes, feeling a numbing vertigo that slowly dissipated. A drizzling rain tickled on his brow. Slowly he realized how clear everything was to him now, all that had happened in the past few hours. For the first time since the operation he remembered every single detail of the past day. The doctors had said that his memory would recover. But why couldn't it have waited a few more days? Finally he felt strong enough to get to his feet.

He went back to the flat rocks by the shore, where he sat down and gazed in the direction the helicopter had flown. It was more than fifteen minutes ago now. Felicia was already in the hands of the best surgeons in this part of the country. That was the victory he had to hold on to. Felicia would survive. Otherwise he wouldn't have been able to tolerate it.

He took out his cell phone and scanned the missed calls. He found Lars's number and punched the green button.

His son answered after the second ring.

"Well, when's the christening going to be?" Singsaker asked softly. A tear slid past his nose, leaving a glistening trail in its wake.

Siri Holm and Odd Singsaker drove back to town through the gray and green landscape of the Fosen peninsula. The rain had let up, and the afternoon sun was breaking through the cloud cover. She tried to ask him about what had happened, but he didn't feel like talking about it, and excused himself by saying he couldn't divulge anything because of the ongoing investigation. All he told her was that Dahle and Vatten were both dead and that Felicia was going to pull through. The news of Vatten's death seemed to make a big impression on Siri. Neither of them said anything for a long time. When they had passed Bjugn, he finally broke the silence.

"What exactly happened between us, at your place," he said, feeling flustered.

"Don't worry about it," she said. Then she gave him a weak smile. "It's a nice but forgotten memory." She sat in silence for a while before she said, "You like her, don't you?"

He didn't reply.

"She likes you, too," said Siri.

For a while neither of them spoke. She was looking out the window.

Finally he said, "And you? You liked Vatten."

She nodded.

"I liked him a lot. He was a man who deserved much more respect."

"You're right about that," said Singsaker.

Again they fell silent. It was a good silence, a silence between friends. They let it go on for a long time.

Brattberg called twice. He thought the ringtone had a rather excitable sound to it, so he didn't bother answering.

Siri Holm nodded approvingly.

"Your boss, right? And you refuse to talk to her because you know she's going to chew you out for not following procedure, or some other absurdity."

He nodded. "Something like that."

"You're getting close, I must say."

"Close to what?"

"To becoming a real crime hero."

"Are there any real crime heroes?" he asked.

They both laughed. When the laughter subsided, they let the silence go on a while longer.

30

Forty-two thousand kroner?" Odd Singsaker rolled his eyes, but he wasn't really mad at anyone but himself. He was entirely unprepared for the exorbitant bill that was presented to him.

"I told you it could be expensive," said the repairman cautiously. "And I seem to recall that you said something to the effect that price was no object."

"Well, this price certainly is," he replied. "I could have remodeled half my bathroom for that price."

"Maybe you're not so familiar with racing bikes," said the repairman. His voice was still calm. "But if you wheel in a practically wrecked Cervelo competition bike and ask us to put it into perfect shape, with all the necessary original parts, then you have to expect it to cost a few kroner."

Singsaker knew he was right. He had made a fool of himself.

"Ahem. . . . Do you take credit cards?"

"No, but I can send you an invoice. If you like we can split it into monthly payments."

"No, the quicker the better," he replied. "Send me an invoice for the total amount." When it came right down to it, he did have a substantial savings account he could draw from.

The repairman made a note of his address and wheeled out the bicycle. Singsaker looked at it, impressed. Even the lacquer had been spiffed up.

"At least I'll have the coolest bike on the street," he said with a laugh.

"You can say that again," said the repairman, smiling, and he slapped Singsaker on the shoulder. All animosity was now gone.

From Sykkelbua in Bakklandet he headed down to Nidelva. He followed the path along the river on the lower side of the row of bungalowlike apartments that enjoyed the second-best view of the Nidaros Cathedral; they also embodied the worst view from the cathedral itself. The best view of the Nidaros Cathedral was still from the path Singsaker was riding along at a leisurely pace. He was pleased by the extreme precision of the gears on his new bike, and thought that the repairs had probably been worth the money after all. He continued to the stadium on the peninsula of Øya. There he turned down the side streets toward St. Olav's Hospital.

For the past three days, Felicia had been in the heart and lung ward at the hospital for observation, after she had been transferred from the ICU. He had visited her every day. Today he wanted to surprise her, so he stopped and bought flowers at the kiosk in the lobby. When he went upstairs to her ward, he asked one of the nurses how Felicia was doing before he went to her room. He'd started doing that on the first critical days. If he asked Felicia herself, she just said that everything was going fine. Even right after they had sewed her up and there was still the danger of internal bleeding and infection, she claimed that there was nothing to worry about. As the days passed, the nurses' evaluations became more in line with Felicia's own. She was on the way to recovery, and everything was healing as it should.

The nurse today was a young man he hadn't spoken with before.

"Felicia Stone . . . she was released this morning," he said.

Singsaker stood there dumbfounded and staring at the young man.

"That can't be true," he said. "Nobody informed me."

"She and the doctor decided this morning that she was well enough to be discharged. I was there myself," said the nurse.

"But she wasn't supposed to be discharged until tomorrow," Singsaker said, walking toward her room. He opened the door and saw an elderly man with a beard and bristly hair sticking out in all directions. He was wearing a robe that was much too tight, and sitting on the bed that used to be Felicia's.

On his way out of the hospital Singsaker tapped in her number on his cell phone and wondered why his pulse was racing. The case was solved. The killer had been caught. And the fact that she'd been released a day early had to be good news.

Felicia's number was busy.

"Why didn't you ever tell us about this, my dear?" Her father's voice seemed so close, as if he were sitting with her in the hotel room here in Trondheim and not over four thousand miles away in a room more familiar to her than any other in the world.

"You must have expected it was something like this." Her voice held no trace of reproach. Guilt was the last thing they needed to come between them.

"We talked about the fact that it could have been something sexual, yes." Her father was honest. Distances sometimes help, Felicia thought. She understood that it was the right time to call, and from the right place.

"The matter isn't settled yet," said her father.

"Yes, it is. It finally is," she said.

Her father understood what she meant.

"You're ready to put it behind you?"

"I don't know. But I don't think I'm afraid of the future anymore. Besides, it might be enough to lock up one Nevins this time around." She laughed.

"A heck of a job you've done with this case, my dear," said her father. "Or rather, with both cases. Who would have believed that the Poe murder would be solved in just a few days?"

"Sounds like you're a little proud of me," she said, noticing that there was something in her voice now, a tone that she and her father had once shared. It had been gone for far too long.

"Not just a little," her father replied.

Felicia Stone had always been slim. But when she put down the phone after talking to her father, giving him as detailed an account as she could about what had happened that night in Shaun Nevins's room, she also felt unburdened and light for the first time in years.

Felicia tried to touch the wound on her back where the knife had gone in. But after the stitches had been removed the day before, it no longer itched and she had a hard time locating the tenderness she still felt in the upper part of her torso. So she just sat there thinking about the case she had helped solve. Odd had updated her every day at the hospital with news from both Trondheim and Richmond.

According to the scholars who had begun to decipher the palimpsest of Johannes the priest and the so-called knife parchment that had been in the possession of Jens Dahle, there were indications that Dahle had been inspired by the man who might prove to be the biggest serial killer in Norwegian history. A twisted priest with an excellent knowledge of anatomy. One thing that had made the work with the Johannes palimpsest easier was the availability of X-rays that had been made by Johns Hopkins University in the United States for the curator of the Poe Museum in Richmond.

These X-rays were found during a search of the office of John Nevins, who'd had his own very personal reasons for not drawing attention to the *Johannes Book* and its missing knives. Nevins, who was familiar with the discoveries that Bond had already made in cooperation with Gunn Brita Dahle, apparently planned to use the revelations to promote his own academic career, but he had wanted to wait until things had cooled off a bit. He had managed to purloin these X-rays from the Poe Museum at the beginning of the investigation while Reynolds was doing the first interviews of the museum staff. In assessing the investigation done by the Richmond police, this was the one event that bothered Morris and his colleagues the most. In the investigators' defense, the X-rays had been kept in a poorly secured storeroom and not in Bond's office. Nevins was the only one who knew where to look. That remained a small yet important oversight. Felicia knew that Laubach had been livid about this, and she expected to hear more about it when she returned.

Now she again picked up the phone and called Morris.

"It's early," he said.

She looked at the clock. It was one o'clock, barely seven in the morning in Richmond.

"Did I wake you?" she asked.

"No, I'm already on my second cup of coffee. But I'm actually off this morning. Things have calmed down over here. How's it going with you?"

"I was released from the hospital today. A day early."

"So I suppose you're anxious to come home? Shall we book a flight for you?"

"That's what I wanted to talk to you about," she said.

Singsaker rode his bike past the Student Society, across Elgeseter Bridge, and followed Prinsens gate all the way to the hotel. When he got there it was twenty past one. He went inside to the front desk, explained that he wanted to see Felicia Stone, and gave her room number to a male desk clerk who had blond streaks in his hair. He was old enough that these streaks blended freely with a sprinkling of gray. He didn't bother to type her name into the computer.

"She checked out five minutes ago," he said. "And left in a taxi."

"Do you know where she was going?" Singsaker asked.

"No, but she's American. I assumed she was going to the airport, although she made her own arrangements with the cab company."

"Damn," Singsaker said, surprising himself by slamming his fist on the counter.

"If you've got some urgent message for her, I'm sure you can catch up with her out at Værnes," said the desk clerk.

"On my bike?"

Outside the hotel he looked at his cell phone, wondering whether he ought to call her or text. But he decided that if she had really left for home without saying good-bye, there was little he could do about it. He'd just be chasing a dream. And he already had enough dreams, which had had a disturbing tendency to turn into nightmares.

He rode his bike over to the state liquor store on Solsiden and bought two bottles of Rød Aalborg. At the grocery store in the shopping center he found some decent Danish rye bread and whole filets of pickled herring, the kind he liked but seldom ate. He had a whole weekend ahead of him, and he wondered how long he'd be able to hold out before he called Anniken.

Felicia Stone suddenly felt as though she'd done something stupid. The case was over, after all. Why couldn't she simply let it drop and go home? Was there anything more to find out now?

She took out the key ring she carried in her pocket, even though none of the keys fit a single lock on this side of the Atlantic. But on it was a lock pick that had no such geographical limitations. It fit in the lock she was now trying to pick with some difficulty. Patterson was so much better at this. She'd often thought that he could have been as good a criminal as he was a cop. For her part, it took some effort, but eventually she managed to get the lock open. She went in and looked around the room, which was exactly as she'd pictured it. And it reinforced her belief that she was on the right track. There was still something left undone; a loose thread was still left.

He biked slowly across Kirkegata. On the way he passed Dahle's house. All the curtains were drawn. The kids had moved in with Gunn Brita's parents, which might be permanent, according to the child welfare authorities. Most probably the house would be sold to cover the inevitable demands for compensation.

There was a lot of investigative work that remained to be done after what had been the bloodiest serial killings in Norway over the past five hundred years. The Norwegian team was using a lot of resources trying to clarify the scope of Jens Dahle's crimes. The boathouse by the cabin out on Ørland had quickly been dubbed "The Boathouse of Horror" by Vlado Taneski in *Adresseavisen*. In general, the press was doing its best to ignore Jon Vatten's next to last wish that Jens Dahle not be mythologized.

In the boathouse there was more than sufficient evidence to link Dahle to the murders of both Edvard and Hedda Vatten, as well as to that of his own wife. In addition, skin had been found from at least one other unidentified individual. So Jens Dahle could be labeled a serial killer according to every definition of the term.

The evidence was strong enough to link him to the murder in Virginia as well. Beside the similarity between the murders and the confirmed connection between Gunn Brita Dahle and Efrahim Bond—which provided a motive for the murder—electronic evidence was found verifying Jens Dahle's travel itinerary. By all accounts he had flown to Washington, D.C., and from there continued in a rental car. He purchased scalpels and other surgical equipment, which he couldn't bring with him on the plane, at a medical supply company in Washington. The equipment had been ordered in advance by the Science Museum in Trondheim. Dahle was back in Norway in a little less than seventy-two hours. The original check of Dahle's alibi had been done before anyone in the Trondheim police was aware of the Richmond murder, so they had only concentrated on the weekend of the murder in Trondheim. Dahle's colleagues, who could not even begin to comprehend what had happened, stated in later interviews that they thought he had been on vacation. Gunn Brita Dahle's parents stated that he had told his wife he was attending a conference.

His alibi had certainly had its weak points, and a stronger focus on Jens Dahle early in the investigation might have revealed his lies. In that sense, his plan to divert police attention by sending them on a hunt for an insane thrill killer had been successful. The police would never know whether focusing the investigation differently might have saved Vatten's life.

The evidence that definitively linked Dahle to the murder in the United States appeared the day after he died. During a search of his home, the police found a copy of the *Johannes Book* that Dahle must have had made before he donated it to the Gunnerus Library. They also found an unopened letter in his mailbox. It was sent from the States the same day Dahle returned to Norway. The handwriting on the envelope clearly showed that he'd written it himself and mailed it to his own address. The envelope contained a small piece of human skin that had not completely dried. The police still needed to ascertain with a DNA test whether the skin came from the victim Efrahim Bond, but this was obviously Dahle's way of keeping a souvenir of that murder. What Dahle had done with the rest of Bond's skin remained an unsolved mystery.

Nor did the police ever find out why the murder in the Poe Museum seemed sloppier and more disorganized than the one in the book vault, since the only person who could have answered that question was dead. Dahle's original plan was probably to make the two murders as incomprehensible as possible. By exaggerating the effects and inserting irrational elements, like putting the head in the garbage can, he wanted to divert attention from the fact that the murders were personal.

But when he killed Gunn Brita, he shifted his MO. The murder was more organized in its execution and done in a confined space. Perhaps it was only the unexpected advantage of being able to hide the body in the vault that made him do it that way. As Felicia Stone said one evening at the hospital: Most killers are opportunists. Even the most organized serial killer can change his method if he has something to gain.

Another theory was that while Jens Dahle had actually enjoyed killing Bond, he wanted to get the murder of his spouse over with as swiftly and efficiently as possible. Some people thought that this could be a sign that somewhere deep inside, Dahle the sociopath had some measure of human feeling. Singsaker did not share this opinion.

The police would probably never find out what had made Jens Dahle into a monster. Despite rumors in his hometown that the fire at the Krangsås farm perhaps was not as accidental as originally believed, there was no concrete proof that he'd had an unhappy childhood or was abused in any way. None of the statements from people who had known him as a child indicated that he'd had any of the problems or behavioral issues that often mark a serial killer. He didn't wet the bed, he didn't torture animals, and he was never caught starting fires or committing vandalism. Once he was apparently caught shoplifting a comic book at the local co-op. That was the only criminal situation in which he'd ever been involved, and it was never reported, since the owner of the shop thought he was a nice boy. Jens Dahle never teased girls, and no one had suspected him of spying or peeping through windows in the town. He never threatened anyone, and nobody had ever seen him in a fight. The only thing the police gleaned from the interviews with people from Ørland where he grew up was that he was a quiet boy who kept mostly to himself, and often seemed lost in his own thoughts. In his youth it was well-known that Jens Dahle would rather lie around in his room reading books and comics than go to a party or spend time with girls. People his own age had seen him as a harmless, intelligent, but rather strange boy.

Singsaker wondered how long it would take until he could ride his bike past Dahle's house without imagining his naked torso and the mask of human skin that had been torn off, revealing two eyes that stared into a world so different from his own—a world that had been shaped inside Dahle without anyone ever knowing.

The sight of Jon Vatten's house a bit farther up the street didn't really put Singsaker in a better mood. When he turned into the back courtyard of his own building to enter his own staircase and apartment, his plan was to forget about the herring and go to bed with an open bottle of aquavit on the nightstand and some sentimental movie on the TV.

But it didn't work out that way.

Felicia panicked when she heard the key in the door. Again she got that nauseating feeling she'd done something stupid. Was it a good idea to do it this way? Could she have ruined everything before it even began? It was too late for such thoughts now. All she could do was follow her plan. She hurried into the bedroom and lay down on the bed. She had to laugh at herself as she unbuttoned the top two buttons of her blouse. This is so dumb, she thought. What if it doesn't work? No, it has to work. I've been waiting fourteen years for this.

When she saw him come into the bedroom with a bottle of aquavit in each hand and his shirt already unbuttoned, she knew that it would be all right. She hadn't done anything stupid; it was the only right thing to do. There was still a loose thread left in the case, and here he was, standing in front of her and saying exactly what she had hoped.

She got up from the bed, went over to him, and put a finger to his lips. Took the bottles out of his hands and set them down. Then she undressed him. He lay down on his back and watched as she took off her clothes. At last there was nothing to see but her black hair and white skin. She crept next to him and kissed him on the lips. From there she moved down to his shoulders and chest. She lingered a long time in the navel region before she finally reached the spot she was aiming for. He was ready to burst, and burst way too soon.

"It was, it was . . ." he stammered afterward, but didn't manage to finish.

"You have no idea what it was," she said. "But someday I might tell you."

He looked at her as she sat on the bed beside him.

"One day I hope you will," he said.

"And I hope you've saved a little ammunition," she said. "That was actually something I *had* to do. What comes next is something I *want*."

"You need to remember that I'm getting older," he said with a smile. "But if we take our time, anything is possible."

An hour later they were sitting in bed watching a rerun of *Grey's Anatomy*. They were still naked. She rested her head on his shoulder, and her long black hair covered his chest like a cape. She sighed with satisfaction. Sometime in the future she would describe the hour that had just passed as weightless, and explain that afterward gravity had taken on a new form. What he remembered best was that it was the first time it felt like the wound in his head was completely healed.

"I hate doctor shows," she said cheerfully.

"Me too," he said, "but in a good way."

"Morris gave me two weeks off."

"Great, then you can come with me to Oslo. I have to go to a christening, and you really ought to see more of the country than just Trondheim."

"That sounds nice. But I like Trondheim. I like the rain and the cold."

"How much do you like it?" he said, feeling a butterfly awaken in his stomach.

"Maybe," she said, "I like it as much as you hope I do."

31

Ørland, 1555

The priest sat in his house and looked down over the meadow outside. A little girl came walking along the path that led up to his dwelling. It was little Mari, who had lost her parents to the plague. That was the week before the bodies of Lady Inger and her daughter were brought back from the shipwreck on the way to Bergen. Johannes the priest had presided at both families' funerals. The one for Lady Inger and her family was resplendent, with oak caskets and family crests in a packed Ørland church. The one for Mari's parents was modest, outdoors. Mari had wept at the burial. The priest had invited her over so that he could see what he could do for her.

Now he sat reading his diary. He had made it himself from calf-skin, and the pages at the back were made of the skin he had brought with him from Bergen, where he had encountered the beard-cutter for the last time. Nothing provided a better writing surface than this parchment. As he read he kept glancing out the open window. Mari was coming closer on the path. She was so skinny, that girl.

His eyes shifted back to the pages of the book. The last pages he had dedicated to them, to the blood and the entrails. Next to the book, on the table in front of him, lay the bundle of skin wrapped around the knives.

What he had written inside this bundle were his worst thoughts. The thoughts from which he couldn't manage to free himself. They dealt with the way he had taken their lives, how he had flayed the skin off them, how he had sliced into them, and then what was concealed within.

But that was all they were. Just thoughts and nothing else. He had never laid a hand on any of them. Ever since the archbishop had sent him out here to Fosen he had been a good priest, first Catholic and then Lutheran. It hadn't cost him as much to convert as he had thought. At some point he realized that religion was not the most important thing. Human beings were more important. He discovered that despite what had happened to him in life, he liked people. He wasn't like the beard-cutter, whose life he had spared that time in Bergen. He had merely knocked him unconscious and taken his knives. The knives and the old skin from the German witch. He had used the skin to make the last pages in this book, and on it he had written his darkest thoughts. Because he did have dark thoughts, there was no use denying it. But by writing them down he had kept them away from the rest of the world. He had found a place to hide the devil that lived inside him. And after that, he was not a bad priest.

Now he wrote one last sentence in the middle of the book, far from those dark pages. It was a sentence that a lucky monkey had once put on paper in Alexandria, at least if one were to believe his great teacher from Padua. When he was done writing, he picked up the bundle, which was also made from the witch's skin. It not only contained the gruesome fantasy about a vivisection, but it served to protect the beard-cutter's knives. The fantasy was harmless as long as he left it where it was, and he had actually saved some lives with these knives over the years. The last time was when a land-owner down by the sea went berserk with an ax and slew five people on his farm. Four others had also been injured, but Johannes the priest managed to save their lives with most of their limbs intact. The five who died were buried at the old grave site out by the chapel. They were the last ones to be buried there, for soon after the superintendent in Nidaros decided that the grave site would no longer be used. The grisly murders were now forgotten. Only the survivors remembered what had happened, and they recalled how Johannes the priest had saved their lives, but not all of their limbs, with his knives and needles.

Mari was so close now that he could hear her footsteps. He had good news for her in these different times. He had already found her a place on one of the farms in the parish, where, for a certain fee, they had promised to take her in. He didn't have much to offer in the way of payment, nothing but the knives and the book he had spent the last half of his life writing. He wasn't afraid to give these items away. The people at the farm couldn't read. He had made them promise not to sell them before he died, and if they were ever sold, the knives and the book must always stay together. Future owners would have to swear to this, too. The farmer had agreed to this peculiar request.

He lay the bundle down behind him on the bed as Mari entered the room.

How he longed to rid himself of these devilish thoughts once and for all. He was approaching old age now, and he wanted to spend it in peace.

AFTERWORD

E*verything of importance in* this novel was made up, and it goes without saying that all the characters are fictitious. Yet the story does contain the names of several historical figures who were real enough in their day. Some of them even play an active role in the plot of the novel. I'm thinking primarily of Broder Lysholm Knudtzon and Alessandro Benedetti. But even though these individuals were once alive, they appear here exclusively as characters in a novel, with traits borrowed from a time long past. This applies especially to Master Alessandro.

The real Alessandro Benedetti (1445–1525), also known as Alexander Benedictus, lived and worked in Padua. We know that he, like Master Alessandro in the novel, traveled extensively throughout the Mediterranean region, and that he collected books. Whether he was a friend of the renowned book printer Manutius who worked in Venice, however, is somewhat less certain. Alessandro was best known for having written the work *Historia Corporis Humani,* in which he describes how a surgeon can transplant skin from a person's arm to his nose. He learned the method from the Branca family of doctors, who performed the procedure in Sicily as early as the fifteenth century.

In 1497 Alessandro wrote down some fundamental guidelines for the design of an anatomical theater: It must have an auditorium that ensured good viewing for all, a well-lit table in the center; good ventilation; and guards to prevent undesirables from entering. We don't know whether Alessandro really managed to build an anatomical theater, but if he did, he certainly wouldn't have done so in his own yard. But we do know that such theaters were erected in several locations during the sixteenth century. At first they were temporary buildings of wood, like that in the master's yard. Near the end of the century, permanent buildings were constructed at a number of universities. This was done first in Italy, and then the rest of Europe followed suit.

Alessandro's own career as an anatomist is not well documented. We do not know how many dissections he performed, or what methods he used. The fictional Master Alessandro is thus based equally on the somewhat later and far more famous anatomist Vesalius (1514–64), about whom we know conclusively that he personally performed many dissections. The cemetery called the Graveyard of the Innocents, which in the story lies outside the city walls of Padua, was actually located in Paris, where the Belgian Vesalius studied and first began his anatomical investigations. He described how in the dark of night he would fetch remnants of corpses from this and similar cemeteries around the French capital. When he later went to Padua and began to work at the university there, Vesalius found the freedom he needed to become the greatest anatomist of his time.

It is also Vesalius who is known for having revised much of the teachings of the Greek physician Galen (ca. A.D. 130–200). As mentioned in the novel, Galen didn't dissect human beings, but animals. Yet most of his knowledge was in reality based on the work of earlier Greek anatomists, primarily that of the famous and infamous Herophilos (4th century B.C.). It is said that condemned prisoners were delivered to him so that he could dissect them alive.

The most famous work of Vesalius is the anatomical atlas *De humani corporis fabrica* (1543).

With regard to Broder Lysholm Knudtzon (1788–1864), it is true that he was born into a family of merchants in Trondheim, and that he was more interested in culture and science than in the business of trading. It is also true that he was a close friend of Lord Byron, and that he collected Byron's books in particular. At his death he left his book collection to the Royal Norwegian Society of Sciences. The collection is today part of the Parchment Division of the University Library in Trondheim, also called the Gunnerus Library. Unfortunately, Knudtzon burned many of his letters. It is said that he did an especially thorough job of burning those from Lord Byron. Did Broder Lysholm Knudtzon ever go out to Fosen, taking with him a book that he thought to be cursed? That is doubtful.

Other historical figures mentioned in the novel, such as Edgar Allan Poe, don't figure directly in the plot. The anecdotes about Poe are true for the most part, or at least based on long-established myths. Small details about Poe were also made up. It would be a mere coincidence should it turn out that Poe actually did own a book by Lord Byron bound in skin that he purchased from a hatter who emigrated from Trondheim to the United States.

Johannes the priest is a product of the author's imagination, and there is also no *Johannes Book* in the book vault of the Gunnerus Library. However, Absalon Pederssøn Beyer's diary, and the same gentleman's history of Norway, are part of the collection, providing one of the most interesting literary sources we have from the 1500s, a time in Norway that was otherwise largely lacking in good writing.

—Jørgen Brekke, 2011